CARNEY

ALSO BY A. F. CARTER:

The Yards

All of Us

The Hostage

Boomtown

Johnny-Boy

CARNEY

A. F. CARTER

THE MYSTERIOUS PRESS
NEW YORK

CARNEY

Mysterious Press
An Imprint of Penzler Publishers
58 Warren Street
New York, N.Y. 10007

First edition

Interior design by Maria Fernandez

Library of Congress Control Number: 2025942611

ISBN: 978-1-61316-726-7
eBook ISBN: 978-1-61316-727-4

10 9 8 7 6 5 4 3 2 1

Printed in the United States of America
Distributed by Simon & Schuster

CARNEY

CHAPTER ONE
DELIA

The phone wakes me at 3:00 A.M. My first thought, to answer it fast before Zoe wakes up, is quickly replaced by the realization that I'm alone in bed. Zoe's my partner, has been for more than a year, but she's currently in Clark County, South Dakota, where the grandmother who raised her has been diagnosed with advanced pancreatic cancer. How much time does she have left? Days, weeks, months? Nobody's sure.

The glowing screen on my phone reveals Vern Taney's name. Vern's my boss, and the commissioner of police in Baxter. As his chief of detectives, I'm always on call.

"Vern, what's goin' on?"

"Got a body. In Boomtown, on the side road they call First Avenue."

Boomtown is a chaotic assembly of Quonset huts, motor homes, single-wides, and just about anything else than can be put up fast, including tents. It developed on its own after Nissan decided to locate their new assembly plant in Baxter. That's when our little city morphed into gold mountain, attracting several thousand workers with no place to live.

Vern clears his throat. "It's one of ours, Delia."

"Who?"

"Rowan Krauss."

Though I consider Sergeant Rowan Krauss a friend, I need to control my emotions. They have no role to play just now, neither grief nor rage. I have to channel a methodical work ethic instead, methodical and unrelenting.

"Tell me there's someone in custody."

"I only wish I could." He clears his throat. "Stu Harrington's on the scene. He's tellin' me they don't have an obvious suspect. It's a goddamned mystery."

"All right, I'll be on my way as soon as I get dressed." I glance at the clock on the dresser. It's 3:38. "Are you coming out?"

"Probably beat you there. And let's keep this as close as possible. Nobody speaks to the press but me."

◆

The Nissan plant-to-be runs north–south on the eastern edge of the city, with Boomtown, still farther east, running parallel. The factory alone is more than a mile in length, with a parking lot at the southern boundary. There are no roads through the property. If you want to reach the other side, you cross the top or the bottom. I approach from the west, stopping briefly at a stop sign. From here, railroad tracks front a view of the assembly plant. On this side, the plant is dominated by a massive concrete yard facing a blank wall broken by loading docks. Three are active at the moment, despite the hour, and the whole area is so uniformly lit that a spider couldn't make it across the yard without being detected. The long flat roof is also lit. Eventually, solar panels will cover it, end to end, generating more than enough electricity to power the plant. The excess will be sold back to the grid, then repurchased on cloudy days.

I turn left, then right at the top of the plant, and finally onto Main Street, the north–south road that separates Boomtown from the construction zone. Our newly minted crime scene unit is already here. They've brought up the LED floodlights and focused them on a patrol car neatly parked at the end of the block. I'm forced to stop behind the four patrol cars blocking traffic, then walk past three uniformed cops who guard the intersection. There's a war going on in Baxter. Not between the cops and the criminals, but between cops and cops, a struggle echoed on the political front. Mayor Harlan Venn has been elected to four consecutive terms, running mostly unchallenged because nobody else wanted to govern a crumbling, rust-belt city.

That's changed, gold mountain being, of course, gold mountain.

◆

First Avenue runs no more than three hundred yards before dead-ending at the edge of a newly planted field of soybeans. At the top of the road, two patrol officers stand behind multiple strands of yellow tape. The effort to preserve the scene has to be made, but there's nothing behind the tents and huts and motor homes but the rear ends of other tents and huts and motor homes. It would take an army to stop somebody from sneaking off to Second Avenue. Otherwise, the scene has been handled in a professional manner. There's one cruiser on the block, the victim's, while another four or five idle outside the yellow tape. The first responders must've shut down the block immediately.

A tall cop, clipboard in hand, nods to me as I approach. The rule is simple. Cops sign in and sign out. Civilians stay right where they are until interviewed. My signature's little more than a scrawl under ordinary conditions. It's worse now. The single cruiser sits at the end of the block. Two sheets, one white, the other blue, cover the top and the windows. I don't know who placed them, but I know why. Gawkers stand in knots on both sides of the road and the sheets provide Sergeant Krauss with a small measure of human dignity.

◆

I meet Stu Harrington halfway down the block. Stu is one my best detectives. Tall and lanky, with a pronounced Southwestern drawl, Stu's laid-back style is only a tease. He's as dogged as they come when he's on the hunt. Ordinarily, I find him with his good old boy smile at the ready. Not today.

"Bad as it gets," he tells me. "One round just above his left ear, in and out. Starburst pattern at the point of entry and heavy stippling. Probably a contact wound."

"That means the window was rolled down."

Stu nods. "Rowan knew his killer. Has to be. No other way he'd let anyone get that close. The man's always careful."

"Unless he was asleep." When Stu merely shrugs, I ask, "Witnesses?"

"Well, that's the thing, captain. These folks, they're mostly working people with no love for killers. Meaning they're eager to help out. But nobody heard the shot."

I look around at the collection of flimsy structures. Barely able to keep out the wind, they offered precious little shelter during the long winter. Not here, but on other blocks, workers too drunk or stoned to start their electric and kerosene heaters were discovered frozen to death in the morning.

"You don't sense they're afraid to talk?"

"Maybe a few, but definitely not all."

I don't have to state the obvious. A suppressed weapon indicates a professional hit, and not some pissed-off civilian with a handgun tucked into his waistband. Or hers. The saddest part is that I'm not surprised. We've almost doubled the number of patrol officers in the city, adding men and women at a rate that short-circuited the vetting process. Last year, two of our new hires were killed while extorting a drug dealer, but the corruption hasn't slowed. Neither has a tendency to handle every hostile interaction by applying excessive force.

Still, not every cop on the job is corrupt, and certainly not Rowan Krauss. Rowan was on the other side, an honest cop who took pride in his work. He was frozen out by a cop gang, determined, with the aid of our chief of patrol, Captain Saul Rawling, to run the department.

◆

We're standing behind the lights erected by the crime scene unit. It's dark enough here to offer the illusion of concealment. That's going to change. I know I have to approach Krauss's vehicle, pull the sheet aside, and view the death scene. Toward no good end, because if there's anything to find, it'll be recovered by the crime scene unit. I'm going because it's expected of me, though

I probably won't be the primary detective on the case. I'll be watching, of course, and offering suggestions, perhaps strongly worded. But Stu Harrington and the team we assemble will be on the street, pumping informants, demanding answers. Their shoe-leather, not mine. Still, I have to look, to bear witness, the task as fundamental as the oath I took to defend the Constitution.

I pass from the shadows into a light that seems more glaring than sunlight. Three techs in the white coveralls we call bunny suits work their way along the edge of the street where it meets what passes for a sidewalk. Another stands at the edge of a soybean field, sweeping his flashlight across rows of green fuzz that quickly merge with the rising ground fog. As I pass the standing lights, my shadow extends before me, cast in three directions by the lights.

I reach the cruiser without pausing and lift the sheet covering the driver's side window. Rowan Krauss lies slumped over, his head resting on the opposite seat. One arm is pinned beneath him, the other hangs over the seat, fingers just grazing the floor. His weapon, a 9mm Glock, is still holstered, the strap meant to hold the pistol in place still snapped.

Rowan's wound is obvious, and especially gruesome. The barrel of a gun forced against a human head pushes gas from the muzzle into the scalp. The gas mushrooms out when it reaches the skull, creating what pathologists call a starburst wound. And maybe, once the wound is cleaned, the injury will resemble a starburst. But here, in the immediate aftermath, there's only the gore, the gore and a hole in the flesh suffused with blood already turning black.

Rowan has a wife, Jesse, and two children. They believe him to still be living, to be drawing breath, to be, in a few hours, on his way home.

CHAPTER TWO

DELIA

I need a quiet moment, away from the crowd of police and paramedics gathered at the Main Street entrance to the block. I walk to the edge of the field where a CSU officer named Ralph Mulligan holds a flashlight, sweeping the beam from side to side. It's possible, maybe likely, that the shooter escaped, not through the field, but north or south to the next block.

"Anything?" I ask.

"Too much, captain." He sweeps the flashlight's narrow beam across the rows of sprouted soybeans and the color instantly intensifies, from the palest mint to a vibrant Kelly green. "What with the ground recently turned, the soil's primed to receive imprints. Too many. I'm thinkin' the residents on the block wander here from time to time, maybe for a quick smoke, or to relieve themselves. Why doesn't matter, though. What matters is how many there are."

Mostly, detectives trust CSU's expertise and the unit's left to its work. Not this time. "If the shooter came this way, before or after, his shoeprints can't be more than a couple of hours old. Photograph and cast anything that looks recent. Anything."

◆

I walk back the way I came, walk into the full glare of the lights as if walking some perverse runway. A KBAX media van has arrived—the media routinely monitor the police band—and a cameraman records my every step. I'm glad the uniforms are keeping them on Main Street. Crime has become a big issue in Baxter, as it has in the country. Drugs are rampant, and rumors that the Baja cartel's become involved haven't helped. At this point, we have roughly fifteen hundred workers in the city, virtually all without family. Prostitutes stroll up and down Main Street every evening, despite enough arrests to overcrowd our small jail, and every other bar has a roulette wheel, a blackjack table, or a craps table in a back room. Again, we bust one of the bars every week, only to find another opening a few doors away.

Vern awaits me. He's standing out of the crime scene, but far enough from Main Street to not be heard. A few years ago, when Vern was appointed commissioner by Mayor Venn, we celebrated, my family and his. Be careful what you wish for? As chief of detectives, I'm under far less pressure than Vern. My division's closure rate is better (not much, but still better) than "that in other cities in the state. The voters and the media seem more concerned with street crime and the fingers are mostly pointed at the patrol division in general and Vern in particular. I think Vern would be up to the job if not for Saul Rawling, our chief of patrol, whose ambition is undisguised. The strain's evident. In parallel, deeply cut lines along Vern's forehead, on the tired edges of his mouth, in blue eyes that seem to be looking backward, as though searching for some elusive explanation.

"First impression, Delia?" he asks.

"He never saw it coming."

"So, he must've trusted the shooter completely?"

"Maybe, and maybe he was cooping."

I ignore Vern's raised eyebrows. Napping is fairly common on the midnight tour. I know because I sometimes surrendered to exhaustion on quiet nights when I first came on the job. Detectives and patrol officers work rotating tours. Eight-to-four, four-to-midnight, midnight-to-eight. My body was never ready for the late tour. I had to fight my way through every time. "Two things, Vern. Rowan's holster is still strapped down and the location just isn't right if he was meeting an informant. Too active."

Vern responds with a grunt before speaking. "They'll say he was corrupt."

I'm not sure who "they" are, but I recognize the process. Charges of corruption by city cops turn up every couple of weeks, and rumors abound, including a claim that the Justice Department has launched its own investigation. Reporters feast on these rumors because they sell tickets. Viewers and readers eat the stories up. But Rowan wasn't on anybody's pad. He's been on our side from the beginning.

◆

Stu Harrington ambles up, looking nearly as tired as Vern. He glances from me to Vern before speaking. "I've got six residents who saw Rowan's cruiser parked at the end of the block. So far."

"The earliest time?" I ask.

"One thirty, about. We're only halfway through the interviews, so there might be more."

We pause as a gray Lexus pulls to a stop and Arshan Rishnavata, our cardiologist-coroner, exits. He nods to us, but doesn't stop to chat. I watch him stride along First Avenue, a warrior rushing to the battlefield. Which is how he likes to think of himself.

"The first call to 911 was recorded at 3:13. He'd been dead for a while by then. I'm figurin' at least an hour, judgin' from how cool he felt when I looked for a pulse. The spatter, too. I didn't touch anything, but it looked pretty dry."

Arshan will have the final say, but I find myself agreeing with Stu. "You said you have six witnesses?"

"Yes, including the man who called 911. See, the men on this block, they live kinda packed in." Stu points to a white, prefab building not much bigger than a home garage. "There's an area at the back with a microwave and a sink and a table with benches. The rest, except for the toilets, is nothin' but narrow beds a few feet apart, ten of 'em with a locker at the foot of the bed. There's ten men livin' there and they spend as little time inside as possible."

"These are workers at the plant?" Vern's incredulous. "You'd think they could do better."

"Woulda thought so as well, commissioner, but these men have families at home. Fact, they mostly have their pay directly deposited in their home banks. Plus, they grab every minute of overtime they can get their hands on and head for a bar when they leave the job. The sleep part is just somethin' to get done before work. Anyway, the time frame for the six witnesses runs from one thirty until three thirteen, but here's the thing. The first five witnesses all report seein' a cop inside the car. Not doin' much of anything, but there. The last witness, that would be Pablo Cruz, came out of that motor home for a quick smoke." Stu points to a vehicle parked only twenty or so yards from the cruisers. "But he doesn't see anyone inside, so he decides to take a closer look and finds Rowan lyin' across the front seat."

Vern steps up. "Any chance he's involved?"

"I'm sayin' no. The kid works private construction. He's part of the meat market." Stu's referring to the gang of day workers who cluster at the northern tip of Main Street, hoping to be hired by small contractors who rely on cheap labor.

"Take a close look anyway." Vern slips a hand into his pocket as he glances back at the assembled media outlets. "Doesn't Rowan normally have a driver? Why was he alone?"

"His regular driver delivered a baby two days ago. Six weeks premature. As for why there's no substitute? I can't say, but I mean to find out."

Vern stares at Stu for a moment, then says, "I'm going to do the notification before some asshole reporter rings Jesse's bell."

"You want me to come along?" I ask.

"No, I want you to manage the investigation. Hands on. Pull anyone you need." He starts to turn away, then looks back at me. "We'll hold a press conference later this morning. Until then, let the assholes go fuck themselves."

◆

We commandeer a large tent, the sort you might find at a county fair, located halfway along the block on the south side of the road. The tent's being used as a bar-casino with a roulette wheel and a craps table in back. Carter Howe, the bar's manager, isn't happy, but we brush him aside. We'll do a hundred interviews tonight and we can't work it outdoors. The alternative, to transport the men and the few women back to headquarters, would only result in a pack of hostile witnesses. Just now, I'm not sensing hostility. Quite the opposite. Stu described them as honest working types and that's how it's playing out. I've called in every detective on the job to conduct the interviews. Mostly, it's just a name and where they live, followed by a disclaimer. They didn't see nothin', not even the marked cruiser at the end of the road. Still, from time to time, we get lucky.

◆

The boy named Pablo Cruz is in his late teens or very early twenties, a handsome kid with a magnetic smile and a head of curly black hair that reminds me of a poodle waiting to be sheared. Cade Barrow's conducting Pablo's interview. He calls me over halfway through.

As I draw close, he tells the boy, "Go ahead, Pablo."

The boy responds immediately, his Spanish accent strong. "So, I'm knowin' this cop. He comes to here . . . how many times I can't say, but always to same place."

"Alone?"

"Sorry?"

"Was he alone when you saw him before?"

"No, before always with . . ." He takes a second to find the right word. "With another officer. A woman."

"Did he always park in the same place?"

"*Sí.* That house?" He points to the caravan next to Rowan's cruiser. "Nobody living there. Very dark, private."

"How long did he stay? Usually?"

"Maybe an hour."

"What about this time?"

"Much longer. Also, he is alone. I think maybe he's sick, maybe needs help. I don' know, so I look and see the blood."

"Was the window raised or lowered? Don't guess, Pablo. Only if you remember."

"*Sí*, I remember. Engine running, but window is down."

I look to Cade. "Did you check Pablo's ID?"

Cade responds by showing me a dog-eared and soiled Social Security card, along with an identity card issued by the Arkansas Department of Motor Vehicles. The photo on the card might be Pablo, and might not be, but I get the point. Pablo doesn't have a green card. Almost surely, he's in the country illegally, working and sending money home.

What do I want to do? That's the unspoken question. And the answer is nothing. He's a witness and we need him.

"Where are you living now, Pablo? In case we have to speak to you again."

His relieved smile actually warms my cold heart. The boy's not much older than my son, Danny. He points to a single-wide parked toward the head of the block. "With two . . . roommates. Yes? Roommates?"

"And you don't plan to move?"

"No, officer."

"Okay, one more question. Did you see anyone else approach the car? Someone you knew, a stranger, another cop, anybody at all?" I watch him shake his head before walking away. Open one door, close another.

CHAPTER THREE

DELIA

It's coming on to 5:00 A.M. when a uniformed officer named Gianni Vetto approaches. She's introduced herself to me several times, each time repeating her desire to join the detective division. She's tall, several inches taller than me, a local whose settler family's been living in Baxter for generations. No friend of Chief Rawling and his insurgents—like most of our female patrol officers, if not all—I read satisfaction in her dark eyes. She's beat the assholes at their own game.

Gianni leads me to the door. "That motor home across the street?" She points to a blue motor home, a small Winnebago with a sleeping loft that extends over the cab. "There's a camera mounted on the cab over."

All I see at first glance is the word WINNEBAGO, spelled out in yellow script. "Where, Gianni?"

She smiles when I use her first name, then says, "Check out

the *i* in *Winnebago*. The dot." She waits for me to focus my attention. "It's a lens, captain. A camera lens."

Gianni's right. Someone's gone to a lot of trouble, not only to install the camera, but to keep it hidden. I don't know when or why, but if that camera's working, I want tonight's video. I motion Stu Harrington over and explain the situation without pointing. "Did you brace the people living there?"

"Person, captain. Man named Keith Moreland. Least that's how he identified himself."

"He inside now?"

Stu gestures to a small group of men gathered near the bar. "Man with the white ball cap. That'd be him."

"He seem reasonable?"

"If seein' nothin' and hearin' nothin' is reasonable, then he was reasonable. But he didn't have an attitude."

"All right, I want you to bring him over to his unit, to the door on the side. Take Cade Barrow." He starts to turn, but I need to make a point. "Try nice first, but get him there."

The man in the white cap stirs when Stu and Cade approach, then shies away. He stops when Stu shakes his head. There's nowhere to go. Faced now by two cops, the man squares up. He's a fairly short man, perhaps five six or five seven, but solidly built. I can't see his eyes from here, but he appears more determined than afraid. I ignore Gianni Vetto's pleading look. She wants to come along, but I have no idea where this is going. The finish line, yeah. I intend to have a look at that video. The route, on the other hand, has yet to be determined.

"Did you put your name on the detective appointment list?" I ask.

"Last year, captain."

"Long time ago." I hesitate, but Gianni doesn't respond. "Be patient. We'll be making appointments from the list next month. And that was good work, spotting the lens. I won't forget."

◆

"This is Keith Moreland," Stu tells me as I approach the camper. Moreland's mouth has firmed. He stares at me. A man who's simply waiting for whatever comes next.

"You've got a video camera inside the camper," I announce. "I'm hoping you'll allow us to review whatever it's captured tonight."

"Didn't capture nothin'." His voice is gravelly and carries an Eastern accent. "It ain't worked in months."

"You mind if we go inside and take a look?"

"If you had a warrant, you wouldn't be askin'. All polite and everything. So, lemme be polite, too. Nope, you can't go inside."

I like it. The determined tone, projecting a confidence I doubt he feels. "Do you have a Department of Buildings permit to park your camper in this spot? Don't answer, shithead, because we both know you don't."

His head jerks back at my use of the epithet, but he doesn't try to come back on me. Instead, he waits for the hammer to fall. "Let's get a tow truck up here, Stu, and drag the camper to our impound yard." I say it without taking my eyes off Moreland. "Course, you'll have to pay the fine before you get it back. Figure a week for processing, if you get lucky and I don't whisper in a few ears."

Moreland's run out of patience. He takes a half step forward before Cade jams the heel of his hand in the man's chest. That stops him and his gaze softens as the truth dawns on him. There's no win here, none at all.

"I ain't done nothin'," he insists. "I'm just a citizen . . ."

I step forward to stand within inches of him. "You don't look stupid enough to believe that I'm going to let you impede the investigation of a cop's murder. Wise up while you still can. I'm going to tow the camper and get a warrant for whatever's inside. And you, Mr. Moreland, will be on my shit list for as long as you stay in Baxter."

"Okay, wait a second." He turns to Cade as he makes his offer. "I got a laptop inside. I'll bring it out and you can watch the video for yourself."

"Video from the camera you said hasn't worked in months?" Cade asks.

I don't wait for Moreland to reply. "Go get the laptop. And, oh, by the way, if you're thinkin' about slamming the door in our faces, I'll have the camper towed with you in it."

"I'm tryin' to cooperate," Moreland announces, once again indignant. He looks at me for a moment, but when I don't reply, he opens the camper's door. I wait until he's in the doorway, then shove him from behind and follow him inside. I don't know what's going on, but I intend to find out.

The camper's small, maybe twenty feet end to end. The only bed's in the back and currently occupied by a child, a girl. No more than ten years old, she's emaciated, and the bones in her face, shoulders, and arms look as if they're trying to escape the jaundiced skin that encloses them.

For just a moment, the girl looks at me through huge dark eyes set far back in their sockets. Then she smiles and says, "Hello."

◆

"The girl's his daughter," I tell Danny and his girlfriend, Gretchen, at seven o'clock in the morning after two hours of sleep. We're enjoying a breakfast prepared by Gretchen. Oatmeal spiked with cinnamon and dried cherries, topped with a slightly overripe banana. "Jane Moreland. She has a rare disease . . ." I check a note in the spiral notebook all detectives carry. "Niemann-Pick disease. It's inherited, and fatal over time, often a lot of time."

"Shouldn't she be in a hospital?" This from Gretchen.

"Should? I don't know. Her father's telling me the girl's terminal. Maybe she's got a day, maybe a week, but not more than a month. What's not in doubt is that Jane loves her daddy, that Keith Moreland loves his daughter, that they want to spend every minute together. Call it a road trip with goodbye the final destination." I pause long enough to shove a spoonful of oatmeal into my mouth. I'll be back at work in an hour. "Maybe she's lucky, in a way. I'm told the disease affects the spleen, liver, and the brain. But Jane's still holding it back. She's rational, or as rational as you can be when you're either in pain or on opiates."

Danny looks up, his expression thoughtful. "What about the camera? What's that for?"

"The camera is for Jane. She can't sit in the front next to her dad. She's too frail for that. So, her father rigged up the camera to feed into a laptop, which he propped in front of her on the bed."

"So she could see where they were going."

"They drove out every day, to look at the farms and the ranches. Jane told me the buffalo ranches were her favorites." I have to stop for a moment. As she described the little calves stumbling after their mothers, the girl had stared up at me through eyes that reached back to some hopeful place at the center of her universe. "That's my favorite part," she'd told me.

Keith Moreland did everything for his daughter, fed her, washed her, changed her, hugged her in the night when she was afraid. It's too much for me. I'd rather deal with the hate that drove someone to murder Rowan Krauss than the love binding Jane and Keith Moreland. I lack the temperament, and the credentials. And that would be true even if Jane's voice didn't resurrect memories of the Covid epidemic when Danny became—I have to hesitate before I can even think the words—deathly ill.

"The camera worked out for us," I announce. "When Rowan drove onto the block at 1:22, he was alone. That's it, though. The camera's field didn't extend to the end of the block. I can only be sure that he didn't leave and return. He stayed put."

I generally share my cop life with Danny, undoubtedly to a greater extent than I should. But though I've grown fond of Fetchin' Gretchen, I'm not ready to share details of an investigation with her. Besides, the truth is that we have a lot of information, while at the same time we have nothing. Twelve individuals admitted to seeing the cruiser at the end of the block. This wasn't the first time and they didn't think much of it. The timeline we constructed is filled with "arounds" and "abouts." A few, though, remembered Rowan and his "girl" driver from other times.

Our patrol officers get an hour off for a meal. The exact timing depends on how busy they are. (The patrol officers on the murder scene last night were lucky to grab a couple of doughnuts and a container of coffee.) Commonly, cops buy takeout at some restaurant and look for a quiet spot in their sector to eat. Now I'm thinking that Rowan and his driver, a patrol officer named Sheila Corning, routinely sought out that quiet spot. On the one hand, he'd still be subject to the radio-god who lives under the dashboard. On the other, he wouldn't have to deal with the

Boomtown chaos centered on Main Street. Except for the tent-bar, First Avenue is generally quiet.

If peace and quiet was Rowan's motivator, it was also his undoing. An assassin hunting him couldn't help but recognize opportunity. Especially with that vacant caravan at the end of the block. In fact, if the caravan was being used by workers, if the lights were on inside, if somebody occasionally stepped out for a smoke, I can't imagine a professional risking an approach. And a professional is what he or she must've been. We interviewed more than fifty men and women who were on First Avenue when Rowan was murdered and none heard the single shot fired. That screams professional. On the other hand, we found shoe impressions leading north to the top of Boomtown, from alongside the vacant caravan to a path wide enough to accommodate a vehicle, along with very faint tire impressions leading back to Main Street. They didn't go very deep into the hardpacked soil and we settled, in the end, for a series of photographs. I think we'll be able to establish the make and size of the tire that left them, but that won't tell us when they were left.

My train of thought is abruptly cut off when Gretchen asks, "What's gonna happen with the girl?" She's moved, obviously, and more than I would have predicted. That makes an honest answer—she's gonna die, and soon—impossible to say out loud.

"Just now, she and her father are at Baxter Medical. In a private room while the docs decide whether or not she can still be treated. But as far as I'm concerned, there's no crime here and I've turned the problem over to Social Services." I slide my chair back and stand. "I have to get going. Sorry to leave you with the dishes, but the squad's waiting for me."

"What about my game this afternoon?" Danny wants to know. "Can you make it?"

"Yeah, probably." Another evasion. The likelihood is that I won't be home, except for a few minutes at a time, for the next couple of days.

CHAPTER FOUR

CARNEY

The cop who leads me to my cell is old enough to be my grandfather. He walks a half step behind me, a hand on my elbow. I don't protest, though I'm wondering how he defines himself. Maybe he believes that he's ready for anything, which he definitely is not. I could break him in half, and long before any help arrived. That's not what I'm up to, resistance, not tonight. If I was, I'd never have been arrested, not by the two cops who cuffed me. Tall and reasonably fit, they paraded their arrogant attitudes like prom queens displaying their tiaras. Nose-in-the-air proud and dismissive. I was beneath them.

We pass the drunk tank on our way. It's pretty much empty, only six or seven men in various states of inebriation from one substance or another. An older man, big enough to be a jailhouse bully, lifts his head, revealing a scar that runs across his cheekbone. He looks like he's about to make some jailhouse threat, but then his head drops into his hands and he groans. Too fucked up even for that.

A smaller cell farther on holds two men. Both lie on their beds, concrete slabs with a thin mattress on the top. They're wrapped in white blankets that wouldn't keep a chipmunk warm, but they seem resigned, a condition you arrive at once the anger and the fear diminish. When you finally admit that time is all you have.

The cells, themselves, might have been imported from a spaghetti Western. Iron partitions between the cells, vertical steel bars in front, cinderblock walls, and concrete floors, a small window too high up to reach, a stainless toilet-sink combo bolted to the floor. The description matches the conditions found in thousands of small jails. Like maybe all these communities hired the same architect. After his lobotomy.

My escort finally stops before a cell containing two sets of bunk beds, one against each wall, but there's only one occupant. He eyes me as the screw unlocks the cell door, not threatening, but not afraid, either. Call it a jailhouse search for truth. Am I prey, or predator, or ally?

I know the man, or at least have met him, but I can't remember his name. Only that he once brought an item of reasonable value to my boss, Benny Kaplan. Benny owns Kaplan Commercial Refrigeration. That's the front. On the back end, Benny Kaplan's a major fence. He'll move nearly anything, but specializes in high-end vehicles.

Kaplan's a big guy with a zigzag of a nose that's been broken at least three times. He's not a punk, just getting old and tired of fronting for himself. I'm his front now.

◆

Somewhere close to one this morning, I got a call from Benny. Harman Broad was coming by with a six-carat diamond ring, or so he claimed. Harman was a burglar and pretty successful. He was also a slimeball con man with a bad attitude when called on his bullshit. And Benny had the means to expose that bullshit, at least when it comes to jewelry. Benny used a Presidium gem tester. How it works, I can't say, but it's small enough to hold in the palm of your hand and identifies gemstones (or glass) with a touch of its metal probe. According to Benny, you can buy gem testers online for a few hundred dollars.

As he came through the door, Harman's bullshit grin was in full effect. It remained in place until Benny applied the probe, then said. "It's not a diamond. It's a white topaz."

"Fuck you, Benny. Topaz is blue."

"Out of the ground, it's mostly clear. That's why jewelers use topaz in place of diamonds on cheap rings."

What Benny didn't add, and which I knew even before I got here, is that you're as likely to find Godzilla as find a six-carat diamond in this dump of a city. Retail, six-carat diamonds can easily run over a hundred grand.

◆

I don't know why, but there are people in the world who expect to be cheated. One of these, Harman Broad, shivered when Benny added, "The setting's not gold, either. It's vermeil."

Harman probably couldn't define *vermeil*, but he was smart enough to know that he wasn't gonna come away with the serious bank he expected. He quickly reverted to his default response. He stepped toward Benny, but I was already between them and prepared to answer back if he threw a punch, which he did. My response was justified, but I carried the lesson a little too far and we had to call for an ambulance. One side of Harman's face had collapsed and he was breathing through enough blood to leave his survival in doubt.

The cops showed up before the ambulance. Two expressionless robots in blue uniforms that appeared black in the low light at the rear of the store. Their bills on their caps gleamed and the creases in their trousers were so sharp they might have used them to shave their near-bald skulls. Initially, they questioned Harman, who only shook his head while his lips formed silent words that were better left unspoken. I was arrested anyway, probably because the knuckles on my right hand were bleeding. I'm sayin' probably because the cops obviously knew Benny. That didn't surprise me and I didn't put up any resistance when they cuffed me. Most cops have a quota to meet, so many arrests each month, and the near certainty that all charges would be dismissed in the morning wasn't relevant. Numbers being numbers.

A night in jail didn't upset me, not even a little, but I admit to just a touch of resentment when they detoured to a quiet street in Oakland Gardens, pulled me out of the back, and delivered a half-hearted tune-up. Punches to the ribs and the kidneys, and not all that hard, just sending a message. Like the polished mirror-bright shields, or the steel-toed brogans.

"Welcome to Baxter," they told me. Several times.

◆

My cellmate watches me for a couple of minutes. I don't know what he's looking for, but his expression softens finally, and he says, "I seen you around. You work for the Jew, right?"

Me, if I was Benny, I'd take offense at being universally called the Jew. Not Benny. What he told me is that being a Jew is something like being a Catholic. You can be lapsed, but you can never be ex.

"Yeah, I work for Benny Kaplan. Name's Carney."

"Sal."

This is where the conversation should stop as far as I'm concerned. The world we inhabit, me and Sal, is filled with snitches, including those of the jailhouse variety. You don't ask your cellmate about his charges, or about what he does on the outside. And you don't enter his house without permission. Your house can be your bunk, or a one-man cell, or an upper bunk in a four-man cell. But whatever little space is left to you becomes your house. Which you are obliged to defend against intruders.

On the other hand, jails and prisons are as much about networking as fraternities at Harvard. As Sarah, Benny's wife might say, "Go figure."

◆

"Cop got himself killed tonight," Sal announces.

Sal's a short man, but heavily built, with a pockmarked complexion and shaggy hair that hangs in curls to his shoulders. When I make no attempt to mask my surprise, he grins, his satisfaction evident. Gotcha.

"When did this happen?"

"Tonight."

"You said that, Sal. I'm askin' when, since I've been around all night and I haven't heard anything about a whacked cop."

Sal raises a stubby finger and wags it in my direction. "I ain't a liar."

"Maybe not, but you can still be wrong. Or maybe have inside knowledge. You know, knowledge that hasn't reached the general public."

Sal is a liar, of course. Jailhouse mutts are all liars when it suits them. But the part about inside knowledge is a lot more important. That's because, if I should happen to be the jailhouse snitch I could be, Sal's gifted me with information I can trade on for the next decade.

I watch Sal's gaze turn inward. What has he just done and how can he undo it? Dumb as he is, the search takes a few minutes. Then he gets up and takes a step toward me, but doesn't cross the imaginary line between our houses.

"Somethin' I gotta show ya. If it's okay."

"Come ahead."

Now Sal's smiling as he kneels at the foot of my bed and presses his fingers to the cinderblock wall at the back of the cell. A few seconds later, an irregular chunk of the wall comes loose. There's a cell phone tucked behind it and Sal holds it up, his smile now triumphant. He carries the phone back to his own house, then says, "You gotta have resources. Jailin's all about resources."

I lean back on the rolled blanket I'm using for a pillow. "You get Wi-Fi in here?"

"Say what?"

"So you can get on the internet."

He's sitting on the edge of his bunk, leaning forward, hands folded on his lap. "Didn't use no internet. Shit, man, the internet's for the naughty-naughty." He stops for a minute, probably waiting for me to laugh. When I don't, he adds, "Pornos, right?"

"Right."

"Anyways, I made a call out. To my partner, okay?"

"Okay."

"That's how I found out." He nods several times. "About the cop."

◆

I have nothing more to say and I close my eyes, hoping to catch a few hours sleep before I'm cut loose. My knuckles hurt, not to mention my ribs, but I'm good at ignoring discomfort. In the army, I saw my share of combat, and learned a basic truth. You take your sleep where and when you can get it. And I'm really close, the hazy edges of a dream already floating through my brain, when Sal starts up again. I hear confidence in his voice and a measure of trust. Criminals commonly believe they're all part of some grand coalition. Us against them, with them being the entire straight world, including cops, even crooked cops.

"You ever take outside jobs?" he wants to know.

I sit up and throw my legs over the edge of the bed. I'm a large man, much larger than Sal, but not into macho displays. You throw a punch at me or pull a weapon, I will hurt you. For the rest of it, I stay calm.

"You have a reason for askin', Sal?"

Sal drags his thumb over the tips of his fingers. A finger snap, only silent. He's about to speak when a scream echoes through the corridors outside our cell. I listen to the sound of running feet followed by a thud, then another scream, then silence. Sal drops his head for a second.

"Some assholes," he observes, "never stop fightin', know what I mean? It's like a principle. Gettin' their asses kicked."

He's tellin' the truth about knuckleheads. Loners, almost always, you can smell the violence from across the room, like a scorched pot. Only you can't know what's gonna set 'em off, and you try to keep out of the way. Not because you're afraid. It's because they're losers, all of them, doomed to be left dead in an alley somewhere, or to rot in solitary confinement.

"So, you were saying . . ."

Sal looks up. "So, yeah, I got popped for a DUI, like, not for the first time, so I'm stuck here for a fucking month. Meanwhile, me and my partner, we gotta pick somethin' up. Out of town." He stops, but I'm not biting. "This thing, it's safe. We done it maybe five times already, but I'm thinkin' George shouldn't do the run alone."

"Why's that?"

Sal runs his fingers through his long hair, exposing his right ear. Half the lobe is missing. "It looks weak." He laughs. "Hell, man, it is weak."

I fall back on the mattress. "Sorry, man, I'm a cautious type. I tend to stay out of caves until I'm sure there's no bear inside."

"I don't blame ya, man." Another hollow laugh, followed by a glance at the ceiling as he searches for the words. "Okay, the last time I was inside, I volunteered for this therapy group. Brownie points with the parole board, right? But to be truthful here, I did learn somethin'. This therapist, Dr. Monello, she . . ."

"A woman therapist? In the joint?"

"Yeah, a true MILF, Carney. It was all I could do not to look up her skirt." He clears his throat. "Anyways, she told us a bunch of times that the main problem with repeat offenders, like me and everybody else in the room, was poor impulse control. We just can't resist temptation. That's why I'm admirin' your cool. You ain't gonna jump into nothin' you don't understand."

What next, a blow job? "Do me a favor, Sal, and get to the point. I'm hopin' for a few hours sleep before they cut me loose."

"First thing, it's a grand on your end, paid when you get back. Maybe five hours, from start to finish. You take two cars, George in front, you following, to a big truck stop off I-80. You'll find a van with a certain license plate in the parking lot. George is gonna drive the van. All you gotta do is drive your own car. You never get out."

"Unless the train goes off the rails for some reason or other."

"Yeah, unless."

Neither of us speaks for a moment, until I ask the obvious question. "What's in the truck, Sal?" I don't ask what's in the car George intends to leave behind. The answer is obvious enough. The payment for whatever's in the truck.

"I know what you're thinkin'. You're thinkin' it's dope."

"Dope? I don't give a shit. Not trafficked women, which runs against the few principles I got left."

This time, Sal's grin is genuine. He's got me. "Not women, not drugs. Cigarettes. Man, these days, what with the fucking taxes, you can sell bootleg cigarettes easier than sellin' dope or speed or blow or just about anything else."

"Hijacked cigarettes?" I put a question mark at the end of the sentence, like I'm thinkin' it over. Which I'm not, not really. "Okay, I'm in. But no bullshit, Sal. I don't care if the truck's empty. I get paid."

"Your end's a hundred percent guaranteed, but we gotta go within the next couple of days. You sure you'll be kicked loose in the morning?"

"One way to find out." I point to the phone. "I need to make a quick call." Again, I'm not really asking, but I'm not confronting, either. He can always refuse.

"Okay." He enters his password, then passes the phone. "But don't say nothin' that I wouldn't say."

I laugh as I tap the phone button and the screen jumps to the keypad. At the bottom, below the keypad, other possibilities are listed: Keypad, Recents, Contacts, Place. I tap Recents, which reveals that Sal's last outgoing call was made to George Pratt at 2:33 A.M. Then I return to the keypad, all the while holding the phone close to my face. A moment later, I'm talking to my pissed-off boss.

"For Christ's sake, Carney. After a terrible night, I'm finally dozing off and you bust into the hottest wet dream I've had in years. Before the fuckin' wet part."

"Just need to know if it's still cool out there."

I listen to Benny's semi-wheeze for a moment. Most likely, he's waking up to the fact that he's talking to someone in a jail cell using a smuggled cell phone. "Yeah, nothing to worry about. You're an innocent man. Now I'm gonna sleep in today. I'll see you tonight."

CHAPTER FIVE

CARNEY

Never mind the circumstances. Even knowing you're gonna walk free after a few hours, you can't help but feel you've escaped some terrible danger when you finally step into the light. And that sense is all the more powerful if the light you step into flows from a bright sun perched in the purest of pure blue skies. I stop to watch three pigeons as they fly across Baxter Boulevard, watch them twist and turn, swoop and soar. And I know what's happening with the pigeons. A mated pair is being chased by an unattached male. It's a bit past nesting season and I suspect the unattached male is fairly desperate.

It's early, not yet eight o'clock, and I'm hungry. A trusty served breakfast inside about two hours ago. Eggs so runny I'd have to drink them, which I chose not to do. Sal didn't hesitate, though. It's slurp or starve for Sal.

I'm tempted to head for a legendary joint called Lena's Luncheonette, only a couple of blocks away. But the restaurant's a hangout for cops and I pass by without going inside. A block farther south, I find a deli where I pick up a fried egg sandwich on a roll and a large container of coffee. I take both to a sunny bench in City Hall Green.

Mostly, I don't see myself as attractive or unattractive to women. Today's a little different, what with the sun, the rising temperatures, and a parade of well-dressed women on their way to city hall at the north end of the park. There's also that other factor, which is that I've lived in Baxter for three months without establishing an enduring relationship. I've taken stabs at it, mutually abortive stabs. Now, my interest isn't so much in checking out the women who pass by, as it is in who might be interested in me. The answer is simple enough. Nobody. And the truth is that I fare better in dimly lit bars after a couple of drinks.

I content myself with my breakfast. The warm sun is consoling, as are alternating beds of crimson tulips and purple iris. Baby-pink blossoms cover rolling azalea bushes, and the still-translucent leaves on the maples glow as if projecting their own light.

I finally dump the remains of my breakfast in a trash barrel and head uptown on Baxter Boulevard. This early in the spring, the air should be filled with birdsong. Instead, I listen to falling hammers, saws cutting through wood, the clang of a pile driver off in the distance. Baxter's gone construction crazy, with contractors operating in every part of town. And this is only the beginning.

On the far side of Boomtown, the newly planted fields of soybeans and corn may not even see the harvest. Two hundred acres have been sold to a national developer who plans to construct a small city on the acreage. Single-family homes on half-acre lots, attached single-family townhouses, two- and three-family homes, six-floor apartment buildings. All neatly organized north-to-south with the best homes on the north end. Add in a small park and a bicycle-jogging path, lots of trees, Main Street in Boomtown given over to stores and barbershops, to dentists and lawyers, to drop-in medical offices, and you have the makings of a self-sufficient community.

I reach Kaplan Commercial Refrigeration, eight blocks north of city hall, a few minutes later. The store's not much to look at, by design. If you want a stove for your home, Kaplan Refrigeration will sell it to you, but that's not what they're about. Kaplan's services apartment buildings, delis, small supermarkets, restaurants, bars, and motels. The décor in its showroom reflects a no-frills business strategy that (according to Benny) makes a more-than-decent profit. Stoves here, refrigerators there, coolers against a far wall, a parts counter in the middle. Whatta ya need? A tiny fridge for a low-end studio apartment? A ten-burner, two-oven stove for your restaurant? Kaplan Refrigeration will supply either at a discount.

My Jeep's parked in the narrow lot at the front of the store. I could jump inside and drive away. I've got an important task that needs attending. But I stop long enough to offer Sarah Kaplan a good morning. Sarah's at least a decade younger than Benny and a seriously good-looking woman. Raven-haired and raven-eyed, her full mouth, curled slightly up at one corner, invites my attention. Meanwhile, the woman's all business. She seems utterly unaware of her appeal.

Today, she wears a navy blue shop coat over blue jeans and a pair of teal athletic shoes. When I enter, she's standing near a door that leads to the stockroom, watching Mark and Joe, two of the store's four workers, wrestle a refrigerator-freezer to what appears to be a draw.

"Ah, it's you," she tells me. "Tell me you're not a fugitive from justice."

"Nope, I'm free as a bird. Seems the victim in this case decided not to cooperate."

"So, whatta ya want from me this morning?"

"Just pickin' up my car."

"And you think it's inside?"

I smile and shrug. "What's up with Benny?"

"Home asleep. He won't need you until late afternoon." Finally, she smiles and nods. "You did good, Carney. Last night. Benny appreciates you steppin' up. Me, too. I like my husband and his big mouth in one piece."

◆

All good, and not because of the praise. My ego isn't so easily stroked. But I've got things to do and the whole day to do them. I hop into my Cherokee and head out of town. My destination is a farmhouse about twenty miles into Maryville County. There's no farm associated with this particular farmhouse. The fields that surround the home's two-acre lot are cultivated by an LLC in Chicago.

A Baxter police detective named Stu Harrington lives in the house, along with his wife, Brenda, their two small children, three dogs, and a flock of chickens that spend their days wandering the fenced yard. All very picturesque, but I'm not here for the atmosphere. I'm a Baxter detective, working deep undercover with the goal of accumulating evidence of police corruption in the department.

Simple as that? The cops in question, the corrupt cops, are also associated with a penchant for unnecessary violence. Dominance is the name of their game. Which is what they showed me last night.

Brenda's in the garden when I step out of the car, on her knees as she yanks what I assume to be weeds from the soil. Her youngest, whose name I forget, is sitting in a four-wheeled contraption that allows her feet to reach the grass. She's jiggling up and down, muttering, "Da-da-da-da-da." Me, I'm from Philadelphia, a city-raised kid with no particular love for the country. I wave to Brenda, who waves back.

I head up to a porch that fronts the farmhouse end to end. Stu Harrington's seated in a rocker, but he rises when I climb the steps. I'm somewhat surprised to find him at home, appointment or no appointment, what with a cop's murder to investigate. But then it comes to me. Delia Mariola, our chief of detectives, is running the investigation, not Stu. Surely at the direction of our commissioner.

"Let's go inside, get some coffee."

I don't particularly like Detective Harrington. The long horse face, a thick mustache that curls around the corners of his mouth, the slow semidrawl. I've got a feeling that he's been cultivating his Sam Elliott look for a long time. But liking him has nothing to do with it. Police departments are paramilitary organizations with top-down command structures. Harrington's running me and that's that. The order came directly from Mariola, who recruited me in the first place. As she and Stu (and maybe the commissioner) are the only cops who know what I'm doing, it pays me to be reasonably cooperative. Sam Elliott impression or not.

The interior of the farmhouse has yet to see the sort of open-concept remodeling so popular these days. Stu leads me into a large family room with chairs and tables and toys scattered about, then straight through a door at the rear into a kitchen big enough to hold a long table. Stu pulls a mug from a shelf loaded with mugs, this one decorated with a Texas longhorn and a cowboy in full regalia.

"Help yourself, Carney. Milk's in the fridge, sugar's in a blue bin."

I dutifully pour my coffee and add a little milk. No sugar. "It's been a busy night. For me, anyway."

"Yeah, so how'd you get yourself arrested?"

Funny thing about working deep undercover. You're supposed to weasel your way into criminal organizations without committing any crimes yourself. Stu's not dumb enough to believe this is actually possible. No, it's more about don't ask, don't tell. Meanwhile, that's not entirely possible, either, paperwork being paperwork. Progress reports must be filed, even if they're initially reviewed only by Captain Mariola.

"I busted up an overexcited asshole named Harman Broad, which is the job Benny Kaplan hired me to do. Not a problem, though. Harman refused to cooperate."

"From jump?"

"Yeah. Wouldn't talk to the cops, not one word."

"So, why'd they arrest you?"

"Juicin' their stats, most likely. Or maybe they only wanted an opportunity to show me what they were about. I'm sayin' that because we made a stop on our way to jail for a quick tune-up. Nothin' heavy, Stu. Just here we are and here you are and we can kick your ass anytime for any reason."

"You get their names?"

"Beale and Stepanik, according to their identification tags. Their names should be on the arrest report as well."

Stu gives it a moment while I sip at my coffee. He's the chief's favorite these days, and seems anxious to keep it that way. That means taking down the corrupt cops in the department, the current priority, and failure isn't an option. Not that Stu Harrington appears anxious. He's maintaining his cool as he tugs at one end of his mustache.

"Something else, Stu, though I have nothing tangible to back it up. Beale and Stepanik? I'm pretty sure they knew Benny."

"How's that?"

"They never spoke to him, didn't even ask his name. I mean, Harman was the one with the busted face and I was the asshole with the bruised knuckles. That made us priorities, yeah. But they're not reasons to ignore Benny altogether."

"You get a tad closer to Benny, he'll probably open up."

"Busting Harman's face was my way of doin' exactly that."

"Well, I do wish you good luck. Extortion and bribery go to the heart of the investigation." Stu's about to say something else when his daughter tears into the kitchen. She's three or four years old and still running like a toddler, head back, legs leading, rocking side to side. A chocolate lab with a gray muzzle follows, its gait as unsure as the kid's. Stu leans forward to pull his daughter into his arms. "You heard what happened last night? To Rowan Krauss?"

"Yeah, I heard." I watch Stu's eyes narrow slightly. I've tickled at the edges of his cop instincts. "I was inside when I heard. My cellie, dude named Sal, told me."

"And who told Sal?"

"Sal had a phone."

"In his cell?"

"Yup. Man on the other end of the phone was his partner, George Pratt."

"Okay, we don't have an official time of death yet, but the coroner's thinkin' between two and about two thirty."

The call from Sal to his partner took place at thirty-three minutes after two. So, how did George know what he did when he did? The answer might be innocent. Maybe George happened to be close to the crime scene, perhaps he heard the sirens and simply followed them out of curiosity. Or maybe not.

I might share this info with Stu. In fact, most likely I'm obliged to report the time of that phone call. But I only smile and wave to Brenda as I head back to my Jeep.

CHAPTER SIX

CARNEY

I make a quick stop at my home, a small trailer off Eighth Avenue in Boomtown. Boomtown sprang up a couple of years ago as workers flooded into Baxter from all over the country. The long road fronting the construction zone they called Main Street. The short east–west streets are deemed avenues and numbered from north to south.

Eighth Avenue is fairly quiet when I pull up in front of my trailer, the workday on the construction site having started two hours ago. Good thing because I'm in a hurry. Still, I find a moment to greet my neighbor, Jennie Adams. Jennie's sitting in a lawn chair, her crutch on the grass beside her, enjoying the early morning sun.

"Morning, Carney, how you feeling today?"

"Never better. And yourself?"

"Can't feel bad on a sunny day in the month of May." Jennie's laugh is infectious, as always. Some sort of childhood infection left her with a severely weakened left leg. On good days, most days, she gets by with a limp. Not today. But Jennie never complains, her husband, either. They're stiff upper lip types from Indiana. "We're gonna barbecue tonight and you're invited to join us."

"Appreciate it, Jennie, but I might have to work at Kaplan's." I draw a deep breath. "Damn, I can almost smell it on the grill." I glance at my watch. "Sorry, busy morning."

"More work?"

My comings and goings are none of Jennie's business. She's curious, sure, because my hours are anything but regular. "Early or late, it's all about gettin' the worm. And, me, I'm one hungry robin."

◆

My rented trailer's basically one big room with a mini-bathroom attached. There's a sink, but no stove, and a refrigerator that's closer in size to a cooler. That's fine because setting the timer on the microwave is as close as I come to cooking. I reach under a couch pushed against the wall and remove a padlocked metal tool chest. I enter the combination, then lift the lid to expose a 9mm Glock auto, a spare magazine, and several boxes of ammo. I'm not especially fond of guns, but as a cop, I'm required to own the service weapon I rarely carry. Benny's not payin' for that kind of protection. George Pratt, on the other hand, for a thousand dollars, gets the full Monty.

I slide the pistol behind the waistband of my jeans, then grab a sweatshirt from the camper's single closet and pull it on. The sweatshirt bears the logo of the Philadelphia Phillies, a blue

Liberty Bell with PHILLIES in bright red letters across the chest. The sweatshirt's oversized and covers the pistol nicely.

The City of Baxter allows open carry but requires a permit for concealed weapons. I don't have a permit, or a Baxter PD badge. Should I be arrested on a weapons charge, my only fallbacks are Stu Harrington and Delia Mariola. I don't know either well enough to be sure they won't, if the occasion calls for it, throw me to the wolves. Did I mention that Mariola's holding my shield?

◆

Twenty minutes later, I walk into Packers Bar & Restaurant on the southern end of Baxter Boulevard, the name an obvious nod to the heyday of a meatpacking industry that once anchored Baxter's economy. I'm meeting George Pratt at eleven, the time arranged by Sal. Call it an audition with all parties auditioning. As a secondary benefit, Packers is known to be a hangout for serious players, but my job with Benny doesn't come within sight of the serious part. Now, I'm walking inside, invited.

The first thing I notice is that the bar's open for business, a violation of city regulations. Restaurants aren't supposed to serve alcohol before noon. The regulation is without effect in Boomtown, but Packers is located on Baxter Boulevard and it isn't a dive. The bar's dark wood gleams, the tile floors are polished, the faux-leather booths along the front wall unmarred, the four-tops down the center already set for business that's yet to arrive. A mural behind the bar on the inside wall depicts cowboys driving a herd of cattle down the main street of a Western town while ladies in hoopskirts and men wearing ten-gallon hats watch from atop a wooden sidewalk.

The man washing glasses behind the bar has to outweigh me by fifty pounds. As my weight generally runs about two-ten, he definitely impresses. But he's a businessman, too, so if I've come for a beer or a burger, great. If I'm trouble, he's prepared for that, too.

"What can I get ya?" he asks as I approach the bar.

"George Pratt. He's expecting me."

"Your name?"

"Carney."

He points to a booth at the far end of the restaurant, well away from the few customers settling into an early lunch. I'm not halfway there before I've taken my host's measure. Pratt's totally wrong for the game. Even beyond a physique that's more bone than muscle, his brown eyes hold no fire, but they're not dead, either. They project a soft desperation that any seasoned criminal will instantly recognize. His pudgy face doesn't help. He looks as though he's still waiting to lose his baby fat. That makes Sal his protector by default.

I don't run into boy-men like Pratt very often in the criminal world I police. Usually, I find people like him among the victims of crime. And that's exactly what Pratt will become if he spends time in prison. A victim.

"Name's Carney," I tell him. "Sal told me you might have a job I could help with."

"Yeah, he called me. Sit down, let's talk." George Pratt's gruff tone doesn't surprise me, just part of the bad-boy facade. "You hungry?"

"I had breakfast."

"Coffee?"

I'm tempted to say that I prefer tea, but I'm pretty sure that Pratt's sense of humor's confined to pulling the wings off butterflies. "Yeah, coffee, great."

A single waiter sits on a stool at the end of the bar. He looks up when Pratt calls him by name, "Hey, Frank, a coffee, por favor."

Frank nods once then heads for the coffee station behind the bar. Pratt looks up at me. "Everybody's got a fuckin' attitude," he tells me.

"True enough." I sit forward, "So, as I see it, I'm supposed to back you up if the shit hits the fan. My kinda job, George. Right up my alley."

Pratt rubs at a thin beard that almost covers his chin. "You work for the Jew, right?"

"Yeah, for Benny."

"Whatta ya do for him?"

This is not George Pratt's business, but I maintain a neutral tone when I reply, "Whatever he wants."

Now that we've disrespected each other, Pratt seems content. "So, yeah, all you gotta do is follow me. You never get out of the car."

"Unless."

"Yeah, unless. But it's not something you need to worry about. It ain't gonna happen."

I pause while Frank ambles up to our table. He's wearing a white shirt and black trousers, a typical waiters' uniform, but something about his attitude tells me there's more to the story. Maybe it's the dead eyes, or the compressed lips, or the complete silence as he drops the cup and saucer on the table, then strolls back to his seat.

"One thing I gotta know, George. What's in the truck?" I watch Pratt bristle. I've put a pinprick in his badass armor. Now I've got to pull back. I raise the band of my sweatshirt, revealing the gun beneath, then pull it back down. "That's my level of commitment, assuming we go ahead. But I can't go in blind. I need to know you're not muling women, or kids."

"Cigarettes." He finally smiles and I know he's about to pump his creds. "A thousand cartons, all neatly boxed. Product of a hijacking in Alabama. Even as middlemen, and with all the expenses, me and Sal are lookin' at ten bucks a carton profit. And this ain't our first rodeo. We done this before with no problems."

"What about the cops in Baxter? If they stop you, how should I play it?" My turn to smile. "I mean they're fuckin' aggressive. Last night, they tuned me up pretty good."

"Forget about it, Carney. We got that angle covered. It's like a fuckin' co-op, this city. Everybody gets a share."

CHAPTER SEVEN
DELIA

I'm behind my desk before eight, sorting through the various notes and witness reports taken by my detectives. Altogether, they interviewed more than fifty individuals. Of these, only twelve admitted to noticing the cruiser. This is bullshit, of course. A Baxter-blue police cruiser with a light bar on top was almost certain to be noted by anybody on the street.

Of the cooperative witnesses, eleven live on First Avenue, while four live elsewhere in the city. We demanded ID from these, thinking that a shooter from outside might stick around to admire his work.

Desperation on our part? Probably. The gap between time of death and the body's discovery argues against sticking around. Nor would a pro linger at a murder scene. And we all believe, given the probable use of a suppressed handgun, the killer was a pro.

The individual witness reports pretty much prove that Krauss and his pregnant driver made the far end of First Avenue a regular stop no matter what tour they worked. That gave the assassin time to plan a route into and out of Boomtown. Still, the presence of Sheila Corning, Rowan's customary driver, would have certainly complicated the project. As would the presence of the patrol officer, Ivy Jordan, newly assigned to the job. Rowan's attacker pressed his weapon against Rowan's head and pulled the trigger. One and done. But Ivy Jordan would be on the other side of the car, snatching at her own weapon. Even if the attacker fired first, he or she would still have to make sure that Ivy was dead. This at a time when every extra second carried risk.

Ivy Jordan never reported for duty last night. Nor did she answer her phone or respond when two cops knocked on the door of her darkened home in Norwood at three o'clock this morning.

◆

My thoughts are interrupted by a knock on my door. A moment later, I'm looking at Patrolwoman Gianni Vetto.

"You asked me to report to your office?"

Gianni has a round face, somewhat soft at the edges, but her dark eyes are sharp. If she'd chosen to wear makeup, I suspect she'd be quite attractive, but there's a no-nonsense quality to her expression, a quality enhanced by her height. She has to be five ten.

"I know you're married," I tell her, "but do you have children?"

"No, not yet. We're . . ."

"I'm not prying, Gianni. I want you to join the task force, but not if you've got young kids. They need you more than I do."

I stop there as Gianni's eyes widen. I haven't offered her a spot in the detective division. She'll remain a patrol officer. If Rowan was murdered by somebody with a grudge, somebody he sent to jail, that wouldn't matter. But if other cops were involved, she could easily become a target herself. Surely, she'll be harassed, and she might be harassed anyway. The power struggle between the detective and patrol divisions isn't lost on either side. I don't think we're quite there yet, but it might come down to which side are you on. No middle ground.

"There's a bar, captain, called Duke's, where the boys hang out. It's not that no women are allowed. It's that no women cops are respected. I stopped in once and there had to be ten cops inside. Nobody spoke to me, or even acknowledged my existence, including cops I'd ridden with on patrol."

"What do you think it's about?"

"I think it's about a sign behind the bar. Not huge, but definitely there. MAKE POLICING GREAT AGAIN. I remember one partner, Jeff Greentree, quoting a nineteenth-century New York cop named Clubber Williams. 'There's more law at the end of a nightstick than in a Supreme Court decision.' That's how they operate and they don't need women cops slowing their play."

"You want to name names?"

"If that's a requirement, I'm gonna have to refuse your offer. Cops don't rat on other cops. Plus, I don't have anything concrete to offer. Just a general attitude along with the occasional joke centered on the external parts of a woman's reproductive organs. That's another thing Jeff Greentree made clear. You turn rat, there's a price to pay."

"What about going forward?"

Gianni crosses her legs as she considers the question. For a moment, I watch her chew on the end of a very blunt fingernail, until she finally asks, "Is that what this is about? Police brutality?"

"I'm not entirely sure what you mean by 'this', but this is about the murder of a good cop. Rowan Krauss was determined to root out corruption and brutality in the patrol division and he paid the ultimate price. I reviewed his file last night, looking for somebody with a grudge. Somebody he arrested. The only thing, Gianni, is that Rowan usually gave collars to the cops he supervised. And I'm a hundred percent sure that he didn't lean toward justice at the end of a nightstick. That's because he told me so."

A sigh now, and a shake of the head as Gianni strokes her cheeks with her right hand. "Rowan broke me in, captain. A good cop who worried about the cops under his command. He wanted to help build a department that served the city's interests. So, going forward, I'll do whatever it takes. No holding back, whatever my assignment might be." She leans toward me. "That's because I want the same thing. I want to be able to hold my head up when I tell people I'm a Baxter cop. But the way it's going now? In this city? If I want to hold my head up, I'm gonna have to find another police force."

◆

Our task force, which pretty much includes every detective on the squad, is already assembled in the department's only conference room when Gianni and I enter. They're consuming whatever breakfast they managed to order up. Most have been awake all night and need to refuel before they pursue their still-to-be-determined assignments. Only Stu Harrington is missing.

I glance at my watch. Just now, Stu's meeting with the job's single undercover cop at Stu's home in Maryville County. It takes a moment to recall his first name, which he never uses. Tom Carney's out of Philadelphia, which might as well be Mars so far as Baxter locals are concerned. All to the good, but I don't entirely trust him. The man's self-contained to the point of inscrutable. On the other hand, should his identity be uncovered, his life will surely be in danger. And not only from the criminals among us, but from other cops as well. Uncovering the organized corruption plaguing our city is his primary assignment. That's why his shield and his personnel file are under lock and key in my house.

Six detectives are sitting at one end of a long table, the only furniture in the room aside from the chairs. There are no patrol cops present even though I'd ordinarily use them for the scut work. I note the angry faces as I take a seat at the end of the table. Anger's sometimes useful, like if the asshole you're about to arrest decides to resist. But there's no asshole in front of us. Rowan's killer will have to be uncovered the old-fashioned way. By careful attention to detail, by turning over each and every stone, then turning it over again. I look from Cade Barrow to Laura Udell to Marcus Goodman to Rena Cafaro to Sam Barret to John Meacham, "the Dink."

"I want to begin with a warning. Whatever evidence you turn up, it stays with the task force. Rowan Krauss put his opinions out there and now he's dead. Understand?"

The question's not rhetorical and I wait for nods of acknowledgment before continuing. I don't mention the patrol division, but I don't have to mention them. My detectives have informants they rely on. These informants have described the beatings and extortion committed by the patrol division. They're not willing to name names, much less testify, because we can't offer them protection. To do that we'd have to draw on the same patrol-division cops they fear.

"All right, let's get started. Rena, did you speak to Sheila Corning?" Sheila served as Rowan Krauss's driver until she gave birth.

Detective Rena Cafaro is new to the squad room. She's clever and smart enough to be ruthless without crossing lines, or at least getting caught. Just now, she seems relaxed, her customary half smile firmly fixed, a gold chain around her neck, gold hoops in her ears.

"I spoke to her an hour ago. And, yes, she and Rowan took their meals on First Avenue, exceptions being when some investigation put them on the other side of Baxter Boulevard. She told me that Rowan was drawn to the fields and the growing crop. The cycle, right, from the sowing to the harvest."

"Did you leave it there?"

"No, I asked her if Rowan was working on some project that might have drawn attention. She whistled, captain. Like I could almost see her shake her head at the stupidity of the question. Rowan hated the new breed. That's how Sheila put it. Hated them. And he was keeping some kind of journal containing allegations made by his own informants."

"Did he personally witness any of these violations?"

"Not to Sheila's knowledge. But she did say that Rowan believed there was an individual running the show, a boss. 'Cut off the head, the body dies.' That's what he told Sheila."

"But no name?"

"No name."

"What about Ivy Jordan?"

"Been out there four times. The house is dark and nobody answers the door. Likewise for her phone."

"You check her personnel file?"

"Yeah. Her folks live in Tennessee, back in the hills. They're sayin' they last heard from her two weeks ago. I also checked with her neighbors. Nobody's seen her for a couple of days."

"And she lives alone?"

"Yeah."

Gianni Vetto chooses that moment to speak. "I know Ivy well. We've partnered together and shared drinks after work. No way she was involved in killing another cop. No fucking way."

I nod to Gianni but address Rena. "Let's get in there. Call it a welfare check, whatever."

"I'll get on it right away, but one more thing, captain. I asked Sheila if Rowan ever took a nap. You know, after his meal. I mean, I've done it myself when I was exhausted and the city was quiet, so it's not that big a deal. Anyway, Sheila told me that Rowan usually had a beer with his meal, which he shouldn't, and that sometimes, especially when they got to the meal late, he did fall asleep. Not for long, but he definitely nodded off."

I look around the room to find my detectives paying attention. Rena's initiative answers a question we've all been asking. The bullet fired into Rowan's head entered his temple just in front of his left ear. He must have been facing forward. Not likely if he'd seen it coming. But asleep, he would have made an easy target, while minimizing the time his attacker spent on the street.

◆

I move on to Sam Barret. Sam's been working through the witness statements, all fifty. We want a reliable timeline, of course, but Sam was assigned to concentrate on the witnesses who saw nothing.

"Okay, first thing, we have domiciles for every witness. I'm not sayin' addresses because Boomtown residences, if you could call 'em that, aren't numbered. Mail to the people livin' in Boomtown has to be collected at the post office. That said, the interviews themselves don't really help us. Too many 'arounds' and 'abouts.'"

Barret's young and good-looking. He's a sharp dresser, too, always in a suit, though suits aren't mandatory in the division. Today, forgivably, he looks a bit disheveled, though he's taken the time to shave. "I think some of them are holdin' back. Same for some who claimed to see nothing. We need to gain their cooperation, but . . ."

If Sam's asking for guidance, he's come to the right place. I shift a bit in my seat and cross my legs. The conference room is as barren as ever, the chairs, if anything, even more uncomfortable. There's a podium against the wall, flanked by our state and the American flags. I've never seen it used.

"I want you to set up the hotline." I gesture to Gianni. "I don't know if you've met Gianni Vetto, but she'll work with you. Once you establish the hotline number, I want you to print up flyers and distribute them by hand to anyone you can find on First Avenue, especially the witnesses you've already spoken to. They're seein' a murdered cop at the end of the block and they don't want to be next. But just maybe they'll place an anonymous call to a hotline. It's no-lose for us. We have to set up the hotline anyway."

Barret merely nods and I'm about to move on when Marcus Goodman raises his hand. "Permission to speak, captain," he says.

Permission? I have to smile. Detective Goodman's a big fan of World War II movies. He told me that he's watched *Band of Brothers* twenty-five times.

"Permission granted, detective. Please be concise."

Marcus Goodman's one of two Black men on the force. Of average height and very broad, he can be formidable, what with the shaved head. Yet his features are relatively delicate and I've seen him work a suspect in the box. The man can do empathy with the best of them.

"We talked for a while before you came in, captain. We feel, all of us, that Rowan's murder was a professional hit. Getting in and out without being seen? A suppressed handgun? Doesn't speak to a street thug with a grudge."

I cut him off. "We've been all over this, Marcus. I'm on your side here."

"Yeah, right, but I have a thought about that suppressor. Now you can legally purchase a suppressor at a gun store, but you have to register with the ATF first. That'd be the Feds and they keep records. Myself, I'm not believing a pro would take that step, knowin' we're gonna check it out."

"Okay, he bought the suppressor illegally. Where do we go from there?"

"That's the point. Last week, we popped an illegal dealer in stolen, untraceable weapons, and I've got three other dealers on my shopping list. You say the word, I'll put serious heat on 'em. In fact, I'll squeeze the bastards till they fucking pop."

This is an area I intended to cover from the outset. To a certain extent, the professional hit man part is only the most likely explanation. The use of a silencer, on the other hand, is a virtual certainty.

"Do it, Marcus, and while you're at it, take a look at any local released from prison in the last couple of months who might fit the definition of a professional."

◆

We take a quick break, mainly for me to fuel up on the doughnut I've been avoiding for weeks. I managed to lose fifteen pounds over the winter and I like the way my clothes fit. Just now, I'm using my two hours of sleep to justify a slip that I hope won't morph into a free fall.

I turn to Patrick O'Malley before I take the first bite. O'Malley's one of our oldest detectives. A tall man with a large belly, he's slow but reliable, the perfect cop for detail work. "Pat, where are we with the shoe and tire impressions?"

"Already uploaded to the FBI's lab at Quantico."

"You call ahead?"

"Yeah, and I emphasized that we have a murdered cop here." He shrugs. "Maybe the agent I spoke with—his name is Paul Horton—got the message. Maybe not. But if you can find a way to goose the process, do it. It'll take weeks if we have to wait our turn."

"I'll see what I can do. Meantime, what about the slug we pulled out of the door?" The bullet fired into Rowan's skull had passed straight through and lodged itself in the padding on the passenger's door.

"Pretty much deformed, but it'll go out to the state lab this morning."

"Good. So, do we have anything on the little camper next to the crime scene?"

"Only that it's been sitting empty for at least a month. That's according to just about every witness."

"Okay, first thing, there's a real estate agency on Main Street. You know the one? Housed in an A-frame."

"Triple-A Realty."

"That's it. Triple-A controls leases for the whole of Boomtown. Every square foot. Start there. I want to know who owns the van, and whose name is on the lease. If they don't cooperate, come back to me. Today, Pat. I want to get into that van today."

"Got it, captain."

Laura Udell's next, the last in line. "Laura, I want you to assume the perpetrator walked across the top of Boomtown and jumped into a vehicle of some kind, probably parked on Main Street. The real estate brokerage has security cameras. Check 'em, and then locate the security cameras on Baxter Boulevard. I don't believe you'll find any to the north, but check for ten blocks south. Approach whoever's in charge and download the data onto a thumb drive. One drive for each camera."

"That it? Because it should take like what? All of two hours?"

"No, Laura. That's not it." Our patrol division is divided up into squads, each supervised by a sergeant. In the civilian world, they'd be called teams because they stay together for the most part. Same sergeant, same personnel, month after month, like platoons in the military. "I want you to pull the files on every member of Rowan's squad. I want you to analyze the files, especially Rowan's six-month evaluations. Who might have been close to Rowan. Any new recruits. Whatever strikes your fancy."

"You want me to use my woman's intuition. That about it?"

I touch my index finger to my lips and look up at the ceiling for a moment. "Well, now that you mention it, I don't think I'd phrase my order in those exact words. I think I'd prefer something like use your imagination."

Ordinarily, I'd ask my team for suggestions, but I don't have time. I've got to be at a press conference at nine o'clock and I need to confer with Vern first. From there, I'm headed to the home of Rowan Krauss's wife and children. I'm going to make a condolence call, which I'm dreading.

"Let's meet again at six. And don't worry about second-guessing. If some trail looks promising, follow your nose. Meantime, I'm gonna have to stand on a dais while our beloved commissioner tells the good people of Baxter that we don't have a fucking clue."

CHAPTER EIGHT
DELIA

"What about Oakland Gardens?" Vern wants to know.

My esteemed commissioner didn't become esteemed commissioner because he's stupid. Oakland Gardens is the obvious flaw in the rundown I've just provided. The Nissan plant-to-be is sited on a stretch of ground formerly called the Yards. Dominated by the decaying hulks of abandoned meat-packing plants, it was the last stop for men and women whose lives had fallen apart. Bipolars and schizophrenics off their meds, tweakers, junkies, crack addicts, and alcoholics who'd abandoned all hope of rehabilitation. They inhabited odd corners of the derelict factories where the roofs were still intact, or outright hovels lacking electricity and even water.

The Yards are gone now, carried off to landfills in a dozen states, but another neighborhood has taken its place. Located on the western side of the construction zone, Oakland Gardens has always been low-rent. Designed for workers at the packing plants, the homes are as small as they are plain. Oakland Gardens was where you lived if you spent your days on the killing floor.

Post-Nissan, the city of Baxter held out great hope for Oakland Gardens. By then, more than half the homes in the neighborhood were abandoned and could be bought on the cheap from the banks who now owned them. Surely, gentrification was on the way.

Surely not, except for the blocks closest to Baxter Boulevard. The vacant lots and most of the homes were bought up, then minimally rehabbed and rented out. But derelict homes remained, as did vacant lots suitable, except in winter, for homeless encampments.

As though drawn by the same instinct that guides migrating birds, the addicts, the homeless, and the psychotics flowed into Oakland Gardens; despite calls for their removal, I don't expect them to be going anywhere soon. That's because they have nowhere to go.

I could make this little speech to Vern as a reason why I didn't search for Rowan's killer in the neighborhood, or why I instructed Laura Udell to inspect the security cameras on Baxter Boulevard. I don't.

"Not enough detectives, Vern, and I can't trust patrol." I hold up a finger. "And I didn't know who we'd be looking for. Meanwhile, Rowan had been dead for at least an hour before we arrived. There were fifty potential witnesses to interview and a crime scene to be processed. And I considered it unlikely we'd find our killer sitting on a front porch in Oakland Gardens waving hello."

Vern flashes that affable grin I know so well, but the smile disappears quickly. We've got a press conference to attend.

Me, I'll stand at the back of the dais, wearing a suitably solemn expression. Vern will have to stand at the podium and admit that we don't have a suspect, or even one of those persons of interest.

Vern walks over to a low table that holds his football trophies, including the game ball he was awarded by his teammates after the state championship. I have to wonder if he's remembering a time when life appeared simple, the handoff, the pass, plays worked or they didn't. As a gay woman growing up in a small town, high school was anything but simple for me. Maybe that's why I rarely think of those years; maybe that's why graduation felt like an escape from prison.

◆

The door opens and Saul Rawling, our chief of patrol, walks inside. Without knocking. He's gotten too big around the middle to wear his belt at waist level. It now circles his body several inches below his navel. The inevitable result of too many drinks after work? Or, according to rumor, during work? Rawling's face is broken by red spider veins that fan out from his nose to run across his cheeks. Doesn't matter, though. Rawling has big-time connections on the city council. Firing him before the election in November would damage our current mayor's prospects, and nobody, including me, wants that. A new mayor will almost certainly appoint a new commissioner. So long, Vern Taney. And if that new commissioner should be Saul Rawling, goodbye Delia Mariola as well.

"Saul asked if he could attend the meeting," Vern tells me. Left unsaid is that Vern arranged Saul's appearance to occur after Vern was briefed. "So, what do you have in mind, Saul? For patrol's contribution to the investigation."

Rawling arches his left eyebrow, a familiar gesture. Most likely, he believes it makes him appear wise. Or, at least, savvy. He's neither. Instead, he's a competent bureaucrat who keeps a close eye on his workers. Their corruption cannot have escaped him.

"Well, I need to know what you have."

"Why, Saul?" Vern asks. "The patrol division patrols, the detective division detects. So, why do you need to know what the detective division has?"

"Because I want to help, Vern. Rowan Krauss was one of mine."

I can't stand it any longer. "Maybe so, but he's ours now. So, unless Vern orders me to share, I'm just gonna have to be selfish."

"How about putting one or two of my guys on the task force?"

"Appreciate the offer, Saul, and we've already pulled one of your guys. Patrolwoman Gianni Vetto."

Saul Rawling's not without pride, despite the drinker's complexion and the beer belly. He looks to Vern, but there's no charity flowing from that direction. Saul's lost the battle, sure, but he's smart enough to know there's still a war to be fought.

"All right, I get it. Brief me whenever it's convenient."

◆

You'd think, with the homicide only seven hours in the past, the media would be satisfied with no suspects, investigation ongoing. You'd be wrong, of course, because the obvious doesn't put fannies in the seats, or sell newspapers. Many of the shouted questions at the press conference were grisly. How many shots, did he die instantly, was the victim being investigated, was it a gangland hit, did Rowan Krauss suffer, suffer, suffer, suffer.

KBAX broadcast the conference live, a real treat for Rowan's family.

I'm en route to the home of Jesse Krauss and her two children. I don't know the kids' names, only that the older can't be more than eight or nine. I'm not rushing, in part because I ran into Stu Harrington after the conference. I instructed Stu to manage the task force moment to moment, leaving me able to respond to any major development. But there was that other bit, too. Notifications are a part of every cop's life, especially early on. I think I was supposed to harden, but I've only grown more reluctant. Yeah, I love the endgame, the "turn around and put your hands on top of your head" part. Confronting the other end, the pain, the devastation, the hurt that never heals, children barely able to walk who look at you and say, "Mommy's in heaven." Or daddy, or brother, or sister.

As I park in front of the Krauss's two-story Colonial in Norwood, I try to console myself. The loss of a mother or father can easily result in financial disaster. That won't be Jesse's fate. She'll receive a line-of-duty pension, three-quarters of Rowan's annual salary, along with full medical benefits, for the rest of her life. As Jesse is an accountant with a good-paying job at Compound Properties, a national developer, she won't have to worry about paying the mortgage.

My rationalization begins to fade as I come up the walk. A dozen mourners crowd a porch that runs across the front of the house. I nod to several I know, then pass through the open front door into a spacious living room with a fieldstone fireplace at one end. Off to my right, the dining room table is covered with food, a reminder, perhaps, that life, with all its physical demands, continues. The mixed odors of casseroles, a roasted chicken, numerous covered dishes, fills my nostrils. Above all, cinnamon from a huge apple pie with a latticework crust.

◆

Jesse Krauss stands before the fireplace, talking with an older woman I know to be her mother, but whose name I can't remember. She looks around the room, seeming almost unfocused, until her dark eyes meet mine. I can read the devastation easily enough as she walks toward me, but there's defiance as well, and a burning anger. We hug briefly, then Jesse steps back.

"Come with me, Delia."

The order is delivered abruptly, almost a parent to a child, and I follow behind as I'm led through an eat-in kitchen to an office at the back of the house. Jesse waits for me to enter, then closes the door behind us. Arms folded across her chest, she turns to me and points off to the left, where a paint can and a brush lie on a tarp spread before the wainscoting.

"A job undone," she tells me. "Like Rowan's life. I told him to go to you with the bullshit he uncovered, but he had this idea about someone at the head of all the corruption. Not just bent cops grabbing what they could, but a comprehensive plan to run the city from beneath."

"Jesse, this isn't . . ."

She waves me off before I complete the sentence. "No, Delia. The bastards have to pay. If they don't pay, Rowan died for nothing. I can't have that. I can't put him in the ground knowing his killers are celebrating."

I'm supposed to say something here, to console with something like "We'll get the bastards." Only she's a cop's wife and knows that not every criminal is brought to justice.

"We're on it, Jesse. We've assembled a task force, we'll have a hotline set up by this afternoon, and we're tapping informants for any and all rumors. Will that be enough? I can't make any promises."

The door opens and Jesse's mom peeks inside. She's a handsome woman, neatly dressed in sweater and skirt, every hair in place. "Sorry to interrupt, but the kids are calling for you."

"I need a few minutes, Mom."

"All right, honey. A few minutes."

Jesse waits for her mother to leave before opening the bottom drawer of a wooden desk topped with a green blotter. I watch her remove a thin laptop with the Apple logo on the cover.

"Rowan was . . . obsessed? No, not that bad. More like preoccupied. I hope I don't have to tell you this, but there's corruption everywhere on the force. And it's open, at least according to Rowan. Pay to play. Not every cop, right? But the straight cops won't testify against the bent cops."

"The blue wall."

"More than that, Delia. The straight cops are afraid because the crooked ones are well organized, extremely violent, with someone at the top giving orders." She hands me the notebook computer. "It's password protected, and what's inside is encrypted. I don't have the password or the key to unlock the encryption, and I've searched every inch of the office for either one. So, for what it's worth, there's a little cluster of cops from Missouri. Only a week ago, Rowan told me they were crooked then and they're crooked now. You might want to look at them first."

We already know about this group. One, Andy Kehoe, was killed last year as he attempted to extort a payoff from a drug dealer. The other six hail from one of three bordering counties: Humphries, Overton, and Bledsoe. I personally spoke with the sheriff in each of the counties, only to be told that the service records of these deputies were confidential and could not be revealed. The identical story, almost the identical phrasing, from each sheriff. Nor would they speak informally except to declare that the decision to part ways had been mutual.

"When do you think Rowan's . . . his body will be released?"

"That's up to the coroner. Probably after they do a tox screen, maybe a week." I lay my hand on Jesse's shoulder. "I've got a million details to cover, but I'll be back to keep you updated. Anything you need in the meantime, you only have to ask."

The door opens before I reach it and a child looks into the room. A pretty girl, her mouth is tight, her blue eyes afraid. She doesn't say anything, only looks at her mother before retreating. Making sure, maybe, that mommy's not in heaven. I look back at Jesse as the door closes.

"Dying is easy," she tells me. "It's living that's hard."

CHAPTER NINE

DELIA

I lied to Jesse Krauss. It's four thirty and I'm sitting in the stands at Goldman High. Rowan's laptop's already in the hands of our computer guy, who admitted that it can't be decrypted, not by any agency, state or federal. A light breeze carries the fragrance of the lilacs that grow on one side of the fieldhouse, along with the pungent odor of cut grass. Fast-moving clouds slide from west to east across a blue sky that seems infinitely deep. The temperature stands at seventy-four degrees.

I need this respite, this R & R. Jesse was bad enough, but I compounded the suffering with a stop at Baxter Medical Center to visit Keith and Jane Moreland. Neither looked up when I reached the doorway to Jane's room and I stood there for a moment, almost paralyzed. Keith sat alongside his daughter's bed, his back to me, an open book on his lap. Jane's eyes were open, her emaciated body a mere rumor beneath the blanket that covered her. Drawn tight over her cheekbones and jaw, her skin was a color that mixed brown, gray, and yellow.

For a brief time, I watched Jane as she drew one shallow breath after another. Then I left without announcing my presence. I found myself inspired, at least on one level. Keith Moreland would see it through. He would not flinch and he would not flee. From birth to death, he would be Jane's protector, although he could not protect, although he could not alter the outcome. Although he could do no more, finally, than put her in the ground.

Rowan Krauss, Jane Moreland. The circumstances so different, the result identical, right down to the suffering of the survivors.

◆

Goldman High's baseball field seats about four hundred fans, and every space is taken as Danny trots out to the mound in the first inning. As a sport, baseball occupies a definite third place at Goldman, behind football and basketball. Seasons past, I'd be lucky to find a hundred fans when I came out to watch Danny and Mike Taney play. The probability that Goldman will go to the state championships, as long as Danny stays healthy, has reversed that trend.

High school baseball teams only play twice a week and Danny's expected to pitch about forty percent of their games.

Lillian Taney sits next to me. Her two-year-old, Cora, is as uninterested in baseball as a girl-toddler can be. She's already fidgeting. By contrast, Emmaline, the Taneys' adopted daughter, is totally involved. She's sitting alongside me, shouting for Danny to "mow 'em down." Two years ago, I pulled Emmaline from a fire that surely would have killed her. Since then, she's become Danny's, Mike's, and Gretchen's little protégé. Gretchen's perched on the edge of the bench next to Emmaline, a little more restrained than Emmaline. But only a little.

I check the stands as Danny tosses warm-up pitches. Lots of moms, lots of fans, and a small knot of middle-aged men, big-bellied for the most part, in a cluster on the other side of the field. These men, and they're all men, are scouts, some for colleges, some for major league teams.

Danny explained the obvious last year. You don't have to have a college degree to play major league baseball. High school graduates are commonly drafted by major league teams. They can look forward to four or five years in the minor leagues, with only a small chance to ever reach the majors. Players with college experience fare better. They often come up to the majors during their third year in the minors.

"So, why not college?" I'd naively asked.

The answer was simple enough. The player drafted first last year, Gretchen explained, received a nine-million-dollar signing bonus.

"Yeah," Danny chimed in, "and the player drafted seventy-eighth got a cool million."

I admit to being thrown off balance by the numbers. Millions here, millions there. This was a universe I've never glimpsed, much less entered. Still, I wanted Danny to have a college degree, and I made a valiant attempt to defend my position.

"Wouldn't you get a larger bonus coming out of college than coming out of high school?"

"You would," Danny admitted, "if you didn't suffer an injury that ended your playing days while you were still in college. That can happen on any pitch you throw. No signing bonus, and they might pull your scholarship. Also, once you enter a college program, you can't be drafted until you finish your junior year or turn twenty-one."

Danny looked over at Gretchen, who took up the cause. "The lowest signing bonus in the first round was two-and-a-half million. That kind of money can set you up for life."

Good old Gretchen.

◆

The numbers still have me off balance. I make seventy-six thousand, plus medical benefits, plus overtime, which amounts to another ten or twelve. So, I'm doing all right. But millions? The numbers tossed around like rice at a wedding? My son a millionaire? At eighteen?

"You got this, chump," Emmaline shouts as the batter, a tall, skinny kid, steps into the batter's box. Prophecy, as it turns out. The boy's tight mouth and narrowed eyes speak to his determination, but he doesn't come close to hitting Danny's first pitch, a fastball at the top of the strike zone. I watch Emmaline clap her hands together. Only a month ago, she announced her intention to be the first woman to pitch in the major leagues.

Danny has a four-seam and a two-seam fastball, along with a changeup. When Danny's in command, his changeup's unhittable, at least by high school batters. When he's not, it finishes in the dirt or so far outside nobody will swing at it.

The changeup's not working this afternoon, often leaving Danny behind in the count and dependent on a fastball that tops out at ninety-three miles an hour. More than enough to cut through the lineup and keep Emmaline on the edge of her seat.

I'm suitably proud of my son, but my thoughts keep drifting to Rowan and the investigation. I need to get back to the squad by six, only a few hours away. I want progress reports on each avenue of the investigation, and a prioritized game plan going forward. That last part, the game plan, grows all the more complicated when I receive a phone call from Stu Harrington at the top of the fourth inning.

I pick up the phone and ask him to hold on as I make my way out of the grandstand. When I find an open spot, not exactly private but the best I can do, I tell Stu to go ahead.

"I'm at Ivy Jordan's house." Ivy Jordan's the patrolwoman who was supposed to act as Rowan's driver, the one who never showed up. "The place is empty, captain. Neighbors are tellin' me they saw her carry suitcases out to her car."

"When?"

"Yesterday afternoon."

"You get inside?"

Stu clears his throat. "Yeah, door was unlocked. All the furniture's in place. Decent stuff, not thrift store. Gaps in the closets, downstairs and up, likewise for the bedroom bureau. Maybe enough to fill a couple of suitcases."

"You find a wallet, credit cards?"

"Neither, or any credit card statements, or utility bills. We have her phone number, of course, but my calls are goin' directly to voicemail. She's on the run."

"Only question, though. Is she running from us, or from whoever told her not to show up for work? I'm betting on the latter. Remember, Gianni vouched for Ivy. She told us that Ivy couldn't be corrupted. That doesn't mean she couldn't be frightened."

"We know the make, model, and plate number of her car, a gold Kia Sportage. I'm already working on a subpoena for her credit cards and bank accounts. She also listed relatives and character references on her application. Like a who's who of her life before she joined the force. So, if she took off in a hurry, she'll have a hard time covering her tracks."

"Yeah, Stu, no matter who's trying to find her."

CHAPTER TEN
CARNEY

Breaking up is hard to do, whether it's with your dearly beloved, or a hustler named Benny Kaplan. I didn't have a problem with Benny. He was fun to be around, an ex-bruiser past his prime, but always in the game and quick with a funny story about the old days. If I wasn't a cop, I would have stayed with him for as long as he'd have me. But the man will never take me where I need to go. He talks a lot, sure, only never about who or exactly what. The way he operates pretty much in the open, he's gotta be makin' the occasional payoff. Benny's refrigeration business wouldn't fool the cops in this town for a day, what with hot merchandise, including high-end cars, finding their way to his warehouse.

Benny doesn't operate a chop shop. He buys stolen cars from the actual thieves, stores them in his warehouse for a few days, then transports them to a destination he won't share with me. I don't know who does the driving, either. That's Benny's secret, and it's smart, no doubt, like never providing an introduction to cops on the take. Unfortunately, as investigating said cops for corruption is what I'd been assigned to do, I needed to find a new job and I broke the bad news on Tuesday evening.

"What happened to fuckin' loyalty?" Benny asked.

"This ain't Cosa Nostra and you ain't the mob, just in case you haven't noticed. America's still the land of opportunity and I've reached an age where I gotta seize the fuckin' day. Workin' for wages, generous as they are, won't get me where I wanna go."

Benny retreated to his desk and opened a drawer. He extracted a bottle of Maker's Mark and two glasses. "Whatta ya say we slow down for a minute. Talk this out." He poured a couple of fingers into each glass and passed one to me. I dutifully sipped, but I wasn't moved. Like all the best criminals, Benny was a pragmatist. Buy for a nickel, sell for a dime. The business of business is business.

◆

We were in Benny's office at the back of the house. Small to begin with, the metal desk and mismatched chairs, including a recliner parked in front of a TV, were dwarfed by a gray safe that had to weigh half a ton.

"If this is only about money, we can talk raise," he said. "I'm a reasonable man."

"A raise won't cut it. Also, what I'm doin' here, Benny, it's just too boring. I need more action."

"C'mon, man, how's it boring when you knocked that prick, Harman Broad, on his ass?" He raised a finger, then pushed a button on his intercom. "Yo, Sarah, can you come in for a minute. Carney says he's gonna quit on us."

To my surprise, Sarah took my side. "You interrupted me watchin' *Sister Wives* for this bullshit? Swear to God, Benny, I'm startin' to give serious thought to brother husbands."

"C'mon, honey, it's not like I got people lined up to replace him."

I thought the point reasonable, but Sarah wasn't having it. "This ain't a war, Benny, and nobody signed up for the duration. He wants to go, let him."

Sarah's spirit was up, her cheeks flushed. She looked gorgeous to me, standing there with her hands on her hips. And Benny wasn't about to get in her face, no way. I saw his eyes withdraw for a moment as his pragmatic side reasserted itself.

"Okay, look," he said to me, his gaze now steady, "I got a car, an X5, on the way. Be here in maybe two hours. I'm hopin' you'll stick around for that long. I don't wanna be home alone."

Sarah raised a slender index finger tipped in crimson. "Careful, Carney. You say yes, he's gonna ask for somethin' else."

◆

But fair is fair. I've taken Benny's money and now he needs me one last time. And I did quit without giving notice.

Let's say a thief turns up with a year-old BMW X5. Blue book value for a vehicle in excellent condition runs about fifty-five large. But if the vehicle isn't mint, or even in good condition, the value changes. That's why the X5 in transit has to be evaluated.

The way it works, a thief drives the stolen vehicle into the warehouse, then comes to the office for a drink while Nate, Benny's mechanic, has a look. If Nate comes in happy, fine. But suppose Nate comes in with something like, "The brake pads and rotors are toast and the engine's leakin' oil." Now a price has to be negotiated.

Thieves typically assume everybody's as crooked as they are, which makes for tense negotiations. My role's not about fanning the flames. It's about preventing combustion.

"Okay, Benny, one last ride. And it's on the house. After we're done, though, I'm gone. And no hard feelings."

"No problem, man, but there is one more . . ."

◆

It's three days later and I'm walking into Packers Bar & Restaurant. The place is fairly crowded with most of the booths and four-tops occupied. I check for George Pratt, but he hasn't turned up yet. Pratt's a mean bastard and I believe he could pull a trigger, if he hasn't done so already. At the same time, he's got an ego problem that forces him to play macho man. Pratt's been fighting his own image for years, fighting it on the outside and on the inside. I've avoided men like him for most of my life. Prison walls are rising up for Pratt on a short horizon he can't see. That's because he's convinced himself that risky behavior will make him a man. Like Trump Jr. thinks killing a water buffalo with a rifle big enough to knock out a tank will make him a man. It doesn't work. It will never work.

The bruiser tending bar nods, but doesn't smile. He calls himself Bear and he never smiles, at least not that I've seen.

"Your boy late again?" he asks.

"Appears so."

"Man has no sense of time."

That's not true, but I don't challenge the observation. Pratt's asserting dominance. Pitiful, but useful. As is Pratt's big mouth. The man can't stop bragging. He knows everything and everybody. As I'm quiet by nature, except for the occasional prompt, I merely soak it up. At this stage, anyway.

◆

Bear draws a pint of Guinness. He places it in front of me without my asking and I lose myself, as I usually do, in the "cattle drive through town" mural behind the bar. There's a signature in the lower right corner, but it's unreadable. Maybe that's on purpose because the mural's pretty crude. The men, women, and children gathered on the sidewalk seem to be looking off into the distance. The cattle are a lot more torso than leg, but their eyes are fierce, and their longhorns actually ferocious. As if the steers are only waiting for the opportunity to impale a careless passerby.

Fortunately, the onlookers mind their manners. None stray from the sidewalks. They leave cattle-management to mounted cowboys, lariats at the ready, wearing hats of all sizes and shapes, from Stetsons to bowlers to sombreros.

I glance at my watch, a suitably inexpensive Casio with the day, date, and time spelled out in blue letters on a black background. Pratt's now forty minutes late. No call, of course, but it's dragging out too long.

"Might be he got busted," Bear observes as he takes my empty glass. "Guy takes mad risks."

"His business, Bear."

Bear's chin jerks, just a bit. He doesn't like being challenged. Tough shit. But I do store the information. Pratt has taken me on several runs. I've stopped asking about drugs because I know he's moving weight. Coke, dope, meth? Don't know and don't care. I make note of the pickup and drop-off points. If Pratt was our target, we'd already have enough to send him away. He's not, though. We're after cops.

◆

Off to my left, a face on the screen of a small TV catches my attention. Calvin "Bute" Stafford declared his candidacy for mayor at a news conference earlier today. Bute received his nickname while serving in the Marine Corps. Rumor has it that Bute was originally Brute or Butt, depending on whether you're a supporter or an opponent. What's not in question is Colonel Stafford's six-year posting to the Marines' Pacific Brig, a level 1 prison.

I'm not a political junkie, or even an enthusiast. For me, it's a pox on both your houses. In fact, I've taken to calling the president, any president, my Deceiver in Chief. Bute Stafford's candidacy only interests me because he's running on a single issue. Crime, crime, and more crime after that. Echoing strident editorials in the *Baxter Bugle* and an independent weekly calling itself *CityTruth*.

◆

Pratt wanders in a few minutes later. He motions to me as he makes his way to his regular booth at the back of the restaurant. I got lucky here. When last I saw Pratt's buddy, Sal, he expected to be released in a week or so. Instead, he was indicted a second time. Charged with armed robbery, he won't be enjoying the spring air anytime soon. Which left Pratt with a hole I was ready to fill.

"What say, George?" I slide into the seat across from my new boss. I don't think he likes being called George, but if he has a street name, he hasn't chosen to share it. Then again, he's not the sharing type.

"It's that shit-and-fan thing, Carney. Cops're bustin' heads. They want the shooter."

"Shooter?"

"Of the cop. What's his name?"

"Krauss."

"Yeah, Krauss. They want the asshole who shot Krauss." He laughs, shakes his head. "Think all they have to do is kick the shit out of a few junkies and . . . And I don't fuckin' know what." He leans across the table and whispers the next part. "Word, Carney, it's cops that hit the cop. And this bullshit on the street? It's all for show."

"Don't matter. It still hurts." I rub my lower ribs, though the pain is virtually gone. "And that was before the murder."

"You wanna work in a city with pussy cops, you gotta move on." He pauses, but I have nothing to say. "Anyways, we got nothin' to worry about."

Pratt's wearing a leather jacket, black, another piece of his facade. He reaches into an outer pocket, comes up with a business card, and tosses it on the table.

Across the top in boldface: FREE OUR POLICE. Below in a smaller font: BAXTER POLICE DEPARTMENT. No names, though. Only a figure contained in a gold circle, a blond cop in full uniform, legs apart, holding a nightstick that runs in a diagonal across his chest.

There's a folding steel baton in his Sam Browne, along with pepper spray, two ammunition pouches, a cuff case, and a radio pouch. At the bottom, a handwritten signature is indecipherable.

"You see what's happening, Carney?" Pratt looks at me for a second before answering his own question. "The cops're kickin' ass up and down Main Street. Their rousting the whores and the pimps and every small-time dealer in Boomtown. Not askin' nice, right? Not, 'Please come along, sir.' And it's only gotten worse since the cop was hit."

My reply is noncommittal, as usual. "Yeah, I been hearin' the same thing."

"And that's where the card does its magic. Cars are bein' searched at every stop. People walkin' down Main Street, mindin' their own business, are havin' their pockets turned out. You have this card on your dashboard, or in your shirt pocket, that ain't gonna happen." Pratt's balding, back to front. He compensates by letting the front grow long and plastering it against the top of his skull. Now he gives the spray holding it down a little pat. "I'm not sayin' you could kick somebody's ass, or rob a liquor store, and use the card. The cops runnin' this show have a major thing about order. But basically, if you keep your shit to yourself, they're not gonna cramp your play. As long as you're not late with their piece."

◆

I commit every word to memory, hoping he'll tell me something about how he acquired the card, but he's not ready. A few minutes later, a man strolls up to our booth. In his thirties and tall, there's something about his erect bearing, shoulders back, that has me thinking ex-military. I don't inquire, though, and I'm not introduced.

"Carney, give us some room."

His tone is boss-to-minion abrupt. The first time he used that tone, I felt the hairs on the back of my neck jump to attention. I'm used to it now, the disrespect. I compensate by telling myself how much a properly subservient response will aid the investigation. And by imagining George Pratt led away in handcuffs.

Bear's pouring me a Coke with lime as I approach the bar. I've never been a drinker and one beer on a working night is all I allow myself. Alcohol makes me stupid and I'm no Albert Einstein to begin with. I slide my ass onto a bar stool and relax. The Free Our Police card is a deliberate echo of the FOP associated with the Fraternal Order of Police, a national organization that lobbies for cops. Something like the VFW for veterans. Of course, the Fraternal Order of Police is a mainstream association. Free Our Police, if you believe Pratt, is playing a different game.

The card answers a question I've been asking myself for the last couple of days. Pratt's a smart guy. If he had his way, I'd be driving the car we've been sharing, but I'm much more valuable, should my assistance be needed, sitting in the back seat with room to maneuver. But even in the back seat, strapped and ready, I couldn't convince myself that I was enough protection. I've watched men deliver packages that could only contain drugs. Fairly large packages, the kind that attract the interests of rip-off artists. At one point, I asked him directly.

"I have skills, George, but I'm only one man."

"Not to worry," he answered, his tone proud. "I got mad backup."

CHAPTER ELEVEN

CARNEY

"So, you're with George."

I turn to the woman seated on my right. She's young, mid-twenties perhaps, and neatly groomed. Honey-blond, highlighted hair, television hair, falls in a soft wave on both sides of her face. She wears a rose-pink skirt that follows the curve of her hips without being tight, and a matching jacket over a white blouse with a scalloped collar. Neither beautiful, nor plain, her green eyes are sharp, likewise for her broad smile. She means to be engaging and I'm engaged.

"Me and George were an item, once upon a time," she tells me.

"Were you the dumper? Or the dumped?"

"And why would you ask that question?"

"Curious is all. Because I'm havin' a hard time imagining you together."

"Why's that?"

I've had enough and I turn back to the mural and my Coke. My still-anonymous companion is attractive and obviously smart. Or, at least street-smart, which I prefer. Only I'm tryin' to get closer to George, and screwing around with his ex-girlfriend isn't likely to bring that about. No matter how the hookup ended.

"George, he's the jealous type. Always lookin' over his shoulder. I have a life, and I like livin' it without having to account for every minute of my day."

A man approaches as she finishes speaking. Much older, late fifties or even sixty, he takes her by the arm, and she gives me a little wave as she slips off the stool. "Bye."

I watch her leave then check on Pratt. He's bent forward over the table, in mid-sentence. I'm looking, but I'm not sensing stress. Back to the longhorns.

"Hey, Carney, this gotta be for you." It's Bear, gathering the woman's glass. He's holding the glass in one hand, in the other a small paper napkin.

I take the napkin. My unnamed companion suddenly has a name, Vangi. And beneath: 432-6161.

◆

"The cocksucker owes me five large," Pratt explains as we drive into the neighborhood of Oakland Gardens. We're on Carroll Street, the only commercial street in the neighborhood. The commercial part is charitable. A few small food stores, one bold enough to call itself a supermarket though it can't be more than thirty feet wide. There are several bars, one with a small herd of chopped Harleys parked haphazardly in front. The no-name bars have darkened front windows that guarantee anonymity to their patrons.

There are streetlights on Carroll, sodium-vapor lights that cast a pale orange light that barely penetrates the gloom surrounding the many boarded-up homes. I'm driving for once, probably because the only trouble Pratt's expecting is trouble he starts.

"Turn here," Pratt orders.

There are no street signs and I have no idea exactly where we are. I've only ridden through Oakland Gardens once, on a look-around with Stu Harrington.

"Where are we, Pratt?"

"Hell, man. We're in hell. I mean, look at this shit."

In fact, the neighborhood is surprisingly vibrant. Music pours from many of the dilapidated homes and people sit outside, on porches or on the small front lawns.

"Wrecks," Pratt assures me. "Junkies and drunks. Later on, they'll be creeping through somebody's window, or ripping off on the street."

"Giving crime a bad name?"

"That ain't funny." Pratt's facing away from me, staring through the window next to him. "Turn here."

I turn to find a police cruiser halfway down the block, with a uniformed cop standing behind it. There's room to get past, barely, but it's too late to back off without looking obvious. While I don't know what might have been concealed by Pratt, I do know that I'm carrying a weapon without having the required permit. If arrested, I won't be able to justify a quick release. I spoke about this with Stu Harrington and Captain Mariola. They didn't have answers either.

"Relax, man," Pratt says. "I know this cop. Lower your window." After a second, he adds, "Be respectful."

The cop's name badge reads THURMAN. Big to begin with, he stands bolt upright, shoulders squared, dark eyes cold, as he approaches Pratt's side of the car.

"You part of this?" The cop gestures to the house behind him as two cops lead a handcuffed man from the house. I can't see the man's face with the light from the doorway behind him, but he's stumbling as the cops propel him forward.

"No, nothin' to do with me."

"Then move on. We'll see you on Sunday."

"No doubt, officer."

◆

I ease around the patrol car, eyes on the road, but I'm hoping Thurman will remember me if we should meet again. Familiarity breeds trust. That's the operating principle anyway. I'm also hoping that I'll be included in Sunday's meet. Or, if not, in the following Sunday's meet. Just now, we need to develop a tight case against a couple of bent cops. After that, again in theory, the dominoes will fall.

"I know the asshole," Pratt says.

"The asshole?"

"The asshole they busted. Goes by the name of Snake. On the street, I mean, and that's his problem, Carney. The on-the-street part. The guy pulls street rips in Boomtown to feed a dope habit. Now he's gonna detox in a cell."

"If he doesn't go to the hospital. Looks to me like they beat his ass."

"That's the point I been tryin' to make. You wanna operate in this town, you gotta keep your business to yourself. Here, turn left."

There's a street sign for this one: Poole Road. I make note of it, though I really don't know where I am. Two vacant lots, side by side, are no longer vacant. They've become a homeless encampment. Tents mostly, with scattered lean-tos pushed against a low wall at the back of the lot. The encampment pulses with energy. Several fires burn in fifty-gallon drums. Men and a smaller number of women gather around the drums, passing bottles wrapped in plastic bags. Others sit off by themselves, in shadows cast by their tents. Several men pace back and forth, gesturing, mouths in constant motion. The others, their fellow campers, pay no attention. Psychosis can't be more than one small piece of their struggle to survive.

"Whatta ya slowin' down for?"

Good question. I step on the gas and we continue on Poole Road for another block, passing houses that look all the more abandoned for the people living there. Sheets cover the windows, not blinds or shades. Doors stand open, and the people sitting in the yards stare at us as we pass.

"Know how to fix the shit back there?"

"The camp?"

"Yeah, the camp. The freaks back there? They contribute nothing. They just take. And take and fuckin' take. Free this, free fuckin' that. You wanna fix the problem, I got the answer."

"And what's that?"

"Napalm."

◆

I think I'm supposed to make a comment, but I don't, and a block later, Pratt says, "That's him. That's Stone."

Stone's at the far end of the block, busy with his cell phone as he walks toward us.

"Let me out."

I slow to a stop and Pratt squeezes through the door, keeping his head low. "Get behind him, Carney. In case he tries to run."

Fifty feet past Stone, I pull the car to a stop and take a quick photo of the card on the dash before jumping out. I'm wearing a maroon fisherman's sweater. The oversized sweater conceals the semi tucked into the waistband of my jeans. I measure Stone as I reach the sidewalk and start to approach him. He's a good four inches taller than Pratt, and heavier without being flabby. Nevertheless, when he finally looks away from his phone long enough to recognize Pratt, he executes a quick half turn and we come face-to-face.

"What the fuck you want?"

Being more about action than words, I snap a quick left jab at his face, but unclench my fist at the last second to cover his eyes with my palm and fingers. Effectively blinded, he doesn't register my right hand until it crashes into his lower ribs with an audible crack. Then he drops to his knees and howls, no fight left.

Pratt's mouth hangs open, but he doesn't say anything for a minute. Then he remembers the point and squats down until his face is a foot from Stone's.

"You think that hurt? Huh? You think that hurt? Listen up, motherfucker, you don't come up with my money, you'll think that was a kiss."

"Jeez, Pratt, you didn't give me a chance."

"What I didn't give you, asshole, was a chance to hotfoot in the other direction." He slaps Stone's face. "I trusted you with a package and now I gotta run all around this fucked-up neighborhood tryin' to find your ass. Man, you could catch the clap in Oakland Gardens without gettin' outta the car."

I've been standing back, waiting for the situation to resolve itself, one way or the other. Then I notice the watch on Stone's left wrist. I grab his arm and yank him to his feet, ignoring the predictable cry of pain.

"How much you say he owes?"

"Three."

Back at the bar, it was five, but I'm not one to argue with the boss. "Man's wearin' a Rolex."

"Real?"

"Can't say, boss. Looks real, though."

Pratt steps close enough to do his own inspection. "Take it," he says.

"Hey, my grandfather gave me that. It's engraved, in the back."

A really stupid thing to say because now Pratt knows it isn't a knockoff. He watches as I slip the bracelet over Stone's fingers. Pratt's almost strutting now and I wouldn't be surprised if he believes that he personally cowed Stone. He takes the watch and shoves it into his pocket.

"Hey, Stone, I'm not a hard guy. I'm just a businessman who can't call a lawyer when somebody owes money and won't pay." He rocks back on his heels. "Tell you what. I'm gonna hold on to the watch for a couple of days. You make good, I'll give it back. Thirty-five hundred, right? Thirty for the debt and another five for bein' a pain in the ass."

◆

Pratt drops me at my car, parked a block away from Packers. He yanks a fat roll out of his pocket and peels off five C-notes. "You did good, Carney. Real good." He shows off the watch, now on his wrist. "A Rolex Submariner? I mean, you're lookin' at fifteen easy, and it could go for a lot more if it's one of the rare models."

Fifteen, easy, and my payoff is a measly five hundred. I'm not surprised. Mobsters are as cheap as billionaires, and like billionaires, they think everyone's out to rip them off. And guess who's never gonna see grampa's watch again.

"What time tomorrow, George?"

"Early, say noon. You know where I live?"

"I don't."

"In Norwood." He rattles off the address. "See you then."

◆

They're waiting for me when I reach my trailer on Eighth Avenue in Boomtown. Two cops in a BPD cruiser, both in uniform. I roll up behind them and wave to Jennie, my next-door neighbor. The front doors of the cruiser open as I'm closing mine and the two cops step out. The one with the stripes on his sleeve has to be ten years older than his partner, who looks to be two weeks out of high school. He's big enough, though. In fact, both are over six feet and well-built. Back in Philly, the cops were fairly casual, but there's not a wrinkle to be found on the uniform of either cop as they approach. The older cop's name tag reads OVERBY, the younger's reads FARRINGTON.

They fan out slightly as they close in. I don't know what they want, but I keep my arms and hands away from my body. No mixed signals. Beyond getting shot for some misjudgment, I'm not worried. The HK is inside the Cherokee's glove box.

"Hands on the car." This from the younger cop, who proceeds to frisk me. He finds nothing of interest and backs off. "Get in the car." He gestures to the BPD cruiser. "In the back."

If I was being arrested, I'd be in cuffs. That doesn't mean I'm not to be tuned up for the second time in a week, but I comply. I have no choice. I'm surprised, though, when Sergeant Overby pushes in after me and shuts the door. He regards me through eyes the color of mud.

"You're from Philadelphia." There's no question mark at the end of the sentence.

"That's right."

"And you were arrested three times while living there."

"That's also true."

"And you have an uncle named Sean Carney, who's currently imprisoned."

"Yeah."

◆

I was in the last six months of my enlistment when I applied to the Philadelphia Police Department. I didn't like my chances because my Uncle Sean was well-placed in what's left of the Irish mob in Philly. They call themselves the Kensington Group, which sounds vaguely corporate, but their main income is from drugs. I rejected the Kensington mob when I entered the military, but I expected the Philadelphia PD to deny my application when they uncovered my relationship to Uncle Sean. Instead, I received a visit from Lieutenant Giordano Grosso. Would I consider working undercover? With my family pedigree, I'd be perfect for the job.

I accepted the assignment and spent the next four years making my way through Philly's criminal underworld. I helped put together numerous cases, and found myself under arrest three times. Twice for burglary, once for assault. Though I was never prosecuted, the arrests were left on the books to bolster my street creds. I hadn't thought to have them expunged before I applied to the Baxter PD. At the time, I simply needed to get away, and not because I feared the gangs or the cops.

"You wanna tell me why you left Philadelphia?"

Overby's a master of the cop staredown, the look that compels a response. I'm not impressed. The three admissions already granted will have to suffice. Seconds tick by until it's obvious that I'm not going to answer and I'm half expecting Overby to punch me in the mouth. He surprises me by pulling away.

"That bad?" he says.

"Time for a change, a new start."

"You're telling me you're not an advance scout for your uncle?"

I'm ready for the question. "If I was working for my uncle, would I have teamed up with George Pratt? I'm living on crumbs, sergeant. Fucking crumbs."

That earns me a nod, followed by a long silence, followed by a second nod before Overby speaks. "What you did in Oakland Gardens tonight, it's gotta stop. I don't expect you to understand, but a functioning city requires order, not chaos. Did Stone, who showed up at Baxter Medical an hour ago, deserve his cracked ribs? I don't know and I don't care. I do know that you need to take your shit indoors. You need to keep your business out of sight." He pauses long enough to pull his shoulders back and take a deep breath, the final line having been reached. "You're new at this, so I'm gonna let it go. But our residents need to go about their business reasonably secure. You cross the line again, you'll be sitting on a Greyhound headed back to Philadelphia."

Contrition time. "I get the point, and if Pratt had spelled out the rules, it would never have happened."

"See that it doesn't." His shoulders drop slightly and the lines across his forehead relax. "You can't carry a gun without a permit in Baxter. And don't bother with the bullshit. I know you were carrying tonight."

"Yeah, I was. Part of the job."

"Tomorrow morning, find your way to the licensing department in city hall. See a woman named Violet. The papers will be filled out when you get them. All you do is sign at the bottom." At this point, I'm expecting him to name his price, but he doesn't. "We'll speak again at the end of the month. Now, get the fuck out of my car."

CHAPTER TWELVE
DELIA

"She's in terrible pain," Zoe tells me. "If the hospice nurses give her enough morphine to kill the pain, she goes under. Not awake, not asleep, like nowhere. When my mom went AWOL, my gramma took me in. I was five years old, Delia, and scared to death until she held me in her arms, until she comforted me. Those first couple of months, I followed her everywhere, clinging to the hem of her dress, and she never complained."

I don't interrupt. That's not my role here, no matter how much I want to do exactly what Zoe's gramma did, to hold my lover in my arms, to ease her pain. I want to tell her that grief is the price we pay for love, but it's too soon for that.

"Her love held, always, even in high school with all the dyke taunts from the other kids and the whispers from the parents. I know Gramma heard them. She went to church every Sunday, and she had her book club and her volunteer work at the hospital. Delia, she never wavered. She told me to find myself and stick with it. When I decided to leave Clark County, she backed me up. And now I've been gone so long that I've missed all the good years."

It's my turn to say something, but what I want to say, I can't. I want to tell my partner that I hope her gramma passes soon, that her tears won't stop until that happens. And it surely will. The doctors have stopped treating her cancer and only treat her pain. This is a journey we'll all take, the message driven home last year when I confronted Paul Ochoa. We fired on each other, almost at the same time. He missed. I didn't. But it could easily have gone the other way.

◆

I can't shake the feeling that I should be with Zoe. For a few days, at least. That's not possible right now, and won't be until we arrest Rowan Krauss's killer, or consign the investigation to the cold case files. Vern's made his position clear on several occasions. He wants me fully engaged. How I'm supposed to be fully engaged while also handling the administrative duties of a department head goes unaddressed. That problem's beside the point. If we don't make an arrest, if we don't confront the assault on the department, we'll both be out of a job come November. Gloria Meacham, president of the city council, echoes that sentiment every time we meet.

I'm on my way to Stu Harrington's home in Maryville County, there to meet with Tom Carney, our undercover. Thus far, the Rowan Krauss murder investigation can be charitably described as proceeding. We recovered shoe and tire impressions leading away from the crime scene. The tire impressions were very faint and could only be photographed. They were laid down by lightly worn Hankook tires of a size that might be found on Accords, Camrys, and several other models.

The shoe impressions ran deeper. We cast those and easily identified the brand and style, Nike Court Legacies. A distinctive cut in the right sole makes them unique. There was an anomaly as well. The impression from mid-sole to the heel was distinct, from mid-sole to the toes more faint. I had my suspicions and they were confirmed by an anonymous call to the hotline. The tipster claimed to have been on First Avenue when he heard a strange sound that he didn't associate with a gunshot. When he looked toward the sound, he saw a woman striding away from Rowan's cruiser. He kept watching until the small camper blocked his view.

"The reason why I'm sure it was a woman," he explained, "is because of her ass."

"Could you explain, sir?"

"Sure thing, officer. See, when a woman's walkin', her ass cheeks move side to side. A man's cheeks move up and down. That's how I'm sure. Her cheeks were rockin'."

I'm somewhat reluctant to call the man a sexist because I'm personally able to confirm the accuracy of his observation. More to the point, the call strengthened a suspicion I developed after studying the shoe impressions. Buy shoes a couple of sizes too large and stuff the front of the shoe with paper towels, a rag, anything to fill the space your toes won't reach. Then wear them to throw off investigators. Even if recovered, they'll be of no use in a courtroom.

◆

There are other dead ends. Laura Udell was assigned to check the security cameras along Baxter Boulevard. The effort came to nothing. Four cars passed within fifteen minutes of the estimated time of death. Each had its license plate registered by a camera designed to identify vehicles exceeding the twenty-five-miles-per-hour limit. The limit is absurdly low and just about every vehicle exceeds it, resulting in virtually every plate being captured. Within a day, the drivers of all four were identified and cleared. A dead end, like the visits to a pair of gun stores where suppressors are sold. Neither showed a purchase within the last year, mainly because suppressors had to be registered with the ATF in Washington, the same ATF and the same Washington that most NRA members fear and hate. Our run of bad luck held when Marcus Goodman reported back. He'd been assigned to check on recently released convicts who might have a grudge against Rowan Krauss. Only one convict released in the past six months had been arrested by Rowan. He was now living with his mother in St. Louis.

◆

Our spell of warm, dry weather has come to an end. It'll be raining soon. Just now, I'm driving through ground fog beneath a slate-black sky. To my left, a gray mare and her chestnut foal canter through a meadow. The foal can't be more than a month old and it suddenly breaks into a gallop, then just as suddenly stops and looks back at the mare. Unimpressed, the mare canters on through deep grass that swishes over her knees and hocks.

No fears. No wolf or cougar. No grizzly bear. A warm stall in the winter, a meadow rich with grass in summer, fresh water within reach. I pass a suitable red barn. Its double doors stand open as two workers muck out a stall. Their work reminds me of my own and I return to my thoughts. The hotline's up and running, but aside from the one anonymous call, it's produced nothing but wasted time.

We've made only grudging progress with the camper parked a few yards from Rowan's cruiser. Triple-A Realty manages leasing arrangements throughout Boomtown and we first approached them informally. We wanted the name of the individual currently renting the camper, which they could have supplied out of hand. Instead, they ran us a bullshit line about protecting their customers' privacy. The subpoena we served two days later finally brought forth a claim that the camper was currently vacant, its last occupant gone for almost two months. Could we then search it? All we needed was Triple-A's permission.

More hem and haw, and another delay that continued until our district attorney, Tommy Atkinson, got off his ass and secured the warrant he might've secured two days ago. We'll serve it late this afternoon.

Unfortunately, I assigned Laura Udell the task of pulling the files on Rowan's squad, all twelve, before the warrant came through. I asked Laura to evaluate them for me. Now I've got four patrol officers scheduled to appear this afternoon. I don't expect them to be happy campers. The interviews are uncompensated.

◆

My brain's beginning to fog out and I need a break. I turn on the radio and tune to the local news. Just in time to catch an interview with Mayor Venn. In contrast to the weather, his interview is determinedly sunny. Spurs from I-80 to the north and I-70 to the south have begun construction. When completed just in time for the plant to open, they'll triple the capacity of the state roads now connecting Baxter to the interstates. Work has also begun on the electric grid with the goal of doubling the voltage flowing into the city, and Windstrom Airfield, ninety minutes south of Baxter, will be upgraded to accommodate midsize airliners. For those in a hurry, a chopper service will get you to a Baxter helipad in less than thirty minutes.

I smile to myself as our beloved mayor shifts to upgrades for the sewers and water mains. Venn's a booster, always has been, and that's all to the good. His problems become apparent, though, when his interviewer shifts to the city's ever-rising crime stats. They get worse when she again shifts, this time to the nightmare of Oakland Gardens. The homeless encampments, the shooting galleries, the undocumented workers stuffed five to a room in homes without running water. Though he fumbles his way through, Mayor Venn has no real answer. Neither do I. Any attempt to weed out the illegals would result in a dozen construction projects grinding to a halt. The developers wouldn't like that, and while they might not have the numbers, they have the dollars that finance campaigns.

A few minutes later, I pull into Stu Harrinton's driveway, still without answers. Even our search for Ivy Jordan, Rowan's assigned driver on the night he was killed, has come to nothing. We know that her credit card was used at a hotel outside Nashville and that she has relatives in the mountains of eastern Tennessee. But efforts to trace her through her phone have failed, as did Vern's effort to enlist the help of the Tennessee state police. As a vaguely sympathetic captain pointed out, Ivy Jordan was only a witness. She hadn't been charged with a crime, and wasn't likely to be. Uncovering her whereabouts in the hill country, if she didn't want to be found, would require a commitment of time and resources the Tennessee Bureau of Investigation wasn't prepared to assume.

"If you can tell us where she is, we'll be happy to get her. Otherwise . . ."

CHAPTER THIRTEEN

DELIA

For just a minute after shutting down the ignition, I sit in the car, watching a half-dozen chickens search the grass for insects. The birds have black bodies and wing feathers tipped with silver. I barely know chickens from pigeons and have no idea what breed they might be. Still, the scene, what with the wide porch fronting the house and the smoke curling up from a pipe in the roof, speaks to an easy peacefulness. I sense that if I return tomorrow, and the next day and the next, these same chickens will be hunting the same insects.

Stupid, that's what I tell myself, but when I step out of the car, a chorus of birdsong rings in my ears. Fuck you, city slicker.

As I come up the porch steps, the door opens and a little girl's face pops out. She stares at me for a moment, eyes widening, then looks back into the house.

"Daddy, the boss is here."

Brenda Harrington steps into the doorway. We've met often enough to be friendly, if not friends. She's smiling as she steps aside to let me pass.

"Welcome, boss."

"That's Ms. Boss, Brenda."

"Okay, Ms. Boss. Your faithful workers are in the kitchen."

The living room still smells of a wood fire that's almost burned out, and I'm reminded, as usual, of the house and business fires I've investigated over the years. The memories are far from pleasant, but they recede as I enter a kitchen dominated by the odor of freshly brewed coffee. There's a mug already laid out and I fill it as I greet Stu Harrington and Tom Carney. There's also a large plate on the kitchen table. A plate loaded with blueberry muffins so fresh they're steaming.

Stu's his usual self, tall, slender, his features dominated by his mustache. I don't waste more than a glance at Stu. I know where he stood, stands, and will stand in the future. Carney's more of a puzzle. I shouldn't be having doubts at this stage. I'm the one who recruited him, after all. But the man's absolutely inscrutable, his expression dead neutral. An advantage, surely, when he's working undercover, but I remember him as distinctly more animated during our prehiring interviews. Today, his small features sit like isolated islands on his face.

"Okay," I announce as I sip at my coffee, "let's hear what you've got."

◆

"I've been working steady with George Pratt," Carney tells me. "I can give him to you whenever you want, gift wrapped."

"We're not after George Pratt, Carney."

"Well, I'm also close to the other part, captain. Maybe another week." He continues on for a few minutes, describing his encounter with Sergeant Overby. As I'd hoped when I hired Carney, his arrests in Philadelphia and his association with Sean Carney were enough for Overby, who appears to have accepted Carney as a player.

"You say Overby had you checked out before he showed up at your trailer?"

"Yup. Most likely prodded by George Pratt. And Overby, he was satisfied with my credentials. He only worried that I was an advance scout for my uncle."

"Sean Carney."

"Yeah, and I reassured him on that issue, too. I told him I wouldn't be workin' with Pratt for peanut wages if my uncle was involved." Carney leans forward to reach the wallet in a rear pocket. "Check this out."

I'm looking at a concealed-weapon carry permit. "How'd you get it?"

"Overby. And without my asking. He told me to show up at city hall, find the licensing department, and see a woman named Violet. Which I did."

"Can you describe this woman?"

"Mid-to-late twenties, average height and weight, red-orange hair, obviously dyed, and eyeglasses with neon-blue frames. Her features are small, her nose unusually thin, her jaw receding. She wore large hoop earrings, yellow gold in color, and a watch with a purple band. Plastic would be my guess."

I have to smile, knowing Carney had anticipated the question and prepared his answer in advance. Looking into his eyes, I detect just a hint of mischief. "Did she say anything to you?"

"Not a word. Just handed me an envelope and walked away."

"Did Overby ask for a payoff?"

"We'd speak again at the end of the month was how he left it." Carney reaches out for a half-eaten muffin on a small plate in front of him. He takes a bite and closes his eyes for a second as he swallows. "More and more, I'm sensing a way of thinking behind Overby and the rest of the cops I've run into. On Pratt's behalf, I hurt a kid named Stone. A street name, probably. I did it in Oakland Gardens, in full view of anybody who wanted to take a look. It's the public part that upset Overby and he said as much. I mean, basically, it was about keeping your business private. Or else."

Again, Carney reaches out, this time for his phone. "You might want to take a look at this." The image on his phone is blurry, but I can make out the cartoon cop at the center and the letters *FOP* at the top of what appears to be a business card. "According to Pratt, if you put the card on the dash or carry it in your shirt pocket, you won't have your car or person searched."

"Did he tell you how he got it?"

"No, but I'm sure he will. The asshole doesn't know how to shut up."

◆

I'm feeling elated as I drive away from Stu's house. Elated because I left that plate of blueberry muffins unmolested. This morning, completely nude, I stepped onto a digital scale in the bathroom to find I'd lost a full pound. This is progress that would have quickly reversed if I'd succumbed. Cut in half, the whole blueberries in the muffin had the allure of sapphires. Precious gems, to be sure.

All good, because I need the psychological boost. Vern and I agree that the way forward will be marked by turning the cops at the bottom of the food chain. In essence, by creating more Carneys, only these will carry badges. The avenue to accomplish this without revealing Carney's role has yet to emerge.

The mist outside has become a steady rain. Good for the farmers, I suppose, but the cows in the dairy farm I pass don't seem particularly happy. They stand in the meadows, water dripping from their muzzles and tails, but continue to graze. I have to think this isn't their first rainstorm and that endurance is their game. No umbrellas for cows. They take what comes.

I come upon a little cluster of country stores and the first red light in the last ten miles. As I wait, I recall a pair of comments, one from Stu, the other from Carney. After Rowan's death, every detective in the division was instructed to pump their informants. The responses were simple to the point of appearing rehearsed. Rowan Krauss was murdered by other cops. Attempts to probe went nowhere. These informants didn't know and didn't want to know.

"They were afraid, sure," Stu explained. "But more than that, they simply didn't know who killed Rowan, and there were no rumors, either. So, if it wasn't the crooks who pulled the trigger, it must have been the cops."

In a way, Carney had echoed the part about a new breed. In times past, the Baxter PD was wildly underfunded. Uniformed personnel were forced to buy their own uniforms, and it wasn't uncommon to find uniforms patched, the fabric thin from multiple washings. Carney wasn't around for that era, but he presented us with an observation that I can't shake, though it had seemed trivial at the time.

"Spit and polish, captain. Like soldiers in their dress uniforms, only all the time. Even in the way they stand and speak. Hair, too, nothing over the ears, some with buzz cuts, a few with shaved skulls. I think I could walk down Main Street and spot these clones from two blocks away."

My mind drifts to images of the state troopers I've met at one or another conference. Their gray trousers were so sharply creased they might have been starched into shape, like they'd stand up without a trooper in them.

All along, I've been thinking opportunists, a group of losers from Missouri who'd recognized the loot to be extracted from a small city with a rapidly expanding force. Now I'm seeing ideology as well. The card read FREE OUR POLICE. I've heard of the organization, a retro movement that looks back to the days when justice was delivered at the end of a nightstick, when cop killers weren't taken alive, when you could shoot a fleeing suspect in the back. Armed or unarmed.

That's not my position, not at all, because I know that in an age of body cams and cell phones and security cameras, justice at the end of a nightstick isn't going to work. Not unless you rewrite the Constitution.

◆

Whatever thread I'm following snaps when my cell rings. It's Patrick O'Malley, who wouldn't be calling unless it was important. It's going to be bad news, surely. Good news can always wait.

"Hey, captain, glad I caught ya. I got good news and bad news. Wha'cha wanna hear first?"

A split decision, more than I'd hoped for. "Lead with the good, Pat."

"We got the shooter, the woman who killed Rowan. Got a gun, got clothes with bloodstains, got oversized shoes stuffed with paper towels. Even got a 2021 Honda with four Hankook tires holdin' it up."

"Where did you find the clothes?"

"On her body. She's wearing them."

"After a week?"

"Well, that's the thing, the bad news. A week's about how long she's been dead."

CHAPTER FOURTEEN

DELIA

Everything's in place. A Ruger .22 semiautomatic with a suppressor still attached. A pair of shoes, still on the victim's feet, toes stuffed with paper towels. Drops of blood, some of them large, on the girl's face and hands and on a black, zip-up sweater. In fact, the one thing missing is an obvious cause of death. She's lying face up on the floor of a small house in Oakland Gardens. The only marks on her body are a pair of healed-over track marks on the back of her left hand. She seems too young to be a junkie, a girl still.

"Name's Deborah Cole, age seventeen," O'Malley says. "Lives in Norwood according to her driver's license. Only other ID is a Covid vaccination card dating back two years."

"No Social Security card?"

"Not on her. But I ran her sheet. She's been arrested three times, all of it petty. Twice for possession of weed, once for less than a gram of meth. Probation all three times, but get this, boss.

Her first arrest was three years ago. The arresting officer was Rowan Krauss."

"Arrest for what?"

"She was caught sharing a joint with three of her friends in a car behind the school. Like I said, petty crap."

As a motive for murder, the bust doesn't pass the smell test. It'll play, though, if there's enough supporting forensics. I look back at what remains of Deborah Cole. The skin on her face and hands is the green of a bruised olive. Her body is bloated and pushes against her clothing and shoes. Now as dull as last year's hay, her dirty-blond hair has lost whatever luster it once had. A bracelet on her right wrist, a bangle, digs into the flesh beneath.

"Who found the body?"

"Four people, three men and a woman, junkies looking for a place to get off. One of them peeked in through an open window in the back and smelled the body. Not the worst sort, obviously. They called it in when they could've walked away."

◆

Arshan Rishnavata, our coroner, stands just outside the house. He's taken a quick look at the body, but now waits for the crime scene unit to arrive before transporting Deborah to our morgue at Baxter Medical Center. I join him on the porch, the steady pounding of the rain on its roof leaving us isolated. I feel a growing anger so familiar it waves hello as it arrives. Did this girl kill Rowan Krauss? I can't make myself believe it. But if she didn't, the setup had to be elaborate, had to be well planned. I now know that I sent Laura on a wild goose chase when I asked her to check the security cameras on Baxter Boulevard. I should have had her work Oakland Gardens.

"Welcome to the puzzle palace, captain." Arshan is the first to speak. "There are no wounds visible on her clothing, no bullet wound, no stabbing wound, not even bruising on her throat." He shakes his head. "Perhaps an overdose?"

Nice and neat. Rowan dead, his killer dead. The tests have yet to be done, but I'd bet my pension that her prints and DNA will be found on the weapon, that gunshot residue will be discovered on her hands, that the blood on her sweater belongs to Rowan Krauss. We'll match her shoes and the tire treads on the Honda to the impressions found at the scene. And if we can't prove that Deborah Cole was murdered, if there's even a small possibility that she died naturally from causes unknown and unknowable? Then it's case closed. A cop murdered, his murderer beyond human justice. Give that mayor a gold star. Give another pair to his police commissioner and the commander of his detective division.

◆

"I want you to run a tox screen as soon as you get the body, Arshan. Forget the state lab. They'll take a week. Run it up to Baxter Medical's own labs." I know from personal experience that when a patient comes into the emergency room unconscious, the docs commonly order a tox screen. If the patient's overdosed, they need to know on what. For my part, I need to eliminate the possibility that Deborah overdosed. Although I believe the chances are very small, the house where she died has been used as a shooting gallery, every room littered with paraphernalia.

"Do the autopsy this afternoon. I'm asking as a favor, and I'll definitely owe you one."

"You have said this before."

"True, but this time it's important."

"This you have also said before, but there are bodies ahead of yours."

"No." I shake my head. "You need to pay careful attention to her neck at the carotids." I've got Arshan's attention now. The man believes himself to be a pathologist-sleuth. Maybe he watches too much television. And maybe, if I give his ego a stroke or two, he'll become personally involved. "Imagine an arm around a neck with the forearm and bicep compressing the carotids on either side of the neck. The crook of the elbow is at the throat, but not making contact. In ten seconds, the victim is unconscious. Three minutes later, the victim is dead."

"There would be bruising."

"Not necessarily. You don't need to apply a great deal of pressure. Just enough to cut off the blood supply. Look for very slight petechiae in the eyes, very minor bruising, perhaps subcutaneous, on the neck. And most of all, look for any sign that she was moved after death. And while you do this, I want you to think about the mindset of the perpetrators who killed her. They have to be stopped, Arshan, and I need your help to pull it off."

And one day Baxter will have a trained pathologist and not a cardiologist to perform autopsies. One day.

◆

I have to move fast now. Deborah Cole appears to be a local. She'll have friends and acquaintances, and probably relatives.

The conspirators behind Rowan's death took a big chance when they set her up. They couldn't know what she might have said to those friends and acquaintances in the days leading up to the murders, his and hers. Now that I have a trail to follow, I intend to find out.

Ten minutes after leaving Arshan, I walk into the squad room. Stu Harrington's in the room, along with Laura Udell and Cade Barrow. I take Stu into my office and quickly brief him on the scene in Oakland Gardens.

"Problem is, I've got members of Rowan's unit coming in for interviews."

"Right, and from what I hear, they're not too happy about it."

"All part of the game plan. The problem is that I won't be here. I'm going to assume that Deborah Cole is a victim, not a perpetrator. If I'm wrong, so what? If I'm right, I need to move quickly."

"I'm guessing you want me to take the lead."

"No guessing to it, Stu. And don't get greedy. They won't give you anything important. The setting's too public. Look for a signal, an invitation to follow up. And watch how they're dressed. You can pretty much assume that the spit-and-polish cops are not on our side. Piss them off if you can. Stir the pot."

Stu's eyes light up as he smooths his long mustache. "I believe I can do that, boss. I believe I will."

◆

My own boss comes next and I arrive at Vern's office to find a ladder in the middle and a workman changing the LED bulbs in a ceiling fixture. Vern's standing at the foot of the ladder, but steps away as I enter the office.

"You know what's wrong with LED bulbs? They don't just blow out. They blink, they glow, they annoy the hell out of me. Swear to Christ, I'm ready to buy candles. In bulk."

My phone sounds before I can manufacture a suitable reply. It's Pat O'Malley, still at the crime scene. I put the phone on speaker and take the call.

"What's up, Pat. I'm with the commissioner at the moment."

"Got it, captain. I'll be quick. The Honda outside was stolen two weeks ago from a mall parking lot in the capital. We found blood inside, a small amount, but for sure it's gonna be Rowan's. We also found hairs on the front seat that could be from Deborah Cole. The right length and color anyway." He hesitates, but I have nothing to say. "Just thought you should know."

"All right, and thanks, but I want that car processed carefully. Don't stop with the hair and blood. Swab everything for DNA. The hair could have been planted but planting DNA from a casual touch would be a lot harder if she was never actually inside it."

I hang up and turn to face a grim Vern Taney. "It gets worse, Vern. We also found blood spatter on Deborah Cole's clothing, on a pair of shoes stuffed with paper towels, and on her body. A Ruger .22 with a silencer lay in plain sight on a table. The one thing we don't have? A cause of death. Maybe Arshan will fix that when he does the autopsy, but I'm betting we'll never pin it down. That means the official line will probably be that Deborah Cole, a local with a record of petty offenses, put a bullet in Rowan's head while he was sleeping, then drove to an abandoned house in Oakland Gardens and conveniently died, thus saving our fair city the cost of a trial."

Vern has no ready answer. I can almost hear the wheels turning. Take advantage of the obvious? The killer of Sergeant

Rowan Krauss has been identified and is beyond punishment. Due, of course, to the superior police work of the Baxter PD's dedicated detectives. And while she might have been discovered by four junkies looking for a safe place to get off, her guilt was established by the Baxter Police Department.

"On the one hand," he says, "if everything checks out, and I'm sure it will, the woman's guilt will be established by that mountain of forensic evidence prosecutors love to cite. On the other hand, it stinks from top to bottom. Tell me, was the house occupied, say, by squatters?"

"I think it was more of a shooting gallery, though I can't say that junkies never spent a night there. But there's no furniture. No fridge or stove or running water. No electric or gas or . . ."

Vern cuts me off. "I'll work on a press release, suitably equivocal. Maybe, maybe, maybe. Still to be determined. Tests not yet conducted. Let's not jump to any hasty conclusions." He smiles. "I don't know how much time I can give you, Delia. Too many cops were at the scene and word is bound to leak out. So, make the best of it."

CHAPTER FIFTEEN
DELIA

Deborah Cole's driver's license carries a Norwood address, a home belonging to Meredith Cole, a relative no doubt. Ordinarily, I hate notifications, but this one should provide a starting point. I want a list of Deborah's friends and acquaintances, and a timeline that accounts for the last forty-eight hours of her life. I discover Cade Barrow still in the squad room and draft him. I'm not expecting trouble, but I'm not taking any chances.

The Norwood section on the southwestern side of the city fully embraces its middle-class reputation. Dominated by free-standing houses, the lucky residents have seen property values skyrocket. Before Nissan, just a few short years ago, these well-maintained homes often remained on the market for a year before they were sold for prices below the original asking price. The average selling price has more than doubled since, and there's no telling how high they'll go. Maybe even to the top of gold mountain.

The neighborhood isn't cookie-cutter. Colonials vie with Tudors that vie with ranch homes. Most are three bedrooms, but there are four bedrooms as well. What they have in common is a ferocious determination to maintain property values. I'm not finding broken pavement or peeling paint or patched roofs or dirty windows. The yards are well tended, the trees trimmed, the grass cut, spring flowers in weeded beds. The same respectability extends to Meredith Cole's home on Maplewood Drive. The smallest on the block, its dormer windows on the upper floor peer from beneath a sharply slanted roof. Below, the Cole front lawn has been recently trimmed and a bed of half-open peonies are far enough advanced to fill my nostrils as I approach the front door.

With Cade at my side, I ring the bell. It's answered less than a minute later by a tall woman, probably in her late thirties. Broad shoulders and hips mark a sturdy torso. When Cade and I display our shields, her hands go to her hips and her chin rises.

"Meredith Cole?" I ask.

"If this about Debbie, I don't wanna hear it. She hasn't lived here in more than two years."

"You're her mother?"

"Stepmother."

"Is her father available?"

"Yeah, you'll find him in the state of New York, town of Peekskill, where he's livin' with his new family." She's glaring now. "So, get it over with. What's that little bitch done now?"

"Your stepdaughter's dead, Mrs. Cole." Beside me, I feel Cade stir. He has a little girl of his own. "We're here to notify her next of kin."

Meredith Cole takes a backward step. Whatever she's anticipated, it wasn't this. But she recovers quickly enough. "Next of kin? That's not me. Like I said, she's my stepdaughter." Another slight pause. "Was it an accident?"

"We won't be sure until after her autopsy, but we're not ruling out homicide."

There's enough dissembling in my reply to fuel a political campaign, but Meredith seems not to notice. "Like I already said, I haven't laid eyes on her for the past six months."

"I understand, but we're beginning our investigation and you can help us. We want to make a list of her friends. Friends her own age, anyone older."

"Anyone older?"

"That's right."

"Well, in that case, come on in. See for yourselves."

◆

I know what's coming as I wait for Meredith Cole's computer to boot up. The video is as disturbing as it is graphic. Deborah Cole and an older white man who appears to be in his forties. The man wears a nylon ski mask that effectively conceals his features. At first, I observe no significant marks on his flesh, no scars, no tattoos, but then Cade points to a spot behind the man's left ear. A skin tag, a wart, a growth of some kind. I don't have to say anything. Videos can be sharpened and enlarged easily enough.

"Shut it down," I tell her. When she replies, perhaps reacting to my tone of voice, I ask, "Is there anything else on there I need to see?"

"Hell, they're just gettin' started." Meredith is wearing bright red lipstick on thin lips that virtually disappear when she grins.

"I don't know when she and her candy man got it on, but she was still fifteen when she sent it to me. That would be six months after she left."

"In what form?"

"In an email. Just threw it in my face. I mean, her father sweet-talks me into marriage with promises of havin' a real family, with cozy dinners and high school graduations and . . . and then he takes off one day. Just gets up and goes, leavin' me with his kid. That was two years ago. And I did my best for a while. Until she got herself busted twice for pot and tossed out of school. I think she blamed me for her old man leavin' her behind. Like I somehow wanted her."

I take a moment to compose my thoughts. I need to identify the man, of course, along with whatever friends she might have had. I need to follow a line, and Meredith is the obvious place to start. But first I have to gain her wholehearted cooperation.

"Are you certain that Deborah sent the video?"

"It came from her email address. Plus, she didn't deny it when she tried to come back. Practically begged me to let her in, and me, I wasn't havin' none of it. Not after the video." She shakes her head. "No whores gonna live in this house."

"Okay, Meredith, this is how it's gonna go. You will answer every question we have, even if those questions last until midnight. Either that or I'm gonna arrest you for possession of child pornography."

"What?"

"You just admitted that the video has been in your possession for months. You should have called the police immediately. And by the way, did you ever consider the possibility that her sending the video was a cry for help?" I don't give her a chance to answer. Instead, I list her rights under the Fifth Amendment to our Constitution.

Meredith proves to be a quick study. She takes a shot at righteous indignation, a brief shot. Then she sighs. "You mind if I smoke?"

"Knock yourself out."

"I think you've pretty much done that already."

◆

My phone gives off a short peep, a message coming in. I take a quick look, hoping for insignificance, but it's Arshan. *Autopsy in one hour. As promised.*

It's true. I asked and he promised. If I want to be there, and I do, I have to leave. Five minutes earlier and leaving would have presented a problem. Now that we've secured Meredith's cooperation, it's become easier. In fact, there's no good reason for my staying. Cade Barrow has proven himself a thorough professional over more than a year of service. I take him outside and explain the situation. He's running the show now. Extract every syllable of information she has to give. No mercy. But don't, under any circumstances, follow up alone. Go back to the squad room and find yourself a partner before you make a move.

"The asshole with the mask in the video? You have to figure he might react poorly if you find him. We've already got one murdered cop. We don't need another. Wear a vest. And take the computer when you leave. It's evidence that was shown to us voluntarily. I want to make sure we preserve the video as leverage in case we need mommy dearest in the future."

◆

I start my car, but leave it in park as I use my phone to call Baxter Medical Center. I don't know what I'm expecting, maybe that Jane Moreland has rallied and gone back to trekking with her father. Instead, a woman informs me, in a voice devoid of emotion, that Jane Moreland is dead. But it's not Jane's image that jumps into my brain. It's Debbie Cole lying on the floor of an abandoned house in Oakland Gardens. Too young, the both of them, but the one, Jane, was loved for every minute of her short life. The other was abandoned, by her father first, then her stepmother. Left to sink or swim on her own, it's no surprise she found herself walking a dark road. I've dealt with throwaways many times, cast-outs bearing injuries that will never heal, and a grudge against society equally deep.

The rain has stopped and the skies are rapidly clearing, west to east. A steady breeze, not quite a wind, flicks at the trees. A long bed of yellow tulips in the yard before me bend, then spring upright. Ten minutes later I'm on First Avenue in Boomtown, walking toward Keith Moreland's small camper. I'm calling it a wellness visit, but that's not what I'm about. I'm acting on impulse, and I don't care. I spend most of my life analyzing, whether it's a crime scene or a deposition. Not this time.

I don't know exactly what I'm expecting to find when Keith opens the door, but neither his composed expression or dry eyes can hide the deep hurt. He attempts a smile, but doesn't quite get there.

"Captain . . ."

"Delia now."

"Delia then, what can I do for you?"

"I called the hospital and . . . and just figured I'd stop by and see how you're doing."

"I'm all right." He steps outside and draws a breath, seeming almost surprised by the pure sunlight now slanting in from the west. "Really, I've been preparing myself for a long time."

I blurt it out before I can stop myself. "I think you're the bravest person I know. And maybe I want to tell you that because I spend so much of my time witnessing every sort of cowardice, because I'm tired of listening to the same sorry excuses for the same sorry failures." I stop for a second, but Keith has nothing to say. "So, from here. Do you plan to stay in Baxter?"

"No. Janey will be cremated tomorrow. Then I'll take her home."

"Where are you from?"

"Wisconsin. My mom's there, and my two sisters."

We maintain an awkward silence for a few seconds. After all, we're not even acquaintances. Finally, I'm about to speak, but he beats me to it. "I've been grieving for years, Delia, and I thought I'd break down altogether when she finally passed. But my inheritance seems to be enough for now."

"Inheritance?"

He taps his chest. "Janey's love. I've inherited Janey's love. I'm taking that home, too. I think it's enough."

◆

Arshan's already present when I walk into the autopsy suite at Baxter Medical Center. He's pissed off, undoubtedly because I've missed my report time by fifteen minutes. I don't mind. My conversation with Keith Moreland was awkward, but worth every second. Tonight, after dinner when Zoe calls, we'll talk it through. For now, I direct my focus to a pair of lab assistants as they unzip a puke-green body bag. Deborah Cole's inside, arms and ankles crossed.

The lab assistants wear gloves, masks, and gowns. The gear will be collected, as will the body bag and the girl's clothing. Within twenty-four hours, the material we gathered this afternoon, along with the evidence recovered at the crime scene and from the car outside, will go to the state's crime lab. Results will be long in coming and we can't press for special treatment. Too much material, too many tests, and we don't want a rush job in any event. Every stain on Deborah's clothing has to be examined, along with the hair found in the car and swabs of virtually every surface in the room where she was discovered. What isn't there could be important as well. When I examined Deborah in Oakland Gardens, the apparent bloodstains on her sweater, especially around the right cuff, were obvious, but I didn't observe bloodstains on her jeans. Significant? Assuming that Rowan was asleep, he would likely be slumped on the seat with his head close to the bottom of the window opening. His killer's hand, the one holding the gun almost level, would have been at her waist or slightly above. The bloodstains on the right wrist of her sweater are very clear because her right hand, the one that held the gun, was closest to the victim. But the waist area of her jeans would have been only inches farther away. If the blowback reached the breast area of Deborah's sweater, and we're sure it did, her jeans should also be stained.

"The sweatshirt does not fit her," Arshan says. "Too large." He raises a finger. "Unless she wished to conceal a weapon beneath."

The observation jars me out of my speculations. And that's just what they were. It's entirely possible that a closer examination of her jeans will reveal the bloodstains I don't want to find.

Deborah Cole lies on an autopsy table. Rigor is long past, and her body is limp, as if her bones had come loose. Yet, despite the bloating, the sweater, when I look closely, is obviously too large. Relevant? Maybe, maybe not, but like her jeans, we're covering every base, and with no suspect, or even person of interest, it's more important to be thorough than quick.

"I think the shoes found at the scene would be too large as well," Arshan declares. "Even with the paper towels stuffed into the toe area."

I don't argue the point, mostly because I know what's coming and I'm trying to prepare myself. Ordinarily, a body is washed and the clothing collected prior to autopsy, but this time I wanted to observe the process from beginning to end. If there's anything to be determined, I want to be here when it happens.

Ten minutes later, a microscopic examination of excised dermis on either side of Deborah's neck reveals a relatively small number of ruptured capillaries. Caused by compression? Possibly, if she died before the leaking blood made its way to the surface. But definitive? So sorry.

A relatively fresh track mark behind her knee might have been used to poison the girl or at least render her unconscious. But her blood, screened a couple of hours before we got started, showed only a small trace of methamphetamine, not enough to produce any effect at all.

An examination of her eyes reveals minor petechiae, but again not severe enough to be definitive. Her organs, removed and examined one at a time, are perfectly normal for her age, her weight as well, even her hair seems healthy, although it, too, will be sent off for testing.

Lividity begins immediately after death when the blood in a body, pulled down by gravity, pools in whatever parts of a body are closest to the ground. Eight to twelve hours after death, lividity becomes fixed. Turning a prone body on its back will have no effect on the pattern left by the now-congealed blood just beneath the surface of the skin. This is why it's so difficult to stage a scene after death. It might take eight hours or more for lividity to become fixed, but it's visible after only an hour as a faint blush that won't go away. If you move the body, but don't pose it exactly as it was, lividity in more than one area of the body will give you away. But the lividity on the underside of Deborah's is consistent. She died where she was found, and the issue now becomes how she got there.

◆

There's good news as well, very good news. Early on, Arshan observed small traces of blood and tissue beneath the index and pinkie fingers of Deborah Cole's right hand. The material he scrapes from beneath these nails will go to the state lab where DNA tests will be performed, but Arshan's certain the material is organic.

"She fought for her life, Arshan. She reached back far enough, or quickly enough, to scratch her killer."

"You are jumping to conclusions."

"Rocketing. I'm rocketing to conclusions."

"Then tell me this. Surely whoever she scratched felt enough pain to notice. And also presumably, as you have said, they were sophisticated enough to disguise cause and manner of death. So why did they not remove this tissue from beneath her nails?"

"For the reasons you just mentioned. The staging here was excellent, and could only be accomplished by someone familiar with homicide investigations. It appears that she simply died, all alone, in that room, a young woman with no sign of pathology in any organ. But if her fingernails were scraped, you'd notice. It would put someone else in the room with her when she died."

I'm feeling better and better. Somehow, Deborah's fight, futile though it was, cheers and motivates me at the same time. Abandoned by her father, discarded by her stepmother, consigned to streets for which she was in no way prepared, she hadn't just surrendered. She'd left us a few centigrams of evidence, a trace of her passing, like the love Jane Moreland left to her father. Remember me.

CHAPTER SIXTEEN
CARNEY

Six days each week, Monday through Saturday, the view from the small front window of my trailer would be of men and women streaming past on their way to work at the construction site. Sunday's the exception, of course, and the street before me is deserted except for the occasional traveler pushing through a morning mist that will soon become a steady rain. A good day to sleep in, but I'm already awake, expecting a phone call at nine o'clock.

I glance out the window at my neighbor, Jennie Adams, as she walks her dog. Time and dogs, not to mention rainstorms and blizzards, wait for no man or woman, which is why I don't have a dog.

Thinking about it, I'm satisfied with my progress, though I've yet to receive a gold star. I've created a persona and sold it to Pratt. I'm the man he needs to back him up. I'm armed and I'm suitably skilled and I've got a mean streak. But I'm not crazy, not liable to fly off the handle and bring down the hammer of the law. Pratt can turn me on and off, which renders him all the more powerful, at least in his own mind.

I've been ordered to meet Pratt at eleven in a Boomtown bar which shouldn't be open on Sunday morning. On a better day, I'd kill the time with a long walk. Not this morning, though.

Breakfast, first, then maybe a light workout. I remove a box of cereal from my undersized cupboard, then a quart of milk and a container of blueberries from the mini-fridge. I have a two-burner hotplate that I rarely use and that's the ball game for home dining.

As I eat my cereal and drink the rancid coffee from my thrift-store coffeemaker, my thoughts drift to Vangi, the girl who approached me in Packers. My first thoughts take a carnal turn. I've been too long between relationships and I'm not big on masturbation. Besides, I know that whatever Vangi has on her mind, it's not love and marriage. So, I'm intrigued, which adds a distinct overtone to the base attraction. That skirt she wore, the color of a pink rosebud, was loose enough to slide over her hips once the four buttons on the side were loosened. I imagine the skirt dropping to the floor, the lingerie beneath, her lips parted, nostrils flaring as she watches me watching her.

Too early on a Sunday morning to make the call, I wash my bowl and spoon in the mini-sink. The woman from Triple-A Realty who rented me the camper listed its benefits as if they were near miraculous. Running water, electricity, sewage treatment, even cable for the TV. All for a monthly rent nearly double what I paid for an apartment in Philadelphia. I have the money to afford better, but it's in my interests to play the struggling immigrant trying to make it in a city where housing of any kind is at a premium. And to give my real estate agent her due, there are campers in Boomtown occupied by two, or even three tenants. Without cable.

I flick on the TV, tuning to the news on KBAX. No surprise, the host runs through the usual bleed-lead stories at the top of the show.

A shooting in Oakland Gardens, a brawl in a Boomtown bar that injured two cops, four household burglaries. As nobody was at home at the time of the burglaries, there's no real bleed to the lead. Burglaries, though, are big news in Baxter these days, and KBAX's coverage includes an interview with the homeowners in a thoroughly trashed living room. Husband and wife are both present, along with a little girl about six who cries throughout because the burglars took her stuffed rabbit.

I'm already tuning out when the segment goes to commercial and I find myself looking at the face of Calvin "Bute" Stafford, candidate for mayor. First impression, the man has presence. A formidable square skull, a full head of salt-and-pepper hair, evenly spaced features held in place by a too-dark mustache. His blue eyes are as sharp as broken glass.

Stafford's seated behind a desk and the shot catches a pair of wide shoulders and a sturdy neck supporting an oversized head. It's a good look, almost arresting, made all the more impressive by a dark suit that fits his shoulders perfectly. I'd have to empty the bank account to afford his tie.

◆

"Good morning, fellow Baxterites. My name is Bute Stafford and I'm running for mayor of our city. This morning, I'm asking for a few minutes of your time while I introduce myself. I was born and raised in Baxter, like most of you voters, and I still have family here. Growing up, I always wanted to be a soldier and I entered the Marine Corps as a lieutenant after graduating from the Citadel. From there, I worked my way to the rank of brigadier general. I've served on four continents, but in my heart, I've never left Baxter. So, after my retirement, I simply came home."

Stafford's a bit stiff, as you'd expect from a career military officer, but his voice is deep and well modulated. Now, he shifts slightly as he draws a breath.

"With three packing plants still operating, Baxter was going strong when I left. But hard times surely followed. The plants closed, the tax base fell apart, the city was on its deathbed, its population declining." Stafford finally manages a small smile that utterly fails to transform his stern expression. "Then Nissan came along and everything changed, including, and especially, our city. The days when mornings were announced by steers bawling in their pens has passed. The very ground on which the packing industry was built, the Yards, has been eradicated. A new Baxter is emerging and we, the citizens of this city, have to decide what it will look like."

Stafford brings his hands up, folds them, and lays them on the table in front of him. He leans forward and his voice drops. "This is Baxter's present."

A series of quick cuts follow. A brawl on the sidewalk outside a Boomtown bar. Four junkies, spikes in hand, huddled around a candle in a shooting gallery. A flock of prostitutes on Main Street. A homeless encampment virtually buried in trash. The segment closes with a long-range shot of a drug dealing crew servicing vehicles that pull to the curb, then pull away as the next car moves up.

"Folks, as part of my duty to my country, I served as commandant of the Marines' Pacific Brig, a level 1 prison. That assignment opened my eyes, and what I say to you now, I learned from personal experience. Thugs, whether in the military or right here in Baxter, live in a might-makes-right world. They respond only to force or the threat of force. They do not respond to reason, or to bleeding-heart sympathy. Respect for authority must be demanded by a police force that won't back down. Police authority will only be respected when there's an immediate penalty for disrespect."

Now Stafford leans back and drops his hands to his lap. Time for the closer. "I know that most folk believe the job of a modern police force is to prevent crime, or even stop it altogether. But crime has been around since Cain slew Abel. It will never be eliminated by any police force. No, the job of a police department is to maintain enough order so ordinary folk, like the folk watching me right now, can go about their daily business safely. And this is what I pledge to accomplish if elected mayor. I will bring order to the city of my birth. I will bring order to Baxter."

A small nod, then, "Thank you very much for allowing me to interrupt your Sunday morning."

◆

I'm impressed. The man's performance conveyed strength and conviction, while the short videos were suitably unsettling. But as I'm not personally threatened by the threats in those videos, I can lean back and ponder the implications. I'm still at it a half hour later when I get my lazy self into gear. I remove one of the drawers from the built-in cabinets and reach behind it to retrieve a slender box. I carry the box to the counter by the sink and remove a burner phone and its battery. I insert the battery, then sit back to wait. The phone rings at nine o'clock, right on time.

"Hello."

"Top of the morning, Tommy."

"Back at ya, Uncle Sean." I know that cell phones are smuggled into prisons, like Frackville where my uncle now resides. How he acquires them at the exact time he specifies in advance eludes me.

"So, what news of Baxter?"

"I'm still putting things together, but I'm sure of two things so far. Some of the cops, if not most, are bent. Only it's not like back East where bent cops followed orders. Here, the cops don't work for the street. The street works for the cops. I had a conversation with a sergeant named Overby two nights ago. What he told me in very plain language was keep my shit private." I stop for a second as I recall Bute Stafford's ad on KBAX. The man's promising order if he's elected. Call it safe streets with crime marching on.

"Did he ask for a payoff?"

"No, but he arranged to get me a carry permit and told me we'd settle up at the end of the month."

◆

I have a complicated relationship with Uncle Sean. Back in Philly, before he was sent away, he played the role of confidential informant to the hilt. The information he provided sent many a scumbag to prison, which usually benefited Uncle Sean and the rest of the Irish mob. One issue, though? Who was running who? I believe Uncle Sean considers me one of the family. I'm talking about his Irish mob family. That's bullshit. I used him as any cop uses any snitch, but I never confronted him. The Irish mob is small relative to other gangs in Philly, a fact of life they counter with ferocity, but cannot change.

"I don't know about you, kid, but I'm smelling opportunity. Who's out there?"

"Nobody. A crew from New York made a move about a year ago, but they were driven off. And that's another thing. Not every cop is bent and I haven't been here long enough to know who's who, or which side's gonna win."

"I'll send one of the boys, Tommy." As always, Uncle Sean ignores information he doesn't want to hear. "You know, take a look around."

"It's too early."

"Just to look."

"No."

"You're tellin' me no? Me?"

"Yeah, I'm tellin' you no."

The pause is shorter than I expect. "All right, Tommy, but when're you gonna wise up? Money's moving all around ya. I'm talkin' about in Baxter. So, where's your end? I tried to put you on to a good thing back in Philly and you jumped onto your high horse. Like a fuckin' cowboy in those movies they used to make. Why, Tommy? Everybody around you has a hand in someone's pocket and you have trouble payin' your rent at the end of the month. Stop bein' a jerk before the train leaves the station. Like forever."

We make an appointment for a follow-up conversation, then I put the phone away. I can't escape thinking that Uncle Sean is the answer to Bute Stafford's prayers. Uncle Sean and his fellow players are sophisticated compared to the street gangs that dominate Philadelphia. They own businesses that launder enough money for them to live comfortable, middle-class lives. And most are smart enough to pay taxes on as much of their income as possible. That's where Uncle Sean screwed up. He skimmed so much cash from his three pizza parlors that he bought himself a vacation in Frackville.

◆

Outside, the rain's picked up, otherwise I'd take a walk. I like to walk while I think things out, but there's not enough room inside the camper to even pace. Still, I manage a final thought before moving on. If Uncle Sean and his boys are perfect for Baxter's new breed of cop, why not George Pratt?

Without giving myself time to think, I dial the number Vangi wrote on the cocktail napkin. It might be too early, but I've never handled boredom well, and I'm not handling it well now. Too much going on.

Vangi answers on the second ring. "Hi, Carney. I'll call you back in ten minutes. I'm not dressed."

I'm not sure why she needs to be dressed for a phone call, but she hangs up before I can ask. I use the ten minutes to retrieve a half-smoked joint from the top drawer of the built-ins. Weed became legal in Pennsylvania in 2018 and I've come to enjoy a few hits from time to time. It does wonders for boredom, and I spend the ten minutes staring out the window at what's now a steady rain. There are more people out there, most likely headed off to find breakfast. The crowded conditions in the campers and huts and single-wides make cooking difficult or impossible. It's like walking the dog. Rain or no rain, you have to get out.

Back home, I'd expect the trudgers to carry umbrellas, but I'm dealing with a macho population here. Only a few carry umbrellas, while a larger number wear some kind of camo rain gear. Most, though, march along, grin and bear it the operating principle.

I'm ready to let off a chorus of "Macho Man" when my phone rings. The caller's name doesn't appear on the phone's screen, only a number.

"Hello."

"It's Vangi, sorry about the wait."

"Not a problem. So, what's up?"

"If I remember right, you called me."

"True, but I'm only responding to the message you left with the bartender at Packers. Cryptic though it was."

Vangi laughs, a throaty chuckle. "I'll give you that one." Another hesitation. "What if I told you I know where a certain person not to be named keeps his stash? Suppose I named a number like mid–five figures?"

"Can I assume that's it? No what, who, or when? Or even how?"

"Pretty much."

"Does that indicate pleasure before business?"

Another laugh. "Bold is what drew me to you in the first place. Before that, I only had Georgie's word for it. He really likes you, by the way. He's decided that you have something his other flunkies haven't even heard about."

I think I'm supposed to react to the word *flunkies*. I don't. "And what would that be?"

"Self-discipline. His other people? When you need 'em, they're stoned out of their minds. Or in a cell after beatin' the shit outta some good citizen. Not you, though, at least according to Georgie, so I decided to see for myself."

"Can I assume I passed the audition?"

"Yeah, so let's meet up. And don't worry too much about the pleasure part. We can take care of that before, during, or after."

"And when will 'during' happen?"

"You tell me."

"I'll call you when I get home tonight. That'll be whenever my boss lets me go."

CHAPTER SEVENTEEN
CARNEY

The name of the bar, written in gold letters on a black background, is SPINNING WHEEL SALOON. But the small neon object below is not an antique spinning wheel. It's a roulette wheel. I suspect that's where the owners went wrong. Inside I find the space divided, with a small bar in front and what's left of a mini-casino in the back. Two roulette wheels, a craps table, and a blackjack–poker table have been smashed to pieces, along with a dozen smaller tables and as many chairs. I can see the ruins clearly because the door separating the bar and the casino has also been smashed and hangs from a single bottom hinge.

Pratt's sitting on a three-legged stool in front of the bar. Curiously, the liquor on the shelves is untouched. What I'm seeing isn't the result of a brawl. I look around for a chair, but Pratt's ass is on the only one still intact.

"The sign out front?" I ask. "That's all it took?"

"That and the loan shark stationed at the bar, and the bookie for sports betting. And the whores."

"The bettors don't know how to play online?"

"They don't give credit online, Carney." Pratt's got a Starbucks container in front of him. He takes a sip from whatever's inside. "Plus, the asshole advertised the casino. Printed business cards and handed 'em out all over Boomtown." He shakes his head. "The idiot was told to stop, but some people can't see that cop fist comin', not until it smashes into their mouths."

"Then it's too late."

"Not for us." Pratt gestures to the mess. "All this, it's ours. As in you and me. I want you to run it. You won't have to be here every night. You'll have a manager for that. Your main job is to make sure the help ain't helpin' themselves. So, whatta ya say?"

"Great, I'll rush out and pick up a tube of superglue."

"Very funny." He raises a finger and shakes it. "I'm gonna make my move, Carney. Now that I understand the game. All I need is a buffer."

"And that would be me."

"Yeah, and you're gonna find out why in a few minutes. Meanwhile, you want a drink, help yourself."

◆

I don't, but rain or no rain, I take a few minutes to fetch coffee from a food truck parked on the block. When I return, I find Pratt has been joined by a short man, his pudgy face made pudgier by a full beard that clings to the contours of his face as though glued to his skin.

"Carney, meet Zacariah McBride. Zacariah, meet Tom Carney. Zacariah managed the casino for the owner who is sitting in a Baxter County jail cell. Now, he's gonna manage it for us. Right, Zacariah?"

"Yessir."

"Only it's not the Spinning Wheel Saloon any more. It's the Blue Skies Tavern. And the new roulette wheels and craps tables are gonna be on the up-and-up, instead of loaded in favor of the house. Right, Zacariah?"

"Yessir."

"Now Carney here? He speaks with my voice. If it comes from him, it comes from me." Pratt looks at me for the first time. "I want you to spend time here layin' out the new casino. Come up with a list of what you'll need and bring it to me. I'll place the order myself, for used equipment, not new. I got a connection that'll get it here in a hurry." He looks to Zacariah, then to me again. "You'll be in for points from the beginning, and it only gets better from there. Now, let's take a ride."

◆

Pratt's driving a Toyota Avalon. The Avalon sits at the top of the Toyota line, but still manages to be inconspicuous. All part of the program, I assume, which includes Pratt biding his time. The gold ring's in sight, almost within reach, but I have to wonder how many other Pratts are listening to the cop message and biding their own time. I also wonder if Bute Stafford and Sergeant Overby have considered the possibility of a gang war to establish supremacy.

At the top of Boomtown, Pratt pulls to the edge of the road. This is the meat market, where a crowd of day workers will assemble tomorrow morning. I suspect they're just as glad the rain's falling on a Sunday.

"You're gonna meet three people this afternoon, three men. They each have their own crews, but they're throwing in with me because I have the connections. What I want is for you to stand in for me. You'll collect, you'll discipline, you'll carry my word, just like in the casino."

"I'm the buffer?"

"You could put it that way."

"You'll have to excuse me, but I gotta ask. What's in it for me? In return for putting my ass on the line."

"See, that's what I like about you. You don't scheme, maybe figurin' a way to rip me off. You come right out and say what's on your mind. Pop the glove box."

I do as asked and find an envelope.

"There's fifteen hundred inside. Take it." He waits until I again comply. "You could figure somethin' like this every week, plus a piece of the casino." He wags a finger in my direction. "This is just the beginning. The men you're gonna meet? Two are runnin' drugs, but quiet, not on the street. The other guy's workin' a string of whores. Only again, not on the street, or in Boomtown. Outcalls only. And you'd be surprised how many of our better citizens appreciate discretion when it come to a taste of the strange."

"Which could, of course, lead to blackmail."

"What can I say? Some guys, they just can't keep it in their pants."

◆

Pratt's got the heater blowing hot air over the windshield to ward off condensation that's already slick on the side windows.

As I slide the envelope into my pocket, I look off for a moment, staring through the window at a distorted landscape. In theory, I'm supposed to hand the money over to my handler. In theory.

"One other thing, George. You said somethin' about me acting as your muscle if one of these crews need correcting. I'll go up against any individual. Just point your finger, but . . ."

"The part about discipline? That's for the future. For now, concentrate on the casino where I gotta put serious money. Zacariah's gonna manage, like I already said, and for the croupiers and the dealers, we gotta use professionals. But the security is up to you. And we wanna go heavy on security, heavy enough to stop trouble before it happens. Hire the right people, make 'em loyal." He looks to the left as he draws a breath. "I'm seein' my chance, Carney. What we have now, it's like the city's bein' born again. Like it's risin', and I plan to rise with it."

◆

I'm a bit tickled by Pratt's crew leaders, Will Duffy, Bradley Owen, and Les Jameson. Whiter than white, these good old boys are like all the others I've met since I got here. Back in Philly, I'd be dealing with Italians, Jews, Blacks, Dominicans, Puerto Ricans, Cubans, or Russians. Not in Baxter where globalization is no more than a hoax. Like Covid.

As I listen to Carney define my role, I recognize how lucky I am to be Irish. Catholic Irish, true, and not Protestant Irish like Will Duffy who wears a Kelly green T-shirt with a silver shamrock on the front. It's the plain gold cross instead of a crucifix that gives him away. The Protestant part, I mean. The cross dangles at the end of a thick gold chain.

The observation made, my amusement subsides, as I pretty much tune out Pratt's faux-knucklehead performance. I'm thinking about Vangi and Uncle Sean's last comments. I'm also thinking about my ex-wife, Joanna. A year after she left me, I left Philadelphia. The neighborhood where I lived was too small. It became a straitjacket, a garotte. Joanna lived only a few blocks away, at first by herself, then with another man after the divorce became final. The divorce was no-fault, based on "irreconcilable differences," but the plural was off base. We had one difference, and while it appeared to be about money, it was in fact about ambition.

You don't dream, is what she said. *You're nowhere and nowhere's exactly where you want to be.*

She wasn't off the mark. Uncle Sean offered me opportunity after opportunity, but I kept on doing my job. Dogged might be the right word. Honest, another. But neither my commitment to the job of policing, or my refusal to take a bribe, made it easier to pay the mortgage on our too-big house. Or the payments on the furniture that filled it, or the new car we couldn't afford. And kids?

We can't afford children, Joanna told me over and over again. Not even with her working. All my fault, of course, because I refused to join the mob that I'd joined the cops to avoid.

I loved her, which was the saddest, not to mention the most pathetic, part. But I loved my job as well. Of all the roles played by cops, from detective to patrol officer to arson investigator, undercover is by far the most dangerous. The bad guys aren't supposed to kill cops. Killing cops brings unbearable heat down on everyone's heads. Undercovers are the exception, and working with Uncle Sean left me all the more vulnerable. He could seal my fate with a phone call. None of this eluded me, but call me a danger junkie if you want, I loved the work. I buddied up to some of the most vicious criminals in my city, only to provide the evidence that sent them away. I never testified publicly, for obvious reasons. Instead, I provided the where, when, and how, along with an assessment of the weakest members of the various gangs, the ones who could be turned.

◆

I was still at it when I left for Baxter, and still at it when I entered the Spinning Wheel. A small flat screen at one end of the bar had been left intact, along with the liquor. I watched the ball game playing on the TV jump to a breaking news segment as Zacariah opened a bottle of bourbon. A woman's body had been discovered in an abandoned Oakland Gardens house. The identity of the individual was being withheld pending notification of her kin, but unnamed police sources claimed that a significant amount of forensic evidence tied her to the murder of Sergeant Rowan Krauss.

I ignored the report. Not Zacariah, who whistled before declaring, "Holy shit, man."

"Problem?"

"Uh-uh, but it's good news in a way. The heat's been like a bitch. They're rousting guys all over town. Maybe they'll let up soon."

"Yeah, great, now back to business. George put you in charge and I'm gonna let you do your thing day-to-day. But I'm also holdin' you responsible for every penny." I leaned forward. "Here's a promise you can bank. If money starts walkin' out of this casino, you won't."

To his credit, Zacariah didn't flinch. He'd been around this particular block too many times. "Yeah, I get it. You can tell George that I'll give him a square count, and I'll make sure the help does, too."

◆

I didn't belabor the point, but I didn't take Zacariah's word, either. Time would tell and there was other work to do. At my insistence, we began a cost estimate on bringing the casino back to life. I'd been promised a percentage of the profit and I wanted to make sure there were profits to be divided. In any event, Zacariah cooperated fully and a suitably impressed Pratt, when he arrived, rewarded me with a curt "Good work, Carney."

By that time, the clean out crew had arrived and were busy loading the debris onto a truck. I told Zacariah that I wanted the casino broom-swept and he didn't argue. Then we were off, me and Pratt, to a farmhouse just past the city line where Pratt again introduced me as his voice. The homeowner, Truman Lane, dealt meth. He serviced numerous retailers inside Baxter, but seldom entered the city himself. Keepin' it private.

CHAPTER EIGHTEEN

CARNEY

Dismissed finally, I went back to my camper to find Vangi waiting for me. I didn't ask how she found my humble abode and she didn't volunteer. Instead, she made good on her promise. More than good, actually. Skillful and utterly uninhibited, at one point she had me flopping on the sheets like a fish at the end of a hook. And being the fair-minded type that I am, I was obliged to return the favor. The camper's sofa bed is barely wide enough for me alone, but we were both asleep, sweaty bodies entangled in sweaty sheets, thirty minutes after we called it quits. Now, it's seven o'clock on Monday morning and I've got to respond to a text from Stu Harrington, my handler.

Vangi's asleep. She doesn't move when I retrieve my cell phone and take it, along with a mug of coffee, out of the trailer. Still fairly low in the east, the sun's light skims over the green rows of soybeans to flood the street before me as I drop to the single step that passes for a porch. The work parade has already begun and workers, mostly male, pass in a long stream. Most wave or call out a good morning as they walk by. Decent people, they nevertheless provide the economic base for entrepreneurs like George Pratt.

I smile as I return their greetings, but my thoughts are of Vangi and her proposal, still without specifics. I'm all but convinced that I'm being set up. A sucker with privileges. The why escapes me, but at this moment I'm not concerned with why. Vangi didn't pick me out of the air. She's a smart girl, and not a prostitute as I first suspected. Last night, she described herself as a "kept woman." The man I saw with her at the bar pays the rent on an Oakland Gardens house reasonably far from the neighborhood's chaos. He pays her utilities, car payments, and medical insurance premiums as well. That leaves her to pay for the online courses she takes at Ohio State.

"Prelaw," she told me. "I'll finish up in about a year."

And how will she pay for law school? Vangi's a paralegal with a full-time job at a prominent local firm. The senior partner, a kindly sort according to Vangi, is also her sugar daddy. She sees him twice a week at her home, and occasionally after hours in the office. That leaves her able to bank most of her paycheck, and to live her life as she chooses.

"I don't mind, really. I like sex."

Me, too, which is part of the reason why I haven't turned her down yet. The other part's that she's yet to provide details and I've always been intensely curious.

◆

I punch Stu's number into the burner. I'm feeling good, buoyed by the unfolding spring and the sun's warmth. The workers who pass seem universally upbeat. They walk in groups, now and again breaking into laughter at some offhand remark.

"Carney?"

"Yup, it's me."

"I don't have a lot of time, so listen up. The victim we found yesterday is named Deborah Cole. There's forensic evidence at the scene that ties her to the Krauss homicide, lots of it. She's a throwaway, kicked out of the house by her stepmother. But listen to this. At her stepmother's house, we recovered a porn tape made when she was fifteen or sixteen. The middle-aged man in the tape wore a mask that covered his features. No scars, either, and no tattoos. What he had was a wart, or maybe a skin tag, behind his left ear."

"Lemme guess, you want me to find a pimp-pornographer with a wart."

Harrington's reply is terse and delivered in his best command-officer tone. "We want this asshole, Carney, want him bad. That's because we don't think Deborah killed Rowan. You keep your eyes open. Got it?"

"Yessir."

My boss hangs up without another word, and I understand his position. He and Delia, and Commissioner Taney, too, are fighting for their professional lives. Not me, though. I'm still looking around, finding my feet, getting the lay of the land or any other cliché you can name. And speaking of the lay of the land, I hear Vangi moving around and get back inside before she's finished dressing. But there's no modesty here as she slips into her panties—a fresh pair taken from her purse—and fastens her bra.

Pleasure done, time for business.

◆

Thirty minutes later we're seated in a booth at the Cowboy Diner and Coffee Shop in a mall off Baxter Boulevard. I'm half expecting Vangi to settle for the yogurt and fresh fruit in season, but she orders a cheese omelet with home fries.

"The home fries are the best in the city," she explains. "Heavy on the garlic and onion bits. With smoked paprika."

I don't argue the point, settling for scrambled eggs and a toasted bagel. I have the feeling that I'm supposed to talk about the caper, but I don't. A few minutes after we're served, as she sips at her coffee, Vangi fills the void.

"So, what, Carney? You're gonna play the fucking sphinx?"

"You want, I'll recite the Gettysburg Address. I learned it by heart in the seventh grade at St. Brigid of Kildare Elementary School."

Vangi lays her fork on the plate. "Here's how George explained it to me one night. Take Mexico and Russia. Gangs and the government are joined at the hip in both. You get it?"

"Sure."

"But there's a big difference. In Mexico, the cartels run the government. In Russia, the government runs the mob. Seriously, Putin lets the mobs function as long as they play ball and kick back and maybe knock off the occasional dissident." She stares at me for a second. "All right, I'm not sayin' what George told me is true, but he named a name and I looked it up. Semion Mogilevich is the shit in Russia. He runs crews all over Europe, and he and Putin go back to the 1990s. And that's not what George told me. It's what I looked up on my own."

"Fascinating, Vangi, but what does this have to do with me?"

"That what I'm gettin' to. It seems people high up in the city, in the cops and on the council, wanna turn Baxter into a mini-Russia. Sounds stupid, maybe, but these assholes, they're serious, and they have the support of some the city's big players. According to George, they're okay with human vices. Whores, drugs, gambling, maybe some hijackings, are all inevitable. You can't stop the crime, so you regulate it."

"And get rich in the process?"

"Right on, Carney." Vangi picks up her fork and begins to eat. I watch for a minute or so, until she once again fills the silence. "Did you know that George used to be married?"

"No."

"His wife, her name was Ashton, died of a stroke three years ago. She was twenty-six, believe it or not. He tell you?" She waits for me to shake my head. "Okay, does the name Colton Steele mean anything to you? Because it really should. Colton's a cop, and also Ashton's father. He was a sergeant when Ashton died, but he's a lieutenant now."

Lieutenant Colton Steele is Captain Saul Rawling's aide. His office and Rawling's are side by side. The position explains why Pratt's so confident, assuming it's true. The bullshit philosophy about crime being eternal and regulating crime being good for the community fits nicely with Bute Stafford's campaign ad. The real question is why I need to give a damn.

"The money's already rolling in. George pays off, and so do most of the other players. The ones who don't will be eliminated, one way or the other."

"And you know this how?"

"George Pratt, who never stops running his mouth."

◆

I don't argue the point because I can't. Baxter's cadre of dirty cops may have adopted a veneer of social philosophy to back their play, but money is honey and they plan to stay sweet.

"I'm still waitin', Vangi. You came to me with a proposition. It's time to get specific or get lost. I have things to do."

"Okay, Pratt's daddy-in-law owns a house, maybe eight blocks on the other side of the hospital. The money's there, George and his father-in-law's. It's hidden in the basement."

"Where?"

"I don't know exactly. George didn't tell me and I was afraid to ask. Only George definitely said 'hidden.' I mean, if it was in a safe, you wouldn't say it was hidden."

"Nice to know, if it's true. And you have to think about that because Pratt's not too reliable. But even if it's true, how do you plan to snatch it?"

"That's where you come in. But I do know this. The family goes to church every Sunday, and out to brunch afterward. They're gone for hours."

I signal for the check, then pay it. Vangi's not finished eating, but I obviously don't care. When I finally speak out, it isn't a question.

"Let's go for a ride."

"Okay, where to?"

"We're gonna make a pass at the father-in-law's house."

But we're not. Instead, I head north on Baxter Boulevard and keep on going after we pass the city line, into Revere County to a small wooded patch ten minutes away. A narrow road leads to a small parking lot and a picnic area with six tables and benches.

I pull to a stop, shift into park, then snatch Vangi's handbag. Vangi's a true amateur. A pro would never carry a gun in a soft-sided purse. I spotted the piece as we left my trailer.

"Hey." She manages an offended tone, but her green eyes betray her fear. What am I gonna do? Why did I bring her to this deserted place? We're surrounded by trees, hidden from the road, which is barely used in any event. "C'mon, Carney, the gun's legal."

I don't know what she's thinking, but I put the issue to rest by wrapping the fingers of my right hand around her throat and squeezing down. She instinctively reaches for my hand.

"You don't wanna scratch me, Vangi, because if you do, I'm gonna have to cut off your fingers." I watch her hesitate briefly, then drop her hands into her lap. She's feeling faint by now, her eyes fluttering. When I let go, she collapses against the window on her side of the car.

I wait for her to recover before I put the bottom line out there. "I'm gonna ask you some questions and you're gonna answer truthfully. You don't, I'll kill you." This isn't true, but Vangi can't be sure, one way or the other. I'm this gangster from Philadelphia. Who knows what I've done, or will do? Certainly not little Vangi. Still, she puts up a front.

"You've got me all wrong, Carney . . ."

"Who told you to set me up?"

"Nobody, I . . ."

I curl my fingers around her throat, this time gently. Call it a reminding factor. "Creep the home of a Baxter cop, a fucking lieutenant, in the hope of finding some buried treasure? There's nothing to discuss, Vangi. Who told you to set me up, and if you think you can lie to me, hear this. I'll find out you lied, then I'll find you. All your fucking dreams, paralegal, college graduate, lawyer, gone forever."

"Just like that?"

"Yeah, just like that."

She stares at me for a moment, then says, "A cop named Overby. Sergeant Overby."

"What's he got on you?"

"Enough to do what you're threatening to do. Just like that."

I'm supposed to meet Pratt in a half hour, so I don't ask the why question. I have a feeling I'll find out soon enough. "When do you report to Overby?"

"This afternoon, and what I'm gonna do is tell him the truth. I asked. You turned me down."

"That's great, Vangi, exactly what I'd do. But I'm still curious. Was George really married to Steele's daughter?" I wait until she shakes her head. "But the house you asked me to rob does belong to Steele?" This time I receive a nod. "Okay, just one more question. If I'd taken the bait and shown up at Lieutenant Steele's house, what do you think would've happened to me?"

She doesn't answer the question, but I didn't expect her to answer. I've been tested and have to figure I passed. I've also got to meet Pratt and have an errand to run first. I have to get back to the trailer and retrieve a GPS unit hidden in the space where I keep the burner. Sooner, rather than later, I intend to attach the unit to George Pratt's Avalon.

CHAPTER NINETEEN

DELIA

We're nine days from the discovery of Deborah Cole's body and the bad news has reached critical mass. The shoe impressions found at the Rowan Krauss murder scene have been matched to the shoes found on Deborah Cole's body. The tire impressions recovered at the scene have been matched to the tires on a Honda parked outside the house where Cole's body was found. While bloodstains found on the clothes she wore have not yet been DNA tested, a simpler test for blood type provided a match with Krauss's blood.

On the other hand, a DNA test on the tissue recovered by Arshan from beneath her fingernails was given priority at the state lab. It produced a result strong enough to bear comparison with the DNA of the male it originally belonged to, assuming we ever find him. We did, of course, run the DNA profile through the relevant databases, but didn't get a hit, a sad fact I learned only an hour ago. That eliminates every member of the Baxter PD.

I find Detective Clyde Norman, resident computer geek, at one of the department's few computers. He's young at twenty-four, and the object of reasonably well-intentioned ribbing, which he accepts with good grace. The ribbing ends when our detectives need Clyde to uncover a hidden bank account or the trail of a fugitive. *Supplicant* is the word that comes to mind.

"Hey, Clyde, you busy?" I ask, ignoring a stack of paperwork next to the computer.

"Not too bad. What's up, captain?"

"DNA, Clyde. I know there's a search for relatives you can do if you don't get an exact match from CODIS."

"Forensic genealogy."

"Yeah, what you said. I know the theory, but not the details. Run it by me."

"It's not that complicated. Customers use services like ForebearsDNA to establish a family tree, for example, or to establish their own origins."

"How about to find lost relatives?"

"Yeah, that, too, but the service isn't open to investigators unless they have a warrant. That said, the searches are very accurate out to third cousins, but they're only useful if you have a relative who used the service in the past." He hesitates for a moment, then adds, "Ya know, you could find a true match. The DNA databanks available to law enforcement only include individuals who've been arrested or in the military or in a law enforcement agency. A citizen who's never been arrested wouldn't be found in the CODIS system, but might be found in a private database."

◆

This morning, Mayor Venn will stand alongside Commissioner Vern Taney at a press conference. Vern will acknowledge the likelihood, although the investigation continues, that Deborah Cole murdered Sergeant Rowan Krauss. Then our beloved mayor will add a few law-and-order remarks designed to bolster his campaign before calling it quits. He really has no choice. Given the evidence, District Attorney Atkinson has made his own position clear. He wouldn't hesitate to charge and try Deborah Cole, if only she wasn't dead.

"Delia," Vern told me when I raised my objections, "if the autopsy provided any physical proof that Deborah Cole's death was a homicide, it'd be different. But it didn't and we can't hold off any longer."

Virtually every incriminating detail found at the crime scene has already been leaked to the press. And despite faint evidence of compression above the carotid arteries, our coroner has determined the manner and the cause of death to be undetermined. I'm only glad he didn't attribute Debbie's passing to natural causes.

◆

I still believe that Deborah Cole is the fall woman in this case, but I'm far from upset on this particular morning. Zoe's finally coming home. Her grandmother passed six days ago and the funeral was held two days later, followed by a memorial dinner yesterday. I would have attended the funeral, wanting nothing more than to stand by my partner's side, but we both knew that my sudden appearance would be a distraction at a time when the family needed to grieve.

So, we're pretending it's a normal, school-day morning at the Mariola house. Gretchen's here, having driven from home to cook a mushroom omelet. I'm dreading the soon-to-be day when she renounces meat altogether, but the omelets are really good. Perhaps because we're excited, all three of us. Gretchen even fails to chide my son when he pours ketchup onto his eggs. As for me, my plate's empty and I'm working on my second cup of coffee. I'll be heading off to work soon.

"I was really worried," Danny tells us. He's been talking to Zoe almost as often as I have. "When I spoke to her, she sounded so guilty. I mean she was really beating herself up about not visiting her grandmother more often."

Or at all over the last few years. Zoe wanted to make the trip. She told herself that the years were slipping away, that she couldn't get the time back, the clock only runs in one direction. Yet somehow it never happened. And I played my part. I never told her to stay in Baxter, to be with me, but I didn't encourage her either. Despite beating myself up over how rarely I visited my own folks.

Gretchen slices the edge of her fork into her omelet. "We need to cook something special for dinner," she announces. "What about fish in that sauce Zoe likes?"

"Lemon-cream sauce." I provide the answer, already planning a trip to the supermarket. I've got work to do this morning, but I'm taking the afternoon off. "With jasmine rice and a salad."

"What about dessert?" Danny homes in on his favorite part of any meal. "Maybe a welcome home cake. An ice cream cake from that bakery."

"Cunning Confections," Gretchen offers. "They make their own ice cream now."

◆

I'm in the car, driving toward Revere County and Stu Harrington's home a few minutes before eight. Tom Carney's expected to deliver a progress report and I want to hear it from his mouth. I've got the recipe for lemon-cream chicken with me, and I'll stop at a supermarket this afternoon to pick up the ingredients. That's all she wrote, though. I can whip together a mean lemon Jell-O, but lemon-cream sauces are on the far side of a line I'll never cross. So, it's TGFG, Thank God for Gretchen. The girl's become more than family. She's become indispensable. If she and Danny should part ways, the Mariola family will default to rubbery meatloaf smothered with canned gravy.

Personally, I think Carney's an asshole. I don't entirely trust him, either, but I can't deny that he produces results. He's become known to several street cops, who address him by name when they happen to cross his path. He's also drawn the attention, positive according to Carney, of Sergeant Thrace Overby. Overby's the probable link, maybe the only one, between the patrol force on the ground and Lieutenant Colton Steele, principal aide to Captain Saul Rawling. If we can turn Overby, the dominoes will fall, or the house of cards will collapse, or any other cliché that comes to mind.

We're getting our first taste of summer in Baxter, but the temperature out in the country seems ten degrees cooler. If so, Brenda's chickens haven't gotten the message. They're clustered in the shade of an old beech, perhaps because that's where Brenda scattered their feed.

I'm still in the car when Tom Carney pulls up behind me. He's wearing that small smile, the one that announces a private joke. I have a feeling it won't stay private for long. I'm sure it'll be important, too. With Carney, you always have the feeling he's a step ahead of you.

"Mornin', captain."

"Morning to you, Carney."

We walk together through the yard and onto the porch where Stu Harrington awaits in a lawn chair. We take seats in lawn chairs of our own while Stu opens a cooler to remove a jug of iced tea.

"Sweetened," he announces, "if that's a problem."

It isn't and Stu pours our drinks into plastic glasses. We sip for a moment, until I nod to Carney.

"That guy with the wart behind his ear?" he announces, "I've got him."

I can't help it. For the moment, I'm speechless. Identifying the man in the video with Deborah Cole is a major development. Even if he had nothing to do with her death, he can point the way to her connections.

"You wanna be a little more specific?" Stu asks.

"Yeah, I do. Start with last night about eight o'clock. I'd been chauffeuring Pratt from place to place most of the afternoon when he decided it was time for a little recreation. He had me drive him to the lower end of Main Street."

"The stroll?"

"Yeah, whore heaven. But Pratt doesn't go for streetwalkers. There's a brothel down there, and he sees one of the girls inside. Or maybe two or three. Pratt doesn't tell and I don't ask. I waited until he got inside, then stepped out of the car. The afternoon was hot and I was stiff from the driving."

Carney gets up and walks to a metal table with a tray on top. A dish on the tray contains slices of coffee cake, probably homemade, along with a pile of napkins. Carney grabs a napkin, but takes his time with the cake.

"I was just sitting there, resting my butt on the fender, when a pimp and a woman, probably one of his, got into an argument. He was shouting, 'Where's the fuckin' money,' but she's not answering. I didn't think too much about it until he punched her in the face and she went down. When he started after her, with his back to me, I noticed the wart—and that's what it is—in the same place behind his ear as in the video. Now, his punching her didn't bother me at first. I'm supposed to be this hard-ass gangster, right? But when I saw the wart, I decided to play the white knight."

"But you weren't going to do anything before that?" This time it's me asking the question.

"Nope, nothing. In fact, if I hadn't been waiting for Pratt, I might have driven away without noticing the wart. Minding your own business is what the street's all about. But in this case, I straightened up and shouted, 'Don't touch her again.' Being a badass pimp, he responded in the only way that he could. He turned toward me and threw a clumsy punch that I slipped. He threw another punch, but this time he stumbled and I hit him in the gut. His gut turned out to be soft, really soft, and he went down. I followed him to the sidewalk and slammed his head into the concrete a couple of times. Then I stood over him and shouted, 'Keep your shit off the street. Hear me? Take it inside.'"

◆

We're briefly interrupted by a pair of Stu's kids, a boy and a girl, who come flying out of the house, cross the porch, and gallop into the yard, scattering the chickens. Brenda follows, announcing, "We're gathering eggs," as she hurries by. For Stu, this is old stuff and he barely reacts, but Carney flashes a bemused smile before he speaks again.

"Two cops, Cowle and Wentworth, showed up a few minutes later, and here's what's interesting. One was new breed and the other old. Cowle appeared to be in his twenties. His uniform looked as if he'd pressed it on the way to the call. The other cop, Wentworth, was old enough to have already retired. But neither reacted when I held up my Free Our Police card. They looked, all right, but then walked over to the pimp and examined his injuries. Maybe three minutes later, Overby arrived. He came up to me and asked what happened. I explained, including the demand to take it inside. Pratt came out as we spoke and that was the end of it. I got back in Pratt's Avalon and we drove away. No harm, no foul."

More bullshit, and I've had enough. "The pimp's name, Carney."

"I didn't get his name. No way I could have asked. No reason I had a need to know. But I'm pretty sure you'll find him at Baxter Medical. When I stood up, I think I accidentally broke his ankle."

◆

Pissed off again, this time at Carney withholding the punch line, I hold my temper while I place a call to the head admissions officer at Baxter Medical. Yes, Beatrice Mueller tells me, a man with a severely fractured ankle was brought into the hospital at 8:37 last night. His name is Brimley Houseman and he's currently in surgery. That's as far as she's willing to go, given the medical privacy issues.

"I expect he'll be with us for the next couple of days, if that's any help."

It most definitely is, and I quickly calm as Carney finishes his report, which includes several names formerly unknown to us. I'm letting Stu take notes, while I plan our next move. First thing, I admit to myself that a growth on a man's neck will never amount to enough evidence to support a conviction, or even an arrest. Unless the man's terminally stupid, it won't be enough to turn Brimley Houseman, either. I need more and I'm still considering the possibilities as I drive back to the house.

Carney responded quickly when I asked him to describe the victim. "Brimley punched the woman square in the eye, full fist. Her eye will be black by now, has to be. I'd look for an abrasion, too. Brimley wore a ring. The woman's a Latina, I think, with curly hair, blue at the ends, like a fringe on an umbrella. She's five seven or eight, heavily tattooed from wrist to elbow on both arms. Flowers and vines, captain, all bright colors. Her eyes are honey-colored, very unusual, and set close together."

"That it?"

"Red fingernails with gold tips."

CHAPTER TWENTY
DELIA

I catch the attention of my part-time assistant, Marcia Blackstone, as I pass through the squad room. "Find Chuck Breyer. He might be in the house, or at home, or in the field. But wherever he is, I want to see him ASAP."

Detective Breyer's our vice division, the alpha and the omega. And that's only when he's not working on something else.

By the time Breyer shows up at my office forty minutes later, I've uploaded a copy of Deborah Cole's porn video to a tablet and printed a face-and-shoulders photo of the girl, along with Brimley Houseman's mug shot. Breyer's a strapping lad, very handsome, with brown eyes and a thick head of hair that runs in all directions without looking rumpled. His features are uniform, nose straight, chin firm without being aggressive, mouth full and sensual. At the station, Breyer's all business. In the field, he's smooth and flirty, or so I've heard. Flies with honey is how he puts it. Personally, I don't have all that much experience with vice, but Breyer's the man you tap when you need information from hookers.

"Captain, you're looking for me?"

"I am." I point to a chair in front of my desk, wait until he's seated, then pass him Houseman's mug shot. "You know this guy?"

Breyer glances at the photo and says, "Sure, that's Brim Houseman. I arrested him . . . about a year ago? For assault."

"You get a conviction?"

"Nope, victim refused to testify and there were no witnesses."

He doesn't offer further explanation and I don't ask. Pimps and violence against women are too closely associated. I hate it and fight it, but I'm no longer shocked.

"Tell me about Brim Houseman."

"Little to tell, captain. There's maybe fifteen street pimps workin' the Boomtown Stroll. He's one of them. No better, no worse than the rest." Breyer's wearing jeans, a dark blue shirt, and a black jacket that's part of a suit he likely wears to weddings and funerals. The Glock he carries is clearly visible in a cross draw holster on the left side of his belt. "One thing, captain. I believe Houseman's out on bail."

"For assaulting a prostitute?"

"For assaulting a john who took his money back. Don't remember the reason why, but we've got the same problem here. I didn't make the arrest, but the john, from what I hear, doesn't wanna testify. Can't blame him really."

"Same old same old." I take a moment to read the description Carney gave of the victim. "Okay, the victim. A Latina, probably, with a blue fringe at the edges of her hair. Tattoos extending up both . . ."

"Got it, captain. Her street name's High Octane. Feisty is how I'd describe her. She used to be one of Brimley's women, but went independent a few months ago. Lives on her own and doesn't pay for protection, which is what probably got her punched. And she's not Latina. Olga Kupchak's her real name and she's American. No trace of an accent."

"How do you know this?"

"She came to me, asked for protection."

"And what did you say?"

"Something to the effect of stop hooking and you won't need protection."

◆

I let that one go. Chuck Breyer's attitude isn't at issue here. I want to find Olga, ask a few questions, and hope that she's sufficiently pissed off to answer them. I lead Breyer into the yard where we pick up an unmarked Hyundai, a near-new Sonata recently seized in a drug raid. I'm surprised to find it in the lot. Mostly, it's snapped up by the first detective out the door.

"So, you wanna tell me what's going on?"

I demonstrate the flaws in my upbringing by answering a question with another question. "How do you know Olga Kupchak?"

"Olga's been on the street for about a year, part of the revolving door. I don't know how many times she's been dragged downtown. More than a few."

Breyer's referring to the sweeps that occur nearly every month. Prostitutes are rounded up en masse and jammed into a holding cell. The most persistent offenders will be charged with the bogus crime of loitering with intent. They're fined, or sent to jail for a week. The rest are let go in the morning, their only punishment a night without work. That's because there's no place to put them.

"But I wouldn't expect to find her on the street," Breyer continues. "It's the wrong time of day for the Boomtown Stroll. The rush after the night shift leaves off is short-lived. By now, lower Main Street's probably deserted. The girls will be elsewhere, catchin' up on their sleep or their drug habits. Or both, come to think of it."

I don't like him using *girls* instead of women, or even workers, but there's nothing to be gained by debating the point. "If finding Olga's hopeless, you might've told me that before we left the house."

Breyer flashes me a smile made all the more engaging by a chipped incisor. "Not impossible, but we need to follow the honeybees back to the hive. That would be the Gardens."

"Oakland Gardens?"

"Yeah, but the name's been shortened by the simple folk who live there. Now it's just the Gardens. Like the Yards back in the day." He smiles. "Every city needs a Yards, or a Gardens. Gotta have a place to put 'em, captain. The unwashed and the unwanted, the crazy and the criminal."

◆

Breyer guides the Sonata along Harmony Road, a north–south Oakland Gardens street, to an unmarked corner. He hooks a U-turn and parks in the shade cast by a huge tree. "This is it," he tells me, "the great Oakland Gardens oak." Breyer takes out his phone and punches in a number. He listens for a moment before saying, "Yeah, usual spot." Another pause, then, "Shouldn't take more than a minute."

I'm watching Breyer closely. His attitude is businesslike, his manner abrupt. He jams the phone into his pocket and says, "The hooker's street name is Verona, for what reason I don't know. But she's local, like me. The two of us grew up together, matter of fact, and she won't bullshit me. If finding Olga's all you want, I can handle that. You wanna ask Verona anything else, I'll put her in the back seat."

"I'll settle for finding Olga, but tell me, why didn't we drive to where Verona's living?"

Breyer looks at me for a moment. "Verona lives in a house a few blocks from here with four other women and a pimp named Julius, aka Julius Caesar. The man has an attitude when it comes to cops. I knock on his door, there's no tellin' where it goes from there. Now, you don't mind, I'm gonna wait outside, have a smoke."

Verona shows up five minutes later. She older than I would have expected, her blond hair rolled into pink plastic curlers. She's not wearing makeup, but a pair of huge sunglasses with rhinestone-speckled frames shields her eyes. She glances at me, then turns her attention to Breyer. I can't hear the conversation, but I note a relieved expression on Verona's face. Whatever's coming down, it's not about her.

The exchange lasts all of a minute before Verona heads back the way she came and Breyer slides into the car. He puts the transmission in gear and pulls away.

"Olga lives a few blocks further south."

"By herself?"

"Can't be sure, but Olga works without a pimp, so it's possible. Possible, too, that she hangs with a biker gang. We'll know when we knock on her door."

We continue on Harmony Road, heading south, until we reach a cross street with a street sign hanging from a lamppost: Sanders Way. Breyer turns right, then immediately pulls to the curb.

"She lives in there." Breyer points to a small house, a bungalow that can't be more than a few rooms and a single bath. The clapboard exterior is suitably weathered, but the roof's in good shape, the shingles still glossy.

With nothing more to be said, we step out of the car and approach the door. It opens before we reach the bell and a woman steps out and closes the door behind her. She's tall and slim with dark hair cut relatively short, a full mouth and large, probably augmented, breasts. Her left eye, purplish-black, is swollen almost closed. Bunched gauze pads conceal what must be a cut on her cheek. She barely glances at me before fixing Breyer with a stare that can best be described as malignant.

"What the fuck you want, cop? I thought I made myself clear last night when I refused to sign a complaint. No way am I gonna testify."

Breyer only smiles. "See, if it was just the two of us, about now I'd get physical, maybe smack your other eye. I have a fondness for symmetry and I'm findin' the lopsided look offensive. But my company this morning . . ." He nods toward me. "She's my boss, Captain Mariola, so I gotta be nice."

I tap Breyer's shoulder and he's smart enough to step out of the way. Olga looks at me, her loathing apparent. I need to reach her somehow, but I have no leverage. When in doubt, as Danny's explained on many occasions, throw the fastball. I'm carrying a shoulder bag that's a cross between a purse and a briefcase. I reach inside to retrieve a photo of Deborah Cole taken at the morgue. Even without an injury to her face, the photo's gruesome.

"You recognize this girl? I'm saying girl instead of woman because that's all she was, a girl."

Olga draws a breath sharp enough for me to conclude that she does, indeed, recognize Deborah Cole. Bad news for her because I don't plan to let her go until she answers my questions.

"Why don't we talk in the car?" As I open the door for Olga, I glance at Breyer and say, "Wait there, detective." My tone is abrupt, but Breyer winks, acknowledging the ploy as I close the door behind Olga.

◆

"I ain't testifyin' and I ain't makin' a complaint," Olga announces, her Southern accent growing stronger. "I'm not a fuckin' rat."

"That would be fine if Brim Houseman wasn't a real asshole. Ask yourself how far he'll go next time. And we both know there will be a next time. That's just who he is. But I'm not here about what happened between you and Brim. I've got bigger things to think about."

This time I put Deborah Cole's photo in Olga's hand. "'The mouse'," she whispers. "That's what we called her."

"Why?"

"The girl was fucked over by everybody in her life. Mother didn't want her, father didn't want her, stepmother tossed her away. By the time she ran into Brimley, she was ripe for the pickin'."

"And he was happy to take advantage?"

"Yeah, and it wasn't no challenge. The girl was slow."

"Slow?"

Olga nods. "Retarded, or real close to retarded. No way she could function on the street. Houseman smelled it on her, like a cat at a mousehole. The bastard played with Debbie. She was his toy." Olga looks at me for a moment, but I have nothing to say. "I left Brim about that time. Had enough with the bullshit."

"And he didn't like it?"

Olga touches her eye, the gesture seeming unconscious. "You could say so." She's about to add something when a BPD patrol vehicle rushes past. The unit's running silent with its lights flashing. Bad for me is what I'm thinking, a reminder of why she hates cops, but Olga surprises me. "Some dealer's gonna be eatin' at a soup kitchen tonight."

I'm tempted to pursue the topic, but I really can't. Maybe later, but not now. I remove the tablet from my briefcase, call up the Deborah Cole tape and set it going. It doesn't run more than five seconds before Olga looks away.

"I seen it before." She picks at her flaming-red fingernails for a moment before adding. "Hell, I was there."

Music to my ears. "The girl, that's Deborah Cole. And the man?"

"Who do you think"

"C'mon, Olga. Name a name."

"Listen, I'm gonna go. I said enough already to get my ass beat."

She touches her eye again, but sympathy isn't on the menu this morning. "No, you're not. You're not going anywhere until you answer every question I ask."

A cold stare follows, but I don't budge. Finally, she says, "I heard you were a hard-ass dyke. Guess the stories were true." She stares at me for another minute, expecting me to react to the epithet. I don't. "All right, here's how it goes. The man in the video, if you can stretch the language by calling him a man, is Brim Houseman. I know he posted the video to some online porn site. For money, okay? With Brim, it's always about the money. Thinkin' back, I don't remember Debbie resisting, but I wasn't there every minute, either. Brim had the girl turnin' tricks, only he never put her on the street. He was sellin' her as underage to certain individuals he didn't name. Like for hundreds of dollars per go, which he bragged about."

When she stops abruptly, I start the engine and flip on the air-conditioning. The sun's pouring through the raised windows and the windshield, and I'm beginning to sweat. Olga's mouth curls up on one side, whether in contempt or in appreciation, I can't tell.

"This here is it, lady cop. Past this, you're gonna have to beat me harder than Brim. Brim has copies of the tape on the computer in his house. Stupid, true, but who said pimps have to be smart?"

"One more question. I know you've heard the rumors about Deborah killing Rowan Krauss. Do you believe them?"

"Get serious. Debbie was a mouse, a point I already made. Outside of a cockroach or two, killin' was not one of her life skills." Olga stops for a moment, her expression growing serious. "Maybe not, though. Thinkin' on it, I'd have to say that Debbie was the ultimate submissive. She did what she was told."

That's enough for me and I dismiss Olga Kupchak, waiting until she's out of sight before retrieving my phone. Breyer stares at me as I shut down the Record function.

"So much for confidentiality," he says.

"Yeah, so much."

CHAPTER TWENTY-ONE

DELIA

As we pull away, Breyer tells me that he's quitting the force. He'll be leaving at the end of the month to work for Blanche Weber at Weber Security. He tells me that he's sick of the merry-go-round. As in round 'em up, let 'em go, round 'em up again.

"It's the pimps and the johns who need to be arrested, but the pimps are payin' off and every time we set up a sting, the Boomtown Stroll ain't boomin'. Like it's deserted. Me, I've had enough."

"Your business, detective. Strictly. But for right now, do you know where Brimley and his stable live?"

"Of course."

Five minutes later, we're double-parked in front of a dilapidated house on Poole Road. The letters that once marked its address are gone, but they were in place long enough to leave a discernible shadow on the vinyl siding.

I instruct Breyer to start driving without giving him a destination. He doesn't ask questions, knowing I want to get away from Brimley's home before we're spotted. A moment later, I'm on the phone with Stu Harrington. He's managing the show while I'm in the field.

"Stu, I need you to work up an affidavit for a search warrant. Address: 455 Poole Road. Resident: Brimley Houseman. We'll be looking for copies of Deborah Cole's porn tape, digital or in any other form. Probable cause is based on the film, of course, but also on a confidential informant to be named later."

Stu laughs. "But she or he does exist, I hope."

"She does, and Stu, I wouldn't put this on you, but we need to move before Saul Rawling and the troops stumble onto what we're doing. Right now, I'm heading for Baxter Medical and Mr. Houseman, who should be out of surgery. Let's see what he has to say for himself."

◆

Unfortunately, fast isn't in the cards this morning. Brimley Houseman's out of surgery, but still waiting for the anesthesia to wear off. Time for lunch, which we find in a newly opened restaurant, 4BaseBurger. No more than a month old, the place has already acquired a reputation for its artery cloggers, double- and triple-stack sirloin burgers topped with anything from a fried egg to potato chips to kimchi slaw. I'm trying to decide whether I can justify the Texas double-burger with the barbeque sauce if I reject the loaded fries when my phone goes off. It's Zoe.

I stand up and carry the phone away from the table. What Zoe and I have to say isn't Stu's business.

"Hey, babe, where are you?"

"On the road, maybe three hours out, maybe a little less."

"You good?"

"Yeah, better than I should be. I was with Gramma to the end, holding her hand. Maybe that's the best you can do for anyone."

I'm instantly reminded of Keith and Janey Moreland, then of Deborah Cole. Nobody to hold Debbie's hand.

"Danny's got a game today," Zoe says. "I should get there right about the time it starts."

I'd asked Danny to back off, to start another game later in the week, but he shook his head. "Births and funerals only," he told me. "Otherwise, you play." I want to tell Zoe that I'll also be there for the first pitch, but I can't.

"Meet you there, honey. Lots of hugs, and perhaps a clandestine kiss."

"Peck on the cheek?"

"Or words to that effect."

◆

It's almost two o'clock before the docs clear us to interview Brim Houseman. The man's not happy to see me, but then he's got a lot to be unhappy about. He has no beard and no mustache, and his head is shaved. The better to display the bruises inflicted by Carney, and there are more than a few. He's in traction as well. His right leg, encased by a thick cast at the ankle, hangs a foot above the bed.

"What the fuck you want?" Houseman tries for pimp attitude, but the painkiller in his system, probably morphine, betrays him and he slurs his words.

"You assaulted a woman last night. On the street in front of many witnesses."

"You tell me that bitch filed a complaint, I'll call you a liar to your cop face."

"So, you're admitting that you committed the assault?"

"I ain't admittin' shit. You get that . . . whatta ya call a female pig? A pigette?"

Breyer's leaning against the wall, but he steps up to the bed and handcuffs Brim's right wrist to the bed rail. "Funny thing, Brimley, you've got the upper hand just now, what with being in a hospital. But complaint or not, we have enough to arrest you. Which means, a few days from now, you'll be in a cell where I can get to you." A smile now. "If you should continue to disrespect my boss."

Brim yanks at the restraint a couple of times, then gives up, his focus concentrating as I tick off his constitutional rights. When he speaks, his tone is wary. "Wha chu want? And don't tell me the famous Captain Mariola gives a flying fuck about a whore who got what was comin' to her."

"Good point, Brim." I make a little show of it, opening my briefcase, rummaging through papers that aren't there, finally pulling out the morgue photo of Deborah Cole. "Recognize this girl?"

Brim's dark eyes give him away. Whatever he expected, it wasn't this. "Never seen her in my life."

"That's not what I asked. I asked you if you recognized her."

"Recognize? Shit, yeah. Bitch has been all over the news. They're sayin' she snuffed that cop. When I said I never seen her, I meant face-to-face."

I go back into my briefcase and remove the tablet. Again, taking my time, I fiddle with the controls, running the only video on the tablet back and forth for a moment.

"Got it. So, now, Brimley, tell me if you recognize the underage girl in this video."

I hold the tablet in front of him and hit the play arrow. Brim closes his eyes and shakes his head, but I'm not having it. I slap his face, hard enough to open his eyes, but pause the video after a few seconds. "I want to draw attention to something. Look behind the left ear of the man in this video. What do you see?"

"C'mon."

"C'mon what? The little growth behind your own ear? You think it's gonna disappear?" I nod to Breyer who pushes Brimley's head to the side, then takes a photo with his cell phone.

"That's bullshit. You can't . . ."

"Can't what?"

Brim finally regains his composure, though he continues to look very unhappy. Ankle dangling in the air, face bruised, I've got him where I want him. "Okay, here's how it'll play out. I'm going to execute a search warrant on your residence at 455 Poole Road. Now, search warrants are self-limiting for the most part. You have to specify what you're after, and that limits where you can search. If you're searching for an elephant, you can't look in a dresser drawer. But when you're searching for something as small as a thumb drive, you can look just about anywhere. I know I'll find a copy of this tape, and I know I'll find drugs. You think the ladies in your house are gonna stand up for you? Think they'll take the weight?"

I open the briefcase. Time for my exit lines. "The mayor's gonna hold a press conference today, probably already has. He's gonna tell our good citizens that Deborah Cole murdered Sergeant Rowan Krauss." I point to the figures on the tablet. "And here you are, humpin' away."

◆

I ignore Brimley's obscene protests. There's too much to do. First thing, I assign Breyer to guard the prisoner. Brim's entitled to a phone call, but he won't make it until after the search of his residence begins. I don't believe that Brimley ordered the death of Rowan Krauss, but his stable was a major stop on the express train Debbie rode to her death. More than likely, Brim can point me to the next station.

Back at the shop, I barely acknowledge the greetings as I cross the squad room to my office. Our coroner refused to call Debbie's death a homicide. I can't blame him. He's a cardiologist, not a pathologist. Murder's too big a limb for him to climb out on. But pathologists working for the state cops are available, including Dr. Joseph Lewin. I've met Lewin twice and know that he loves a mystery. I'll persuade Vern to forward Arshan's results to Lewin ASAP, then follow it up with a phone call emphasizing the urgency.

That's for later. It's already two o'clock and Danny's game will start at three thirty. I spend the next thirty minutes reviewing the search warrant affidavit drawn up by Stu Harrington. It's ready to go after a few minor changes. Then it's off to find a judge with a handy pen. Ordinarily, I'd let the primary on the case handle this task. It's a good policy because on those rare occasions when I show myself in a courtroom or a judge's chambers, they know whatever's on my mind is urgent. That's the reaction I get when Stu Harrington and I enter Judge Thomas's courtroom in the middle of a trial. Five minutes later, she announces a short recess and motions me into her chambers. I offer the affidavit, swear to its accuracy, and the judge quickly signs.

"Happy hunting," she offers.

Outside, I stand in bright sunshine as Stu and I discuss the next steps. "We'll serve the warrant at five o'clock tomorrow morning," I tell him. "It's too late for this afternoon. The women will be working on Main Street and I want to corral them in the house."

"You won't be there?"

"No, I will be. Only now I have something to do. Zoe's on her way home." I glance at my watch. "Hell, she's probably home already."

Zoe and I have had dinner with Stu, Brenda, and their kids. I don't need to convince him. He nods once, and says, "Take off. I'll text you as we go along."

◆

I point the Sonata at Goldman High's athletic field and begin to wind my way through traffic. In the distance, I hear a pile driver, or maybe a pair, clanging rhythmically at the worksite. I turn on the Sonata's radio just in time for a report on Mayor Venn's news conference. He did, in fact, name Deborah Cole as the likely killer of Rowan Krauss, but added a bit of good news as well. Our state university's decided to open a campus in Baxter. A junior college to be sure, specializing in teaching skills that complement the needs of the plant when it finally opens. Computer maintenance and repair, obviously, but robot maintenance and repair, too, as well as accounting and computer engineering.

"Baxter," he told his audience, "is moving forward."

My brain is still buzzing with the day's developments when I pull into the Goldman High parking lot and hunt for a space. I'm asking myself if we should serve the warrant immediately. More than likely, we'd find the double-wide nearly deserted, but we'd be certain to seize Brim's computer and any related devices. Waiting carries the risk that Brim will find a way to communicate with one or another of his cohorts on the outside, that the computer will vanish in the middle of the night, or even that a co-conspirator might eliminate the middleman by setting the house on fire. I have to assume that Brim's paying off, which is why he wasn't immediately arrested after the assault on Olga last night. Suppose one of Brimley's women shows up at the hospital, a casual visitor. If she realizes that Brimley's under arrest, she might reach out to one of our bent cops.

A cheer from the stands a hundred yards away drags me into the here and now. I spend so much time wallowing in the dark side of human nature, it can be hard to remember that crime is something most people read about or hear about on television.

I can see the scoreboard as I walk toward the field. It's the top of the second and there's no score. Danny's gotten through the first inning without giving up a run. He's now on the mound. Suddenly, I find myself trotting, almost running toward the stands. Zoe has to be waiting. I couldn't bear it if she's still on the road. I come out thirty feet behind the plate with the stands to my left.

I hear the pitch thud into the catcher's mitt and a muttered "Shit" from the batter. I ignore both as I scan the crowd until I find Zoe. She's sitting next to Vern and Lillian Taney. Vern's holding his baby, Cora, in his arms. Emmaline, Vern and Lillian's daughter, sits on Zoe's lap. Emmaline's getting a little big for long-term lap sitting, but Zoe's got her arms wrapped around the girl. The seat next to Zoe is empty, and obviously meant for me. Fetchin' Gretchen's sitting beside the empty seat, leaning forward with her elbows on her knees, focused on the game.

Zoe turns to look at me as I make my way through the crowd, ignoring a sudden cheer from our side of the stands that has to signal a strikeout. She's smiling a smile that lights up my heart.

As I finally take my seat, I want to put my arms around her, to kiss her for the next two hours. But that's not gonna happen, and not only because we're in a public setting. Before I can open my mouth, Emmaline turns to me and raises a finger to her lips.

"Shhhhh," she demands, "Danny's pitching."

◆

I settle for holding Zoe's hand as we watch Danny toss a one-hitter, the one hit being a dribbler down the third base line that wouldn't roll foul. Just as good, Vern's son, Mike, who played center field, had three hits, including a home run that we all agreed must have traveled four hundred feet, but surely didn't.

Doesn't matter, of course. The afternoon deserves a celebration and Lillian suggests we celebrate at her home. A barbecue is in order. Happy tidings, because I didn't have time to shop for the lemon, the cream, or the fish.

The only place I want to be is alone with Zoe, but she seems willing, almost eager, and off we go. The barbecue is impromptu. Burgers and hot dogs, potato salad and coleslaw, beer for the grown-ups, pink lemonade for the kids. For Zoe, it's a first step, and she seems hesitant until Danny and Mike show up after showering at school. Both carry gym bags filled with stinky uniforms they drop as they approach Zoe. She hugs each, fiercely, pulling them to her. This is family life rolling along, the sun rising and setting. This is why we bear the inevitable losses, and this is the greatest loss for the Deborah Coles of this world. No family, no comfort, loss upon loss upon loss. I'll roll out of bed at two o'clock this morning. At three, I'll lead the task force assigned to serve the warrant on Brim Houseman's trailer. The women in that house will be transported to Baxter PD headquarters where I will spend the rest of my day tearing at their psyches. I'll appeal to their sympathies. I'll threaten to prosecute if we find drugs. For this one day, they'll cease to be human beings. They'll become means to an end.

◆

An hour later, I spot Gretchen off by herself. She's standing on the edge of the lawn, watching the first fireflies of the year display the visual equivalent of a mating call. I walk over and lay a hand on her shoulder.

She speaks without looking at me. "Danny's gonna be off to baseball camp in August."

Yes, to Aspirants Baseball Camp in far off California. Danny was personally recruited by the camp's owner, Gene Famello, who's promised to teach Danny how to throw an effective slider. More than the learning part, at least according to Famello, scouts from colleges and from major league teams will attend.

"I'll miss him" is all I can say.

"Me, too."

Gretchen finally turns to look at me, her green eyes softer than I'm used to. The girl's confidence can be unnerving at times. Not now.

"Well, I was just thinking . . ." She hesitates briefly, then says, "I'm just wondering if it would be all right if I still came around? You know, while he's gone?"

The question earns a quick hug. "Thank God," I tell her. "For a moment there I thought I'd have to eat my own cooking."

CHAPTER TWENTY-TWO

DELIA

Disappointment and frustration mark the careers of all cops, especially detectives. You're supposed to roll with the punches. You're supposed to keep on keepin' on. Maybe next time it'll go your way. Only forbearance isn't on the table when we roll up to Brim Houseman's home at four o'clock in the morning. Ten of us, including a SWAT team in full regalia, pound on the door twice before taking it down, only to discover a fully furnished, entirely unoccupied house. The closets are empty, likewise the bureaus. More to the point, the computer mentioned by Olga Kupchak is nowhere to be found. We're too late.

We can't simply walk away. The house has to be searched in the hope that something has been left behind. Drugs possibly, or an incriminating device, a DVD or a thumb drive. We find empty closets in the bedrooms and hallways, but the kitchen's fully stocked and a large bookcase holds several dozen books that have to be fanned in search of photographs.

"The man's a scholar," Stu observes. "I wouldn't believe it if I wasn't lookin' right at it."

As I run my fingers over the spines, I realize these weren't the sort of popular histories churned out every year, or young-adult histories suitable to high school students. The one I pull out, on the Mongol invasions, carries forty pages of endnotes.

◆

An hour after we enter, with the search team still at work, I walk out the door, headed for home. I expect deserted streets, but a thin stream of men walk north, toward the meat market at the top of Main Street. Early birds in search of that worm. The contractors who employ day workers generally arrive between six and seven.

I stop a group of three as they come past Brim's house, flashing my badge. They respond with rapid-fire Spanish, which I can't translate. But I catch the drift. Their lives are about minding their own business, their fear of ICE a weight across their shoulders almost from minute to minute.

Baxter's not a sanctuary city by any means, but immigration is a federal problem and we have enough problems of our own. I watch the men go as I walk toward my car. I'm almost there, keys in hand, when a man pulling a shopping cart filled with plastic trash bags turns onto Poole Road. He walks in front, pulling it over a cracked and broken sidewalk. I don't have to ask what's in the bags. The man has been up all night, collecting bottles and cans.

You can find these men, along with a few women, in every neighborhood on the night before recyclables are collected.

I've never tracked them, but they must put in miles every day, checking each container, untying plastic bags, searching through them, retying when they're finished. Men like the one who comes steadily forward, invisible to most, but street-smart.

I'm wearing a tan bomber jacket with BAXTER PD written on the front and back, yet the man doesn't hesitate as he approaches. In his sixties, he has long gray hair and a beard to match, finally stopping when I hold up my hand.

"You don't mind, I want to ask you a few questions." The "you don't mind" part is strictly rhetorical and the man doesn't protest. He's been here before. "What's your name?"

"Cray Justice."

"Where you headed?"

"Homeless sweet homeless." He points to an encampment at the far end of the block. "How can I help ya?"

"Yesterday, probably in the afternoon, the people in this house moved on."

"True enough." He grins, running his fingers through his beard. "Gonna miss them girls. They used to sit outside on warm days. Smart mouths and sassy attitudes."

"Did you see them leave?"

"Nope. I was sleepin', but some of my fellow campers seen 'em."

"You think they'd talk to me?"

"Could be. You'd have to ask 'em." Another grin, revealing several missing teeth. "Course you'd most likely do better across the street. Lady there's a paranoid type. Sits out on her lawn with a shotgun next to her chair. Has a camera, too. One of those Ring bell cameras. She'd be the one I'd go to first, I was you."

The brick house across the street, partially hidden by an overgrown rhododendron, is tiny, no more than two bedrooms.

Reasonably well kept except for a roof that needs repair, the home's front door faces Brim Houseman's property. I can see the camera from where I stand, but I'm not impressed. Only the most expensive door-mounted cameras can record detail beyond fifteen feet, roughly the distance from the door to the sidewalk. The busybody part, on the other hand, has me intrigued.

"One thing, though. What I'm told, some of our people . . ." Cray gestures toward the homeless camp. "They're sayin' they watched a white van drive up. Big, right, like a small school bus. Four men got out and went inside. Maybe a half hour later, the girls come through the door carryin' suitcases and hop into the van. Hour after that, the men come out carryin' boxes. Our people told me the men were cops."

"They wore uniforms?"

Cray shakes his head. "Uh-uh, but a good number of the folk in the camp been to prison. Me, too, come to say it. We know cops when we see 'em."

◆

I want to head home for breakfast, but the woman across the street remains in play. Every window's dark and I have to assume she's asleep. Like I have to assume waking her in the middle of the night will leave her in no mood to cooperate. I slide into the cruiser and settle back to watch the sun rise. Marcus Goodman sits beside me, wearing a nearly identical Baxter PD bomber jacket. The difference being that his jacket's four sizes larger than mine.

At a bit after seven, a light comes on at the back of the house, bright enough to be reflected in the windows of the house next door.

"Go in?" Marcus asks.

"Let's give her a little time to wake up."

And use the bathroom, which I don't say. There's also that shotgun Cray mentioned. So, yes, a chance to wake up. Less chance to panic. But as it happens, Addis McCourt proves affable when we ring her bell a half hour later. I can see the why of her shotgun, even without it in her hands. The small woman has to be in her seventies, a bit stooped, with lively blue eyes that weigh and measure.

"How can I help you?"

"Your door camera, was it active yesterday afternoon?"

"Well, sure. It's always on. Not that anyone 'cept the postman comes close enough to set it off."

"Can it reach the house across the street?"

"Ah, you're here about them women movin' out. Good riddance to 'em."

She steps toward me, staring over my shoulder. "And to the animal who ran 'em."

"Please, Addis, about the camera . . ."

"Sorry to disappoint, but the picture only reaches this side of the street. The rest is a blur."

I take out my phone and pull up a photo of Deborah Cole. "I understand you like to sit outside on warm days. With a shotgun by your side."

"Ain't no law against it."

"Nope, none at all. Long guns don't have to be registered, not in this state. But I am curious. Why do you think you need it?"

"Look around, detective. This ain't Beverly Hills." Addis's mouth curls into a sneer as she makes a valiant, if unsuccessful attempt to straighten. "This house? Moved in with my new husband forty years ago. Rented first, then bought. There's no mortgage now, and the property tax is next to nothin'. That's the good news. The bad part is it ain't worth a bag of spit, not in the Gardens. Had a man come by two or three months ago, offered ten thousand dollars. And how long would that last with me survivin' on Social Security and food stamps?"

I let her run on, nodding from time to time. Elderly and isolated, Addis's life has to be a lonely one. Finally, I turn my phone to show her Debbie Cole's photo as she grinds to a halt, her questions still unanswered.

"You ever see this girl at the house across the street?"

"Yeah, I did. Little girl, too young really. Stayed across the street for months, then disappeared."

"You don't recognize her, though? Not from the news or . . ."

"Don't get me started on the goddamned news. I got enough problems with depression and the meds I can't afford without listening to bad news every damned day. And television? Can't afford cable and my antenna barely gets two stations. I mostly listen to the radio." She sobers abruptly. "Did I miss something here? About this girl?"

"Yeah, she's dead. Murdered."

"By them cops took the women out yesterday?"

"What makes you think they were cops? Did they wear uniforms?"

Addis shakes her head. "I was sittin' out front, mindin' my own business. Man told me to go inside. Big guy. Well, I had my shotgun next to me and I don't like bein' told what to do, so I just kept on sittin' till he showed me his badge. As puttin' a load of birdshot in a cop's behind wasn't on my to-do list, I complied."

◆

I confess to Vern Taney as soon as I return to the house. Vern sits behind his desk, taking it in, his face composed, his championship football in his hands. So, yes, I could have served the warrant as soon as Judge Thomas signed it. I would probably—no, make that almost surely—have recovered Brim Houseman's computer if I'd taken that course. But just as surely, the women living inside the house would have been walking the Boomtown Stroll. They would not have returned, not once they learned of a cop raid on their home. Nor did we have any info on their identities.

"We know Deborah Cole recently lived in that house," I continue. "So, where did she go from there? The other women in the house could have provided us with important information and we wanted to round them up when we served the warrant. So, I decided to wait until I was sure they'd be home. Me, and nobody else. The mistake was mine and I don't want it falling on my detectives."

Vern folds his arms across his chest. "I've already decided to fire Stu." He maintains his grave expression for a moment, then laughs. "Woman proposes, but God disposes. I'm in the mood for clichés this morning, so let's call it water under the bridge. Where do we go from here?"

"We win is what I think."

"Win? Go ahead, tell me."

"Brim's house was scrubbed by cops an hour before the warrant was signed. How did they know?"

"Tell me."

"Fine. Street cops brought Houseman to the hospital. Cops took the names of the victim and several eyewitnesses. All by the book, all about covering their asses. But they had to know that Houseman was in trouble and there was evidence linking Deborah Cole to

Brim Houseman. For sure, through the other women, and maybe they knew about the tape as well. Word on the street, universally, is that Rowan was murdered by other cops. Only there's Deborah Cole and all that evidence linking her to the murder. Well, if she's linked to the murder, then she must be linked to the cops as well. So, they panicked. I'm talking about Thrace Overby and Colton Steele. When they chose to empty the house in broad daylight, they must've known we'd uncover their role. Costs and benefits, right Vern? They had more to lose by allowing us to search Brim's home than by us knowing they cleaned the place out."

◆

We go with what we have left. The only person who can now tell us where Deborah Cole went after leaving Brim Houseman is Brim Houseman. And we do have leverage in the person of Olga Kupchak. Present when the Cole–Houseman movie was made, I had her on a record I can use to pressure Houseman. So far, we only have Brim's assault on Olga, a charge that's hanging by a thread.

Will Olga's testimony, plus the wart behind Brim's ear, be enough to convict him for sexually assaulting a minor? As cops, we collect evidence and offer it to the prosecutors. Whether or not that evidence is presented to a grand jury is a decision that belongs to them. But there's no hope at all without Olga Kupchak to verify that it's her voice on the recording. Olga's already experienced Brim Houseman's capacity for violence, and then you have Deborah Cole whose body rests in the morgue.

For now, Olga believes her conversation with me was private. More than likely, she'll stay put. But the next moves, a sworn statement and an appearance before the grand jury, won't be received well. Given the opportunity, she's very likely to place our little city in the rearview mirror. That's what I'd do in her position. But she doesn't have to be given the opportunity, as I find out when I consult our district attorney, Tommy Atkinson.

"Ask her, kindly, if she'd be willing to appear before a grand jury. If she refuses, which you think she will, take her into custody while I seek a court order to hold her indefinitely as a material witness. Now, show me what you've got on her." Always jumpy, Tommy's hands dance in front of him as he watches the Deborah Cole video, then listens to Olga claim that she was present when the video was made. "Yeah, this'll do. You say Olga's a prostitute?"

"Yes, no doubt."

"That means no visible means of support and no ties to the community. Couldn't be better."

CHAPTER TWENTY-THREE
DELIA

I find a stack of files on my desk when I return to my office, cases in progress, cases headed for trial, all in need of review. I sit down without touching them. I have a decision to make. Yes, I can take and keep Olga Kupchak in custody pending an appearance before the grand jury and a trial that won't be held for at least six months. Six or seven months in a cell will turn her life, tough as it already is, upside down. Does she have dependent children? An elderly relative who needs help?

I don't care. Olga referred to Deborah Cole as the Mouse, yet stood by as Houseman systematically exploited the girl. I have no desire to rip Olga's life apart, but mercy's not on the table, either.

With these thoughts still tumbling through my little brain, the ancient police landline on my desk rings. A few days ago, we faxed Arshan's autopsy report to Dr. Joseph Lewin, a state pathologist. He apparently expedited his review of the material as a personal favor. We'd met, Lewin and I, at a seminar on the "Police–Pathologist Relationship."

"Joe, I've been hoping you'd call. How have you been?"

"Got a dose of long-term Covid a few years ago, but I'm almost back to normal now. And yourself?"

"Hale and hearty. So, what's the news?"

"I reviewed the autopsy report you sent. Deborah Cole was murdered."

Joe Lewin has a flare for the dramatic. I can almost hear the score for *Jaws* in the background. "You're sure?"

"Nothing's sure, and the injuries were subtle, but I've observed similar injuries on a number of occasions. Minor bruising around the carotids, minor petechiae, they generally result from what the police call sleeper holds. Forearm and bicep are placed to either side of the neck, with the crook of the elbow at the throat. Pressure is then applied to the carotid arteries without damaging throat cartilage or the hyoid bone. I might ignore the damage if Cole was ill, or her tox screen revealed heavy narcotics use, but the girl was in perfect health."

"How many times have you seen this sort of injury?"

"Not that often. Maybe fifteen times over the last twenty years. The number began to tail off as police departments banned choke holds." He pauses long enough to clear his throat. "Sleeper holds aren't easy to administer. You need training and you need to be a lot stronger than your victim. Personally, I've never reviewed a case with no police involvement."

"Great, Joe. Now, if only I can convince our beloved coroner to change the manner of death."

"Already done," Joe declares. "Flies with honey. I spoke to Arshan a few minutes ago. Told how much I admired his work.

Told him that his autopsy was spot on, which it was. Told him he didn't recognize the cause of death only because the cause was so rare. I might not have recognized the homicide either if any other possibility existed. But a young woman in good health? Wasn't it Sherlock Holmes who said that once you eliminate every other possibility, the one that remains, no matter how improbable, must be the truth?" Again, Joe clears his throat, then coughs. "Anyway, he's going to change the manner of death on his autopsy report to homicide, and the cause of death to strangulation. You're good as gold."

◆

I call Stu Harrington into my office and explain the situation. Decorah Cole is now a homicide victim. Stu's smile stretches from ear to ear. "That's great news," he tells me. "Now we can operate."

Commissioner Vern Taney, by contrast, is less than pleased when I confront him in his office. "Are you kidding me? I just held a press conference announcing her cause of death as undetermined."

"Undetermined pending further investigation, which we've done." I take a breath, then outline our Olga Kupchak strategy. I intend to snatch her off the Boomtown Stroll this evening because I don't know who else lives at her home address. Maybe that biker gang Chuck Breyer mentioned.

I take a moment after I leave Vern to review my strategy, along with the steps I've taken and the steps to come, which include an aggressive interview with Olga Kupchak, followed by a more aggressive interview with Brim Houseman. Then I order lunch, a grilled cheddar and tomato sandwich from Lena's, before settling down to review the files on my desk. I feel good though I'm far from a natural administrator and have no love for paperwork. But I need the break. I've been living inside the Rowan Krauss homicide bubble almost from moment to moment.

◆

I eat my sandwich with some relish, my optimism a virtual condiment, and work steadily for the next couple of hours. I hope to finish with the open files, then spend the evening at home before joining Stu for a trip to the Boomtown Stroll and Olga Kupchak. A phone call blasts those hopes out of the water. A robbery at a liquor store on Baxter Boulevard, a fatality, a wounded bystander in critical condition. The press is already there, along with a crowd of gawkers.

Commissioner Taney and I arrive almost simultaneously. We view the scene together, but keep away from the store's owner, John Gentry. Security cameras have recorded the confrontation from two directions. We'll review the data soon enough, but for now we're relying on the store's clerk, who witnessed the confrontation from beginning to end.

The robber, Jerry Stiffle according to his driver's license, had entered the store and immediately drawn his gun. John Gentry responded, also immediately, drawing a 9mm Glock and opening fire. A quick inspection of the robber's weapon, a .22 with the serial number filed off, revealed that it couldn't have been fired because it was unloaded. Nevertheless, John Gentry had a right to defend himself. Within reason.

The reason part flies out the widow after Vern and I examine Gentry's weapon. The Glock's magazine holds fourteen rounds, fifteen with a round in the chamber. We can't be sure about the one in the chamber because the magazine proves to be empty. Gentry had pulled the weapon from a holster behind his right hip and emptied it in Stiffle's general direction. I say general direction because at least six bullets passed through the front window, one of them entering Sandra Berman's abdomen.

Legitimate self-defense or criminal negligence? Almost surely, John Gentry's body was flooded with adrenaline when he saw the gun in Stiffle's hand. Just as surely, his visceral reaction had been devoid of reason. So, when did Stiffle drop his gun? Did Gentry continue shooting after Stiffle was neutralized? The security cams will tell the story. But should Gentry escape the hands of the state, he won't escape the lawsuit sure to come.

I look over at Stiffle's body. He wears a St. Louis Cardinals tank top, filthy, like his torn jeans. Pockmarked from wrist to elbow, his arms extend from his body. Drying blood mats tangled brown hair that partially covers his face. He can't weight more than 130 pounds.

"The fact that we lost the war on drugs doesn't mean we won't keep on losing."

Laura Udell stands beside me inside the store, the pair of us ignoring the mixed odors of cordite and booze. Four or five bottles of wine, arranged on a table beneath the window, have also fallen victim to Gentry's fusillade. Across the street, Bute Stafford's mouth continues to move while reporters stand at attention. Their microphones are raised, like they're already toasting the juicy story they intend to write.

"How do you want me to play it?" Laura's the primary on the case.

"It's your show, Laura."

"Yeah, so here's what's gonna happen. I'm gonna kid-glove Mr. Gentry. I'm gonna tell him that he isn't a suspect—which he isn't, technically—but I need to hear his version. I'll let him run through the confrontation once, then ask him to write it down and sign it. After that, it'll be up to the DA."

◆

I pause to consult with Vern on my way out of the crime scene. That affable, good old boy smile I know so well has been replaced by a pinched mouth and a pair of dark circles under his eyes. He rubs at his eyes as I approach, and I find myself glad, not for the first time, that I turned down the commissioner's post. Cops don't prevent crimes before they happen. We're reactive, not proactive, an obvious truth the public chooses to ignore.

"The woman, Sandra Berman, she's in surgery. Her condition's critical." Vern looks up at the sky for a moment. "Berman's an engineer, Delia. Directly employed by Nissan. One of a team assigned to keep an eye on the project."

Call it lose-lose. Businessman Gentry, community pillar, defended himself against a lowlife junkie with a gun. Sandra Berman, pillar of a much larger community, walked in front of a stray bullet and is now undergoing surgery at Baxter Medical Center. Arrest Gentry or don't arrest Gentry, doesn't matter. Stafford will exploit the situation either way.

Across the street, Bute Stafford finally makes his exit, stepping into the back of a gleaming Cadillac Escalade. The driver wears a suit and tie and has both hands on the wheel. Free at last, the reporters and camera staff begin to move in our direction.

"Something else," Vern says. "I just got a call from Sheriff Bascomb in Revere County. You mentioned a man named George Pratt in one of our conversations."

"Right, he's currently employing our undercover."

"George Pratt's dead. Murdered. His ID makes him a resident of Baxter, so . . ."

"Lemme guess. Bascomb wants our help."

"Any help we can give. A courtesy they're prepared to return if we should need them in the future."

◆

I quit the scene a few minutes later. Gentry and Berman will dominate the news for the next few days, but Olga Kupchak and Brim Houseman are a lot more important. I find a shady spot a few blocks south on Baxter Boulevard and park, my thoughts turning to Detective Tom Carney. Should I call him? Warn him? Revere County detectives will find him sooner or later. Too many people know of his association with Pratt. But there's that lingering doubt, that mistrust, and I can't eliminate the possibility that Carney had something to do with the killing, not entirely.

For the next few minutes, I allow my thoughts to run where they will, until they finally settle. Then I place a phone call to Sheriff Bascomb.

"Afternoon, captain, how can I help you."

I resist an urge to laugh. Bascomb wouldn't have taken my call if he didn't need the department's help. "Think it's kind of the other way around, sheriff. More like what help I can offer on the Pratt investigation."

Bascomb chuckles the chuckle only a seasoned politician can manage. "Got me there, captain. So, how can you help us."

"A name. Tom Carney, Pratt's regular driver and full-time muscle."

"I take it that George Pratt's known to your department."

"Not a major player by any means, but active enough to come to our attention. But here's what I can do for you. I'll have Carney brought into the house tomorrow morning for an interview. To be conducted by your detectives. How's that work for you?"

"Works just fine, captain, and I appreciate the cooperation. You need our help in the future, you've got my number."

◆

Thursday isn't through with me. No, the hits just keep on coming. Even as I prepare to snatch Olga Kupchak off the Boomtown Stroll, meeting with Marcus Goodman and Rena Cafaro, results for the DNA collected in the camper parked close to Rowan Krauss's vehicle on the night he was murdered, and from the car parked outside the home where Deborah Cole's body was found, come through.

The DNA was collected from the obvious places. From the door handles, dashboard, and steering wheel on the car, from cabinet handles, the flush handle on the toilet, the arms of a couch, the faucets inside the camper. Deborah Cole's DNA was recovered in numerous places, in the camper and in the car.

I've been living in denial from the moment I learned Deborah Cole's name. And I've made a mistake I should never have made, one I'd been avoiding for decades. Deborah was victimized by a hard, hard life. She'd gotten the crappiest end of a crappy deal, rejected and exploited almost from birth. But her suffering obviously hadn't equated with virtue. It rarely does.

Deborah Cole walked up to Rowan Krauss while he slept, pulled the trigger on the gun she held, and walked away. Our hotline had produced a single witness. Though he'd refused to be identified, his description of a small woman dressed in black walking toward Main Street jibed with the evidence. So, yes, the clothes were a bit too large, likewise for the shoes. So what? I've fueled my wish for her innocence with bits and pieces so flimsy they now dissolve before my eyes.

◆

I drop down a notch. Deborah Cole was, indeed, a victim. A homicide victim. I'll pursue her killer as I'd pursue any other killer. And now I have a piece of evidence that advances the ball to the far end of the field. Other DNA recovered inside the camper and the vehicle matched DNA recovered from the tissue beneath Deborah's fingernails. The CODIS database has already been searched, while the genealogical search through the Forebears website is ongoing. CODIS failed to produce a match, but the man—and the DNA definitely belongs to a male—was too intimately involved to be very far away. Still, he hadn't accompanied Deborah as she made her way from the camper to Rowan's vehicle, as she pulled the trigger, as she walked toward Main Street. In some important, if perverse, way, she surely trusted or feared the man who eventually killed her.

Everything I've learned about Deborah so far leads me to believe she wasn't close to anyone. Estranged from her parents, without real friends, exploited by a pimp known to be vicious, then suddenly vanished. It would be easy to conclude that she'd been passed off to another pimp, passed against her will. It's equally possible that she ran into someone who gained her confidence, who promised her support, who worked her mind instead of her body. A young girl desperately in need of a daddy.

◆

We head out to the Boomtown Stroll shortly before the day shift at the plant finishes work. Me, Stu, and Chuck Breyer. Broken by pure white clouds, the skies are a sheet of blue paint, close enough to touch and infinitely far away at the same time. The Stroll's truly up and running when we arrive, crowded actually. The boys from the plant are finishing up their shift and the hookers, some half-naked, stand in little packs, most of them smoking cigarettes or weed. Olga's not hard to find, what with the neon-blue fringe at the ends of her hair.

I'm sitting in the back of an unmarked car, a Toyota with smoked windows, and I send Stu and Chuck to fetch Olga. There's really no point to it, but I'm in the mood for a little drama and I don't want the woman to see me until she's pushed into the back seat. I can't hear the exchange when Stu approaches, but knowing Stu, I'm pretty sure he makes it simple. Go gently, or go kicking and screaming, but you're going. Olga demonstrates the expected indignation, mouth tightening, chin lifting, but her protest is short-lived. There's nothing to be gained by fighting cops. Stu leads her to the car, opens the back door, and guides her inside.

"Hi, Olga."

"You, you're the one, you bitch."

"Nice to see you as well."

Olga's face reddens, her outrage seeming more personal this time. I think, given her temper, she'd be quick to use her hands. Not here though. I maintain eye contact, my expression neutral as I give her a minute to calm down.

"Didn't I tell you already. I'm not a fucking rat and I'm not gonna help you. I helped you enough already."

I respond by holding up my phone and pressing play. Olga draws back, releasing her breath in a long hiss. "You already have," I explain, "and now you're gonna have to back it up. We're gonna hold you as a material witness pending a grand jury indicting Brim Houseman for sexual assault, based mostly on your testimony. Under oath, Olga. Under oath."

Olga's fear, a fear she's been concealing all her life, replaces her hostility. I've witnessed this transition many, many times. Now, she'll bargain.

"I've got my mother at home, detective . . ."

"Captain."

"All right, captain. She needs my help."

"Who's with her right now." I can read the answer on Olga's face: nobody. "You stood by while a fifteen-year-old girl was abused and exploited. Because you were afraid? I might buy that excuse if you never broke away from Brim. But you did. You declared your independence and faced the consequences."

I give it a few beats, then say, "Not even an anonymous phone call to social services, alerting the city to the nightmare that haunted every minute of Deborah's waking life. No, not even a phone call. Well, you're mine now, get used to it."

CHAPTER TWENTY-FOUR
CARNEY

It's been two days since I passed Brim Houseman's existence on to my superiors, but nothing, so far as I can tell, has come of it. Nothing in the papers, or over the air, and those same superiors have yet to get in touch. I'm surprised, but not disappointed. It's nine o'clock in the morning and I'm still in bed, propped up on two pillows, my eyes glued to Vangi's fetching butt as she makes coffee. I'm pretty sure that Vangi's been tasked with keeping an eye on me. The who part is still a mystery.

Vangi's focused on her long-term goals, like a law degree and a social life "far away from tiny town." And little old Tom Carney? Who's living in a tiny trailer in tiny town? Obviously not what you'd call a long-term investment. So, why is she here?

Last night while Vangi slept, I attached a GPS unit to her Mustang. The unit was originally meant for George Pratt's car, but George Pratt is dead. Executed yesterday morning as he drove through Revere County. Curiously, Bute Stafford was on the phone to reporters an hour after the murder went public, describing Pratt as an "up-and-coming entrepreneur."

I don't give a damn about George Pratt. It's my own ass that worries me. Vangi thinks cops pulled the trigger on Pratt, though it makes no sense and she's offered no proof. In the meantime, the casino's already been refurbished. The Blue Skies Tavern will open tonight, Pratt or no Pratt. Or so I decided before Stu Harrington and a uniformed cop knock on my door.

Vangi takes one look before demonstrating her street-smarts by hustling across the yard to her red Mustang. Whatever's going down, she wants no part of it. Stu doesn't try to stop her, or even appear to notice.

◆

It's just past nine o'clock on a workday, with the temperature in the seventies and steadily climbing as the sun rises into a cloudless sky. The flow of pedestrians has reversed, with stragglers heading home after working all night. They barely glance in our direction, but they don't matter. The only important witness at the moment is the cop in his immaculate uniform. Surely one of Overby's.

"What do you want?" I ask Stu.

"You're comin' downtown. There's a couple of deputy sheriffs from Revere County who want to speak with you. Turn and face the wall."

When I hesitate, the uniform, who hasn't introduced himself, spins me around and begins a close search of my person. I complain, of course, like any other hard-ass gangster. "What the fuck, what the fuck." That earns me a slap on the back of the head a moment before I'm handcuffed behind my back. Personally, I think the cuffs are overkill on Stu's part, but I'm not here to reason why as I'm hustled into a marked patrol car.

I don't speak on the way downtown, and I'm not asked to speak. There's no point in protesting because the show must go on. And that's what this is, a show. At the station, I'm marched past a dozen cops in the reception area, including Sergeant Overby, who glances my way before turning back to whatever he was doing. Then it's up a flight of stairs and into the squad room, empty except for a pair of Revere County deputy sheriffs. They don't acknowledge me as I'm led to an interrogation room where Stu Harrington points to a hard-backed chair behind a small table and says, "Sit."

I'm thinking that Stu left out the asshole part, as in "Sit, asshole." But I obey, hoping the cuffs will come off. They don't, and both Stu and his over-starched muscle exit without a word.

◆

Always leave 'em waiting. That's Interrogation 101. The length, however, is determined by numerous factors, including the whims of the detectives running the case. So, what'll I do? Complain about the cuffs: "Hey, my fuckin' hands're goin' numb." Demand to use a bathroom? "I'm gonna piss on the fuckin' floor." Pounding on the table is another good one, but I'd have to use my head, what with my hands cuffed behind my back.

Speaking of which, I have to wonder how I ended up in this room, waiting to be interrogated. The only way the sheriff's office in Revere County could know about my relationship with George Pratt is if my handlers told them. That would be Mariola and

Harrington, my protectors. The obvious question is why, and the obvious answer is they don't trust me. They believe I might have killed Pratt because I want the Blue Skies for myself. Well, they're right about the last part. I intend to be at the Blue Skies Tavern when it opens tonight and I hope to operate the bar-casino far into the future. The jump, from Pratt's flunky to businessman, can only enhance my status in Overby's eyes. Whatever payoff he demands has to come from me.

Across from where I sit, some wag has written *casa de Dios* in pencil, the letters traced over and over again. I lose myself for a time in speculation. Is the God referred to merely the state exercising arbitrary justice? Or did the prisoner bring God with him or her, sanctifying the room? And where did he or she get the pencil? A pencil can surely be used as a weapon and should have been taken away. Is it possible that the detective who overlooked the pencil compensated for this error by kicking the shit out of the prisoner? That would pretty much eliminate the possibility of an interrogation room as a house of God. Or, maybe not. Maybe it depends on the character of the god you worship.

◆

I'm still at it when the door opens and the two deputy sheriffs, unaccompanied, walk into the small room. Both are large males and they dominate the space. They seem to know it because for a long moment, they glare at me without saying a word. Finally, the older of the two pulls out a chair and introduces himself. "I'm Detective Holliday." He doesn't bother to introduce his partner, who leans against the door as he slides a toothpick into his mouth.

I have a number of options here. I could exercise my right to a lawyer, or ask if I'm under arrest, or demand to leave because my rights have not been read. At another time, I might try any of these, but not this time. I didn't expect to be interviewed this early—and I'm still blaming Mariola—but I'm glad it's come. That's because my alibi is beyond challenge.

"What do you want?"

"I'll ask the questions."

"Not if you want answers." When Holliday takes a step in my direction, I add, "You wanna hit me, go ahead. I can use the money." When he stops, I make the facts of our confrontation clear. "You have no jurisdiction in Baxter and you haven't read my rights. That means I'm not under arrest and I can walk right on out. If you want answers, you're gonna have to ask nice."

Holliday's small eyes are almost hidden beneath a heavy brow. They open as wide as they can as he jabs at me with a long, thin nose. Most likely, he's considering what he'd do to me if the interrogation room was located in Revere County.

"Where were you yesterday?"

"From when to when?"

"All day." He watches me shake my head, before leaning back on his heels. This isn't going the way he hoped. But if I have an alibi, it's better to get it on the table. Otherwise, he and his troops might spend days running it down on their own. "From two till eleven."

"Two in the afternoon?"

"Yeah."

"I spent the day, from around eleven in the morning until near midnight, at the Blue Skies Tavern. The bar's at the tail end of a renovation. It'll open tonight. I never left, not even to eat. Food was brought in."

"Anybody else there?"

"The on-site manager, Zacariah McBride, along with a pair of day workers. We also received deliveries at different times throughout the day."

"And you never left?"

"Never."

"This bar, where can we find it?"

"There are no legal addresses in Boomtown. You look at city records, it doesn't exist. But you can find the Blue Skies Tavern on a road they call Sixth Avenue, which also doesn't exist. No fear, though. The cops who picked me up can take you there. There's a sign outside."

Detective Holliday stares at me for another few seconds, then abruptly turns and leads his flunky out of the room. I didn't kill Pratt and he knows it, whether or not he checks my alibi. That doesn't mean I didn't have my boss killed, but proving a conspiracy requires the identification of a co-conspirator. Until that happens, I am, apparently, free and clear.

CHAPTER TWENTY-FIVE
CARNEY

I leave *casa de Dios* ten minutes later, grab a fried egg with bacon sandwich at a deli, and head for my trailer. I've missed Uncle Sean's phone call, but I'm hoping he'll call back. That's the rule of thumb. If I can't answer at the arranged time, he'll try again two hours later, assuming there's a phone available. I don't know who killed Pratt, but I can make an educated guess about where he was headed. Only one of Pratt's crews operates in Revere County. That would be Les Jameson's crew. But I can't make myself believe that Jameson, a hillbilly who samples too much of his own product, pulled it off a few days after he aligned himself with Pratt. While Pratt was on the road, no less.

Inside my trailer, I fetch the burner and unlock it. There's a one-word message from Uncle Sean: *noon*. My watch reads 11:30, close enough. I roll a joint and drag a lawn chair outside. It's too hot to sit in the sun and Boomtown might as well be an arid plain for all the shade trees available. My camper does come with an awning that once upon a time provided shade, but is now rusted in place. I sit anyway, mainly because I need a little room after my brief confinement.

Off in the distance, a dozen vultures describe slow circles, their wings tipping up and down as they navigate breezes I don't feel. That many, packed so close together, can only mean they've found something on the ground, something tasty, something dying but not quite dead. I'm wondering if buzzards occasionally starve because there's not enough dead animals to feed them all. And I'm wondering if I'll survive, or if I'll die because some high-up cop decides there are too many criminals unwilling to follow rules that include a regular payoff.

I'm expecting Overby to arrive tonight or tomorrow. By then, he'll know the casino's up and running. He'll demand his piece, of course, and I'll probably agree to his demand. But what if I can't make the payment, say because one or more of the gamblers has a good run? We're not like those Las Vegas casinos with dozens of tables and hundreds of slot machines. They can absorb a big payout. Me, I have one craps table, one blackjack table, one roulette wheel, and a moneymaker designed to facilitate the payoff. I'm adding a poker table with a professional dealer. The dealer won't play any cards. Instead, I'm going to rent seats at the table by the hour, a strategy to protect against losses and insure there's enough cash to make my payoffs on time. I hope.

◆

The burner in my pocket, set to vibrate, interrupts my calculations. But it's not Uncle Sean on the other end. The voice I hear belongs to a man a good twenty years older than my uncle. Some believe that Aloysius McKinney sits at the head of the table, that he quietly runs the Kensington Group in Philadelphia. Myself, I've seen him on and off since I was a child, usually at the odd wedding or funeral. The same relationship was true for most of the Irish kids in Philadelphia. We all knew him well enough to say hello if we ran into him at the supermarket, and he generally recognized us. The rest, the if and what, remained hidden.

I'm supposed to be shocked when he pronounces his name, but I've been at it too long to advertise my feelings. "So, what's up?" I ask.

"You must be surprised to hear my voice."

"I was expecting someone else."

"Yeah, Sean. But Sean's in prison and he's gonna be there a while longer. I'm in Baxter and I'm hoping to speak with you."

I give this a moment to settle before asking, "How long have you been here?"

Ally McKinney laughs, a sound more like he's clearing his throat. "Sean told me you were sharp, Carney. But why don't we meet. I won't take up more than an hour of your time. Promise."

"I'm not inviting you here."

"Good thinking. I'm at the Hilton, got a suite. C'mon by and have a cup of coffee?"

◆

Forty minutes later, after a phone call to Zacariah at the casino, I'm walking through the Hilton's lobby. The hotel bears only a passing resemblance to the chain's major hotels, like the Hilton in Las Vegas. Eight stories high, the outer facade is vanilla, in architectural detail and color both. The best you can say is that it's not cinder block. Inside, the lobby is a bit more dramatic with bright, abstract paintings, heavy on the red and gold, lining the wall behind the reception desk. A wide set of stairs with a dogleg to the right leads to the hotel's bar and restaurant.

I pass through the lobby to the elevators without being challenged, and ride up to the top floor. Ally's suite is at the end of the hall. It opens at my knock to reveal a large man wearing blue slacks and a silk polo shirt. I don't recognize him, but I'm sure he's the bodyguard. He steps aside to let me into a large room furnished exactly as you'd expect. A green, tweedy couch sits before a giant flat-screen with a leather coffee table between them. End tables to either side of the couch bear metal lamps with narrow green shades that match the wallpaper and the rug. Ally McKinney's seated in an armchair at the far end of the couch.

"You want coffee?" he asks. When I shake my head, he nods to his man. "Kenny, give us a little room? Maybe go out for a smoke?"

◆

My host is so typically Irish, I have to suspect that his appearance was sculpted by an AI program. In his seventies, he's allowed what's left of his hair to go unbrushed, so that tufts curl away from his skull in stiff gray waves. His complexion is suitably flushed, his drinker's nose swollen at the tip and set above a slash of a mouth. His blue eyes are small, yet still twinkle, as if he's enjoying a joke he's yet to tell.

"How long have you been here?" I ask as I take a seat.

"You begin with a cross-examination?"

"How long have you been here and how many of you are there?"

His features tighten for a moment, but then he smiles. "We're coming, Carney. We have no choice. Philly? It's overrun by . . . See, at one time I mighta said the colored. Now there's so many shitheads of color, I don't know where to begin. The mayor, the city council, and the mobs, too. There's nothing left for us, not even a small piece." He leans toward me. "When Sean first mentioned Baxter, I figured I'd hate it. I'm a big-city type, born and raised, but the town's grown on me. Back home, I leave my neighborhood, I stand out like a sore thumb. Here I'm one of the crowd. I'm operationally anonymous, and it's gonna stay that way for years to come. Thousands of newcomers here to build the plant, followed by thousands of newcomers to work it. Strangers livin' alongside strangers."

I'm wondering how long it took him to come up with the word *operationally,* but I get the point. "You're not the first, Ally. Couple of years ago, a crew from New York tried to do exactly what you want to do. They were driven out, and pretty quick. You wanna succeed, you'll have to deal with the locals. Soon as one or another gets busted, they'll give you up. You're an outsider, not one of them."

Ally shakes his head and glances at his watch. "Me, I don't really want you or need you, but Sean asked me to give it a shot. So, here's how it's gonna play out. We're not gonna work the street. We're gonna wholesale. We already have a connect with the Baja cartel, and they're not dumb. They also know opportunity when they see it, which means they're willing to make the kinda deals we can't refuse. Now, even wholesaling, we'll take hits from time to time, but who cares? It's just how the game is played. So, you want in or not?"

"I have a bar in Boomtown with a little casino in the back." While Uncle Sean knows I worked undercover in Philadelphia, I wasn't stupid enough to let him know tell him that I'm doing the same in Baxter. Plus, there's no way he can out me as a cop without revealing that he, himself, was a snitch. "I'm gonna build from there, slowly and carefully. It won't make me rich, but it's mine all mine."

"And who do you have to thank for that? If not your Fenian friends from Philly?"

CHAPTER TWENTY-SIX

CARNEY

Ally was making several points. That he's been here longer than I thought, that he's been keeping an eye on me, that murder is a line he's willing to cross. As I sit in the small office I partitioned off at the back of the casino, I find myself grateful. Cards on the table is a strategy I appreciate. Now I have to decide what to do. If I let my handlers know what's happening, Mariola will surely ask me to go along. Or, not exactly ask. Order me is more like it, and my decision, when I make it, will have nothing to do with loyalty to the old neighborhood. In Philly, I trusted the job to protect me. Can I also trust Mariola and Harrington, or that my role won't accidentally leak? If I set up Ally and his crew, Sean will surely seek revenge.

I shake myself back into the present. I've got a business to run and crooked cops to catch. To that effect, I've concealed a tiny camera inside a digital clock on a shelf to my left. The camera doesn't run continually. Instead, it can be activated by a button attached to the bottom of my desk, a button I can reach by moving my right knee about six inches to the side.

◆

The system's not in use when Anniston Lowell enters the office. Anniston's my newly hired poker dealer and it's time I made things clear. The woman's in her late thirties and matronly, the mother of two children. You wouldn't believe her dexterity until you watched her manipulate a deck of cards.

"You asked to see me, boss?"

"Yeah, take a seat." I wait until she's sitting in one of the hardback chairs on the other side of my desk. "Before you take offense, what I'm gonna tell you I already told Joe." Joe Jones is our blackjack dealer. "If I catch you dealin' seconds, I'll take a hammer to your fingers. I want every card turned legit."

Anniston's color rises. For a moment, I'm thinking she's gonna tell me to go fuck myself and walk out. But she settles down—she's got kids to support—and crosses her legs.

Anniston's and Joe's wages are too small to live on. Both depend on tips supplied by wining players. This is something I don't get, what with the odds already being stacked in favor of the house. But the gamblers keep coming, drawn by an addiction to a god they call luck.

"All right, I get the fuckin' point. But you could've given me a chance before you started makin' threats."

I watch Anniston leave, closing the door behind her. Pratt's office is long and narrow, much like Benny Kaplan's. And like Benny's, the office contains a tall, heavy safe. There are no tumblers on the safe, only a keypad requiring an eight-digit PIN. Out of necessity, Pratt shared that PIN with me. If I was to manage the casino, I needed access to the bank.

Every casino has a bank, a money reserve in case somebody wins big. In Vegas or Atlantic City, the bank can run to millions of dollars. In my case, the cash in the safe amounts to $9,432. Not enough, really, and for a time this afternoon, I was tempted to shut the casino down and pocket the money. I didn't, though, and here I am, gambling on the stacked odds at the roulette, blackjack, and craps tables to see me through.

◆

A few hours later, I'm standing on the sidewalk outside the Blue Skies, greeting customers as they enter the tavern. The bar is already crowded. Good news because the bar's revenue isn't subject to the whims of fate. Beyond the money, I want to put my face out there. A new player in town, check him out. And I get a few hits, one from a pimp who wants to know if he can put one or two of his women inside.

"Ya know, discreet like." When I turn him down, he shrugs his shoulders. "Cops are fuckin' everywhere now. I gotta get my girls off the street."

"Not in my bar, no disrespect intended."

The pimp doesn't protest. He simply walks off, no harm and no foul. I'm left to myself for the moment, left to enjoy the pulse. Friday night, paychecks handed out or direct deposited, money sent home, the rest to spend. It's party time for Boomtown workers, mostly male, but with enough women to brighten the evening. Alcohol naturally tops the entertainment list, and drugs, of course, often sold by resident dealers inside the bars. Not in mine, though.

Most of the strollers are white, though not all, like most are male but not all. I don't give a damn either way, unlike Ally. I do care, however, when a Baxter PD patrol car pulls to the curb. My old buddy, Sergeant Overby, is seated on the passenger side. He takes his time opening the door and stepping out, rising to his full height, then looking right and left.

For the first time, I make him as a narcissist. Is he being noticed, shown the proper respect, even admired for his regal bearing as he dons his regulation cap with its polished bill? The strollers do react, giving him plenty of room, and I have to feel that they recognize him. An asshole with an attitude.

"Do we need to talk?" I ask.

"Yeah."

"In my office?"

"That'd do."

◆

Overby leaves his driver behind as we march through the bar, then the casino, to my office in the back. As I take my seat behind the desk, I slip my right leg to the side, activating the camera hidden in the digital clock. Overby's expression doesn't change. No light comes on behind his eyes.

"You did good," Overby tells me, "getting the place up and running. Only you're operating under a false impression. Pratt thought we took the joint apart because it was too out front." He pauses long enough to shake his head. "Our law enforcement action was all about the tax."

"As in, they didn't pay it?"

"Yeah. And before we go any further, are you in trouble over Pratt?"

"Nope. I have a good-as-gold alibi. I was here all day with multiple witnesses to back up the claim. I had nothin' to do with the hit on Pratt."

A silence follows as Overby looks around. Moment of truth time. He's naturally cautious, but there's no way to collect the tax without naming a price. I could prod him, maybe ask how much, but that might be construed as entrapment. I content myself with looking up expectantly, ready to conform to whatever demand he makes.

"All right, Carney, let's start with a grand a month."

"Can I ask what's in it for me?"

"You get to operate, for one. For two, anybody tries to muscle in, we handle it. Third, if a raid's coming down, you receive advance warning." Overby tries for a smile, his thin lips expanding at the edges. "It's good you asked. Show's you got enough brains to go places."

I lean back in my chair and spread my hands. "The tax, does it start at the end of the month?" Which is only a week away.

"Now, Carney." He glances at the safe. "Now would be good."

"That's gonna leave me low on the bank, but what the fuck." I use my body as a shield as I punch in the safe's PIN. There's a tray lying on a shelf and I carry it back to my desk. Overby watches closely as I count out the bribe, stuff it into an envelope, and hand it over.

"One more thing. Change of plans. What you did the other day, steppin' in with the pimp? You ordered him to keep his business private. Forget that. Stay low yourself, but for the rest, the worse, the better. We win the election in November, we own the city."

I don't bother to ask if the "we" includes Bute Stafford. Just yesterday, a boy, a teenager, attempted to rob a liquor store on Baxter Boulevard. The boy was armed, but so was the store's owner. The shootout ended with the boy dead and a bystander on the sidewalk in critical condition. Stafford arrived in time to be interviewed by reporters he beat to the scene. An hour later, Mayor Venn announced that the runways at Windstrom Airfield in Coombs County had been extended far enough to handle commuter aircraft and the largest private jets.

For Venn, Baxter was moving up and out. For Stafford, the city had already descended into a hell of its own making. Guess who got the headline and who found his way to page eight of the *Baxter Bugle*?

I retrieve the burner from the back of the safe and punch in Ally McKinney's number. He answers on the second ring and I get right to business.

"If you're lookin' for outlets for your product, I can supply you with a few leads. Pratt's customers."

"Not even a hello first?"

"What could I say, Ally. I have a business to run."

CHAPTER TWENTY-SEVEN

CARNEY

The business of business is working your ass off. It's hard-focused eyes on the bottom fucking line. The rule applies to every business, legit or crooked. Is the Blue Skies Tavern legit? Is a tolerated vice legit or criminal? Doesn't matter. We're doing as much business in cash as on credit cards and I spend the next couple of hours moving between the casino and the bar. I drink Cokes with a lime wedge, no alcohol. Only once do I retreat to my office and have a few hits on a joint I rolled before I left the trailer I call home.

I spend most of my worknight at the bar, chatting with the regulars, paying attention to what they drink, what they eat. Outside of bagged potato chips and pretzels, we don't serve food, but that can change. I'm imagining a food truck parked outside (owned by yours truly) dispensing tacos, or loaded hot dogs, or even Midwestern pizza. How 'bout Philly cheesesteaks?

Carney the entrepreneur. Like George Pratt the entrepreneur who's now in the Revere County morgue awaiting an autopsy.

But I'm sure of one thing. All by itself, the crowded bar's a serious moneymaker, and not due to any effort on my part. I simply rehired the club's original bartender, a woman named Brenda Farb. Brenda's in her forties and hefty, a plain woman with a broad nose that dominates her face. No matter, she flirts with the regulars and rattles off dirty jokes as she pulls mugs of beer and pours shots of whiskey. She's also very active online, with a following that includes hundreds of workers at the construction site. The best news is that her salary (and that of her coworker, Jackie) is relatively minimal. Her living depends on tips.

I'm deep in these fantasies, actually considering whether I want to buy the blue Maybach with the white top or the white Maybach with the blue top and hood. I get to the part where Vangi slides onto a leather seat, her short skirt riding up, when she walks through the door.

Vangi's not alone. She's with her lawyer sugar daddy, who looks absolutely regal in a dark blue suit, pale blue shirt, and a silver tie pulled tight against his throat. Vangi doesn't look at me as she's led across the barroom and into the casino, but every eye on the bar turns toward her. The woman's not beautiful, but she projects a physicality that's undeniable, and I find myself thinking her arm should be linked to the arm of a gangster, not a lawyer. The perfect moll.

◆

"Hey, are you Tom Carney?"

The man addressing me is the polar opposite of the man escorting Vangi. He's in his forties, and his face is a series of planes accentuated by a prominent brow that leaves his eyes in shadow. Close to six feet, his shoulders are broad, his manner confident. He wears a checked flannel shirt, green and blue, with the sleeves rolled up. Perhaps so I won't miss the gold bracelet on his wrist.

"That's me. What can I do for you?"

"Name's Bud Murphy." He hands me a card: MURPHY AND SON/ WHOLESALE SPIRITS. "From Brooklyn, if you could believe that."

I shake his hand. "Tom Carney, from Philadelphia."

"Yeah, two migrants workin' the dark side of the moon." He offers a short laugh, but when I merely nod in return, he states his business. "When it comes to sellin' booze, there's no quality angle. A case of Bud is a case of Bud, no matter who you buy it from. So, it's all about price and I'm offering, sight unseen, a ten reduction across the board, plus same-day delivery."

I slide the card into my shirt pocket, figuring I can play Murphy off against my current supplier. "Not the time right now, but have a drink on the house."

"Nah, gotta turn ya down. I'm a Christian. I don't drink."

"Only sell?"

"Yeah, you could say that. I got my own rules for myself, but I ain't a crusader. If you take my meaning."

◆

I go back to my office and settle down before my computer. There's an app that allows me to access the security cameras in the bar and the casino. I'm no tech nerd and it took me a good fifteen minutes to get the software up and running, but the stream of images the system now produces are sharp.

First thing, I look for Vangi in the casino, but she and her escort are already gone. I turn to the cameras in the bar next. Zacariah urged me to use a computerized system that requires servers to enter drink orders before they're pulled. That would make it hard to cheat, but I turned it down in favor of a cash system with no record beyond the ring of an old-fashioned cash register. I plan to maximize the skim, to show only a small profit while I fill my pockets. The mob in Las Vegas lived on the skim for decades. Can I do less?

The drawback to this strategy doesn't require a lot of analysis. A piece of that skim can easily be skimmed by my employees. I'm not seeing that as I watch Brenda work the drinkers at the bar, but I do find myself regretting every credit card purchase.

Toward one o'clock, a man named Crandall "Crank" Rivera knocks on the door of my office. I need security and I put the word out a couple of days ago. Thus far, applicants have been limited to pure knuckleheads. Men who spend their lives in search of an excuse to throw punches, if not elbows and feet, not to mention clubs, knives, and bullets. Meanwhile, I'm looking for a peaceful, yet secure, environment. There will be the occasional degenerate gambler who needs to blame someone else for his addiction. They'll get loud and threatening and must be quieted. With a few words, if at all possible.

I met Crank Rivera when I was still working for Benny. Convicted of manslaughter, he'd served the better part of ten years in state prison before his release earlier this year. Not an uncommon story, but what caught my attention was the account Benny related when we were alone. Rivera had refused parole, remaining in prison for an extra year before his unconditional release. That means no parole officer and no drug tests. Crank decided to regain his independence, no matter the price, and he made good on it.

"Don't mean to get in your business," he now tells me, "but I heard you're lookin' for muscle."

"Nope." Crank's well over six feet tall and prison-hard. It wouldn't pay to disrespect him and I don't. "I'm lookin' for security. A quiet presence acting with . . . let's call it restraint."

"I can do that." He hesitates for a few seconds. "Word on the street, you're a serious man. And me? I don't do well on my own. Where you're goin', I hope you'll take me along."

Music to my tone-deaf ears, but I have a reservation. As a convicted felon, guns are a no-no for Crank. My safe? Yeah, nobody's gonna run away with it and four incorrect PIN entries will shut the lock down until I contact the manufacturer. Fine and dandy, but a gun put to my head short-circuits every other precaution. Instantly.

"I need someone with a carry permit."

"Already have one."

"How'd that come about?"

"A couple hundred dollars to the right cop . . ."

"Which cop?"

Crank's most prominent features are a pair of large ears that jut from the side of his head like flattened teacups. They flare red now. I'm asking for information he'd rather keep to himself. But I'm not moving. He doesn't want to answer, he can walk out the door.

"Sergeant named Overby." Crank's sharp enough to understand my concern. Has Overby planted him here? Maybe due to my association with organized crime? "Look, I don't give a flyin' fuck about Overby. You want, I'll put him in the dirt. Just say the word."

◆

Sometimes in life you gotta go with your gut. The main vibe coming off Crank is hunger. He's always been a criminal, always will be. No way he's gonna take a job sweeping the floor somewhere. Only he's lost a lot of time and he needs to get his career on track. I hire him, explain the long hours and that I'll hire a second man as soon as I can find one. In the meantime, this early in the game, I can't pay him more than five hundred a week. He doesn't exactly jump at the number, but doesn't turn me down either. A moment later, he's out the door with instructions to return tomorrow around four, an hour ahead of the tavern's opening.

I take a quick walk through the casino and the bar. The rush is over, the casino's almost deserted. A few committed drunks still linger at the bar, nursing their drinks. I get Brenda's attention and tell her, "Last call at two forty-five." Then I return to my office and open the safe. Today's receipts and cash will be tucked inside, pretty much secure. Nobody can put a gun to my head if I'm not here.

An hour later, just before three, I catch a break. I've just closed the safe when Sergeant Thrace Overby strolls into the office and comes to a halt, looking down at me through eyes that radiate pure contempt. Maybe it's an East Coast thing, but preening narcissists trigger the lizard in me. Not to mention the crocodile. I activate the camera, then lean back to wait. Overby hesitates for a moment as well, perhaps expecting a polite greeting that's not coming.

"We've been keeping an eye on the operation. Seems like you're goin' strong, in the bar and the casino both." Again, he pauses. Again, I fail to respond. "So, what we're gonna do is up the tax. Let's say two thousand a month with another thousand on account. Like now."

"No."

"What?"

"I'm not givin' you another penny." As I stand, I shut down the camera with my knee. I'm wearing an unbuttoned jacket that leaves the pistol I'm carrying in plain view. If forced, I plan to use it. A cop like Overby wouldn't last an hour back in Philly and I'm pretty sure the asshole knows it.

"Do you have any idea what's going to happen next?"

"Nothing, Overby. You made a deal that you're gonna have to honor. Now, if you don't mind, it's been a long day and I need my beauty rest."

Moment of truth and I'm betting that Overby's sorry he left his driver outside. Not that backup would have changed my attitude. Overby's right about one thing. The Blue Skies Tavern is a little gold mine and I intend to hang on to as much of that gold as possible.

The contempt in Overby's eyes suddenly changes to a barely controlled rage. There's nothing a punk hates more than being exposed as a punk. But he doesn't have it in him to act on his anger and he finally turns toward the door. I wait for him to take a step before I make a final point.

"Oh, by the way, I almost forgot. Uncle Sean says hello."

"Sean Carney's in prison," Overby says without turning around.

"So he is, sergeant. So he is."

CHAPTER TWENTY-EIGHT

DELIA

Wild cards, also called unforeseen contingencies, have a way of turning up at the worst times in my professional life. Danny and Gretchen went for an early morning run at seven, trying to beat the rain. I don't think Gretchen's a natural runner. The girl's a yoga type, with maybe a few Pilates tossed into the mix. She's out there anyway, protecting her investment. Last night, while Danny was on the phone with Mike, Gretchen confessed that she worries constantly about Danny dumping her for a newer model.

"He's become a prize," she explained. "You should see the way they look at him. How they say, 'Hiiiii, Danny' when they pass him in the hall."

"How does he react?"

"He seems oblivious, but for how long. And if we end up at different schools? Gone, goodbye."

I like Gretchen because I believe she's on Danny's side, that she keeps him grounded and focused on his studies. So, I tell her that Danny genuinely cares for her, which is true, but not really consoling. Teenage romances are notoriously short-lived, which is why Gretchen's out there, jogging through humidity thick enough to spread on toast, leaving Zoe and me to entertain ourselves. Which we enthusiastically do.

◆

My thoughts turn to work when Danny and Gretchen return, ready for separate showers. Then the phone rings and I read Vern's name on the little screen. No way is he calling this early to wish me a pleasant day.

"Morning, Delia." He doesn't wait for a return greeting. "Look, Arshan released Rowan's body last night and Jesse's scheduled a viewing at the Fulton Funeral Home this afternoon. We have to be there."

I don't argue the point, because there's no argument available. Rowan's time with the Baxter Police Department must be acknowledged. Still, it comes just as the investigation's gathering momentum. By now, Overby, Steele, and Rawling know we have DNA and that we have Brim Houseman in custody. I'm hoping they haven't heard about Olga, but I can't discount the possibility. Bottom line, with the good guys only a couple of jumps away, they have to be scared, if not actually desperate.

"I'm going to pay a condolence call on Jesse before I go to work," Vern tells me. "So, bring me up to date. Quickly."

"A couple of questions, Vern. Where did Debbie Cole go after she left Brim Houseman? Olga claims not to know and I almost believe her. Debbie was still with Houseman when Olga walked away. But Houseman almost surely knows, if not exactly where she went, who she was close to before she split. I'm going to squeeze him out like a tube of toothpaste. I don't care if I have to threaten him with a murder charge. Arshan changing the manner of death was a lucky break for us. Killer or not, Debbie Cole was a homicide victim."

"Okay, sounds good. We'll talk again at the viewing."

◆

Once I reach work, I call down to the jail and ask for Olga to be brought up and deposited in an interrogation room. Sorry, but she's eating her breakfast is the response, whereupon I lose my temper. Whereupon the deputy in the jail hangs up. I've almost decided to fetch her myself when Stu shakes his head. He's smiling, amused, but I know we're feeling the same excitement. We've been working Rowan's murder for a long time, working one dead end after another. Now there's a shaft of sunlight peeking through the blinds. Or two shafts, one named Olga Kupchak, the other Brim Houseman.

"I heard from our undercover this morning," Stu tells me. "He wants a meet tomorrow. Promises he'll brighten our day."

Another wild card. "I can't promise, Stu. Depends on how far we get today."

We're in search of a man whose DNA matches the DNA found beneath Debbie Cole's fingernails. Her killer must've known he'd been scratched. At that point, he might have scraped her fingernails, or even amputated her fingers. But then we'd know she'd been murdered when the plan likely called for the Baxter PD to pin the murder on Debbie, then write off her death as natural. So, he took a chance. He left her as she was and all we have to do now is find him.

◆

Escorted by a pair of corrections officers, Olga finally makes an appearance. I watch her carefully as she's led across the squad room to the box. I'm not seeing the anger, the defiance. They've been replaced by a composure that's been forced upon her. She'll bargain first, then take the best deal on the table.

We let her sit for ten minutes before following her inside. She's in a chair with her back to a graffitied, windowless wall. There's a small table in front and we take up positions in chairs between her and the door. I don't have to spell it out. Olga's a vet.

"Right now," she tells us, "I'd do anal for a cigarette."

"Right now, you're just gonna have to do nicotine withdrawal. Call it tough love."

"You're not gonna bribe me?"

"Bribe you to do what?"

Olga's wearing the same clothes she wore yesterday, a neon-pink dress made of a glittery synthetic that might be used to wrap birthday presents. The makeup has mostly disappeared except for a smudged black circle around her bruised eye. "You're not gonna bribe me to rat on Brim?"

"Now, see, you've got it backward," Stu says. "You've already ratted on Brim and we've recorded your ratting."

Olga points an accusing finger in my direction. "She tricked me with that picture of the Mouse."

"Save it for the grand jury."

"I'll take the Fifth."

"Nope. You're not a suspect and you've committed no crime." Stu's tone is patient, but not condescending. "The Fifth

Amendment only protects suspects against self-incrimination. The judge will order you to answer. If you refuse, he'll jail you until you comply."

"I'm already in fucking jail."

Stu's about to go on, but I raise a hand. "Olga, didn't you speak to a lawyer last night?"

"Yeah, she told me I was screwed. Like I'm nothing but a filthy whore and no judge will let me out until I testify. Like material witness is worse than bein' convicted. It's like a life sentence. They don't let you out till they feel like it."

"In that case, you received good advice. So, are you hungry, want coffee, a soda? We can run out, bring back a breakfast that's gotta be better than what they serve downstairs?"

"See, I knew you were gonna bribe me."

◆

We leave Olga to further contemplate her condition, returning thirty minutes later with a large latte, a bacon-and-egg sandwich, heavy on the ketchup, and two of Lena Luncheonette's frosted doughnuts. I'm thinking, as I watch her eat, that Olga would prefer to show some small element of restraint. But her jailhouse breakfast must've been even worse than I imagined, because she wolfs down the sandwich before starting on the doughnuts. Without saying a word, not even a thank-you.

"I'm dead, ya know," she finally says. "Thanks to you."

I shake my head. "Brim won't see daylight for the next thirty years. Pimping a fifteen-year-old girl? With his priors, he'll be tucked away in the most miserable hole this state has to offer."

"It ain't Brim."

"Then who?" I know the answer, but we're recording the interview, video and audio. It needs to come from her.

Olga picks up a doughnut, then abruptly drops it before sipping at her latte. "My lawyer said I don't have to talk to you."

"That's right, Olga. You're not a suspect and you don't have to cooperate." I lean forward, the odor of fresh-baked doughnuts suddenly filling my nostrils. "It's strictly up to you."

"I'm havin' a little trouble here, captain. I mean, what's my motivation? What's in it for me? Besides takin' a shank?"

"A shank from who?"

"From the kind of people who can reach you in jail. From the kind of people who might already be workin' at the jail."

"Okay, that's reasonable. But suppose I can arrange a trip to somewhere safe."

In fact, it's already arranged. Sheriff Bascomb in Revere County owes me for making Tom Carney available and he didn't hesitate when I asked. He's willing to house—and protect—Olga for at least the next month. More than enough time to put her before a grand jury.

"So, that's it? That's the bribe? A couple of years in a different cage? When you admit that I didn't commit a crime."

"Not one that can be prosecuted, but you left that child to her fate. You were an enabler."

"No." Olga shakes her head. She's pissed off again. "You don't know shit about her, or me, or my life. I came up hard, cop. Really, really fucking hard. I worked the street younger than Debbie, and the only people who gave a damn were the social workers who placed me with a foster family that treated me worse than my own parents. So, you can save that bleeding-heart bullshit for someone who cares."

Stu raises both hands, palms out. "I get the parallels, Olga. Young girls turned loose in a hard world to learn hard lessons. But you gotta admit, there's one big difference. You're alive and Debbie Cole is dead." He glances at me out of the corner of his eye. "You go to Revere County, you'll be housed away from the other inmates and we'll give you a phone. And maybe it won't be all that long. We have Brim on tape sexually assaulting a minor. All we want from you is a signed statement in your handwriting."

"Sayin' what?"

"Sayin' exactly what you've already said. Between you and your two statements, I got a strong feeling that Brim's gonna cop to rape. He's gonna do what you're doin' now, which is latch on to the best deal he can negotiate. That happens, we'll cut you loose."

Olga stares at Stu for a long minute before saying, "Shit, gimme a pen."

CHAPTER TWENTY-NINE

DELIA

Mission accomplished, I'm heading over to the hospital to confront Brim Houseman. I find Laura Udell in the squad room, pecking away at a keyboard. Laura's the primary on yesterday's shooting.

"Any word on Sandra Berman?" I ask.

"Upgraded to guarded but stable. Whatever that means."

"You get a statement from John Gentry?"

"Nope. Asked for a lawyer right away. Sandra Berman's family, too. They've hired their own shyster. But I've got a half-dozen witness statements, so there's no question about what happened, and the security cams show that Gentry continued to fire after Stiffle dropped the gun." She turns back to the keyboard. "Once I get everything on paper, I'll take it to the DA, drop it in his lap."

◆

I open an umbrella (that Gretchen urged on me) as I step into a steady rain. It's only twenty yards to a free unit, but my feet are soaked before I get there. Likewise for the half-block walk from my parking space to Baxter Medical Center. I'm on my own because Stu's transporting Olga to the Revere County lockup. Her phone's been returned, along with a warning. Contact friends and relatives, but don't tell anybody where you are. We'll stop by your house sometime in the next few days and pick up your clothes and anything else except your drug stash. I don't have to ask if she has one.

There's a bin filled with plastic umbrella sleeves near the Center's main entrance and I slide my umbrella inside. My thoughts are already turning to Brim Houseman as I deposit umbrella and sleeve behind the reception desk. Like any cop, I try to keep both hands free.

I intend to arrest Brim Houseman for sexual assault on a minor and have him transported to a small locked ward, currently vacant, on the hospital's top floor. That's if he chooses to remain silent or demand a lawyer. On the other hand, should he decide to cooperate . . .

What can I offer? I'm still considering the possibilities when I step out of the elevator, look down the corridor, and find a small crowd of medical personnel in scrubs, along with a patient clinging to a portable IV stand. They're facing away from me, staring at a pair of uniformed cops outside Brim Houseman's room. I recognize Thrace Overby and a patrolman I've met before, Tony Mellone. In the doorway, Chuck Breyer blocks their entry. I ordered him to remain with the prisoner and it appears that he took me literally.

I stay silent as I approach, placing myself against the far wall. Chuck can see me, I'm sure, but the two uniforms don't react.

"Are you deaf or stupid, sergeant?" Chuck says. "I already told you. You're not comin' in." A patrol sergeant and a detective share the same rank in the Baxter PD. Overby can't order Chuck to move.

"We're visitors," Overby says. "Mr. Houseman has a right to receive visitors. You have to let us in."

Chuck's a big boy and fit. His brown eyes are darker now, and hard as glass. "No," he says, just the one word, and I have to figure he's looking for a fight. I can't see Overby's face, but his back is stiff, his shoulders raised. It's two against one and he'll lose face if he backs off. Poor baby.

"Overby." I finally speak up, aware of the witnesses behind me. "What do you think you're doing here?"

He spins to face me, as does his backup. The stripes on his sleeve don't matter now. Like any other police department, the Baxter PD is a paramilitary organization with a fixed chain of command. Insubordination is a punishable offense.

"I want to visit Mr. Houseman. He's allowed to have visitors."

"So, you're Brim's buddy, his pal?"

No way Overby can admit this, even if it's true, which it's not. "I don't answer to you," he finally says.

"How about Commissioner Taney? You answer to the commissioner?" The question's greeted with silence. "Houseman's a prisoner. He's been charged with physical assault, and now I'm going to charge him with sexual assault. That means he has no right to privacy except with his lawyer. You still want to visit him, that's fine with me, but I'll have to record every word you say."

◆

Overby, as it turns out, no longer wants a face-to-face with Brim Houseman. I watch his back as he leads Mellone down the corridor, then turn to Breyer. He's smiling as he shakes his head.

"You ruined my fun, captain."

"Did you plan to take him on by yourself?"

"No, I planned to back him down. Word on the street, he's all bluff."

"I think you've been awake too long."

"I'm ready to go home whenever a replacement shows up." He hesitates long enough for me to absorb the rebuke. "But for now, I'd like to be in the room when you confront Houseman. The guy's a total prick. He brags about the women he turned out. Desperate druggies. He kept them high, as long as they worked the street."

Houseman's game plan doesn't surprise me. The man's telling an old, old story. In any event, I plan to bring him down a few pegs. Houseman, given his priors, could easily spend the next thirty years in prison if he's convicted. Not a happy prospect when you're thirty-five years old. "Tell you what, Chuck. I'm gonna start by showing Houseman just how fucked he really is. I'll let you take it from there. Debbie Cole's the issue, specifically where she went after she left Houseman's stable."

Breyer's smile lights up the corridor. "I got your back," he tells me. "A hundred percent."

◆

"What the fuck you want?" The expected defiance falls flat. Houseman's on the wrong end of a long run of bad days and it shows.

"I'm here to formally place you under arrest."

"For what?"

"For sexually assaulting Deborah Cole, and for selling her services to the highest bidder."

"Assault? The little bitch never said no to nothin' she did."

"Well, see, there's your problem. A child under the age of seventeen can't assent. Not in this state. Her very age is a no."

Houseman takes his time processing the information, then says, "I never had nothin' to do with nobody named Deborah Cole. And what have you got? A fucking wart?"

"Uh-uh. I have a written statement from an individual present when the film was made. Within a week or so, she'll testify before a grand jury. Face it, Brim, you're up that proverbial creek and you'll never get your hands on a paddle."

Houseman yanks on the handcuff chaining him to the bed rail. "Olga, right? You know what I'm gonna do to her when I get out of here?"

"Get out of here? Brim, you're lookin' at a half-million-dollar bail, if you get bail at all." I take a small recorder from my shoulder bag and turn it on. "Now I'm going to read your rights again. Slowly and carefully, while you think about spending the next thirty years in prison."

I can't say how much thinking Houseman does, but when he confirms his understanding of his rights, I step back to let Chuck take his best shot. At this point, Houseman has no lawyer and hasn't asked for one.

"You and me, Brim, we've been around the block enough times for you to know I'm not a bullshitter." Breyer steps to the side of the bed. "We played the game straight, you and me. I never pretended I was a social worker and you never pretended you were a humanitarian lookin' out for homeless women. Now, I want you to take a glance out that window."

There's only one window in the room, against the far wall, and the view is of blue-gray clouds and rain spattering against the glass. Yesterday, you could have seen the top of city hall. Not today.

"You been throwin' the dice for a long time. You've tossed your share of naturals, made your share of points, but this time the dice are reading snake eyes and boxcars on the same roll. And at thirty-five, you're old enough to understand the difference between the gates opening twenty years from now, when you're fifty-five, and thirty years from now, when you're sixty-five. Or just maybe, if we can hang Debbie Cole's murder around your broad shoulders, burial in a prison graveyard."

◆

Houseman's trapped and he knows it. I watch his mouth soften a bit as his jaw loosens, as he weighs the pros and cons. Yes, there's a big difference between parole at fifty-five and sixty-five, but Houseman's in a bind. The man wants to cooperate. He's been in the game too long to believe that silence is the manly thing, that you never put your time on someone else. Houseman's problem is that he can't inform without first admitting his own guilt.

"Where'd she go, Brim? Did she have regular johns? Somebody with a special appetite for young girls?" Breyer's speaking softly now, a seductive whisper, a lover's tone. "Debbie murdered a cop, yeah. But can you really imagine she did it on her own? That she just decided, one day, I think I'll put a bullet in a cop's head?"

Brim's beginning to sweat. His shaved head glistens. "Girl didn't have no will. Do anything you tell her to do, but you gotta tell her." He looks away from Chuck and toward me, his eyes almost pleading now. "Why would I want to kill a cop? Do I look stupid? Besides, everybody knows it was cops who took that sergeant out. Ain't even a rumor out there about no one else."

I step close to the bed, hold up the recorder, and shut it down. "Let's go off the record for now. Make you more comfortable. Later on, after you find a lawyer, we can work on a formal deal. But understand one thing, and I mean you should take it to heart. Any deal is contingent on you telling the whole truth. You lie to us, I'll whisper in the judge's ear, and there's plenty to whisper about. You'll serve every day of a maximum sentence on every count I can dream up."

◆

Brim begins to laugh, and once started has a hard time stopping. I wait him out, until he begins to cough, then lapses into silence. Still, I wait, arms folded across my chest, eyes hard-focused on his.

"I am truly fucked," he finally says. "No matter what happens. But I'm thinkin' whatever deal I'm gonna make, I should make through a lawyer. I'll even take a fuckin' public defender. All those assholes ever do is bargain. Plea bargain I believe they call it."

"Your choice, but you might wanna think about something. The DA's not gonna cut a deal until he knows exactly what you have to say. You'll have to make what they call a proffer. This is what I have to sell, whatta you wanna pay for it? Now that proffer is strictly off the record, like we are now. It can't be used against you."

"You tellin' me there's no difference? I gotta . . ."

I cut him off, take a step closer to the bed as Breyer backs off. "By the time you find your lawyer, create that proffer, offer it to the DA, and the DA finally makes a decision, your revelations might not reveal anything. Maybe we arrest Debbie's killer without your help. Maybe you're no longer a link in the chain of evidence. Maybe your testimony isn't needed. Then what?"

Brim takes a minute, then laughs again. "Lady, you got yourself a real mean streak. Know just where to plant that needle. But we're off the record for true?"

"We are."

"So, where you want me to start?"

"Start with Debbie Cole. How she came to live in your house."

"First thing, if the girl wasn't a retard, she was the next thing to it. Slow, man, like almost stopped. When the witch dumped . . ."

"The witch?"

"Her stepmother. Can't remember the woman's name." Houseman turns his eyes to the ceiling for a moment, then takes a deep breath. "So, when Debbie got dumped, she didn't have no place to go, no real friends and nada by way of street survival skills. I took her in, fed her, gave her a safe place to sleep." He waves a hand in my direction. "Ain't claimin' to be some kinda hero. My motives were purely financial. But I did take my time bringin' her around. And she wasn't no virgin, either."

Brim stops for a moment, his eyes closing. "Damn this pain. I'm tryin' to stay straight, only my ankle hurts like hell. Pain runs right up my leg. I need painkillers."

"Now, see," I tell him, "that's some great motivation in itself. Because you're not gettin' so much as an aspirin until we're finished."

"Figured as much." He reaches behind his neck to raise the two pillows beneath his head. "The video came first, and it come outta nowhere. Man from out of town, works at the plant, and don't ask me at what because I don't know. Name's Rob and he liked my girls. Somehow, he got wind of Debbie and come to me with a proposition. Ten thou, up front, for a twenty-minute sex tape. First, he wanted to use more than one guy, only Debbie wasn't ready for that. But she didn't say no to a one-on-one, didn't argue. Didn't argue when I started arranging her dates. Didn't argue, didn't haggle. A mouse, which is what the other girls called her."

◆

I need a break. Over the years, I've probably interrogated a couple of hundred men and women. I'd say that one out of ten could have been Brimley Houseman's doppelganger. The dead eyes, the cold, empty voice. I did this, then I did this, then I did that. Starting out, they were angry or wheedling or even charming. But when they finally broke, I realized they were empty inside, hollow, the ultimate pragmatists. Whatever works.

Houseman's eyes were blue and bright when I walked into the room. They're cobalt now, focused on nothing, his voice a drone, as though he's reciting a story written by someone else.

"You need to get to the point, because I'm startin' to think you have nothing to sell."

Houseman continued on as though I hadn't spoken. "Debbie's trick list was small, had to be. Word got out, I'd be up that creek you mentioned before. The one I'm up right now. So, she had this one john she saw every week, a regular. Only I don't know his name."

"You serious?"

"Hang on. In fact, lemme back up. One day Debbie left to meet up with this particular john and never came back. And like I said, I don't know his name. Or hers, for that matter."

"You never asked Debbie?"

"Nope, because I didn't wanna know. See, the man who picked her up and paid me cash on the spot is a cop. The new breed, captain. You fuck with them, you catch a beating makes my ankle feel like a mosquito bite. That day, and I don't recall the exact date, maybe a month before she killed the sergeant, same cop picked her up and didn't bring her back."

"And the name of the cop?"

"I give you that, what do you need me for?"

"You can ask the same question in reverse. Why do I need you if you don't? So far, you've told me nothing."

"No way, captain. I've told you everything but the punch line. Now I think it's time you got together with the prosecutors. The name is all I have and I ain't gonna give it up until I know what's in it for me. But I will give you this. I said there's no rumor on the street except cops were behind Krauss's murder. But there's another rumor makin' the rounds on the street. Sayin' the same cops took out your sergeant, are lookin' to hit another cop. Lookin' for someone to do the job."

"The rumor include the name of the target?"

"Yeah, the commissioner, Vern Taney."

CHAPTER THIRTY

DELIA

I carried that thought into the corridor, Chuck Breyer trailing behind. Later, I'll work out whether or not the threat was more than Houseman bravado. It does make sense, though. With Vern out of the way, Mayor Venn will be forced to name an acting replacement. The list will likely include two names, mine and Saul Rawling's. Once in charge, Saul will likely keep Colton Steele's storm troopers safe until after the election. And me, I've already turned the job down. I call Vern and give him a quick heads-up, but neither of us is overly impressed. Houseman's just too unreliable.

"There's a jail unit upstairs," I tell Chuck after hanging up.

"Yeah, I know about it."

"Right now, it's unoccupied, but I've already notified corrections and they'll be sending personnel in a couple of hours. I need you to stick around until Houseman's tucked away. I know you've been here . . ."

"No big deal, captain. I want to watch the cell door close on good ol' Brim, wanna hear the key turn in the lock."

I start down the hall, but pause in front of the elevator without pushing the down button. Instead, I take out my phone and tap Stu's number into the keyboard.

"Hey, boss. I'm at the sheriff's station now, making appropriate arrangements."

"How's our lady doing?"

"Jumping back and forth between pissed off and resigned. But she's right here if you wanna ask her yourself."

"Yeah, put her on."

Olga comes on a moment later. "Hey, captain, couldn't go another minute without hearing my voice?"

"Shut it down, Olga. This is important. Brim had Debbie Cole turning tricks, is that right?"

"Yeah, outcalls."

"Did she have a regular customer, someone she visited once a week or more?"

"Come to think on it, she did. The mystery man. But I wouldn't say 'visit' is exactly the right word."

I endure Olga's chuckle. I'm trying hard not to put words in her mouth, but my heart picks up the pace as we continue. "Mystery man? Explain."

"Nobody knew who he was and she wouldn't talk about it. I don't even think Brim knew."

"The visits took place away from Boomtown or the house in Oakland Gardens. Is that right?"

"Yeah."

"So, how did she get there?"

"Gee, I thought you'd never ask. Usually, with outcalls, Brim took us back and forth. For all his bein' a scumbag, he was protective. Only with Debbie, she was picked up and brought back by someone the john trusted."

If I was in the room with Olga, at this point I'd probably slap her in the head. As it is, I have to be patient. Not my strong point. "Olga, you don't stop fucking with me, I'll ask the sheriff to house you in the drunk tank."

That draws a laugh. "Ya know, I haven't thought about Debbie's mystery john in a while, but I can still close my eyes and see the cop that picked her up and brought her back. A real asshole, captain."

"His name?"

"I want a pizza, and a pint of ice cream."

"C'mon, Olga, cut the crap."

"You're tellin' me the name isn't worth a pizza and some ice cream. And no rum raisin. I hate the flavor." She pauses here, but I'm not biting. "All right, captain, you called my bluff. Besides, a deputy already asked me what I like to eat. The cop's name, the one who transported Debbie, is Stepanik. A shitkicker, captain. The kinda asshole cop who likes usin' his hands."

On that she was absolutely right. Not long ago, two cops arrested Tom Carney for assault. On the way to the house, they tuned him up. Almost by habit, since he offered no resistance. One of those cops is named Beale, the other Stepanik.

I hang up on Olga, then make a call to my part-time aide, Marcia Blackstone. I ask that she stop whatever she's doing and find a quiet spot in front of a computer. "I want to make sure we have a DNA profile for every new hire going back a full year." I'd order her to perform the task if I had the authority, or if I had a full-time aide. As a civilian employee, Marcia answers to a dozen superiors.

"Is this about Rowan?"

"It's part of the investigation, but you need to keep the inquiry to yourself. Just make sure the profile is there. Don't investigate anything."

I hang up, my thoughts almost joyous as I consider Brim Houseman's fate. Brim had only one thing to sell and he should have sold it when he had the chance. Too late now. Brim will do every minute of his thirty years. It couldn't happen to a nicer guy.

◆

I've still got a couple of hours before Rowan's viewing and I'm too stoked to spend it in my office. I call into the squad room and find Cade Barrow at his desk. When I ask him if he's tied up, he gives the response he knows I want. Another perk of being the boss.

"Nothin' life-or-death, captain. What's up?"

"I'm headed for city hall. I'll pick you up on the way."

Ten minutes later, we're parked two blocks south of the hall. I've briefed Cade, who's obviously disappointed with his wholly passive role here.

"C'mon, boss, I haven't shot anybody in months." His grin extends to his brown eyes, but I'm not fooled. A special forces vet, Cade misses the combat rush. He's cool for the most part, but always ready for battle. Cade's the cop I most want at my side when a doorway's about to be breached.

Unfortunately for Cade, my attack this morning will be wholly psychological. I dig out my cell and phone the general info desk at city hall, where I ask for the licensing and permit division.

Most city agencies are closed on Saturday, but a few remain open due to high demand and long backlogs. The woman I need to contact, Violet, works in the busiest of these offices. Contractors must secure a permit, or multiple permits, at each stage of construction, and nothing turns a construction boom into a bust more than endless permitting delays.

A man answers on the second ring. "Knowles." Just the one word, spoken with great confidence by a unionized civil servant.

I respond with an equally confident, "Violet, please."

Knowles should resist, should at least ask me to identify myself, but he's either indifferent, or knows about Violet's indiscretions and wants to keep his distance. "Hang on."

"Grinnell." Just the one word, the voice hoarse, the tone harried. One of those days, maybe, and I'm about to make it a lot worse.

"Violet Grinnell?"

"Yeah." Her tone cautious now. "Who's calling?"

"Captain Delia Mariola, Baxter PD."

A long breath here, audible over the phone despite the rain pounding on the roof of the car. "What do you want?"

"You know what I want, Violet, and I'm giving you a choice. You can come to where I'm parked and we can talk in private. That's choice one. Choice two is that I come up there and pull you out in front of your colleagues. Then we have the same conversation in an interrogation room. You choose."

◆

Violet's choice isn't a choice. She could, of course, refuse to cooperate, maybe call a lawyer. But then she'd have to answer questions from supervisors only too happy to throw her to the wolves if that's what it takes to save themselves.

"I'm parked on Baxter Boulevard, three blocks south of the hall. If you're not here in five minutes, I'm coming after you."

Cade and I settle down to wait. Despite the air-conditioning, it's so humid inside that Cade's standard buzz cut has given up the fight. It's lying flat. But his spirits are surely high. We already have enough on Violet to make an arrest. Once she accepts the reality, I believe she'll turn on whoever's running her, probably Overby. Her handler might have considered that before he approached her. The prospect of passing a single night in prison terrifies ordinary citizens.

Violet's not hard to spot as she hustles along beneath a purple umbrella that barely covers her head. She wears a raincoat that's a little too pink to match the umbrella, a heavy woman, half running with her mouth open. Cade steps into the rain as she approaches and opens the back door. She pauses only long enough to close the umbrella before sliding inside.

Violet's eyes close for a moment as she catches her breath. Potentially, she's one more nail in that coffin I'm building for Saul Rawling and his merry men. I can use the word *men* without fear of censure by the politically correct because I can't name a single woman cop associated with the Rawling crew. There's an old saying out there. Keep your friends close, but keep your enemies closer. Rawling, Steele, and Overby never learned the lesson. They've made enemies of the Baxter PD's female cops and I'm sincerely hoping they live to regret it.

"Well?" Violet's recovered enough to pretend she's a falsely accused citizen.

"Violet, you've been handing out carry permits to men who never filed a formal application. I've got two witnesses with the paperwork to prove it. They were told to show up at the licensing division where you handed over their carry permits without demanding ID. 'Just ask for Violet.' That's what they were told and that's what they did."

"It's my word against theirs."

"It would be, except for a change we made last year. We used to delete the data from our city hall CCTV cameras every six months. Now that data's stored in the cloud. Forever, Violet. And what else do you think we might find after we examine every document you've filed over the last year?" I hesitate for just a second, then list her rights under the Constitution, then fall silent.

Violet's composure slowly dissolves and I have the feeling she's been dreading this visit, at the same time knowing that somebody was going to show up, sooner or later. The whole business was just too blatant.

"From what you're sayin', you could've arrested me in the office, but you didn't. Am I supposed to ask why not? Don't answer. You're after a shark and I'm a minnow. That about it?"

"Yup, right on the mark." I settle back to wait for the story, the one she needs to tell before she agrees to cooperate. Her eyes retreat for a moment, her small features seeming to melt into fleshy cheeks and a prominent double chin.

"My name is Violet Grinnell and what I'm supposed to be is what you're lookin' at. A civil servant who ate too many doughnuts while she waited for her pension to vest. And that's exactly what I was until a year ago. One of the gray people who staff bureaucracies everywhere. You mess with us, your application winds up in the circular file. Then one night, around ten, I get a call from my daughter. She's about to be arrested and there's a cop wants to speak with me."

"Have a name?" This from Cade, his tone sharper than I would have liked, but Violet doesn't appear to notice. She stares at Cade for a moment, as though surprised to find him in the car.

"Overby. I didn't know that at the time, mind you. All I knew is that Angeline was about to be arrested. Fifteen years old, right? And I'm scared to death, a divorced woman with a single child I love with every inch of my heart and soul." She stops here, but I have nothing to say. It's her story, not mine. "So, this cop starts out by tellin' me that Angeline's in deep trouble. Caught riding in a car with a gram of cocaine in the driver's shirt pocket and a kilo in the trunk. I remember his voice, matter-of-fact, almost uninterested. But he made his point clear enough. Angeline hadn't been formally arrested and if I drove out to meet him, we could talk about it."

"Why you, Violet?" Cade asks. "Anybody else, they make the arrest first, then allow the arrestee that single phone call."

"Angeline told them I worked for the city. In the licensing division. I don't know what she thought, but she was terrified. And she had no drugs on her, and no drugs were out where she could see them. What she told me later was that she only went for a ride with this dealer—name of Knox—because he had a cool car, a Mustang. Stupid, yeah, but what's fifteen if it isn't stupid?"

"Okay, I get it. Angeline's as innocent as the angels she's named after. Why don't we cut to the bottom line."

"The bottom line is simple. I'm a supervisor in the licensing department. There's a director, but she's a political appointee who spends her mornings on an indoor tennis court. So, you can basically say that I run the show. Overby wanted me to approve applications without a review."

"Carry permits?"

"That and construction permits." Violet leans back and draws a long breath as the tension finally breaks. "Look, I don't wanna go to jail, but it's more than that." She touches a finger to her chest. "I've been a good citizen all my life. Church every Sunday, communion on the first Friday of every month, confession the day before. So, first, I'm blackmailed into committing one crime after another, and now I'm caught. So maybe it's time for a little payback. The way it works, you can find applications for permits on the city's website. The idea is for you to print them and fill them out before you show up at the department. Saves time, reduces department outlays. So, that's how the applications came to me, already filled out, delivered to my home at night. Meantime, I copied every application and kept a record of when they were delivered. By cops, okay, only not in uniform. They didn't identify themselves, but Overby, that bastard, came by a few times. Wrote that down, too."

I step in. There's a point that needs to be established. "Are you prepared to testify, Violet? Are you prepared to turn over the documents?"

"Better believe it."

"What about your daughter?"

Finally, a vicious sneer. "She's living with her father in Oregon. They took Angeline away from me, too."

◆

Cade and I drive Violet to her home in Norwood. On leaving the licensing department, she'd claimed a family emergency, and home is where her notes and records are stored. On the way, I brief Stu. With Olga tucked away, he's returned from Revere County. I want Violet on the record as soon as possible, with nobody outside Stu, Cade, and myself the wiser. Stu's responsibilities are overwhelming at this point, which leaves Cade Barrow to take up the slack. I assign him the job of monitoring Violet until we have a written statement and her records in hand. As both are sure to be complex, I expect the job to last for the rest of the day. Cade accepts his fate without a complaint, though I'm sure babysitting witnesses isn't his favorite activity.

Violet settled, I have an hour before I have to meet Vern at the Fulton Funeral Home and I spend it at a table in Lena's Luncheonette. The table's located in a quiet corner beneath a large poster. Rice paddies in tiers on the terraced side of a mountain, peasants included, even a water buffalo lounging on a bank. The earthy posters seem out of place, given the polished chrome décor, but I can't complain about the grilled chicken or the Caesar salad it sits on.

I'm just about finished when my cell chimes. I read Danny's name and experience the short jolt of adrenaline that runs through my body every time he calls. Like I spend my life just waiting for a disaster I know is coming but never seems to arrive.

"Hey, Danny."

"Hey, Mom."

"So, what's up?"

"My game's canceled. Rained out."

"This I already figured. Tell me why you really called."

"Gretchen's gonna make dinner tonight. Gretchen and Zoe. They're gonna make ravioli."

"From scratch?"

"Yeah, and get this. They're making pumpkin ravioli. Pumpkin? I mean, what is it, Thanksgiving in May?"

Every so often, my son demonstrates the kind of jock mentality common to high school athletes. The attitude includes a rejection of anything new, anything uncommon, anything that hints of sophistication. But that's not my focus at the moment. All morning, almost from moment to moment, I've been in pursuit of a murderer. I've squeezed Brimley and Olga, a pimp and a prostitute, along with Violet, a corrupt civil servant. I made myself clear to each from the outset. Give me what I want or face consequences you're not ready to face. Danny's coming at me with the other side, with ordinary, everyday life, with pumpkin ravioli. Still, I know what I'm supposed to say and I say it.

"I'm sure it'll be delicious. What kind of sauce are they making?"

"Not tomato, not even cream. Brown butter with walnuts."

"That's terrible, Danny, and I can only think of one solution."

"What's that?"

"Flu-like symptoms. Gastrointestinal, if at all possible."

CHAPTER THIRTY-ONE

DELIA

The Fulton Funeral Home is Baxter's biggest and best. A two-story white Colonial located in the Mt. Jackson neighborhood close to the Revere County border. Across the street, a small kiddie park is deserted, as are the cornfields to the north.

The rain has slowed to a fine drizzle and I leave my umbrella behind as I hustle from the unmarked unit to the funeral home's front porch. I remind myself that we've done all we can, that there's no bringing Rowan Krauss back to life, no resurrection in this material world. His killer's been identified and beyond punishment, murdered herself, perhaps the ultimate justice. Mouse or not, Deborah Cole pointed a gun at Rowan's head and pulled the trigger.

I come through the front door to find the home's owner, Frederick Fulton, at a small desk. He nods to me and gestures to a corridor with doors on either side and at the end.

"The rear door, Delia." Then he shakes his head. "A sad day. I can deal with the elderly come to the end of life, but the young, the fathers and mothers, the children . . . they're harder."

I nod and walk down the corridor, composing my expression as I go. Inside the viewing room, flanked by folding chairs, I find a path leading to the coffin. The plain cross on the wall behind the coffin stands as tall as a man. I'd never known Rowan to be religious, but, then, outside of work, I barely knew him at all.

To my right, Vern's chatting with Gloria Meacham, president of the city council, and Mayor Venn. Scattered here and there, other cops, many from the patrol division, pay their respects. I recognize some, but can't put names to their faces. They're old school, though. The new breed is unrepresented. Perhaps some'll show up later, or maybe none, not even Overby, will find the courage to look into Jesse Krauss's eye. She's sitting in a chair at the front of the room, flanked by two older women.

Rowan and Jesse's children are absent, and I find myself grateful as I approach the coffin. There's a kneeler in front and I think a prayer is expected, but I'm not the one to make it. I stand for a moment, staring down at Rowan. Somehow, the Fulton Funeral Home has restored his skull just enough for an open coffin. The result, the face thick with makeup, is grisly. I want my own coffin closed, no matter the condition of my body. I've made this clear to Zoe, along with my wish to have my body cremated after whatever mourning period she decides on.

◆

"Captain?"

I look to my right, then up, to find Gianni Vetto standing beside me. I'm thrown for a moment by her height, but then remember. Gianni was the one who spotted the CCTV camera in the Winnebago that housed Keith and Jane Moreland. I'd attached her to the original task force, but soon lost track of her role, if any.

"Gianni, how are you making out?"

"I'd like more responsibility, but I'm not complaining. I appreciate the opportunity." Gianni's standing behind me, her body partially shielding my own as she slips something into my front pocket, a folded page by the feel of it. Her voice softens as she adds, "Need to see you there, captain. You wanna bring someone, be sure it's someone you trust."

Her point made, she drops onto the kneeler and folds her hands. I stay where I am for a few seconds, then walk over to Jesse. What follows is what you say when there's nothing you can say. Condolences, a quick hug, introductions to a sister and a cousin, a few moments of awkward conversation. Jesse tells me that identifying Rowan's killer made a difference, and that Deborah Cole's death at the hands of another killer is as close to justice as she'll get. But it doesn't bring Rowan back to life, or console her children.

I react by not really reacting, by absorbing her pain as I've absorbed the pain of so many others over the years. Cops are 50 percent more likely to commit suicide than the general population, though usually after they retire. I think that's when it catches up to you. I think you can keep your finger in the dike while you're going to work every day, but when you have too many empty hours, it all catches up with you. Better to be a mall Santa than the career you chose.

◆

Obligations met, I approach Vern, who catches me out of the corner of his eye. He nods to Gloria and the mayor as he turns to me. "We need a moment?"

"Yeah, let's talk on the porch."

I sweep the street as I come through the door. An old habit born on the day I walked into what I thought was the aftermath of a convenience store robbery, only to have a fusillade of shots fired in my direction. Since then, I let my eyes take a quick survey whenever I leave or enter a new environment. I make the same quick search this time, ready to brace Vern, when my brain, some part of it I can't reach, forwards a sharp warning. A second later, I know what it is. Farm fields often have what amounts to a broad path that traces their borders. Unpaved, they allow farm machinery to reach the various fields without running over the plants. What I'm seeing, though, isn't farm machinery, but a black minivan stopped about two hundred yards from where Vern and I stand.

When a head pops up to lean over the hood from the far side, I don't wait to evaluate the danger. I slam both hands into Vern's chest.

"Get down."

Two rounds slam into the side of the house before I hear the report of what has to be a rifle. There's no time to think now. The Fulton Funeral Home is sided with shingles over plywood. Bullets, even from a deer rifle, will likely pierce every wall of the house before exiting into the backyard. I dash for my car through a drizzle that's slowed almost to a mist. With a little luck, the mist will coat the lens of the shooter's sight, forcing him to wipe it off, giving me enough time to reach my car. Instead, two more shots ring out, though I have no idea where they were aimed.

I enter the car through the passenger's door, which I should have locked but fortunately didn't, and wiggle across the seat as I press the starter button on the key fob. I have to come up now, to raise my head above the dashboard, and my heartbeat accelerates until I can feel it against my ribs. Some part of my brain is screaming at me, demanding I preserve my own life and to hell with everyone else. I ignore the demand, but press my body against the door, offering the smallest possible target, as I put the car in gear and slam my foot down on the accelerator.

A road only fifty feet from the funeral home runs parallel to the unpaved track inside the field, perhaps twenty yards distant. An overgrown drainage ditch and a barbed wire fence keep them separated. I'm expecting the shooter to run because I can't get to him, while he can almost surely reach some unseen road at the far end of a planted field that has to cover thousands of acres. But the vehicle, a small van, remains in place, and no shots are fired in my direction.

I'm within a couple of hundred yards when I discover why. A night and day of heavy rain has turned the unpaved track into a mud pit. Maybe the shooter took his time coming in, but he's heavy-footed now and his right rear wheel is spinning madly as it digs its way into the muck. I don't think he's even aware of my approach, not until I slam on the brakes and roll out of the car on the driver's side.

My weapon's in my hand as I crawl to the back of the car and raise my head just far enough to look out over the trunk. I see a man's head and shoulders leaning through the van's window. His dark tangled hair reaches to his shoulders and a thick, half-grown beard runs to the top of a green T-shirt. To my right, from the direction of the funeral home, I hear a vehicle approaching.

Probably Vern. But I'm hearing a second vehicle, and when I glance to my left, I see a marked patrol car, it's light bar flashing, within a few hundred yards.

On the other side of the fence, the man steps out of the truck. Short and thick, he's holding a rifle with the barrel pointing up at the sky. He looks terrified.

"Drop the rifle." I can pull the trigger right now and walk away a hero. I don't want to do that, in part because killing people doesn't get me off. But also, because I can't believe this asshole acted on his own. I want him alive and talking. "Don't be a fool. Put the gun down and your hands on top of your head. You haven't killed anyone." I don't know this to be true, but I have to say something, to keep communication open. Then my voice, even shouting, is drowned by the cruiser's siren. Why switch it on now, when you're at the scene and there's no traffic to get around? I have to assume it's deliberate.

The cruiser brakes hard and two cops emerge, brogans spit-shined, hat brims gleaming, uniforms crisp. The younger of the two, Abott according to his name tag, carries a shotgun in his hands. Shotguns are standard equipment in our patrol cars, but they're always mounted on a bracket in the trunk, which is now, of course, closed.

As they step onto the pavement, the man on the other side of the fence drops the rifle and runs around the van and into the cornfield beyond. I'm considering how I'll get past the ditch and the barbed wire, about to give chase, when the boom of the shotgun slams into my ear, and the running man, his back turned, pitches forward onto his face between two rows of corn. He manages to lift himself a few inches off the dirt, hanging there for a second before dropping back down. I can see a single hole in the back of his T-shirt from where I stand. Not bird shot, or even buckshot, but a solid slug, the kind used to kill bears. To my right, I see Vern approaching. From the other side, I hear a voice, obviously happy, obviously proud.

"Now, see, folks, that there was some fancy shootin'. Sure enough."

CHAPTER THIRTY-TWO

CARNEY

Saturday morning's a washout, and I don't have to look out the window for confirmation. The rain on the trailer's metal roof is incessant, a hundred psychotic drummers on crystal meth. And me, I didn't get home until three o'clock, only to have Crank Rivera call at seven thirty. He had a candidate for the second security guard I needed.

"He's good, Carney. Reliable like. And cool. He don't lose his head over bullshit."

"What's his name?"

"Stell. Johnny Stell, but mostly he's called by his last name. Like you."

I've never heard of Johnny Stell, and though I'm reluctant to hire two buddies, I'm willing to take a look.

"Bring him around this afternoon."

"See, here's what it is. Stell's workin' a shit job at the UPS warehouse and he goes in at three. Could we do it in like a half hour?"

"A half hour? You're pushing my buttons, Crank, and I don't like to have my buttons pushed."

"No, man, it ain't like that."

I find what I was hoping for in his tone. Not quite fear, but surely respect. The man's too slow to be acting. "Then what's it like?"

"Like maybe I shoulda thought a little more. But, hey, if you got somebody there and you don't wanna see us, that's cool. We'll pick another time."

In fact, Vangi never showed up last night. Not that we'd made an appointment. Vangi will always come and go as she wishes. I wouldn't have it any other way.

"All right, Crank, bring your boy around. Like in an hour. I need to clean up and eat some breakfast."

"Got it, boss."

◆

An hour later, almost to the second, Crank and his buddy knock on the door. Way too macho to use umbrellas, they're soaked. I let them in, toss them a couple of dish towels, none too clean, and watch them closely while I consider my position.

First off, the Blue Skies Tavern's a little gold mine, the bar especially. Our bartender, Brenda Farb, has the knack of making every customer feel special. Her raucous laugh is loud enough to be heard over the pile drivers on the construction site. Most of the time, she's laughing at her own jokes, but the regulars laugh with her.

I'm not an accountant, or even a bookkeeper, and I can't accurately subtract costs from revenue, but it seemed to me, as

I locked the safe last night, that my opening day profit had to be over a thousand dollars. And it'll be a lot more if I somehow manage to attract high rollers. As it is, my working-class gamblers toss five- or ten-dollar chips (no cash, never) on the craps and blackjack tables. They mostly lose, of course, but their losses are relatively small. They can't afford to take a big hit and still send money home.

I don't blame them. In fact, on many levels, I admire them for their restraint. But I find myself already wanting more, and maybe my ex was right. As I strove to limit the crimes I was forced to commit, I remained content with being small. But this opportunity dropping into my lap has me wondering if the luck god has finally glanced in my direction. Right now, an irresistible force is tugging on a very movable object named Tom Carney.

That I'll go nowhere on my own doesn't really need stating. I have to assemble a crew ferocious enough to keep men like Uncle Sean and Sergeant Overby at a distance. Johnny Stell has the look. Thick neck, heavy brow, small mouth, thick beard. On the other side, his blue eyes are quick, and his prison tattoos are limited to his arms. His hands, neck, and face are clean, as his beard is trimmed and brushed.

I shake Stell's hand before offering both men a seat on my couch-bed. The trailer provides a useful ambience. I won't have to convince either man that I'm not a big-time player in Baxter's underworld economy. I offer coffee, which both refuse, then reinforce Stell's first impression.

"I'm not gonna bullshit you, Stell." Which I am, of course, by not revealing that I'm a cop. "Right now, I'm one day into operating a casino. Business was good last night, very good, but I can't offer you any more right now than a security job inside the casino. Five hundred per week, same as Crank. As for the future? Well, it's the future and time will tell how far I get. Life has a way of sorting things out."

Crank and Stell exchange a glance, then Stell speaks up. "Truth, Carney, I'm workin' at UPS under someone else's Social Security number. No choice because UPS doesn't hire ex-felons. They got enough problems with theft already. So, I can use the job, and I appreciate you not askin' about what I done or how many years I spent inside. And . . ."

A knock on the front door brings Stell to an abrupt halt. My Glock is on the fold-down table, left there to be noticed, but I don't pick it up. I do, though, take a moment to glance through the window at the man standing in the rain. I recognize him immediately. One of Ally McKinney's, Mike Mulligan is the man you call when gamblers or borrowers fall behind in their payments. Mulligan's tall and strongly built, with sleepy eyes, a permanent smirk, and a reputation for enjoying the pain he inflicts.

I motion Stell and Crank to either side of the door, then open it. Mulligan's standing on a pair of cinder blocks that serve as my steps. There's a small overhang above the door, but even so, a steady rain pounds on the top of his head, matting what little hair he has left.

"What's up, Mike."

"Same old. And you?"

"A new adventure every day. Like you showin' up without callin' first. Don't remember how we're such close friends."

Mulligan's smirk remains steady, the rock upon which he's built his ego. "Boss wants to see ya, Carney. Asked me to pick you up, give you a lift."

"Ally didn't call me, either."

"He mighta been busy, what with tryin' to set up in a new city." He stares at me for a minute, but I've got nothing to say. "Look, you gotta come in. Simple as that, Carney. When the man calls, you gotta come in."

Mulligan's tone doesn't waver. He's a man reciting a truth so ancient its very existence demands compliance. In fact, the command is little more than a memory from the time when Irish mobs had real clout in Philadelphia. No more, and not for the last fifty years.

I take a step forward and slam the heels of my hands into Mulligan's chest. He flies off my cinder block step and lands on his back in the mud. I step down, followed by Crank and Stell. The smirk vanishes as Mulligan slowly rises. Not all that sharp to begin with, his eyes betray his confusion. He came to summon me into what he imagines to be an exalted presence.

"Go home, Mike, and tell Ally there's no *gotta* between us. And never will be."

CHAPTER THIRTY-THREE

CARNEY

SATURDAY, MAY 24

It's noon and I'm weaving my way back and forth through Baxter's future. One part of it anyway. Still in its birth throes, the Gardens, formerly Oakland Gardens, is a crime district in waiting. Boomtown will be a relic of the past once the factory's completed, and even now, the vice, the gambling, whores, and drugs are too visible to law enforcement and rival gangsters. The Gardens, with its unmarked roads and broken streetlights, its homeless encampments, its squatters and shooting galleries, its undocumented immigrants, is far better suited to provide the anonymity I want.

The high rollers on my wish list will never gamble in the Blue Skies. We're too vulnerable, apt to be raided at any time, and the business types and the professionals need to guard their reputations. You'll find most of them in church every Sunday morning. They volunteer on hospital and school boards, operate charitable foundations, seek dark corners when they indulge their pet vices.

I slow as I pass a two-story house in decent condition, imagining a sleek modern barroom on the first floor, perhaps with an in-house cocaine dealer. The second floor, its windows covered with thick, luxurious drapes, will be set aside for gamblers. Right now, I'm thinking no-limit poker tables with the chairs rented out by the hour, as in the Blue Skies, only for a lot more money. A craps table, a blackjack table, a roulette wheel . . .

My fantasy is interrupted by my phone, encased in a holder on one of the dashboard's vents. I'm wearing earbuds, but I'm not inclined to answer. I'm enjoying myself too much. Then I read the number on the screen and know it has to be Uncle Sean calling from Frackville. I pull to the curb and shut off the wipers.

"Hi, Uncle Sean." I maintain a casual tone, but he isn't having it.

"Don't play that game, like nothin' fucking happened. Not with me, Carney."

Only I'm not playing a game. Back in Philly, I found myself seriously threatened more than a few times. I feel now what I did then, my pulse raised, my adrenals packed and ready. I feel alert, mood elevated, ready to rock.

Joanna, the beloved ex-wife, had been quick to observe this change. "Swear to God, Carney, sometimes I think you wanna die. You wanna go out in a blaze of glory. Only there's nothing glorious about the dirt lyin' on top of your coffin. It's just dirt."

"Nothin' did happen," I tell Uncle Sean. "Ally summoned me and I said no. I don't work for him. I work for myself. And Ally? Well, with assholes like Ally, you have to make yourself clear. No mixed signals."

"You punched Mike Mulligan."

"Nope, just pushed him."

"Into the mud."

"What could I say? The man has balance problems."

"And you're not worried about what he might do? Him or Ally?"

"Nah, too early. Ally and his crew just arrived and they can't afford to draw attention. Later, maybe, once Ally establishes himself. Assuming he does establish himself, which is far from certain."

In truth, I'm not that concerned with Overby, either. I put a thousand dollars in his hand and promised to do the same every month. Maybe he wanted two, but if he takes me out, he's got nothing. And even if I disrespected him, which I surely did, there were no witnesses. Overby can bide his time, just like Ally. Meantime, knowing what I know about Mariola and Stu Harrington, Overby has a lot more than me to worry about.

I lean back and watch the raindrops splatter on the windshield, watch swollen drops break into little rivers that race across the glass. I'm tempted to flick on the wipers, just once, across and back. I would if there was anything out there to see.

"You still there, Carney?"

"Yeah, I am. And let me put it like this. I moved to Baxter because I wanted to get away from Philly and all the mob bullshit. So, you could excuse me if I catch an attitude when Mulligan shows up and tells me 'You gotta come in.' Like he's Sammy the Bull delivering a message from John Gotti." I take a breath. "If I remember right, Uncle Sean, I already told you this."

"All right, Carney, I get it. You don't let nobody order you around, never did. But what do you say to a meet? Just you and Ally? And by the way, Mike Mulligan's on his way home."

"I'm always ready to cooperate, Uncle Sean. As long as the cooperation runs both ways. Tell Ally to come by the club tonight. We can talk in my office."

◆

I reach for the shift, then stop. Earlier I put in a call to my handler, Stu Harrington, asking for a meet tomorrow morning. He hasn't called back to confirm and I'm thinking I should have told him I had Overby tied up with a pink ribbon. Audio and video of the man soliciting a bribe which I dutifully paid. I also have Overby returning for a second bite of the apple, though not our confrontation. I'd wanted to see Stu's face, and Mariola's, when I opened the gift box, so I kept the news to myself.

Surprise!

Of course, I can always place a second call, this time pushing the urgency. And I would if there wasn't a problem yet unaddressed. Sure, I've got the audio and video, but in order to use it in court, prosecutors will have to reveal how they got it. They can't do that without also revealing that I'm a cop. That'll put a quick end to my undercover career.

Do I care? I just don't know. Don't know whether I care about remaining undercover, or whether I stay a cop at all.

My phone rings before I answer any of these questions. It's Vangi and I answer quickly. I lost her on the GPS last night, perhaps because she parked the car in a garage with thick walls, or because the tracker's internal battery went dead. A fully charged tracker battery lasts between four and seven days, but I can't be sure, tech challenged as I am, that the battery was fully charged.

I'm not a stalker, and my use of the tracker had nothing to do with jealousy or control. I really couldn't care less. But I need to know if she's legit, or if she's collaborating with Overby or some unnamed rival. I need to explain to myself why she approached a perfect stranger at Packers. I can't make myself believe it was related to my good looks.

"Hey, Vangi. What's doin', girl?"

"Just hangin' out. And you?"

"Schemin' and plottin'. I'm on the road."

"Where?"

"In the Gardens. I'm having a look around."

"Seriously? The place is polluted. Not the water, Carney, or the air. The people."

I'm tempted to laugh. I grew up in Philadelphia's Kensington neighborhood. You do a search for most dangerous neighborhoods in the city, Kensington's always near the top of the list. The Irish section is marginally safer than the Hispanic and Black areas, where street gangs compete for turf, but you still have to watch your back every minute. The Gardens, by comparison, are unthreatening. Sad, poor people for the most part, with a few hoods, like Brim Houseman, thrown into the mix. Back in Philly, gangs of well-armed adolescents with hair-trigger tempers and no stopping point roamed the streets I worked.

"Guess I'll have to watch my back. Or stay in the car. Anyway, I miss you. I was hoping you'd stop by."

"Couldn't, but I have some time this afternoon."

"Can't do it. Tonight instead? At the Blue Skies?"

"I'll try, Carney, but I'm not promising. It's Saturday and I'm usually busy on Saturday nights."

◆

I check my phone after hanging up. Still no signal from the GPS unit on Vangi's car. The rain hasn't yet slackened, though I see brighter skies in the distance when I turn on the wipers. More roaming, more thinking. Ideas are fine, and I can easily imagine a sleek operation somewhere in the Gardens. But dreams, no matter how elaborate, don't come true without money and I don't have the money to build a casino. I'll need backers and just now the only backer in view is Ally McKinney.

Take money from Ally McKinney and you go from partner to employee in a hurry.

I let these thoughts hopscotch through my brain as I continue to search the streets. What I discover, for the most part, is misery, the homeless encampments especially. The tents are topped with pools of water and look ready to collapse, while huts made with bits and pieces of discarded lumber and plywood are far from waterproof. And what will these people do in December when the downpours are replaced with snow driven by a relentless western wind?

Pratt suggested napalm. Even under Bute Stafford, the city won't go that far. Drive them out of town? Where will they go? And where will the druggies in those shooting galleries go? From time to time, I see children playing on porches. Whose are they? How did they end up in the Gardens? The younger ones appear innocent, but for how long? The children of the poor grow up early, maturity forced upon them by the failures of the adults around them. The older kids, eleven or twelve, stare at me as I pass, their eyes betraying equal measures of hostility and distrust.

I finally turn north on Harmony Road, the only through north–south road in the neighborhood. Unlike Boomtown, mature trees mark every block here, leaving many of the homes in deep shadow. All to the good, but one thing's becoming obvious. Despite my ambitions, I'll never attract the clientele I want to these lower depths. The media, TV and print, offer terrifying descriptions of the Gardens. As if you took your life in your hands even driving along its streets. Bullshit, of course, but reputation is everything.

Early this morning, I did a Google search for Baxter city neighborhoods and a fifteen-minute YouTube video: "Welcome to Baxter." Its creator bore the name Harry Young, but it might have been a chamber of commerce booster film. So, yes, the video mentioned Oakland Gardens, but only displayed footage of the few developed blocks close to Baxter Boulevard. I remember laughing, but then I noticed that the northern end of the Gardens, though it narrowed and hooked to the west, extended beyond the construction zone to the border of Mt. Jackson, the most affluent neighborhood in Baxter.

◆

Imagine driving through an urban slum, along filthy streets, past abandoned stores, feral street dogs, the helpless, and the hopeless gathered on stoops and corners, listless, almost lifeless. Then suddenly, upon crossing a simple intersection, entering a middle-class neighborhood of large homes on generous well-tended lots. Now imagine most of those same homes empty, their windows dark, no cars in any driveway, no children playing outside, no parents carrying groceries through welcoming front doors.

Harmony Road had come to an abrupt finish against a thin line of trees that marked the boundary between town and farmland. The only turn was to the west along a narrow, unmarked street. A sign, new by the look of it, read NO TRESPASSING. I ignored it.

The homes I find are brick, some Colonial, some Tudor, some single-story ranch homes. Despite the rain, I can see at a glance that they're in good shape. These roofs will not leak.

The enclave covers about a square mile and there's only one road in and one road out. I stop for a moment, a moment too long as it turns out. A Baxter PD cruiser turns onto the block, flicks its siren on and off, finally pulls to the curb behind me.

I pull my FREE OUR POLICE card from the pocket of my denim shirt and lay it on the dash as two cops, old school by the look of them, walk up, one to my side of the car, the other to the passenger side. I let down the window, but keep both hands on the wheel.

"Driver's license and registration, please."

I haven't been told why I've been stopped and I'm not dumb enough to ask. I do notice the cop's eyes drop to the card on the dash. She's fairly young, probably in her late twenties, but she has the look of a veteran. Staying cool, maintaining control. Her name tag reads LARRIMORE.

Patrolwoman Larrimore takes my documents, but only glances at them before handing them back. "I stopped you because you're trespassing."

"Trespassing? I'm only looking for a place to rent."

"These are private roads, Mr. Carney. They're not open to the public."

"So, I need permission to enter this section of the city?"

"That would be correct, sir."

"Can you tell me from who?"

"I can't, but I will tell you to drive out the way you came in."

◆

I need to get back to the Blue Skies. There's a lot more to running my bar/casino than trying to look important. Both casino and bar should have been cleaned this morning by a pair of locals recommended to me by Zacariah. Did it happen? Was it thorough, or slipshod? And maybe there'll come a day when the Blue Skies includes enough storage to keep the bar stocked for days at a time. As it is, I need to restock every day. Zacariah will supervise, but I want to watch the operation, to meet the vendors and the delivery personnel. Just now, I'm totally dependent on Zacariah McBride, and I really, really hate being dependent.

Still, I decide to make one more pass along Carroll Street, the Gardens main drag, where I come upon Garden Groceries. A sign in the window offers sandwiches and I'm hungry enough to step inside. The offerings are meager, a scattering of groceries, including cans of refried beans, *chiles poblanos,* and tomatillos. A large freezer contains frozen chickens, ground beef, and sausages. A cooler is filled with beer and soda.

An elderly man stands in front of a small flattop grill behind the counter. His hair is long, gray and shaggy, but he's clean-shaven. Tattoos run up both arms including a Marine Corps bulldog. His blue eyes are small, with pronounced folds in the outer corners.

"How do," he says. "What can I get ya?"

I point to a pair of sausages on a corner of the grill. "Italian?"

"Chorizo. Lotta Mexicans in the Gardens. Far from home." He lays both hands on the counter. "You want, I can put one on a hot dog roll."

Ever the optimist, I ask, "And top it with *pico de gallo*?"

"Mustard or ketchup." A hesitation worthy of stand-up comic, then, "Or mayonnaise."

I settle for the ketchup, then introduce myself. "Tom Carney here. I run the Blue Skies in Boomtown."

"Which is?"

"A bar and casino. Just opened last night."

"Name's Ken. Ken Lawrence. What brings you to the Gardens?"

"Real estate."

"You lookin' for a new home?"

"Yeah, for my business. Someplace more private."

Ken forks the chorizo onto the untoasted hot dog roll, tops it with ketchup from a squeeze bottle, drops it onto a paper plate, and hands it over. "Ain't no lack of empty houses in the Gardens. Empty lots, too, if you're lookin' to build."

When I take a bite of the sandwich, the casing on the sausage cracks beneath my teeth, releasing the trapped juices inside. I stroll to the cooler and grab a can of Bud.

"I was just roamin' around, like at random, and I found this little area up north of here. Nice homes, well kept, but nobody livin' there. Then cops showed up and told me I was parked on a private road. Ran me off."

"I been up there, but I thought those blocks were in Mt. Jackson."

"Says Oakland Gardens on a map I used. Not that it matters. What caught my attention is that all those unoccupied houses were in very good condition. What with the housing shortage, they should be sold or rented out." I pull a twenty from my pocket to pay for my food. Ken takes the money and I wave off the change. "What you have to figure is that someone's got plans for those homes, and what I'd like to find out is who that someone is."

Ken slides the twenty into his shirt pocket. "I been livin' in Baxter my whole life, except when I was inside for a few years. Or maybe more than a few. There's only a few wheeler-dealers in this town. Rumor is they own Boomtown. Together, right? Man named George Temps is one, another could be Xavier Reade, and maybe Zack Butler. As for the properties that caught your attention, I couldn't say."

CHAPTER THIRTY-FOUR
CARNEY

I'm in the Blue Skies, sitting at the bar, a Coke, plenty of ice, and a wedge of lime in front of me. I did an inspection when I got here about an hour ago and found sticky spots on the bar top and streaks in the mirror behind the bar. Like someone had swiped a wet rag across the glass and walked away. I'm wasn't happy and I made my unhappiness known to Zacariah, who promised to speak with the agency that supplies the cleaning staff. That's not good enough for me, in part because I think we're paying too much.

Where to go? You can find house cleaners at the meat market on the northern end of Boomtown. Day workers, sure, but who's to say a crew couldn't be assembled? Cheaply. And if they're not in the country legally? I wonder how many of the millions of American households that hire non-natives to sweep and mop and mow their lawns ask for green cards? Or deduct Social Security payments from these workers' salaries?

And when you get right down to it, my little casino isn't legal to begin with. The tavern's tolerated, just like all those foreign-born housekeepers.

I reach for my phone as Zacariah walks away and quickly punch in Stu Harrington's cell number. The phone rings several times before he finally answers. I repeat my request for a meeting tomorrow morning, but follow up before he can turn me down.

"You want Overby? I can hand him over, Stu. Video and audio soliciting a bribe. Twice."

I think Stu wants to turn me down, but this is the offer he can't refuse. After a short pause, he mutters, "Early, goddamn it. Early."

◆

The bar's already up and running for the night, with maybe ten or twelve patrons enjoying their drinks, when the man seated two stools down points a finger at a small TV at our end of the bar.

"Hey, Brenda, you think we can take a look at the Cardinals game?"

We subscribe to the MLB channel, which allows us to watch any game in the country, but when Brenda presses the remote's power button, it's Bute Stafford's face that appears on the screen. He's praising the courage of a cop named Louis Abott. At the bottom of the shot, a legend reads FULTON FUNERAL HOME ASSASSINATION ATTEMPT.

It only takes a few minutes to gather the bare facts. Stationed inside a cornfield, an unidentified man fired six shots at our chief of detectives and our police commissioner as they stood alone on the porch of the Fulton Funeral Home. Inside, Rowan Krauss, a murdered police officer, lay in state. The shooter missed his prime targets, and though several rounds penetrated the funeral home's exterior and interior walls, no one inside the building was struck. Only the assassin failed to survive, killed by a police officer named Abott, in uniform at the time.

The accompanying video reveals a body lying between two rows of knee-high corn and little else. Attended by a pair of uniformed cops and a man I know to be our coroner, Arshan Rishnavata, the investigation is obviously ongoing. Seconds later, the piece turns to an earwitness, an unidentified worker at the funeral home who claims to be an avid hunter. Gunshots from a rifle came first, he tells the reporter. Four or five, he isn't sure. But he is sure that a few minutes later, he heard the deep boom of a shotgun, followed by silence.

◆

The station, KBAX, breaks for a commercial and everyone in the bar speaks at once, as though someone had thrown a switch. I don't participate. Instead, I step outside, away from the alcohol-fueled discussion. Questions pop into my brain, bounce around for a few minutes, then pop back out. First thing, the shotgun blast that killed the shooter occurred a few minutes after the shots were fired. So, how did Officer Abott get to the Fulton Funeral Home so fast? I'm not one of those cops who claim that coincidences don't exist. Instead, I try to calculate probabilities, and this one doesn't pass the stink test. First thing, the uniforms who responded to the shootings had to be close enough to actually hear the shots. Second, in some jurisdictions, shotguns are mounted between the front seats of patrol cars. In Baxter, they're in the trunk. That means the cop who killed the shooter heard the shots fired at Taney and Mariola, drove to the scene, instantly evaluated the circumstances, retrieved the shotgun, then fired off the fatal round. All in the space of a "few minutes."

As a casino owner, even newly minted, I can safely state that the odds against that particular sequence of events are astronomical.

Cut off the head and the body dies. Of course, the opposite is also true when it comes to human flesh. But I'm thinking just now that Overby, Steele, and Rawling must be very frightened. About what? Debbie Cole's my first thought, though I haven't been briefed on the investigation into Cole's murder. But if Mariola can make a solid case, whoever she accuses will have a strong incentive to cooperate.

My thoughts are interrupted when my neighbor Ernie, who runs the coin laundromat down the street, walks up.

"Hey, Carney."

"Ernie, how's business?"

"Not as good as it would be if I had space for another ten machines. But I'm gettin' along." Ernie's a small man, perpetually worried, like most of the Boomtown business owners I've been meeting. "This is bad, Carney," he tells me. "What happened at the funeral home. I'm tellin' you, the city's out of control. We gotta have new blood."

"Like Bute Stafford?"

"Yeah. You'll notice, he got to the scene before Mayor Venn. He'll put a stop to it." Ernie's mouth tightens. "By any means necessary."

I glance away to find Vangi coming to the rescue. She walks straight up, ignoring poor Ernie, and hugs me.

"Is that a gun in your pocket," she asks, "or are you just glad to see me?"

Vangi's got the gun part right, though it's in a holster and not in my pocket. "Both, Vangi. The gun and the glad."

She leans forward to whisper in my ear. "I have something you need to know. In private."

I lead her into the Blue Skies, and up to the bar. "You want anything?"

"A margarita?"

The rain stopped a couple of hours ago, but the air remains sultry. I've got fans going in the bar, but it's a bit too cool for the air-conditioning. Vangi's wearing a print dress, blue with tiny red flowers, very light, very summery. The dress isn't tight, nor does it appear expensive, but it drapes her body as though designed for her waist and hips. I walk behind her as she carries her drink through the casino to my office, admiring the view, as do most of the men in the casino.

"These chairs are hard on the butt," she says.

"Give me time. I'll do better." I punch a random key on my computer's keyboard and the monitor springs to life. "Need a minute here. Something I have to check on."

What I have to check on is the whereabouts of Vangi's car, assuming the GPS tracker's still working. It is, and I find her little Mustang in Mt. Jackson. I file the information away for later as I close the tracking software.

"So, is this about Overby?" I ask.

"Uh-uh. I told him what you said. That I asked about the burglary and you said no. I can't tell what he thought. The asshole's a hard read. But I haven't heard from him since. No, it's something else. I mean I'm not supposed to talk about it, but I like you Carney. Seriously, and this you really need to know." She sips at her drink, her eyes narrowing slightly, until she finally draws a deep breath. "I told you about this guy I'm seeing? You remember?"

"Sure."

"You didn't get jealous. I don't know what to make of that." She waves me off before I can make a comment. "Anyway, there's someone else I've been seeing. Like once every couple of weeks. That's where I've been." She stops there, maybe waiting for me to jump into the conversation. Only it's not a conversation. It's some kind of recital, maybe a confession, but whatever she's about doesn't need my input. "Okay, this man, he's really old. Like on oxygen, and he has a regular health aide and a visiting nurse who shows up three times a week. So, like, he can't do regular sex, or really any kind of sex. I do wear something sexy when I visit, maybe a microskirt, or an almost see-through blouse." She manages a small laugh. "But all we do is talk."

"And what's in it for you?" I finally open my mouth.

"A gentleman wouldn't ask that question."

"I'm glad we've settled the issue."

"Look, I wouldn't be talking about this because it's none of your business really. But last night he asked me to keep an eye on you. Like Overby."

"He knows who I am?"

"Worse, Carney. He knows you're a cop."

I can't keep the surprise off my face, not entirely. "Knows?"

"What he said was, 'Tom Carney's a cop.' Just like that. Like there wasn't any doubt."

"Did he say anything else?"

"Only that he wanted me to keep an eye on you. See, mostly what we do, me and Zack Butler, is talk. I mentioned you a couple of times, not knowing he'd have any interest."

"And who did you tell about the cop bullshit? Besides me?"

"Nobody, I swear. I mean I don't want any part of this. And I shouldn't even tell you."

"Then why have you?"

Vangi stands up, hesitates for a moment, then sits back down. "Can't I just like you? Can't that be what it's about?"

For the first time, I find a hint of vulnerability in Vangi's green eyes. I'm accustomed to a teasing confidence, the look of a woman who believes she's in control. No longer. She's opened the door just a sliver and I don't think either one of us is all that comfortable with the view inside. But I'm not ready to give her up, not even close. I reach across the desk and take her hand.

"I hear you, Vangi, and I believe you. Maybe I've grown so used to being . . . maybe not disliked, but hard to read. Like, keep this one at a distance because you have no idea what he's thinking." I give it a couple of beats, then ask, "Who's Zack Butler? This is the second time I've heard his name."

"Zack never talks about his business, not with me. But he lives in Mt. Jackson, in a big house, and most people think he owns a major piece of Boomtown. The land, right. And he did advise me to buy a house somewhere. Said it would be worth double five years from now."

"The bit about his having a piece of Boomtown, where does that come from?"

Vangi laughs. "Okay, I gotta fess up. It came from George Pratt, now deceased. But that's it, Carney. With Zack Butler, everyone has a theory, but nobody knows."

◆

I get an almost-commitment from Vangi to meet me at the trailer after I leave work tonight. Then I step out onto the sidewalk to greet customers as they enter. Gamblers or drinkers, it's all the same to me. I want my visitors to feel at home, to know that I value their business. Again, I'm struck by the vibrancy, the clean, positive energy given off by the men and women who crowd the bars and the restaurants. In Philly, you're always watching out. Everyone gets a look, a quick evaluation, even in neighborhoods like Rittenhouse Square with its upscale galleries, boutiques, and restaurants.

Not in Baxter, despite the media insisting there's a mugger lurking inside every shadow. The atmosphere is electric early on a Saturday, as it should be. The unemployment rate in Baxter is too small to measure. This is truly the city where everybody who wants a job can find one.

I keep it up for the next several hours, in and out, meeting vendors and salespeople, men and women, who want to supply something they're absolutely sure I can't do without. I take their business cards, shake their hands, listen at least briefly to the pitch. Most call me by name. Mr. Carney, if you can believe that. Toward eight o'clock, I head back inside, through a crowded bar and a busy casino to my office. I carry my dinner in a bag, Chinese food delivered by a restaurant on Baxter Boulevard.

I'm interrupted only once, by Sherri Utrecht, our cashier. Her basic job is to exchange chips for cash, or vice versa when someone leaves. Now she tells me that we're sitting on too much cash and I need to put some of it in the safe until needed. I don't argue the point because she's right, but wait until she leaves to open the safe.

More than likely, I'll be performing this task several times before the end of the night, with money moving in both directions. I know I can't be in the Blue Skies every night for the entire time it's open. That job belongs to Zacariah, who doesn't know the code to open the safe. Another problem.

◆

I've just tossed the remains of my dinner in the wastebasket when my door opens and Ally steps into the room, shortly followed by Mike Mulligan, who's not on his way home. Shortly followed by Stell and Crank.

"Sorry, boss," Crank says. "They got past us before we figured out where they were goin'. You want them out of here?"

I look from Ally to Mike Mulligan. Their whole attitude, from pushing their way into my office to lying about Mike Mulligan going home, is wrong for the neighborhood. But Ally can't help himself. The jerk has no plan B, which is why he'll ultimately fail. Mulligan's smirk is back, as is Ally's practiced twinkle. I begin to rise, activating the camera in the clock, then quickly settle back down.

"It's cool, guys. Give us some room."

"No problem. We'll be right outside."

I wait until the door closes, then motion for Ally to sit down.

"So, what brings you to my place of business?" Though far from friendly, my tone is more indifferent than confrontational.

"You wanna play hard . . ."

I stop him right there. "What you're doing? The same thing over and over? It's the definition of insanity. I'm not coming into the fold. You're never gonna control me. So, whatever comes next, let it come."

I watch his drinker's nose grow even redder. Leaning against the door, Mulligan's hands are in his pockets. I'm supposed to be intimidated, but a gunfight in the Blue Skies is off the table. The only way out is past a hundred witnesses.

"The cops found us," Ally tells me.

"Lemme guess. A sergeant named Overby."

"How the fuck you know that?"

"I'm payin' a tax, Ally. To the Baxter Police Department. Overby's the bagman. He collects." I push my chair away from the desk and stretch my arms. "You were dumb. Where you came to ground in the Hilton? Except for the cleaners, every single worker's a local. That includes the hotel's security. So, when hoods from Philly show up, they notice. Your fantasy about being just another face in the crowd was just that, a fantasy. Plus, they already knew about my connection to the Sean Carney crew. Overby asked me, point blank, if I was here on my own, or as an advance scout. That's before you showed up."

"You finished?" He waits a moment, then says. "First thing, Overby likes the idea of one organization working the dark side of the street. Reliable, cooperative. That's what they want. In the long run, anyway."

"They'll bleed you dry."

"Why don't you let me worry about that?"

"Why don't you tell me what you want? Or better yet, tell me what Overby wants, being as he's a nothing-for-nothing kind of guy."

Ally runs his hand over his hair, smoothing it down, only to have it pop back up when he moves his hand away. He looks around for a moment, then his eyes return to mine. "They want someone hit. A cop."

"They tried that already. This afternoon, Ally. It didn't work." Again, I'm struck by the apparent desperation. Rawling, Steele, Overby. Their game is falling apart. "A free piece of advice? No strings attached? When Overby and his running dogs, Chief of Patrol Rawling and Lieutenant Steele, go down, they're gonna take you with them."

Ally's eyes harden. No more twinkle. "The name of the target is Stepanik. He's a street cop and he lives in a small house in Coombs County. I'm talkin' about cow country, nobody livin' within a mile of the place. And get this, he had a girlfriend stayin' at the house, her and her kid, but she walked away more than a month ago. He's livin' alone, Carney. It's a fuckin' gift."

Stepanik's the cop who beat my ass after the incident at Benny Kaplan's and I have to believe he's tied to Cole's death. Rawling and the crew made an attempt to short-circuit the overall investigation, but they failed. Now they want to eliminate the weak link.

"Why don't you do it yourself, Ally? Why come to me?"

"We ain't been here long enough to know players or the terrain. But you could get out there while Stepanik's on patrol. You could be waitin' for him when he comes home." He points a finger in my general direction. "Bang, gone, over and out. And don't tell me you're too good for it. You took out at least two men in Philly."

True enough, but self-defense isn't murder. "Whatta ya say we do the bottom line? What's in it for me?"

"Ten large."

"Payable when?"

"After it's done."

I shake my head. "Nope. I'm not sayin' I'll do it, but if I take the job, I want fifteen. Half up front."

CHAPTER THIRTY-FIVE
DELIA

I've just witnessed what I believe to be a murder. I don't know the name of the victim, or why he tried to kill Vern Taney, or who sent him. I'm sure that he failed, though, because Vern's car, with him behind the wheel, is fast approaching. The murderer is a cop named Abott. He's tall and broad with a narrow head bisected by a thin sharp nose and muddy brown eyes that project his confusion. Like he doesn't know how he came to be standing next to me with a discharged shotgun in his hand, though it had seemed like a good idea at the time.

I tap a finger against his chest as he begins to move in the general direction of his victim's body. "Stay off my crime scene."

Abott lifts his chin. "He had a gun. I saw a gun."

"Save it for the statement you'll be giving. And I'm going to remind you, right now, that the department allows you to remain silent until you've consulted an attorney."

I don't wait for a reply as I turn and make my way across the ditch and over a low-hanging strand of the barbed wire fence. Unintimidated by my advance, a small flock of crows, carrion birds, drop onto the field a dozen yards from the fallen man. The vultures won't be far behind. I pass between parallel rows of knee-high corn, my eyes focused on the unmoving body. I didn't see a gun, except for the rifle dropped before the man fled, but I'm not taking any chances.

I needn't have bothered. The entry wound high on his back is wide open, revealing his severed spine. I don't see an exit wound because he's fallen straight down onto his stomach and chest. I want to leave the scene undisturbed, but I can't ignore the bulge of a wallet in his back pocket. I pull it free, then carefully retrace my steps.

By the time I get back to the road, Vern has taken charge. Patrolman Abott, no longer smiling, leans back against the cruiser. I hear Vern's voice as I approach. My boss is angry, but appears unshaken.

"Leave the shotgun where it is. I'm ordering you to report to headquarters and remain there until I personally authorize your release. You will surrender your weapon and be placed on administrative leave pending an investigation. Now, do you have anything you want to say?"

"I saw a gun. He had a gun."

Vern looks over at me, but when I shake my head, he turns to Patrolman Abott's partner, a twentysomething named Youngman. "Take what you need from the trunk and close off this street. From intersection to intersection."

From intersection to intersection covers a distance of about three hundred yards, but Youngman doesn't argue. He pops the trunk and gets busy.

I think I know what Vern's about. Youngman, though not the shooter, and who appears not to have drawn his weapon, is still an important witness. When, for example, was the shotgun taken from the trunk? How did they get here so fast? Separating the two men before they coordinate their accounts is par for the course. And while Abott's protected by an officer-involved shooting procedure, Youngman is not.

Youngman unloads crime scene tape, a box of nitrile gloves, and an evidence-collection kit, then closes the trunk. Abott moves to get in, but Vern stops him. "The vehicle is part of the crime scene. It stays where it is."

"How am I supposed to get back to the house?"

"Right at this moment, I don't care if you fly. Just get the fuck away from me."

◆

Finished with Abott, Vern shifts his attention to me. "You can't run the investigation, Delia. I'll assign it myself. I want you to return to the house and write up a report, then wait for me. We'll go see Tommy together."

Tommy is Tommy Atkinson, our district attorney. Bad news for Patrolman Abott, who's looking more and more forlorn. Maybe he's beginning to understand just how deep a hole he's dug for himself. I think the plan called for Abott to show up while Vern was receiving medical attention (or, maybe, last rites). He never expected me to beat him to the scene, or for the shooter to throw his rifle away and take off running.

I'm more or less obliged to hand the shooter's wallet over to Vern, but not before I take a peek at his driver's license. I find

Edward Smith's photo predictably fuzzy, and his address, in the Coombs County town of Attica, is of no help. I finally pass the wallet to Vern and turn away.

◆

Being the humanitarian I am, I offer Abott a ride back to the house. He sniffs once, suspecting a trap I'm sure he'll fall into, then resigns himself.

"Yeah, thanks."

My phone rings as I'm opening the door on the driver's side. It's Marcia Blackstone, my part-time assistant. It takes me a moment to remember that I tasked her with checking the DNA profiles of all new department hires over the last year. Still outside, I close the door and step away as I answer.

"Marcia, what's up?"

"I finished that review." She's almost whispering. "So, yes, we have a profile for every new hire. But it's, like, not always the same."

"The same as what?"

"Like, if the applicant already has a profile in CODIS, say if they were cop somewhere else, we download it into our own database. If not, we do the profile ourselves."

I glance over the field, my gaze finally centering on Edward Smith's body. "You checked the files individually, that right?"

"Each and every one."

"Did you happen to notice the file on a cop named Al Stepanik?"

Now it's Marcia's turn to pause. "Like, I'm not a hundred percent sure. Maybe ninety percent. But I remember he came to us from some sheriff's department. I can't tell you the county or even the state."

"So, you would have uploaded his DNA profile?"

"If I'm right, yeah. We upload to our own servers and also print out a copy for our files."

"Great work, Marcia. Really great. But I need you to keep this to yourself. Don't even tell your parrot."

"I don't have a parrot, but I get it, captain. No slip of this girl's lip."

◆

I take my time driving back to the house, first past the Fulton Funeral Home where several people stand outside, including Rowan Krauss's wife. She doesn't wave and I face forward as I come by. Abott sits beside me, his tiny mouth now pursed, as if he's about to cry. I can't blame him.

Everything went wrong for Abott and his pals. I'm speculating here, but there's only one line that makes sense. Edward Smith was hired to kill Vern Taney. Abott was tasked with killing Smith while he still possessed the rifle. Smith missed, and not because he was a bad shot. He missed thanks to a pimp named Brim Houseman who warned me of the upcoming assassination attempt. Now Abott's shot an unarmed, fleeing man. He won't be arrested immediately. That will come after a grand jury indictment. The investigation, on the other hand, has already started.

I can feel Abott's discomfort. He needs to speak, but he can't. Instead, the pressure's building. The fingers of his right hand, resting on his knee, are trembling. As for myself, I'm trying not to laugh. Men and women on probation or parole, facing a drug test, will commonly smuggle clean urine into the testing room. Stepanik's DNA profile was first recorded at some unknown sheriff's department where he might easily have substituted a swab from somebody else's cheek. Somebody whose DNA wouldn't appear in any database, a category that includes more than 90 percent of the American people. His reason? His own DNA was already stored in the CODIS database, and not in a category that would facilitate his working in law enforcement.

I admit that I'm jumping to conclusions. True, Stepanik had contact with Debbie Cole on a regular basis. True, he acted as a semi-pimp, driving her to some unknown encounter. That doesn't mean that he killed her. That job could have been handed to someone else. But Stepanik's the cop who put a beating on Tom Carney even though Carney offered no resistance. So . . .

"Whatta you think's gonna happen next?" This from my companion, spoken softly.

"An investigation, obviously. You shot an unarmed man."

Abott's head swivels back and forth. "He had a gun. I saw a gun."

"Uh-uh. No gun. His hands were empty, not even a cell phone. And by the way, I could see his spine through the hole in his back. Completely severed. Damn good shooting, officer. Damn good." I pull to a stop at a light. We're only a few blocks from headquarters. "You need to become more focused on the practical. Why was the shotgun in your hands when you pulled up, and not in the trunk? And why did you ignore the presence of a superior officer with her own weapon drawn? And why, even if he was armed, did you shoot him in the back as he fled?"

Abott has nothing more to say and I wait until we're parked and he's opening the door to get in one last message. "When you finally figure it out, when you finally realize there's only one way forward, reach out to me. I'll be waiting."

◆

Due diligence, my trademark. I spend the next two hours writing a report that begins with an offhand remark by an arrestee named Brim Houseman, and finish with Ed Smith's body in a cornfield. I leave nothing out, though I'm careful to use the emotionless language, sequence by sequence, beloved of cops everywhere. By the time I finish, I know the investigation has been assigned to Detectives O'Malley and Meacham. I don't care for Meacham's inclusion, at best he's a reliable errand boy. But no one's asking for my opinion. As a material witness, I have to leave the grunt work to others.

That doesn't mean I can't, as the chief of detectives, ask for routine progress reports, or meet with the team. Which I will, in time.

CHAPTER THIRTY-SIX

DELIA

Toward six o'clock, I attend a meeting with Tommy Atkinson that includes Patrick O'Malley and Vern. By now, much of the preliminary work has been done, and the most salient fact, that Edward Smith was unarmed, well established. The man was shot in the back by a slug from a 12-gauge shotgun fired by Patrolman Abott.

I mostly keep my big mouth shut. My report speaks for itself, and my credibility isn't hurt when Vern insists that I saved his life. There's no evidence to support the assertion, but the fact that I pushed him to one side isn't in dispute.

"And you did this on the basis of an offhand remark by a pimp?" Tommy already knows the answer because he's scanned my report. He now wants to hear a few of the thrilling details firsthand. In my experience, prosecutors are often cop-wannabes.

"When we walked onto the porch, I looked around and noticed something out of place. A van parked in a cornfield. If not for Houseman's tip, I might have dismissed it. As it was, I took a closer look and saw a man with a rifle. That was enough for me to react."

By now, we've got a preliminary report on Ed Smith. A hero marine who earned a Silver Star in the first Iraq War, he'd fallen apart after he came home. This is a story I've heard many times over the years. Which came first, his descent into a serious crystal meth addiction or the dissolution of his marriage, is unknown. What is known is that shortly after the divorce became final, his wife took herself and their two children to Spokane. Also known are a series of arrests, for possession or the sale of small amounts of methamphetamine. Smith received probation four times, until a judge got sick of his inevitable return to her courtroom. Two years later, released from prison, he returned to the druggie life. A series of arrests and short sentences followed, mostly to the county jail in Revere, until his last arrest for operating a meth lab.

Tommy's hands are flying about, as always when he's the center of attention. "That doesn't connect him to Patrolman Abott or any of the others. But I agree with Delia. Abott could only have gotten to the scene that fast if he was waiting somewhere close by, ready to go. I'm going to open a grand jury investigation on Monday. And you, Vern, you need to have your ducks in a row."

"We've been installing GPS units in the older cars for the past month. Abott was driving one of them. The data's being downloaded as we speak. As for his partner, Jim Youngman. He refused to give us a statement, although he's not a suspect. I'm hoping he'll come around. Doesn't really matter, though." Vern nods at me. "The unit's dashboard camera verifies Delia's account. Abott's looking at life in prison. I have a strong feeling that he'll try to cut a deal once he's indicted."

◆

The meeting continues for another hour, until we're going around in circles. The lead detective, Patrick O'Malley, the most important player in the room, isn't consulted until the end of the meeting. No surprise, O'Malley has his investigation in hand. Everyone present at the Fulton Funeral Home has been interviewed, despite having little to offer. The trajectories of the bullets that penetrated the building have been established. The rifle and the spent cartridges found in the van are with the state police lab, undergoing analysis. Edward Smith's family, a brother and a father, have been notified, and Detective Meacham is running down his friends and acquaintances. Thus far, Smith's cell phone, if he had one, has yet to be discovered. It wasn't found on his person or in the van.

Does any of this matter? Unless Edward Smith blabbed to his friends, probably not. More important, does any of this matter to Patrolman John Abott? He'll claim he saw a gun and fired in self-defense, but it won't fly. Smith was running away when he was shot in the back. I know because I was there.

◆

I gradually put these thoughts away as I travel home, hopefully in time for my lover's pumpkin ravioli. Abott's not my problem anyway. Stepanik's my problem and I don't intend to worry about him until Monday morning, the day after tomorrow. Danny's game, postponed today, will start tomorrow at one o'clock. I expect to be there, if not cheering my head off, at least encouraging little Emmaline to act as my surrogate.

I don't have to worry about Emmaline because she's in the house when I come through the door, along with Danny's best pal, Mike Taney. The table's set, with a huge salad already laid out. I accept multiple hugs, every one of which I need, before we sit down.

Zoe gives the blessing. More and more now, she's become the mom. Danny's mom and whatever stray happens to show up for a meal. I'm too hungry at the moment to care all that much. I wait my turn as Danny serves Emmaline. He and Mike embraced her after she was rescued from a burning house, and her adoption by the Taneys hasn't altered the fundamentals. Personally, I think Emmaline should spend more time with kids her own age, but I'm not prepared to say it out loud. Minorities of one must know when to keep their mouths shut.

The salad's a little masterpiece on its own. Wedges of orange, toasted walnuts, and crumbled Gorgonzola cheese. The pumpkin ravioli's even better. I'd been expecting to bite into a big blob of pumpkin, but the pumpkin's been mixed with ricotta and the pasta is pillow soft and chewy at the same time. Flavored with garlic and sage, the sauce does a break dance over my palate. Even Danny's impressed, and the proud smile on Gretchen's face is enough to melt this hard-ass heart.

After dinner, the kids prove they're still kids by tuning into a Godzilla vs. Kong movie. That leaves Zoe and me to step outside. Our porch is just large enough for a two-seat swing and we sit with our arms thrown across each other's shoulders.

"Been that bad?" Zoe asks.

"You can tell?"

"You look like you're ready to collapse."

"Beat up and beat down?" I wait a moment, but Zoe has nothing to say. She's waiting for me to unburden, but there's no escape from this burden. "Say you're putting a puzzle together, one piece at a time. With most jigsaw puzzles, there's only one possible outcome. If you persist, you'll eventually get it right. But what if there's two possibilities? Or three? What if the fate of your city depends on getting it right? The good guys are on a roll at the moment, but I can't allow myself the luxury of making one or two arrests, then reading about my exploits in the *Baxter Bugle*."

"Delia, you're acting like the whole department's on its way to being corrupt. That's pretty far out there."

"You think so? In the past, entire departments in major cities like New York and Chicago were systematically corrupt. In New York, they called it the pad. So much for patrol, so much for sergeants and lieutenants and captains right up the ladder. And even now, sheriffs control law enforcement in small counties. As the sheriff goes, so goes the county."

"Like in Coombs County?"

"There ya go."

Coombs County lies south of Baxter. One or another member of the Judson family's been elected sheriff for more than fifty years. And it's no surprise that the shooter this afternoon, Edward Smith, lived in Coombs County. Word is that Edson Judson, who currently wears the badge, gets a piece of any illegal activity. As a direct result, more than half the crystal meth we find in our city begins life in Coombs County.

CHAPTER THIRTY-SEVEN

DELIA

My small front yard isn't much. Danny mows the lawn and I've planted a bed of yellow irises, now in full bloom. My two rose bushes are a couple of weeks from blossoming but covered with buds. Homely is the right word, or maybe homey. Still tired, I now feel almost at peace as I look forward to a night with Zoe, breakfast in the morning, then Danny's makeup game. A full day, leisurely, leisurely, leisurely.

Then I remember Stu and Tom Carney and Carney's insistence on a meet. Tomorrow morning. He's promising to deliver Thrace Overby and I have to show up.

"Something wrong?" Zoe asks.

"Yeah, I just remembered. I have to drive out to Revere County tomorrow morning."

"Have to?"

"One of those puzzle pieces I've been talking about. Too important to ignore. But I shouldn't be more than a couple of hours. For sure, I intend to be back in time for Danny's game. I'd walk away from . . ."

I break off as a sedan, a small VW, comes slowly past the house before parking a few houses up. A figure emerges, a woman wearing a dark hoodie, black or navy, with the hood pulled over her head. I'm guessing she's trying to disguise herself, but that's really not an option when you're nearly six feet tall.

It's Gianni Vetto, and only as she approaches do I remember her standing next to me before Rowan Krauss's coffin. She'd slipped a folded piece of paper into my pocket. And shortly afterward forgotten altogether.

"Speak to you, captain?"

I make eye contact with Gianni and hold it. "Zoe, this is patrol officer Gianni Vetto. I need to speak with her for a moment."

Gianni stares at me for a few seconds, then nods to Zoe. "Nice to meet you." She looks back at me until I stand and lead her back toward her car. "You didn't show up tonight."

"I had other things on my mind." I'm not in the mood to coddle Gianni, or to apologize, or to wait until we get into her car. She was at the funeral home when Edward Smith fired off those shots. "So, let's hear it."

"No, in the car. I can't be seen with you." Her hands go to her hips, leaving me to look into a pair of dark eyes made darker by the deepening twilight.

"All right, but this better be good."

Gianni opens the back door, then piles in after me. I don't know what she has to say, but I'm sure it puts her at serious risk should it come to light. I soften my tone, suddenly a cop again.

"All right, Gianni. Sorry for being so short. What's up?"

Gianni slumps down in the seat, then begins to speak. "I've been working with the other women on patrol. Organizing, you might call it. Remember, they ride with the asshole brigade, so they see things you'll never see." She pauses long enough to cross her legs. "I was hoping they witnessed one of their partners taking a bribe, but if that's happening, they're keeping it private. What they have seen, though, is police brutality. Almost routine, right? And not necessarily in front of witnesses."

"Except for your witnesses."

"Yeah, except for them."

"So, why haven't they come forward?"

"Two reasons. First, they're scared. Second, who do they approach? They don't trust their bosses, like Sergeant Overby, and they don't trust you, either." The words are coming fast now. "What they planned to do is quit. And why not? There's no place for them to go in this department and they're being propositioned on every tour. But like I said, I've been meeting with a few women cops. Privately, real privately." Finally, a pause long enough for her to draw a deep breath. "What they decided to do, when they were driving units with dashcams, was position the cams to capture the abuse. I'm talking about prisoners in cuffs. Slapped, punched, sometimes kicked."

"How many?"

"Five, all different."

Is this a big deal? Maybe after we handle Debbie Cole's killer. And Edward Smith's, too. Prosecuting cop violence is tricky in any event. Elected district attorneys like Tommy Atkinson want no part of these prosecutions, and that's especially true when the political opposition is screaming about our high crime rate. On the other hand, they can be quickly fired.

"Take statements if you can, including the call number of the units with the dashcams, dates, and times of occurrence, and the names and ranks of the cops on the video. Give whatever you get to me. I'm going to sit on it initially, and I want to make sure it stays private."

We sit there for a minute, listening to a dog barking inside a home at the end of the street. The barking is deep and punctuated by snarls. An intruder trying to force entry? Or a raccoon walking through the backyard? To a dog, it doesn't make much difference.

"They're scared, captain. After Rowan and the attempt on you and the commissioner . . ."

"We're all worried, Gianni. And what you've done, it's superior police work. If we get through this, you'll wear that detective's badge. But we have to get through it. I plan to hit the asshole brigade so hard, and from so many directions, they won't have time to organize a response. Now, if you don't have anything to add, I want to get back to the family I haven't seen all week."

CHAPTER THIRTY-EIGHT

DELIA

The sun's been up for less than an hour when I head off to Stu's home in Revere County. The night, once Gianni drove away, was everything I'd been needing. A two-tiered chocolate ice cream cake from Cunning Confections provided the dessert we ate after watching a movie. *Godzilla vs. Kong* hadn't lived up to its name. By the end of the film, the two enemies had become frenemies, just in time to overcome the evil forces arrayed against them. With the help of another monster, this one named Mothra.

Only a few hours before, I'd stared at the severed spine of a man who tried to assassinate Vern. Or, maybe, me. Perhaps that's why I couldn't summon up the slightest concern for the fates of Kong, Godzilla, and Mothra. But I could bathe in the atmosphere. Real life, not blood, not sudden death or wasted lives or battered women or abused boys. Nope. Real life is Godzilla vs. Kong. Much better. Much, much better.

The atmosphere held when I drove Gretchen and Emmaline to their respective homes. Both sat in the back, with Emmaline asleep on Gretchen's shoulder as Gretchen discoursed on her next culinary triumph. The secret, she explained after escorting Emmaline to the door, is Asian pear juice. When I asked about the difference between pear juice and Asian pear juice, she looked over at me.

"Asian pear juice is made from Asian pears."

At that point, I had the good sense to keep my ignorant mouth shut. I did not, though tempted, ask, "What is an Asian pear?"

◆

Danny was in his bedroom when I got home. Dimly, I heard the cheers of a crowd through the closed door. I'd bought him an MLB subscription for his birthday that allows him to watch any game in the country on his laptop. There are times I regret the gift, but not tonight. Zoe leads me into the bedroom, then turns for a first kiss that stretches on and on. No hurry, now, despite its being way too long. No hurry thirty minutes later when we shower together before returning for a long cuddle that eventually leads to a second shower.

Nights like the last compensate for the wasted lives, for the murders, for the overdoses, for the battered women and children. They do not, however, make rising at six in the morning on your theoretical day off a pleasant experience. I like to think of myself as Suck-It-Up Delia Mariola, but I'm having a hard time. And the weather isn't making it easier. The sun's been up for an hour and now dances in and out of sight behind rapidly retreating clouds. To the west, the blue skies appear as slick as satin. A perfect day for a high school baseball game. Especially if your son's scheduled to start.

And maybe it's not a bad day to visit a farm. Stu's outside by the chicken coop when I pull up. He waves to me, then opens the coop and begins to toss some kind of feed onto the grass. I watch the chickens emerge, one at a time, heads bobbing, wary despite Stu's presence. Maybe that's just the way it has to be when you're dinner for every predator in the neighborhood. But they go straight for their breakfast and I flash on what should have been obvious. The need to sustain themselves is exactly what makes them vulnerable.

"Mornin', captain."

"Mornin', Stu. Everybody else asleep?"

"So far. Look, I've got coffee going in the kitchen. Let me bring it onto the porch while we wait for our insistent undercover."

"You think he has something real?"

"Delia, there's times when I think he's smarter than both of us. I can't read him and I never trust people I can't read. Not entirely. But he claims he can deliver Overby, so . . ."

◆

Tom Carney rolls up fifteen minutes later. He's carrying a laptop and what appears to be a digital clock as he comes up the steps. We exchange the mandatory good mornings, then Stu nods at the clock with its dangling plug.

"You need an outlet for that?"

"No. I've already uploaded the data. But the camera that recorded the data is inside the clock and I wanted you to see it. I have a tiny office at the back of the Blue Skies . . ."

My turn now. I'm far from comfortable with the crimes being committed by a member of the Baxter Police Department. "Your casino, I assume."

"I think I'm more like a squatter, the way it came to me. But I knew somebody from the goon squad would turn up. I've been spending time on the street, speaking with other business owners. Payoffs are pretty much universal, even when businesses are legit. Or semi-legit, which is key. See, no Boomtown business has the required permits because the land they sit on has no legitimate address. They can be shut down without notice unless they pay off."

From inside the house, I hear a young girl's outraged voice. "That's mine. Give it back." A second later, a woman's voice, Momma's I assume, sounds out. "Stop teasing your sister."

Stu tugs at the end of his mustache. "We're gonna need privacy. Let's take it around back."

He heads off with me and Carney trailing behind. I'm still pissed off. Back when Carney was being recruited, I demanded that he not commit any crimes without consulting me first. He nodded agreement, but he never intended to comply. He's sitting pretty now, running his own little gold mine, almost daring me to do something about it.

Stu leads us to a large shed at the back of the lawn. There's a padlock on the door that he opens with a key. A glance inside explains the lock. Tools hang on the walls, including sharp-edged saws and awls that could pass for ice picks. A garden tractor at the back is surrounded by attachments, mower blades, a snowplow, and a harrow with sawtooth blades. This is a no-kids zone if I've ever seen one.

Carney sets the laptop on a long workbench, opens it, and turns it on. I read confidence in his movements as a familiar tingle builds in my temples. I still don't trust Carney. I'm still thinking I made a mistake hiring him. At the same time, I know that whatever he's got, it's gonna be exactly what we need to put the screws to somebody.

"I didn't run the camera all the time," he explains. "Mainly because storage capacity on the chip is limited. So, I had a switch hidden beneath my desk that I could activate with my right knee. I was outside when Overby approached me. I suggested we go back to my office where it was private and he agreed. I closed the door after he entered, sat down behind my desk, and immediately activated the recorder inside the clock."

◆

I insist on watching the video twice, then a third time. I'm looking for any nuance, but there's none to be found. I'm tempted to say that Overby solicited a bribe, but that's not entirely accurate. With almost every word issuing from Overby's mouth, I become more certain that I can charge him with extortion, a far more serious crime.

"You ready for part two?" Carney asks.

I don't know if I'm exactly ready, but Carney taps a key and off we go. Overby again, returning for a separate bite of the apple. And Carney basically telling him to go fuck himself.

"How did you pull it off?" Stu wants to know. "How did you convince them to trust you."

"Simple enough. I worked for Benny Kaplan, worked for George Pratt, kicked some ass, and got my own ass kicked by a pair of cops and never complained." He scratches the back of his neck for a moment. "Arrogance, too. I don't know how long

Overby's been the bagman for whoever's running the show, but they've been at it long enough to feel above the law. Like they can't be touched."

I have enough to arrest Overby right now. Can I turn him? Will he take the whole charge on himself? And what about his regular driver? What can he tell us?

"I want you to take the clock back to your little tavern and set it up again. Write a full report, in longhand. I'm going to take the laptop back to my office and lock it up. But . . ."

Carney brings me to halt. "There's more, captain. Much more."

"Tell me."

"The Irish Mafia, as they like to call themselves, has come to Baxter. How many? I don't know, but it can't be all that many because the Irish mob in Philadelphia doesn't amount to more than a modest crew. They've been forced out, at least the way they told it to me, by mobs and gangs of every color and nationality. Baxter is where they see their future."

"And they came to you?"

My tone's abrupt, but Carney only smiles. "All disclosed, captain. My relationship with my uncle, Sean Carney, now in prison, and my connections to the Kensington Group, as they also like to call themselves. Before you hired me."

My quest for an undercover is sounding more like be careful what you wish for. Still, the man's come through. Overby's finished. I could arrest him today, and maybe I will. Overby's a middle rung on a ladder that I'm sure has Colton Steele and Saul Rawling perched on the top rungs.

"All right, Carney, let's see what you've got."

Carney advances the video, then pauses the data as two men walk into his office, shortly followed by two more.

"The older guy is Aloysius McKinney, called Ally. The other is Mike Mulligan. You can think of him as a debt collector. The pair behind them work security in the Blue Skies. My employees."

That said, Carney hits play and the video advances. Carney sends his employees from the room first. Then McKinney orders Mulligan to leave. He complies after shooting Carney what I'd call a withering glance. Carney doesn't wither. In fact, I can't detect any emotion as he pushes back against McKinney's bullying attitude. Neither can McKinney, apparently, because he doesn't respond to Carney's insolence, but continues on, dropping the proposition in Carney's lap. There's a cop in the Baxter Police Department that other cops want to kill.

I'm expecting to hear Vern's name at the end, or even my own. So much for my cop instincts. Debbie Cole's killer, Al Stepanik, is a lot more to the point. And there's no doubt now. I don't know what evidence Rowan Krauss managed to accumulate, and I'll probably never know. There's no getting into his laptop without the password, and too many false entries will lock it up for good. I'm told that federal agencies have tricks unknown to the rest of law enforcement, but they're only employed in cases where our national security is threatened. So sorry, obscure jurisdiction.

◆

The video shuts down and except for a mumbled "Shit" from Stu, we fall into a momentary silence. I'm struck by Carney's noncommittal response to McKinney's request. And by McKinney's casual mention of two men slain by Carney in Philadelphia. Carney disclosed both killings when I interviewed him, but

I didn't leave it there. I checked back with his superiors in Philadelphia. Both were justified, line-of-duty homicides investigated by shooting boards. That, apparently, was far from the impression on the street. No, Carney has played the game beautifully since he arrived in our little city. Working for a pair of gangsters, Pratt and Benny Kaplan, operating a completely illegal bar-casino, and now a two-time killer. And killer is the right word, justified or not.

"Stepanik lives in town," I finally say. "Not on a farm in Coombs County."

Carney doesn't hesitate. The man has an answer for everything. "Captain, the only thing I know about Stepanik is that he and his partner went out of their way to kick my ass after I was arrested at Benny's. I didn't hold it against them at the time, and I don't now. Meanwhile, I need instructions. Tell me what you want me to do."

CHAPTER THIRTY-NINE

DELIA

Our strategy session would likely be more productive if I'd been forthcoming about Patrolman Al Stepanik. Carney doesn't ask me why Overby wants Al Stepanik eliminated and I choose to keep my theories to myself for the moment. But I hardly doubt that Carney's already figured it out.

One item, though, we did settle. Carney's intelligence is of little use unless we explain—to our district attorney, to the judge hearing the case, and to a jury—exactly how we acquired it. That means Carney will have to come in from the cold. His response, when I put it to him, is exasperating, though it comes as no surprise.

"I work for you, captain. I'm good either way."

That's enough for me, and all I'm likely to get. I leave it there and head for Goldman High's baseball field. Beyond the six or seven uniformed cops scattered about, I discover the usual suspects sitting on the Goldman side of the field. The Taneys with their kids, Emmaline and Cora. Zoe with Gretchen seated beside her. Danny hasn't thrown a pitch yet. He's warming up on the right side of the field. I wave and he flashes me a quick smile. Enough.

Vern Taney interrupts me as I head for my seat. "I'm glad you got here before the game started. I received a call this morning from an attorney named Eustis Prout, now representing Jim Youngman. Youngman wants to come in this afternoon."

Youngman was partnered with John Abott when Abott killed Edward Smith. Should he open up, I've no doubt he can put his buddy in a cage.

"He's prepared to give a statement?"

Vern shakes his head. "Prout wouldn't commit. Even after I explained that should Youngman fail to answer our questions, he'll be suspended without pay. On the spot." A slight hesitation, then, "I'd like a briefing before Youngman arrives."

I don't argue the point, though I can surely use the time off. But there's Carney's revelations, too, and we need to develop a cohesive strategy. Should we hold fire until we have enough to make a mass arrest? Blow Rawling and his team apart, one piece at a time?

"All right, Vern, I'll be there."

◆

I haven't taken two steps when my phone rings. It's Patrick O'Malley, the primary detective investigating yesterday's shooting. Edward Smith, the shooter, Pat tells me, has a long record and was out on bail, charged with possession of crack cocaine with intent to sell.

"A sad story, captain, but one we've heard before. Three tours, two in Afghanistan, one in Iraq. Diagnosed with PTSD and blast damage from his posting to an artillery unit. He held it together while he was active but fell apart once he was discharged. After his wife left, he went back to his parents' house. Then his father passed, and his mother kicked him out because he wouldn't stop stealing."

"Any idea who approached him?"

"Not so far, but get this. Smith was caught running a meth lab in the Gardens. By street cops who were dispatched to investigate an altercation of some kind. When Youngman answered the door, they smelled marijuana inside and one thing led to another. Now, here's the good part, captain. I checked in our evidence room and the crystal, three ounces, is missing. The paraphernalia's still there, but not the drugs."

◆

The game, finally the game. I turn my phone off, knowing I need to make myself available, but not giving a damn. The rewards begin early when Danny strikes out the first three batters and Mike Taney hits a two-run homer in the bottom of the inning. Emmaline's beside herself, her hazel eyes astonished, her laughs and her grins contagious. And Gretchen's not that far behind. She folds her hands on every pitch Danny tosses. The stakes are high and Gretchen knows it. One thing about scouts, you can always spot them. They're middle-aged, male, and huddle together at the far end of the stands. Two of the three currently watching wear narrow-brimmed fedoras, the other a beige Kangol cap.

Zoe takes my hand as the seventh inning begins. "Whatta ya think, love? Does the real world have any appeal?"

"I wish I could bathe in it, Zoe. Just wander into the maze and never find my way out. Sometimes I think about leaving the job. You remember Blanche Weber?" Blanche paid a big part in taking down a serial killer whose real name still isn't known.

"Yeah, sure."

"She left the force and opened a private security business. I ran into her a couple of weeks ago and she told me that running a business was less than fun. The bills chase the earnings, with the possibility of a cash crunch at the end of every month. But her hours are close to regular and she's home with her husband almost every night and no one's shooting at her. I feel . . ."

Zoe stops me with a laugh. "Uh-uh. Sitting behind a desk, wondering if the next check will be large enough to keep you afloat? I'm not seein' it. But you do owe yourself a vacation. Why don't we take off while Danny's at baseball camp? Just the two of us."

The worst thing about a conscience is having a conscience. There are moments when I almost envy psychopaths and the simplistic lives they lead. Just a few days ago, Gretchen asked me if she could still come over while Danny's in camp. I'd not only agreed, I'd hugged her close. So . . . so I could suggest that we take Gretchen with us, but I'm pretty sure that's not what Zoe has in mind.

I let Zoe's suggestion sit and turn back to the game. Danny doesn't falter, even knowing the stakes. His expression just before he starts his windup is intense, mouth a sharp line, eyes slightly narrowed. He doesn't relax until the pitch leaves his hand. The score's irrelevant. By the time Danny takes the mound, Goldman's winning 8 to 0. Danny's still pitching like the game's tied in the bottom of the final inning. Most parents of adolescent children wish their damn kids would grow up. I find myself wishing that Danny would grow down. It's not going to happen, though. Not today and not in the future.

One of the scouts approaches me at the end of the game. From the University of Texas, he offers a business card and suggests that we get in touch. I take the card, but resist any further conversation. We're headed, all of us except Mike and Danny, to Theo's Waffle Shop on Baxter Boulevard. Danny and Mike will join us after they shower.

Emmaline can't stop talking as we ride to the restaurant. Not about Danny, but about Mike who went five-for-five, including a pair of home runs. Mike's been a lot more disciplined recently and the boys now talk about attending the same college. On full athletic scholarships of course.

Theo's Waffles offers a full brunch menu and we take advantage. Waffles with just about anything on top you can imagine, pancakes with blueberries, strawberries, pineapple, or mango, eggs Benedict with a hollandaise sauce that should be eaten by the spoonful. Only a couple of years ago, brunch was a foreign concept reserved for elite cities that consistently rejected the likes of us. Now we're growing up and the meal, once Danny and Mike join us, delivers the familial punch I need. The conversation is necessarily centered on baseball, but I don't mind. Zoe sits to my right and Danny to my left, and there's absolutely zero talk of crime and punishment. Praise the Lord and pass the pancakes.

CHAPTER FORTY

DELIA

I leave early for my afternoon meeting with Vern and Tommy Atkinson. In addition to the briefing, Jim Youngman, Louis Abott's driver, is coming in with his lawyer. Work and more work, but I'm nothing if not a glutton for punishment. I park outside Baxter Medical Center and make my way to the top floor and the jail-custody unit. I find a patrolman sitting outside a closed door. She comes off the chair and all but salutes when I come out of the elevator.

"Captain."

I'm in too much of a hurry for chitchat. "Brim Houseman back there?"

"Sure is."

"Anyone else?" I'm thinking about other arrestees, but Marie surprises me.

"Detective Breyer. Got here at nine o'clock."

"With breakfast for Houseman?"

She points to a paper bag next to the chair. "And me."

The door to the locked unit is, in fact, unlocked. Inside, I find an empty nurse's station and four rooms with the privacy curtains open. Houseman's in the first of these rooms, sitting on a chair with Detective Chuck Breyer, also seated. They're playing cards, rummy by the look of it.

"Afternoon, captain," Breyer says. Handsome as ever, his jeans and white Western shirt with its snap buttons are neat and clean. At least the man's been home.

I point to a large bag of potato chips, unopened. "That the stakes?"

"Yeah," Breyer says. "First one to a hundred wins the pot."

"And I'm almost there," Brim growls. The hair's started to grow on his shaved head, or at least the part that's not bald, which is almost the whole of the top. He appears a lot less threatening now. "Eighty-six points. Then you show up."

Establishing a rapport with prisoners undergoing interrogation is a basic, taught in every academy. Breyer's taken it to the next level. Circumstances have allowed him to spend virtually unlimited time with Houseman and he's turned it to good use. I'm about to find out how good.

"Up and about, Brim?" I ask. "I'm told you'll be ready for discharge in a few days."

Houseman gestures to the crutch beside his bed. "My ankle's fucked. I'll be needin' this for the next three months. And maybe, if the rehab goes sideways, for the next three years."

"Not much fun when you're locked up." I'm trying for sympathetic, but empathy's a hard slog when the subject of that empathy doesn't know what empathy is. I gesture to Chuck Breyer. "You wanna open those chips?"

Breyer pulls on the edges of the bag and the tops split apart. He offers me first pick, but I shake my head. Houseman goes next and snatches almost half the bag.

"What's in it for me?" he asks.

"Why should anything be in it for you?"

"You wouldn't be here if you didn't want somethin'."

"Got me there, all right. I want something and maybe, if you cooperate, I can offer a short reprieve."

"Like how? And, please, without the bullshit."

Unfortunately, bullshit's all I have at the moment. I have no authority to make an offer of any kind. "Bail. You help me out here and the prosecutor won't oppose the judge's ordering a reasonable bail." I watch Brim's dead eyes reach back as he considers the offer. Lots of calculations. Like if he runs, where will he go? How will he get there without leaving a trace? "And here's the thing. I only want a single word from you. A name, Brim. The name of the cop who regularly picked up Debbie Cole and brought her back. This is a name I already have, but I need it confirmed."

"How do I know you're telling the truth?"

"Because I'm a cop and cops don't lie?" I get the contemptuous laugh I was hoping for, then go on quickly. "I'm not asking you to write anything down. And nobody can make you testify when the grand jury meets or at a later trial. You'll have a bail hearing before either can happen, so if I'm bullshitting, you'll know it."

Brim stares at me for a long moment. Hope to the hopeless, I'm beginning to feel like an evangelist. To my right, Chuck Breyer is staring at Brimley, his gaze so intense it seems as if he's trying to rip the word from Houseman's brain. Finally, Houseman lays a hand on the crutch by his side. In jail, it'll be his only weapon.

"Stepanik," he says. "Yeah, fuckin' Stepanik. A shitkicker cop with a nasty attitude. He picked her up and brought her home. Wouldn't tell me where she was goin', and I even tried to bribe him. That brought me a slap in the face. So, yeah, Stepanik."

◆

I speed-write an application for a search warrant when I get to the office. In the form of an affidavit, I include everything we know about Stepanik, that he regularly carried Deborah Cole to an unknown destination and returned her to the rented home of Brimley Houseman afterward, that he picked her up on the day she disappeared and never returned, that his DNA profile was downloaded from another website and not taken by Baxter PD personnel, that DNA from a single, unknown male was found beneath Deborah Cole's fingernails, inside a camper parked within feet of the Rowan Krauss murder scene, and finally in a car parked a few yards from the murder scene.

I don't request a search warrant for Stepanik's residence, or even for his person. The request's for DNA, fingerprints, and hair samples, and I have no doubt a judge will authorize the warrant if Tommy Atkinson goes along. That's why I don't initially mention the affidavit when I walk into the meeting ten minutes late. Tommy and Vern are sitting at the table in our conference room, along with Patrick O'Malley. I offer a quick apology, then grab a coffee container, add a dollop of cream, and take my seat.

"Glad you've finally arrived," Tommy says. "I've got a fund-raising BBQ scheduled and I need to be there in an hour."

"I may be late, Tommy, but the news is good. Better than good. Lemme start with Sergeant Thrace Overby. Our undercover recorded him, video and audio, demanding a payoff to allow an illegal casino to operate. No ifs and no buts. Flat-out demanding, and not once but twice."

"And your undercover? He'll testify?" Tommy's asking the right question, but I'm ready.

"I don't want Overby to know what's coming, so he'll stay undercover until after we arrest Overby." In fact, I'm imagining the look on Overby's face when he sees Tom Carney wearing a badge. "I'd like to have a pair of warrants in hand, an arrest warrant and a search warrant for his residence and his cell phone. We know Overby's working with at least one ranking officer and maybe two. All we need is the proof, which Overby can supply."

Tommy's smile is infectious. Most of the time, he's the one at the table who can't sit still. But I'm flying right now. "Lemme guess, Delia. If he gets the right deal?"

"Doesn't need sayin', Tommy. But as we all know you're the kind, empathetic type, so I'm sure you'll be generous."

Vern's sitting back, looking hopeful for the first time since Rowan Krauss was murdered. He glances at Patrick O'Malley, he of the belly and jowls. "What do have you so far, Pat?"

"Anybody watch the morning news?" O'Malley's small blue eyes roll back as he shakes his head. "Interviews with Ed Smith's relatives and friends. How sweet and kind he was, always ready to help his neighbors. How he loved his children and his ex-wife, even though he hasn't seen either in years."

"That's good for us," Vern notes, "even though it's bullshit. The public will demand justice, which has to begin with Louis Abott's arrest."

"Give me everything you have so far," Tommy says, "and I'll put it before a grand jury early this week."

"You think they'll indict?"

"Yeah, once they hear Delia's testimony." Tommy nods at me. "You chose not to fire, even though you were armed, right?"

"The rifle was lying in plain sight and Smith was running away. I planned on running him down."

"By yourself?"

"I wanted him alive. For obvious reasons." I don't offer further explanation. Instead, I outline the information supplied by Gianni Vetto. "I'll have a list of the units and the dates by tomorrow morning. The data from the dashcams is stored in digital form in somebody's cloud. I'm going to pull that data, and if it confirms the allegations, I'll bring it to you. Whether or not to bring assault charges will be up to you . . ." I glance at Vern. "But I assume they'll be fired immediately."

Vern smiles, but there's no affability to it this time. "Patrolman Houseman and his lawyer are due in about an hour. You can't be here, Delia. You're a witness and your testimony can't be tainted by knowledge of what Houseman's going to say, if anything. So . . ."

Great news. The absolute best. Now, if I hustle home, I'll arrive just in time to watch *Alien: Romulus* with the kids.

CHAPTER FORTY-ONE

CARNEY

I'm driving back from my rendezvous with Delia Mariola and Stu Harrington. I don't have a problem with Mariola. She's dedicated to the craft of policing and to the welfare of her city. That said, I do find her naive about undercover work. I'm sure she's familiar with short-term undercover stings. Female cops who dress slutty, then parade the goods up and down an established stroll. Johns are drawn to them, in part because the women appear healthy, unlike the tweakers and junkies who make a living on the street.

Deep undercover is a way different game. Hooker-cops deal with johns, almost all of whom are ordinary men from ordinary walks of life. These undercovers change clothes and go home at the end of their tours. Back in Philadelphia, I spent months in the company of hardened criminals. I'm talking about prison-savvy men and women for whom violence is a default setting. I never took part in crimes like armed robberies or debt collection, but I did participate in burglaries and sometimes rode shotgun on drug runs. As long as I disclosed these foul deeds, my handlers accepted the inevitable. Their choice, in fact, was simple. Put up with the indiscretions or give up on deep undercover campaigns.

I think Mariola wants it both ways. Like I should wave a magic wand and make myself invisible. Now, she's hinting about taking me off the street because she doesn't have the stomach for the work I do. Not when she has to authorize it.

Do I want to come up for air? The short answer is no. I didn't sign on to conduct routine investigations, to process crime scenes, or interview witnesses. Interrogations do hold some charm, but not enough.

◆

The morning weather finally calms me. As does a large horse farm with mares and foals grazing in an impossibly green meadow. The blue skies, almost cloudless now, are complemented by a breeze that whips through the open windows of my Jeep. I've been warned about the summers in this part of the country, but that's for later. I don't care to waste my day by fearing what's to come. I suspect the horses don't either.

Fifteen minutes later, I park in front of my trailer and shut down the engine. Still asleep when I left, Vangi's up and dressed, sitting outside with a plate on her lap.

"Bacon and eggs," she tells me. "There's more in the pan. And fresh squeezed orange juice."

I'd skipped breakfast, expecting more of Brenda Harrington's baked goodies. Last time out, the blueberry muffins were light enough to pass for balloons. Instead, we spent our time in a shed, surrounded by gardening tools.

I fill a plate, then carry it outside. Vangi's set up a lawn chair next to hers and we sit there, side by side, watching our neighbors as they pass. Most at least wave and we return their greetings. I'm wondering how many are on their way to church. Well inside the Bible Belt, Baxter has many. The only other possibility is breakfast. The plant is all but shut down on Sundays.

"Whatever you were up to, did it go well?" Vangi asks.

"Reasonably. I got a lot done."

What I didn't get done may be more important. I didn't tell Mariola and Harrington that I've been outed. "There's something we need to do together."

Vangi turns her sharp green eyes to me, her expression defiantly noncommittal. I get the feeling she likes playing close to the edge, but not too close.

"And what's that?"

"I'm going to pay a call on Zack Butler and I want you to help me get inside."

I give my tone a demanding twist, but I don't make an actual demand. The distinction's lost on Vangi, whose expression grows almost contemptuous. I know nothing about Vangi's past, but somewhere along the way she decided that nobody was gonna push her around.

"You gotta do better, Carney. Need, for instance, instead of want."

"Yeah, maybe, but I'm thinking that if I show up alone, I present Butler with one set of calculations. After all, I'm not gonna force my way inside. But if I show up with you, the calculations change in my favor. You said that he's sick. How sick?"

"He's on oxygen during the day, but he has to use a ventilator when he sleeps."

"Does he have a daytime nurse?"

"No, Miranda takes care of him. His housekeeper." A hesitation. "Miranda's very protective."

"Let's go find out how protective." When she hesitates, I add. "Butler told you I was a cop. Why would he do that?"

"Don't know and don't care. Remember, ignorance is strength."

Vangi's head is shaking back and forth, slow but deliberate. She's not coming and I can't say I blame her. She doesn't know what motivated Butler, or what's motivating me, and she's not the kind of woman who walks into dark rooms without turning on the lights.

◆

Zack Butler's brick Colonial in Mt. Jackson impresses. I make it to be at least five bedrooms. The brick's painted white, the shutters black. I don't see flaking paint anywhere and the shingles on the roof are so flat they might have been cowed into submission. The grounds are immaculately tended, with a large bed of butter-yellow roses halfway between bud and blossom off to one side. There's even a small bunny at the edge of the yard. The bunny rises up for a moment when I open the Jeep's door, then goes back to feeding on the grass.

I make my way along a curving flagstone walk to a front door with a knocker in the form of a lion's head. I assume it's for show and ring the bell. The diminutive Latina who answers a moment later positions herself in the doorway.

"Yes?"

"I'm here to see Mr. Butler."

"Do you have an appointment?"

"No. But you tell him Tom Carney's standing at his door." I watch her dark eyes narrow. She doesn't like me showing up out of the blue and if she could refuse on her own, she'd do it. But however much Butler relies on her, she doesn't decide who he sees or when he sees them. The best she can do is tell me to wait and close the door in my face.

The wait is short enough to encourage speculation. When Butler told Vangi I was a cop, he wanted her to let me know. He assumed I'd need to answer a basic question. Who else knows?

"Mr. Butler will see you," Miranda announces in heavily accented English. Her expression hasn't changed, though. Middle-aged and naturally suspicious, she only moves enough to allow me inside. Then she leads me slowly through a series of rooms to a sunroom at the back of the house. I'm struck by the heat and the humidity. Though not a conservatory, there are enough houseplants to make the prevailing odor verdant. Butler's seated in a leather wing chair, his feet on a matching ottoman. He has thin tubes in each nostril, while a machine on his right makes a small humming sound.

"Mr. Carney," he says, his voice soft and hoarse, "please have a seat."

The seat in question, a lawn chair with tubes for arms, is positioned about six feet from Butler's chair. I sit down, wondering if the woven seat will give under my weight, that's how far down it sags. This leaves me in the sort of vulnerable place that any detective would instantly recognize. My ass is below my knees, with my chin, even given my height, below Butler's.

"Now, Mr. Thomas Carney, please tell me why you've come to my house uninvited, demanding a face-to-face."

"Mister?"

"Detective, then."

The saggy brown pouches beneath Butler's eyes run so deep, they lie on his cheeks. The man's not in good health, but his eyes are sharp enough to draw blood. Unfortunately for him, having spent time in the company of murderers, this cop is not intimidated.

"You told Vangi that I'm a cop because you knew I'd come calling. So, let's dispense with the bullshit. I have questions that need answering."

"You'll have to excuse me. I'm not used to being threatened."

"More bullshit? I'm going to ask the questions. You can refuse to answer. But I don't think you will. You didn't lure me here to send me back out the door."

Butler finally smiles. On one level, he's enjoying our back-and-forth. On another, he's weighing and measuring. Me, of course. "Fine, ask your questions."

"Who told you that I'm a cop? Who told him or her? Who else did you tell? How many others know?"

"That's it?"

"Two more, Mr. Butler. What do you want from me? And how long do I have to sit in this fucking chair?"

Butler finally laughs. Or maybe he's coughing. I can't be sure. "Would you like the long answers, or the longer answers?"

"I'll settle for true answers."

"Well said." He raises a sleepy finger in a half-hearted salute. "So, I've come to an age where I need to define my life, and not necessarily in glowing terms. I'm not a politician offering up his greatest hits." He pauses, maybe expecting me to comment. When I don't, he goes on. "What I am—what I've been—is that proverbial big fish in a little pond named Baxter. I might have moved on to bigger and better opportunities. I thought about it many times, but always chose to remain. Being human and still relatively young, I armed myself with plausible reasons. The city's decay offered opportunities of its own. Assets were available, almost for the taking, and the local cops were small in number, pitifully underpaid and risk averse."

Butler stops suddenly as Miranda walks into the sunroom bearing a tray with a silver coffeepot, a cup and a saucer, cream and sugar. She leaves the tray on the table and hustles out of the room without speaking.

"I'd do the honors, but these days my hands tremble. So, please, help yourself." Butler resumes as I walk over to the table. "I've thrown off those excuses as I've aged. I don't really know what made me stay while so many others left. I don't really care anymore. I only know that I've become . . . possessive might be the best way to express it. The city of Baxter belongs to me. I don't want to see it fall into the hands of Bute Stafford and his storm troopers. In their eyes, crime is not to be fought, but to be managed. At a price."

I settle back in my chair and sip at my coffee. "You haven't answered any of the questions that matter. Do I need to repeat them?" I smile. "Or maybe I don't care either. Maybe I only need to measure the level of threat."

"Then let's make it simple. I know because I have friends in low places. Anonymous civil servants who might, for example, work in the city's payroll department. So, I can only tell you that the same individual who told me, probably told others. For certain, she's willing to gab away for a price and you should take precautions. The people in question are more than willing, even eager, to eliminate threats.Sergeant Rowan Krauss was first, and the failed assassination yesterday won't be the last."

In fact, I've been taking the threat seriously ever since the words spilled from Vangi's mouth. "Believe it or not, I haven't come because I want answers to any of the questions I put to you. I came to ask you about a small residential section of Baxter that might be in Mt. Jackson and might be in Oakland Gardens."

Butler's nostrils flare as he draws an involuntary breath. I've caught him off guard. He repairs the damage so fast that I doubt anyone but a cop would have caught the tell.

"Funny thing, Mr. Butler, almost all of the homes in that little neighborhood are empty, despite being in good repair. I'm assuming you have plans for the area. Me, too."

"You're quick, and I generally like quick, but why would a few square miles of real estate in an obscure section of the city interest you?"

"Currently, I'm operating a tiny casino in Boomtown. Locals, mostly, with limited funds. It's nickels and dimes, but I won't say they don't add up. I think I'd be satisfied if the Blue Skies Tavern wasn't so exposed. I'm paying off because if I don't, I can be closed at a moment's notice. And that remains true no matter who runs the Baxter PD."

"I already know about the Blue Skies, and I sympathize. I don't disagree with your analysis, either. But what's that have to do with me?"

"Do you dream, Mr. Butler?"

I watch his eyes soften, then turn down. "If you're talking about dreams of the future, about hope, the answer is no."

"I can't say I blame you, but as you're still in the game, you must be interested in other people's dreams. I don't want a casino open to the public. I'm dreaming of a club open to members only. Members and their guests. I'm seeing my private club operating out of a home in a quiet neighborhood, far from the chaos in Boomtown. A sleek bar-restaurant on the first floor, gambling upstairs. And no slot machines. High-stakes poker, instead, dealt by a professional dealer. A baccarat table, a craps table, and that's it."

"Baccarat?"

"What can I say? I love James Bond."

Butler leans back in his chair, closes his eyes, and takes a deep breath through his nose. Suddenly, I'm thinking that he's not as old as I thought. Sick, yes, but in his seventies, not his nineties.

"Let's see if I understand. You, a perfect stranger I'm meeting for the first time, are asking me to provide you with real estate so you can open a private club for gamblers."

"Right, the real estate and the financing."

Butler's still laughing as Miranda shows me out.

◆

On the way home, I stop behind the Nissan construction site before turning north. Maybe it's Sunday, and maybe the weekday construction workers are enjoying a leisurely morning, but the huge yard before me hums with activity. A dozen eighteen-wheelers are parked side by side, rear cargo doors raised. Almost as many forklifts dart from one to another, lifting pallets, ferrying them to the loading docks. I'm reminded of just how inconsequential I am. Whether I dress every night in a tux or end up in a body bag on a morgue slab is of no consequence to Nissan. Nor do they care if Bute Stafford wins the election, or if his robocops beat the crap out of every unemployable in Baxter. The plant will open, workers will be found, cars will roll through the doors at the end of the line. Ready for sale.

Zack Butler described his relationship with the city as possessive. It's not, though. Nissan is Baxter's present and future, and Baxter's government will do everything in its power to keep it that way. As long as they can skim off a piece here and there, they're willing, even eager, to allow Nissan to possess the city.

◆

Vangi's already left by the time I park in front of my trailer. Just as well because it's time to get to work. Ally will return tonight. Assuming I agree to the hit on Stepanik, he'll pay me. Maybe not half up front, but enough to get me going. And after he leaves? What would I be thinking, right now, if Butler hadn't warned Vangi? If I thought my undercover identity to be secure?

I'd be walking right into it.

I reach the Blue Skies at four o'clock, an hour before our Sunday opening. I'm not expecting a big crowd on a Sunday night and I don't get one. The casino is especially quiet. I have dinner brought in at six, then take a walk along Main Street. Again, the streets are quiet. I'm offered drugs from street dealers hawking their goodies from the shadows. They look at me as I go by, then quickly turn to the next man coming. Farther south, hookers cluster in little groups, smoking, complaining. They're more insistent than the dealers, and offer quick and very negative comments on my sexual orientation when I pass.

I'm glad for the exercise. I needed to get off my butt, to stretch my limbs. But I have another purpose. All along the way, I've been checking (surreptitiously, I hope) for anybody focused on me or on the Blue Skies. If I'm being watched, moment to moment, I need to know. I don't find anything out of order, which doesn't mean nobody's out there. A minder might even be drinking at the bar in my little tavern, or watching from inside one of the trailers parked on the block. I'm sure only that I'm not being followed, though I am being approached.

"Hey, honey, tell me your dreams and I'll make them come true."

◆

I'm sitting at the bar, nursing a short beer. Even with it being a Sunday, the money's been rolling in all night. Too much for the safe. I need to cut out four or five thousand dollars, but I have nowhere to put it, something I might have already considered. Still, it's better to have money and nowhere to put it, than a vault and empty pockets.

Ally walks through the door a few minutes before midnight. He's accompanied by Mike Mulligan, smirk firmly set. Ally stands at the entrance for a moment, perhaps expecting me to jump to my feet and bow. I take my time sliding off the barstool before walking off to my office. With no choice, Ally trails in my wake.

"Not you, Mike," I say when Mulligan tries to follow his boss. "Let's keep it cozy. Just the two of us."

Ally nods, then closes the door on his bodyguard. I take a seat behind my desk, but don't activate the camera. I've got enough already.

"Okay, Ally. You're up."

"I've come for your answer." The man's pissed. He's been giving orders for a long time. "To the offer I made last night."

I nod once before getting down to business. "What about the terms, Ally? Half up front, half once I murder the cop."

"I'm willing to go five right now. Five thousand if you agree."

"See right there, Ally. You're already chiseling, and that leads me to think you won't come through in the end. You know what they get in Philly for hitting a cop? Thirty large."

"This ain't Philly."

"So, what? Life is cheap in Baxter? There's a descending scale of values? Cause from where I sit, a badge is a badge. Either way, you're lookin' at execution if you get caught." I stare up at Ally, but the money here is irrelevant. Bargaining is expected.

"I can go six," Ally finally says. "But that's it. I gotta know it's done before I come up with the rest."

Again, I stare at him, but only for a few seconds. "Let's hear it, then."

Ally's twinkly eyes almost dance in his head and his smile appears genuine. "What I've got is a photo and a map. I don't suppose you need the photo—you and Stepanik have already met—but I brought it anyway. Now, as to the map. Stepanik's home is on County Road 12 in Revere County. Also called Pettus Road. As you get close, you'll see a couple of abandoned buildings about a half mile before you reach the house. It says Mueller Dairy on the biggest of them. Faded, right, but you can read the words. Stepanik's house is painted white with a green door. There's one chimney, on the north side. You really can't miss it because the next house down is a mile away."

"What's in between?"

"Some kinda crop. Me, I ain't a farmer, so I can't say what. Green, right?" He taps the desktop. "Stepanik lives alone. That's what matters. He might be in the house tonight and he might not. But tomorrow morning, eight o'clock, he starts his shift. He'll be working all day. When he comes home, you'll be waiting."

CHAPTER FORTY-TWO

CARNEY

I start the drive out to Pettus Road at one o'clock. Even using the GPS on my phone, it takes longer than I expected. I'm forty-five minutes and thirty miles north of the city when I reach the abandoned dairy. It's early to bed and early to rise in farm country. The few, widely spaced homes I pass are completely dark. I'm running slowly, with my lights off, guided by a nearly full moon in a sky marked only by a few wispy clouds.

I'm almost past the dairy when the obvious finally makes its way into my thick brain. I have to approach the house on foot and I can't just leave my car at the edge of the road. Though the chances are small, any gambler will tell you that long shots occasionally win. The odds against a sheriff's cruiser patrolling on Pettus Road at this hour may be tiny, but the possible remains possible.

A wide break in a ditch that runs to both sides marks the entry to the dairy. I wouldn't call it a driveway. It's too beaten down for that, but it is firm enough to bear the weight of the car. I come in slowly, watching for obstacles like glass embedded in the dirt, and circle behind the Mueller Dairy building. From here, I see fields and more fields, broken only by a grove of trees perhaps a quarter mile away.

I don a pair of nitrile gloves, a Covid mask, and a baker's cap, then step out of the car. Back in Philly, light on the ground virtually obliterated light from the stars. Even on clear nights, only a few stars were bright enough to be seen. I'm tempted to say the sky above the fields that surround me are ablaze, but the white-on-black heavens seem too cold for that. Too cold and utterly indifferent to the warmth of this planet, maybe to life itself. But the life on this planet is apparently unimpressed. Dozens of bats turn, swoop, and soar, changing direction so fast my eyes can't follow them.

Nothing cold and remote about the bats, nothing that hints of the infinite. Flesh and blood, life feeding on life, the price of survival. There's no escape for the bats and no escape for me. I can't see the house from here. There's a grove of trees between where I stand and where it's supposed to be. The trees will shield my approach.

I don't know what's growing in the fields, but the evenly spaced rows travel in the wrong direction and I have to step over the knee-high plants, one after another. The athletic shoes I'm wearing are wrong for the yielding soil and it takes me a good twenty minutes to reach the trees. Immediately, I discover why this grove was left intact while all the surrounding land was given to farming. Rocks poke through soil, most the size of footballs. They surround a giant boulder that has to be the size of a small car. For the most part, the loam runs deep in this part of the state. What I'm looking at was left by a glacier from the last ice age.

The where and how of it is irrelevant, and I don't linger. I cross between the trees until I'm staring at a small house no more than a quarter mile distant. This time I catch a break. The evenly spaced rows between the grove and the house travel in straight lines. Eventually, the rows will meet, but this early in the growing season, the plants are still a shoulder-width apart. I raise my eyes to study the house. A two-story box, it appears to be in reasonably good shape. By moonlight, anyway. But the residents, whoever they might be, made a mistake common to homeowners. The shrubbery on the side of the house is in flower. I can see the blossoms clearly, though it's impossible to determine their color. They're also high enough to conceal an intruder as he forces an entry.

I'm carrying my Glock in a holster near my left hip, and a Colt .32 automatic, an untraceable throwaway, in a holster on my right ankle. I'm trying not to drag either through the dirt as I crawl on my belly toward the house. That's clearly impossible, but I do the best I can. The good news is that the growth around me is tall enough to reduce me to a shadow within shadows. But so is everything else that moves through the night and twice I'm startled by small animals that I only hear as they flee. And there's always the possibility of running into a snake, a possibility that fueled my childhood terrors. Spiders, okay, likewise for mice and rats, but not snakes. Never snakes.

It's slow going, but I've got all night, and I pause often to check the windows on the side of the house facing me. A waste of time because the moon's reflection on the glass is bright enough to conceal anybody behind it. I look anyway, a reflex, or perhaps only a pitiful attempt at reassurance. Either way, I keep going until I'm within fifty yards and a light comes on. The light projects from a window on the second floor onto a tree outside. I can't see the window from my position, but I drop down flat, burrowing into the soil, until the light goes off a couple of minutes later. Somebody using a bathroom, then returning to bed. I hope.

◆

As I crawl behind a large bush covered with blossoms, I'm in one piece except for a stinging cut on my neck from a branch I never saw. Here I'm invisible to passing vehicles like the two pickups that drove by as I crawled across the field. Better yet, my head rests against the side of the house just below a windowsill. I'm going to take a look. I have no choice. Call it a moment of truth, but when I raise my head, I'm looking through an empty, unlit kitchen into an empty living room. I place my ear against the glass, but there's nothing to hear, not even the ticking of a clock.

I settle back to check my weapons, making certain there's a round in the chambers of both pistols. I need to get inside the house, to ask questions in a way that inspires truthful answers. Again, I put my ear to the glass. Again, nothing.

The window is double-hung and in reasonably good condition. Maybe it won't be frozen in place, the worst-case scenario, but it is locked, as I discover when I push up on the lower window. Not a major problem. I remove a pocket knife I always carry, work it between the upper and lower windows, and cut into the sash, stopping every few seconds to listen. The wood is old and very dry. It comes off in small chunks, finally exposing the tab on the lock which emits a small squeak when I pull it toward me.

Now for all the money. I put my fingers on top of the lower window and rock it back and forth. There's give, which I expected, and I can feel the window loosen before I try to raise it. Still, it's surely possible, maybe even likely, that the wood-on-wood friction will produce a squeal loud enough to shame a terrified piglet.

A part of me wants to put all my strength into raising the window, to get it the fuck over with and shoot anybody who responds. I resist, mainly because I'm too chicken. I raise the window an inch at a time, adjusting when it threatens to jam. Then repeat, then repeat. By the time the window lifts far enough for me to climb through, I'm sweating despite the cool night air. Again, I listen, this time for anyone coming down the stairs; again there's only silence.

◆

I spend the rest of the night in a coat closet near the front door. The closet's empty, confirming my belief that nobody, definitely not Al Stepanik, lives here. The squatter, or squatters, upstairs are just that, here temporarily, their purpose to kill me. That, you'd think, would be enough to heighten the senses, that I'd immediately come to full alert. Instead, after a time I can't measure in the total darkness that surrounds me, I fall asleep.

It's better to be lucky than good. I awake to voices coming from a short distance away, but not right beside the closet. Orienting myself takes a moment, but then my adrenals pop and I come fully awake. I have to force myself to listen, until I'm sure that I'm hearing two voices only, and that a persistent odor I can't avoid is from brewing coffee.

I pull the .32 from its holster, then rise to a crouch, open the door and step into the living room. As I do, I remind myself, once again, that the two men in the kitchen, one sitting at a small table, the other standing, mean to kill me. The man standing by the sink is Mike Mulligan. The other I don't recognize, but there's a gun lying on the table within a yard of his right hand. We stare at each other a few seconds, the silence as loud as a scream. I'm daring him to make a move, an offer he finally refuses by stepping away from the table and raising his hands.

"Hey," he says before making an attempt to smile, an attempt I short-circuit by shooting him in belly. His eyes widen and his lips move convulsively though he doesn't make a sound. Not even when I shoot him a second time and he drops slowly to the floor. He's alive, though, and strong enough to pull himself into a sitting position with his back against a cabinet.

"What the fuck, Carney?" This from Mike who raises a forearm when I level the gun on him.

"What's his name?" I gesture to the man on the floor. He's young, in his mid-twenties at most, with green eyes that seem inwardly focused. Like he's still trying to understand why the man he meant to kill shot him.

"Kevin."

"All right, Mike. Now Kevin, as you can see, is gutshot. He's gutshot and I'm using a small-caliber weapon, which means he has a decent chance if he receives medical treatment. Like pronto. But that's up to you, Mike, because I have a few questions and you have the answers."

"Okay, Carney, just take it easy. Think this thing out."

"I've been sitting in a closet for the last four hours thinking it out. You came here to kill me. That's not a question by the way. No, there are two questions that need an answer. Who wanted me dead, and why."

"For shit's sake, man, tell him." Kevin has both hands clutched to his belly. His hands are bloodstained and blood drips from his fingers. He speaks in bits and pieces, each word more painful than the next. "We didn't come here to kill nobody," he says. "It's supposed to be like a warning."

"Warning about what?"

"About you bein' a fuckin' cop."

"Ally told you that?"

"Yeah," Mulligan says.

"And who told him?"

I've had enough and I let the .32 slide toward Kevin, who closes his eyes and turns his head. "The cops," he says. "They want you gone."

"Didn't you say something about a warning? Now it's about making me gone." I look from one to the other, but they have nothing to say. "What cops want me gone? I wanna hear names this time."

"Overby's the only one I know. He offered Ally the city."

"Like the works," Mike finally adds. "The whores, the gambling, the dope. The whole fucking city."

I watch Mike nod, his brown eyes almost childlike. He's been a good boy, so can he go home now? Instead, I pull the trigger and send him to hell. Then I do the same for Kevin. I feel nothing afterward. No sympathy and no regrets. They came here to kill me. If I'd let them go, they'd only try again. I couldn't arrest them, either. Intentions aren't crimes until they're carried out.

Behind a closed door, I find a set of stairs leading to a dirt basement. I drag both men to the edge of the steps, then watch them slide to the bottom, banging over the steps, beyond pain or caring. They have cell phones and wallets, probably with IDs inside, but I don't take them. Mulligan's been to prison and his DNA is registered in the CODIS database. He'll be identified, even if his body isn't discovered for months.

Ally faces a different problem. When he doesn't hear from his killers, he'll order somebody to investigate. The bodies will probably be found at that point, and Ally could inform the Revere County sheriff. But toward what end? I've left no physical evidence and Ally's in it up to his neck. Better to let dead dogs lie.

I'm home by ten. Vangi's not there and I'm glad. I need rest, time to think. I'm counting on the bodies not being officially discovered for weeks, at the least. The longer the time between death and discovery, the harder to determine time of death. It's one thing if you need an alibi for a three-hour period, another if that period covers several weeks. I may become a suspect at some point, but I'll never be convicted in a court of law. The only thing I have to fear is the extralegal judgment of men like Overby, Stepanik, and Colton Steele. These are men who never take the death penalty off the table.

CHAPTER FORTY-THREE

DELIA

I've been up since three o'clock. Me, Stu Harrington, and Vern Taney. Scheming, as you'd expect. We've got enough now to dismantle Baxter's robocops. The how part, though, is tricky. Which chicken comes before which egg? Or maybe *chicken* is the wrong word, the wrong gender. *Fighting roosters* might be a better way to understand what's to come. These men—and they're all men—have made violence a first resort and appear to have no stopping point.

It's almost seven now and the detective's squad room is crowded with new arrivals. Patrick O'Malley, Sam Barret, Cade Barrow, Laura Udell, and a bedraggled Tom Carney. Carney showed up fifteen minutes ago after numerous calls that went directly to voicemail. I don't ask and he doesn't tell, but we both know that his undercover days are over. The good guys, meaning the detective division and Vern, can't afford to have one of ours running a casino.

Gianni Vetto's not here, though she's why the rest of us are. Gianni provided us with a list of patrol vehicles whose dashcams captured incidents of police brutality. Or, so she claimed. Early this morning, I reviewed the data from those dashcams and it was conclusive. Helpless arrestees, hands cuffed behind their backs, being punched, kicked, even slammed with telescoping steel batons. Four videos involving four different cops, all but one providing clear evidence of an assault. And just in case some future defense attorney should claim they're AI-generated fakes, I also have signed statements from the women cops who witnessed the brutality. More than enough for the arrests we plan to make a few minutes from now. As for Gianni, she'll have to wait a bit for her reward. She organized her sisters, but she's not a witness and will never testify. Better to keep her name out of it.

◆

We've decided to lead with these crimes, though we could easily begin elsewhere. The evidence against Overby is clear and convincing, as is the evidence against Ally McKinney, on the hook for soliciting a hit on a police officer. The case against Louis Abott, who shot Edward Smith, is ongoing, but it's only a matter of time. Abott's partner that afternoon, Jim Youngman, came into the house with his lawyer, Eustis Prout, and refused to give us a statement. He's been suspended without pay, but not until after a lecture, meant as much for his lawyer as Youngman. You don't want to get on the wrong side of a murder investigation. The stakes are too high and the GPS data from your vehicle proves you meandered through Mt. Jackson for an hour before the shooting. Mt. Jackson has the lowest crime rate in the city, but it's conveniently close to the Fulton Funeral Home. Have a nice vacation.

Gianni Vetto's work has changed our strategy. Instead of picking off the bad cops, one by one, we're going to blitz the patrol division. Thus far, we've kept the media in the dark. That's about to change and Vern intends to control the narrative. We'll orchestrate one takedown after another. The four cops first, followed by Stepanik and Overby, then Louis Abott. We'll leak information in bits and pieces after each arrest, enough to inspire new stories about our heroic commissioner's battle to cleanse the Baxter PD.

Of course, we've yet to get our mayor on board, or even to brief him. Likewise for Tommy Atkinson, our district attorney. They'll be pissed, even infuriated, but they won't be able to stop the investigation before it gets started. Both are up for reelection and both are pragmatists. Maybe they'd prefer to let sleeping dogs lie until after the election, but with that option gone, they'll stake out positions and shoulder on.

◆

The four cops named by Gianni's recruits, along with the rest of the cops working the day tour, are currently in the muster room, enduring a pre-tour briefing. We're going to take them down in front of their brothers and sisters in blue (tan, actually). Stepanik will come next. He'll be forced to contribute DNA that will likely tie him to the murder of Debbie Cole. Vern's already worked his buddy network at the state police lab and Stepanik's sample will be given priority status. Once we have it in hand, he'll be arrested and charged with murder, thus clearing an open homicide file. And who could say no to that?

A few minutes from now, Thrace Overby will bear witness to the arrest of four of his boys. We'll let him take that out on the street until we finish with Stepanik and his DNA's on the way to a state lab. That done, Overby will be ordered into the house and arrested. Will he turn, maybe tell us who got what share of what money? For sure and certain, once he lays eyes on Tom Carney wearing a badge, he'll know cooperation is the only way out of the maze. All other paths lead to prison.

◆

The arrest of so many cops, all from the patrol division, will give Vern the excuse he needs to transfer Saul Rawling, our chief of patrol, along with his top aide, Colton Steele. Baxter's media will be briefed at each stage, with resulting pressure on Tommy Atkinson, our district attorney, who's on the ballot in November. Turning him, we hope, into a hang-'em-high prosecutor, which he's never been.

There's a negative here as well. As the electoral arena heats up, our beloved Mayor Venn will have to choose. He can back Vern, claiming that our efforts to cleanse the department of its sins proves that Vern's the right man for the job. Or he can fire Vern's ass, claiming that he has no faith in a police commissioner who allowed his department to become corrupt. Vern's aware of the stakes. He made that clear when he gave me the go-ahead.

"The mayor fires me, I'll consider it a blessing. I haven't had any fun since I came off the street."

◆

We march, the eight of us, all armed, out of the squad room, down the stairs, across the main floor, and into the muster room. Everything stops at our appearance and all eyes turn to us, including the eyes of the sergeant at the front of the room. That would be Thrace Overby. He sees me first and his eyes narrow, his anger apparent. Then he sees Tom Carney. Carney's badge is pinned to the front of his Crimson Tide sweatshirt. Dead center. I suspect Overby would like to conceal his reaction, but he's not up to it. His mouth opens and he sucks in a long breath, hoping against hope that we haven't come for him.

I step far enough into the room to give the rest of my crew enough space to follow, then fan out behind me. Laura Udell and Cade Barrow carry shotguns, but we haven't donned body armor.

"Patrolmen Guardino, Jackson, Buell, and Worth." I speak loud enough to be sure that everyone hears. "You are under arrest. Put your hands on top of your heads. The rest of you move away."

More than twenty cops, all standing, fill the area in front of Overby's podium. They freeze initially, shocked by our appearance. Then some begin to move, the women first, all of them, then the regulars. They're easy to identify in their well-worn uniforms. Should the remaining ten or so, all men, decide to resist, I'm hoping these others will back our play.

"I told you to move off. If you don't, you'll be arrested yourselves. Sergeant, control your men. That's an order."

I suspect Overby's run through his emotional spectrum and come to the end of the line. Surprise, fear, and now hate. Maybe he's watching his dreams as they circle round and round before vanishing down the toilet. He stares at me through dark brown eyes that seem to absorb the light. Can he bluff his way out of this?

"Do you have a warrant?" he finally asks, his voice weaker than I would have expected.

"That's not your business, sergeant. Control your men."

On either side of me, Cade and Laura hold their shotguns at port arms with the barrels extending above their left shoulders. If it turns out to be a gunfight at the OK Corral, Overby will be in the line of fire. I glance quickly to my right, at Tom Carney. He's staring at Overby, a small smile lifting the corners of his mouth. No fear and not really smug. Not afraid, either. Like he's almost hoping the bust goes sideways.

Overby's right hand curls into a fist. Maybe he'd rather bite off his tongue than issue the order, but a shotgun blast is another matter. "Just tell me what they're being charged with. Please."

"Second-degree assault."

Overby nods to himself. Charges like bribery might come back to bite him, but in this case, Guardino, Jackson, Buell, and Worth don't come close to justifying a battle Overby can't win.

"Move away," he says.

Six of the ten cops walk away, joining their colleagues already off to the side. Four men now stand in front of us. How do you appear enraged and lost at the same time? The other cops at the muster, including men they believed to be allies, are on one side of the room while they stand there, isolated, humiliated, fully armed but in no way prepared to use their weapons.

"Put your hands on top of your heads," I tell them. "If you don't comply, we'll add resisting arrest to your charges."

More humiliation as they, albeit slowly, lay their palms on top of their brush cuts. As planned, Sam Barret and Patrick O'Malley step forward to relieve them of their weapons and apply the cuffs. They range in age from early twenties to post-forty, but they all wear the same bewildered expression as they're led out of the room. They wear the same expression and their heads turn in the same direction, toward their boss and mentor, Thrace Overby.

CHAPTER FORTY-FOUR

DELIA

Mayor Venn is a no-show, but he sent his closest aide, Jenny Ivorson. Tommy Atkinson makes a personal appearance, accompanied by a pair of assistant district attorneys he never introduces. Reporters from KBAX, the *Baxter Bugle,* and two independent websites, alerted by an anonymous leaker, beat all of them. They've set up on the sidewalk, mics at the ready.

I only have a few minutes before I brief our esteemed guests, but I stop by the holding pen in our jail. All four men have demanded lawyers, but I'm not here to ask questions. I stand in front of the pen for a moment, staring through the bars. I hope—no, expect—to turn at least one of them and one is all we need. Let the rest spend a few years in a prison where they'll have to be protected night and day.

I look from one to another. They're still spit-shined, but that'll change when they're booked. Our booking process includes a mandated strip search. I finally settle on Jordan Buell. He's shorter than the others and sports the beginnings of a gut. Balding from front to back, he's allowed his hair to grow a bit longer than the others and combed it forward in a failed attempt to conceal his naked scalp. Just now he's trying for a snarl, but his eyelids droop ever so slightly and I know he's afraid. Of the four, Buell's the only one who's married. With two kids.

"Okay, listen up. You've asked for lawyers and been given a chance to make a phone call. So, I'm not going to ask you any questions." I take a step closer to their cage and say, "I've got video and witness statements proving that you assaulted unresisting prisoners with their hands cuffed behind their backs. Brutal assaults, fellas. The kind that motivates jurors and judges alike. You wanna save yourselves, you need to get on the train before it leaves the station. That's because once it's gone, it's not coming back. The next decade of your life is in your hands. Your life, and your family's."

◆

The meeting starts an hour later. Me, Stu, Vern, Tommy, and Jenny Ivorson. Jenny's plump and middle-aged, fond of reading glasses with pink frames that dangle from a chain around her neck when not in use. I said that Tom Carney's hard to read, but he could take lessons from Jenny. At first glance, you'd take her for that nice lady who lives next door and never misses church on Sunday. But Jenny's the perfect stand-in. She's absorbs every nuance, but projects nothing.

Vern thanks our guests for coming, then turns the meeting over to me. I've got the data on all four assaults loaded into a computer with a thirty-four-inch-wide monitor. The presentation takes forty-five minutes. At the beginning of each segment, I name the suspect, but otherwise allow the images to speak for themselves. Only Tommy Atkinson reacts as the beatings take place.

"Holy shit, holy shit. Why the fuck . . ."

◆

"A couple of things," I announce when the last segment plays out. "The data was recorded by dashcams mounted in four different vehicles. We have the unit ID numbers and the video is time- and date-stamped. We also have statements from the partners riding with these cops at the time the incidents took place. Within a week, we'll identify the victims and have statements from them."

"So, there's no escape?" Tommy asks. "It's airtight?"

"The guilt of these officers isn't in doubt, and they've already been arrested," I say. "That leaves you with two choices, Tommy. Indict or cut them loose."

Tommy shakes his head, not at Vern, but at me. He lays a hand on his heart, then grins. "I'm running for reelection."

"And there's twenty reporters waiting for you when you walk out the door."

"I love you, Delia, but you can be a serious pain in the ass." He waves off a response. "I'll send up an ADA, maybe a pair, to review and prepare the evidence for a grand jury. But please, please, please. Tell me there's nothing more coming, no more surprises. My cardiologist, what he's sayin', I need to ease off on the stress."

I can't make that promise and I don't. I let Vern, as commissioner, speak for me. The four arrests, he tells them, pale in comparison to the arrests we plan to make in the near future.

"Bribery, murder, an attempt on my life. I survived the bullets. Will I survive professionally? I don't care. And I really am to blame. We expanded way too fast and the vetting process sucked. That's on me." Vern turns to Jenny. "Go tell your boss that I'm going to correct my mistake. It's like having surgery, like if they take out a tumor. The tumor has to go, no question, but your gut still hurts like hell the day after. And by the way, I'm going to fire—well, demote, I can't fire him—my chief of patrol. That would be Saul Rawling. And I'm going to reassign Lieutenant Steele, his aide." A grin, finally. "Your boss, Jenny, our beloved mayor, once told me I was too idealistic for my own good. Tell him he was right."

Tommy Atkinson takes the pocket square from the pocket of his jacket and dabs at his eyes. "Beautiful, Vern, beautiful."

"Fuck you, Tommy."

"I'll take that as a compliment. But let's talk about Louis Abott, who shot Edward Smith. I've read your summaries, but I want to hear it from our star witness."

That would be me and I retell my story for the tenth time. Shots fired from a field, suspect's vehicle trapped in mud, rifle tossed away, suspect fleeing, no weapon visible, shot in the back. I add the part about Abott's patrol unit aimlessly cruising in a low-crime area for a considerable length of time before speeding to the crime scene.

"Abott had a partner that day. His name is Jim Youngman and he never drew his weapon. He showed up with his lawyer yesterday and refused to give a statement. He's been placed on administrative leave with no pay."

Tommy raises a finger and waggles it in my direction. "You say you came out on the porch with Vern, saw this vehicle in a field, and pushed Vern out of the way. What made you think Vern was a target?"

"A pimp named Brimley Houseman, currently in our jail unit at Baxter Medical. Brim claimed that persons unknown intended to have the commissioner assassinated. At the time, I thought he was trying to get under my skin. Almost taunting me. That's not the way it went down." I raise my hands. "But I do get it. Who told Brimley? That's the question. For right now, the man isn't telling. Later on, who knows? Brim's going from the hospital to our jail, accused of sex with an underage girl. The case is locked down and he's looking at fifteen years, minimum. So, right now, it's about the low-hanging fruit. We took four bad cops off the street, five if you count Youngman's suspension. Within twenty-four hours, we expect to make another arrest, this time for soliciting a bribe. Within a week, I believe we'll arrest the cop who murdered Deborah Cole. That done, we'll start squeezing. You wanna get up a pool, I'm betting that a patrolman named Buell will crack first, but I wouldn't be surprised if Overby beats him to it."

Jenny leans forward, her glasses at the end of their chain swinging out and back. "Do you know what just about every woman in the mayor's office says about you, Delia? They don't wanna be like Mike. They wanna be like you." Now she leans back, ready for the punch line. "Except for the sex."

Am I being complimented? Or insulted? With Jenny you can never be sure. She should have been a con artist. Or maybe, as she works in politics, she already is.

I really don't give a damn. For the first time in months, I can say we're winning and believe it. I'm talking about the Baxter PD. Because the rats are gonna turn and I expect other cops on the force to come forward with tales of their own. And maybe, just maybe, I'll answer a question I've been asking myself for weeks. According to Houseman and Olga Kupchak, Al Stepanik transported Debbie from Brim's house to a rendezvous with an unnamed trick. I want that man's name and what with Stepanik facing life without parole, I'm pretty sure I'll get it.

CHAPTER FORTY-FIVE

CARNEY

It's the Delia Mariola show and she's more than adept. I'm in the squad room for the first time and it's as dingy as I expected. Our commissioner's here, along with Stu Harrington, my handler, and four other detectives, none of them known to me. They introduce themselves when I arrive, but I'm too spacey to do more than nod. I killed two men this morning, and forget the obvious, that they were trying to kill me and would certainly try again if I let them go. Forget that Ally McKinney imagines himself a mobster and mobsters are obligated to seek revenge by a sick and perverted ideology. I killed two men this morning and something's shifted in a part of my brain I can't access. It's there, and I know it's there, but the rest, the consequences, remain out of reach.

Mariola's going on about arresting four cops on an assault charge. I don't know what she's revealed to the commissioner, her justifications, but she's not sharing them with the rank and file.

We're to go down to the muster room, fully armed, and make the arrest in front of the assembled day tour. Get yourselves together.

I find myself indifferent. Sure, let's go, but I don't really care at this point. I am, though, taken with Mariola, not for the first time. Police and military share a concept, command presence, that divides commanders into a pair of categories. The first blusters, threatens, yells. The second secures obedience by their presence alone. Mariola fits into that second category. She expects compliance and I'm sure she'll get it. From me, too, if called to testify before a grand jury or at trial. I handled Ally and Overby without all that much trouble, but Mariola worries me.

◆

We march down a flight and into the squad room, then fan out, as instructed. For a few seconds, nobody moves. We're scrutinizing the uniformed cops at the briefing. Will they resist? It's not impossible, especially with Thrace Overby standing behind a podium at the back of the room. But despite Overby's obvious outrage at the detective division's intrusion, his eyes come back to me again and again. I'm supposed to be dead, but here I am. Now what?

Overby's voice is surprisingly strong when he demands to know why his cops are being arrested. His eyes shift when Mariola announces the men are being accused of assault. He's thinking, evaluating, and I'm not surprised when his eyes find mine as he accepts the arrests. Maybe he's hoping for some sort of reassurance. If so, he has to be disappointed. My expression is closer to that of a scientist examining a specimen through a microscope. Inside, though, I'm also formulating plans. Mariola's no fool, and my personal jeopardy isn't imagined. You'd think, if she wanted to dangle me at the end of her line, she'd tell me.

◆

She doesn't. Instead, she assigns me and three other detectives to deliver a warrant to Patrolman Al Stepanik. The warrant allows us to collect a DNA sample. On the spot if he complies. Back in the house if he refuses. That's because Stepanik is the only suspect in the murder of Debbie Cole. While I don't know the details, Stepanik's DNA is expected to provide the sort of irrefutable evidence that juries have been conditioned to embrace. The gold standard.

My three companions on this errand are again introduced: Cade Barrow, John Meacham, and Laura Udell, who's in charge. I have full confidence only in one of them. Barrow radiates physical competence. Ex-military, almost for sure, and probably Special Forces. Laura Udell appears reliable and unafraid, but I'm not finding the competence of a combat veteran. As for John Meacham, I can only hope he's stable enough to call for backup should that become necessary.

"Okay, listen up," Mariola explains. "Al Stepanik didn't show up for work this morning and he doesn't answer his phone. He's not married, but might be in a relationship. We have no intelligence either way." She looks from one of us to another. "Stepanik is dangerous and definitely armed. He doesn't know you're coming, or even that he's under investigation. That means he's liable to panic when he learns you're after his DNA." She stops long enough to take a breath. "Carney, you'll find body armor waiting for you in the supply room. Strap it under your . . .

your sweatshirt. Remember, you've only come to serve a warrant. Remember, also, that you can't exclude the possibility that children might be in the house. At the first sign of resistance, I want you to retreat and call for backup."

Udell raises her hand. "What if nobody answers?"

"I've reviewed Stepanik's file. He's never been late or taken a day off that wasn't scheduled. Now he's not answering his phone. Knock hard, ring the bell multiple times, announce yourselves. Then, if no one responds, force an entry. We'll call it a welfare check."

◆

With Mariola gone, Udell thrusts forth a shovel of a jaw as she turns to me. "We'll have portables, but it's hard to use a radio and return fire. Someone needs to stay at a distance in case we need backup in a hurry. You want that job?"

"You're the boss. Do whatever suits you."

"That's not an answer."

"It's the only one you're getting."

Udell takes a step toward me, eyes locked on mine. Am I supposed to be intimidated? Maybe dominated? But I'm not feeling particularly submissive and I stare right back until she heads across the squad room to Mariola's office.

Fine with me. I ignore the stares of my fellow team members and find a quiet corner before punching Zacariah McBride's number into my cell phone. When he answers, I make it quick.

"I'm gonna be away from the bar for a few days. I want you to run the business while I'm gone. I'll text you the PIN number for the safe. The bank's inside." At this point, I'm supposed to list the awful things I'll do to him if the money's not right. I don't bother.

"When do you think you'll be back?"

"Can't say right now. The bar's yours, though, if I don't make it."

◆

Udell doesn't tell me, or anyone else, what she said to our boss. I don't ask, either. Right now, I'm carrying my weapon in a cross draw holster. I'm glad for the protection, but I recognize the half-assed nature of our little squad. Our handguns should be snugged into gunslinger holsters strapped to our thighs. We should be carrying shotguns and assault rifles. We should have sniper backup, like any SWAT team. But you can't justify those precautions when you're serving a DNA warrant instead of an arrest warrant. End result? We're not only underprepared for an attack from inside the house, we're underprepared to put up a strong defense.

Stepanik's rented home is on Portland Street in a neighborhood called Norwood. I've never visited Norwood and I'm buoyed somewhat by the middle-class, single-family homes lining the quiet streets. The lots are well tended and spring flowers blossom in every yard. Azaleas, rhododendrons, lilacs, even a few late-to-the-party irises. It's after ten and the workers have left for work, the kids for school. There's nobody sitting on any of the porches, though I see figures moving behind some of the windows.

"Stop here, John," Udell says as we turn onto Portland Street. Stepanik's home is at the other end of the block. "Final rehearsal before the show. John, you're to step out, but stay behind the van. If the shit goes bad, we're depending on you to summon backup. Carney, Cade, we'll stay a shoulder width apart as we approach the front door. I'll be carrying a manila envelope, which should be enough to indicate our peaceful intentions. Again, John, don't forget that your primary task is to secure backup. Once that's done, if we're fired on, you're to provide covering fire. I mean fast, John. Don't worry about hitting anything. Empty your weapon in the direction of whatever threat presents itself. We'll be counting on you."

Udell's instructions fit the circumstances well. We'll make for easy targets as we approach the house, and no matter how alert, we're unlikely to see it coming. Filtered through a sheet of thin, white cloud, the sun's behind the house. The windows in front are deeply shadowed. Anyone standing more than a few feet behind them will be invisible to us.

I sense our vulnerability, but it's not like I haven't been here before. Every traffic stop presents the possibility of sudden violence, and it doesn't matter how many routine stops you've done. The next driver or passenger might be armed, might have multiple warrants out, might be the ex-con who's decided never to go back. So, I'm feeling the threat, but under control as we walk toward the door, a shoulder width apart, eyes constantly in motion. I'm still wearing my cross draw holster, and I keep my right thumb hooked behind my belt buckle. Stepanik's yard is neat enough, but there are no lilac or azalea bushes, or even a tree. It's wide open.

I hear Laura Udell release her breath when we reach the door. She glances from me to Cade Barrow. "Stay apart," she tells us, though we don't need telling. Then she leans on the bell, standing right in front. The door is wood and obviously heavy. You'd need serious firepower to shoot through it, but it doesn't come to that. The door opens without warning to reveal Al Stepanik. He's almost as I remember him, a soft, pudgy face above the shoulders of a heavyweight boxer. The only change is in his dark eyes. They tore into me on the night of my arrest, but he's not looking at me now, and probably doesn't remember me. Leaving me to wonder how many tune-ups he's delivered since last we met.

"What do you want?" he demands.

"I have a warrant, patrolman," Udell responds.

"To search my home?"

"To collect a DNA sample."

Stepanik flinches, a slight movement, but all the more noticeable when he swallows, his prominent larynx bobbing up and down. "I already gave a DNA sample."

"Actually, you didn't. Your profile was transferred from your last posting." Udell raises the manila envelope. "I have a copy of the warrant here, signed by a judge. So, this isn't about choosing. If you don't give us the sample voluntarily, you'll be taken to the house and the sample extracted by force."

Stepanik considers this for a few seconds, then jumps back and slams the door. I listen to the deadbolt snick home, certain now that Stepanik's a murderer. The details remain unknown to me, but they're unimportant. Stepanik's desperation is another matter. Cops don't do well in jail or prison, especially asshole cops like Stepanik, which makes him all the more dangerous.

Udell takes charge, as she should. She turns and shouts at John Meacham: "Make the call." Then to me: "Get to the back and keep Stepanik confined." She doesn't wait for a response and I don't offer one as she leads Cade back to the van. Plan B is now in effect. Contain and wait.

CHAPTER FORTY-SIX
CARNEY

Stepanik's backyard is large. There's a rusted swing set to one side and a small shed, probably containing much the same assortment of mowers, snowblowers, and tools I found at Stu Harrington's. I back through the open space between myself and the shed, weapon in hand, eyes jumping from window to window. I'm not fooling myself, even when I take cover behind the shed. First thing, I can't keep an eye on the back door to the house without exposing myself. Second thing, a round from any large-caliber rifle will tear through the shed's thin walls, barely slowing on the way. I'm holding my weapon against my right thigh with my finger outside the trigger guard. I'm not really panting, but I'm drawing deep, rapid breaths. I will myself to stop, but I don't.

There's nothing to do but wait and hope Stepanik doesn't spot me before backup arrives. I assume I'll be reinforced at that point, the goal to make contact, to start a dialogue resulting in his surrender. Time, then, is on our side. Or will be, though not at the moment. In a fight, you don't let your opponent throw the first punch.

I shake out my shoulders, tamp the adrenaline down. Good thing, because a minute later, the back door opens and a woman holding a child runs, full tilt, directly at me. I feel my hand jerk, the one holding my weapon, but I don't bring it to bear. As she passes, I call to her.

"Anybody else in the house?"

She glances in my direction and despite her haste, she's composed. Her answer confirms the impression. "Yeah, the asshole."

Twenty seconds later the asshole makes a personal appearance. He's carrying an AR-15 in one hand with the barrel pointed down. He doesn't appear surprised when I step into view, or when I train my weapon on the center of his chest as I come within ten feet of him.

"You gonna drop that, Officer Stepanik?"

"Don't believe I will."

"You think you can bring it up before I put two or three rounds in your chest?"

He takes his time thinking it over, his eyes locked on mine. Then he shakes his head and I know he wants me to kill him. At the same time, he hasn't made an aggressive move. So, not yet.

◆

"I don't want to kill you."

"Then let me pass."

I point to the rifle with my free hand. "Can't do that, Al. Sorry."

"Then it appears we have us a standoff. I'd say Mexican standoff, but I ain't too fond of the beaners."

"That means you won't flee to Mexico? Or Guatemala, Ecuador, or El Salvador."

Stepanik manages a snort that passes for a laugh. "Not this week." He glances at the gun in my hand. "I don't suppose money would change your mind. I've got five thousand in a money belt."

"Nope, not money. Knowledge, though? Well, that's another thing. My boss, that would be Captain Mariola, has all kinds of questions. The man who provides honest answers might buy himself a deal. Like, for example, why was Rowan Krauss killed? It had to be something big."

Stepanik's eyes open wide. Maybe he's been assuming that we already know. If we don't . . .

"Think I'll keep that one to myself for now."

"Then how about Debbie Cole. Little Debbie."

"What about her?"

"What was she like?"

Stepanik shakes his head. "The little bitch was born to be used. A fucking retard."

"And that's why she put a bullet in a cop's head?"

"Let's say that God fell asleep before he got around to building your brain. Let's say you were kicked out of your house, that you lived on the street for a while, that you're currently being pimped out. Let's say you've got nowhere to go and no money to get there and not enough brainpower to deal with either. Then someone shows up with a way out in the form of a cash payment. A lotta cash. And let's say that someone tells you the cop is dirty, that he hurts women, that he hurts kids, that he eats kittens for breakfast. I mean, how hard could it be?" He stares into my eyes for a moment. "Yeah, you get it. You're as hard as I am, maybe harder. You do what you have to do. That's what real life is all about."

"Not exactly." I shift my weapon to the left and pull the trigger. The round slams into Stepanik's arm, spinning him around, and the rifle drops to the ground. In the vacuum following the gunshot, I hear approaching sirens. Then Udell and Barrow come flying around the side of the house.

"I would have killed him," I explain, "but I think our chief wants to ask him a few questions."

◆

I'm not surprised when Udell stashes me upstairs pending a "thorough debriefing." She wants me out of the way in case reporters show up. I'm a wild card that needs to be temporarily buried in the deck. But I'm close to shocked at what I find in Stepanik's man cave. Facing me on the far wall as I come through the door, a large poster depicts two figures, one carrying a rifle, the other in Klan robes. They reach across a skull and crossbones to shake hands. Beneath the skull and crossbones, a Black man and woman, the woman cradling a child, kneel in the dirt. On the floor, a discarded printout of a Celtic cross, red, inside a white circle, lies face up. WHITE PRIDE rolls over the top, WORLDWIDE curls up from the bottom. To my right, an upside-down American flag hangs next to a Gadsden flag, yellow with a coiled rattlesnake and the familiar words: DON'T TREAD ON ME.

I find a copy of *The Turner Diaries,* a book written long ago that predicts a war to the death between Black and white Americans, lying on a table. The cover, in red, bears the images of a man and a woman. The man holds an assault rifle, the woman a handgun, both aimed at some distant, and surely Black, target. A pile of tracts, crudely printed, rest beneath the novel. I skim the one on top: *Secrets of the Hebrew Peoples*.

I'm expecting an antisemitic screed and I'm not disappointed. In the course of a long introduction, the unnamed author claims the ten lost tribes of Israel, the true chosen people, migrated across Europe, founding Aryan nations as they went. Germany, Holland, Sweden, and Great Britain. Left behind in the Kingdom of Israel, the Jews of Judea are the children of Cain, himself the result of a prurient liaison between Eve and Satan. That bad girl.

I finally take a seat, wishing now for a cold beer and a fat joint. I expect the wait to be a long one and it is, more than two hours. Plenty of time to consider my present and immediate future. Speaking of which, my phone rings five minutes later. It's Uncle Sean. He starts in before I can say hello.

"What the fuck do you think you're doin'?"

"Cutting you loose. And you might tell Ally that he'll be arrested within a day if he sticks around."

"He's already gone. The man's not an idiot."

"Tell him to stay away. Him and his crew. I have plans and he's not included. You either."

"Tom, we're family, me and you."

This is really unbelievable. No way did Ally try to kill me without Sean's permission. "Great, invite me on Thanksgiving. Or better yet, check the mail on Valentine's Day. See if I sent you a card."

I hang up and settle back. I'm going to leave the department, but how to break the news to Mariola. She definitely needs me, now that I've shot Stepanik. In fact, she should thank me because I've left Stepanik alive. As she should thank me for spotting Brim Houseman and making sure he'd stay put. I don't think she will, though. She's not the grateful type. But she is goal oriented, especially now. Given what's in this room, the effort to identify and rid Baxter of all those bad apples has to be her priority. Not some poor immigrant operating one of a dozen small illegal casinos. Mariola won't dirty me up, not before the plea bargains and trials are over. That gives me plenty of time to contemplate a future I fully intend to enjoy.

CHAPTER FORTY-SEVEN

DELIA

I don't have time for him, but when he's agitated, Tommy Atkinson's a force of nature. I can't resist and I don't try when he charges into my office a few minutes after I dispatch Laura Udell to collect Stepanik's DNA.

"I spoke to Vern and he told me to speak to you," Tommy declares.

"About what, Tommy?"

"About John Gentry. What we're gonna do about him. I've been fielding a dozen phone calls every day. From people who matter." Always fidgety, now Tommy's pacing. "Well, not me. I'm not taking the calls. My aide's taking the calls. And guess what, Delia. They're leaning on me from both sides. Prosecute, don't prosecute, nobody's above the law, everybody has a right to defend themselves. And the worst, the absolute worst? The calls are comin' from people I'd rather not offend when I'm running for reelection."

It takes me a second to shift gears. Faced in his liquor store with an armed robber named Jerry Stiffle, John Gentry emptied his licensed Glock in Stiffle's general direction. We recovered fifteen shell casings, so we're not guessing. Jerry Stiffle died at the scene, but he had a long criminal record, too long for Baxterites to mourn his passing. And that's how it would have played out if a bystander hadn't been struck by a stray round that passed through the front window. Taken alive but in critical condition to Baxter Medical Center, Sandra Berman died last night.

"Talk to me, Delia. Indict Gentry? Call it a horrible accident, but insist that Gentry had a right to defend himself? I mean no one gives a flying fuck about Stiffle, but Sandra Berman was an engineer. She worked for Nissan."

Who to offend? Pro-gun voters? Or anti-gun voters? Tommy's always been good at dodging bad news, but there's no escape here.

"I feel your pain, Tommy, but I don't know what you want from me. Your office has the paperwork, all of it."

"Please, do me a favor. Take me over it again. Maybe there's something I can use."

I don't ask, Use for what? I don't have any good news, either. "With Stiffle, it's justified. Armed robber confronts store owner. Store owner kills robber. Give this man a medal. Gentry meant to hit Stiffle and only Stiffle. But when you fire off fifteen rounds as fast as you can pull the trigger, when you never learned to shoot and never practice, when the adrenaline rush eliminates the possibility of rational thought? Well, the law of unintended consequences inevitably kicks in. Was Sandra Berman simply in the wrong place at the wrong time? You could make that argument if Stiffle hadn't dropped his weapon and fallen to the carpet before Gentry pulled the trigger a fourth time. If he didn't pull it eleven more times after he neutralized the threat."

"How can you be sure?"

"By going, frame by frame, through the video generated by a CCTV camera. By comparing the accounts of two people in the store at the time. By the statement Gentry gave voluntarily. So, there's no escaping the evidence. We can charge Gentry with anything from manslaughter to reckless endangerment."

Tommy stops in his tracks. "But you haven't."

"Waitin' on you, Tommy."

"To do what?" He stares at me, expecting a response I don't make. "You think I should take the evidence to a grand jury? Let the jury decide?"

"Ya think? Look, for my part, there's no arrest to make if a grand jury fails to return an indictment. My hands are tied. Yours, too."

"What if they do indict?"

"Same thing. We still have no choice. I have to make the arrest and you have to prosecute." I give him a few seconds to think it over, to nod agreement. "But that approach won't work for Patrolman Louis Abott. Abott shot an unarmed man in the back with me standing next to him. I plan to arrest Abott later today."

Tommy smiles for the first time. "Not a problem, Delia. I got a call this morning from Eustis Prout. Prout's the lawyer for Jim Youngman, Abott's partner. Youngman wants a deal and he'll talk if he gets the right offer. What's the name of the man Abott shot?"

"Ed Smith. And Jim Youngman never drew his weapon. He was barely out of the car when Abott pulled the trigger."

"From a prosecutorial point of view, it couldn't be better." He waggles a finger in my direction. "On the other hand, I don't know if you caught Bute Stafford on KBAX this morning. The man's painting the two of them, Abott and Gentry, as heroes defending Baxter against anarchy."

"And what about Sandra Berman? You know, the woman Gentry killed?"

"Never mentioned her name."

◆

Laura Udell calls fifteen minutes after Tommy heads back to his office. Is the news good? Stepanik's been shot, but expected to survive. Shot by Tom Carney. And why am I not surprised? This is the guy who fractured Brim Houseman's ankle. Who, without my knowledge, installed a video system in the office of an illegal casino to snare Overby and a Philadelphia mobster named Aloysius McKinney. So, what to do with a cop who gets results, but will never accept the chain of command? Fire the man? Not when he'll be forced to testify at trials that might not take place for a year.

"Can you tell us why you were fired, Mr. Carney?" That would be the first question any competent defense lawyer would ask.

"I assigned him," Laura Udell explains, "to cover the back of the house."

"Alone?"

"Yeah, alone. I wanted to contain Stepanik until backup arrived."

"Okay." I take a moment to add and subtract. "I want you to do this right away. Stand where the incident took place and look around. Any house with a view of the backyard? Knock on the door, find out if the confrontation was witnessed. Do it now, Laura. And don't send John Meacham."

"Got it, boss."

◆

On the way out, I hesitate before a photo of Danny on the mound at Goldman High. I have framed photos of Danny and Zoe on my desk, taken myself a year ago. But the photos of Danny on my wall behind my desk were shot by a friend whose father works for the *Baxter Bugle*. The photos are exquisitely detailed, even those taken in mid-pitch. In this one, Danny's leaning in for a sign, his focus so intense I have to believe there are no other thoughts running through his mind, only the pitch, the one he's going to throw. School, scholarships, Gretchen, his mom. All, for the moment, banished.

I find myself wishing that I could limit my own focus to a future that ends when a baseball leaves my hand. No such luck. Too many baseballs in the air. Meanwhile I have to catch them all before they hit the ground. I drive first to Baxter Medical Center, arriving a few minutes after Stepanik. He'll live, but I can't speak with him, not even for a minute before he's hustled into an operating room. I have to settle for informing hospital personnel that Stepanik is under arrest, then ordering a cop named Wade Wentworth to shadow Stepanik wherever he goes.

"The ICU, radiology, a private room? I don't care. And no visitors, especially cops."

"What if a lawyer shows up?"

"You'll have to leave. But wait by the door."

"You worried he'll try to escape?"

"More like he'll try to kill himself. He's up for murder."

◆

Twenty minutes later, I pull up behind several units, including our crime scene van, parked outside Al Stepanik's home. Laura Udell's in front, calmly writing in the small spiral notebook all our detectives carry.

"Hey, boss."

"Everything quiet?"

"Under control. And no witnesses."

"Besides Stepanik and Carney."

"Yeah, besides them. And I checked the backyard. Only two neighboring houses have windows looking onto the yard and there's nobody home at either one."

"What did Stepanik have to say?"

"Ouch."

"And Carney?"

"I was in back thirty seconds after the shot was fired. A single shot. Stepanik was on the ground with an AR-15 right beside him. Carney was on his knees, taking Stepanik's pulse. Carney claims that Stepanik made the first move, forcing him to pull the trigger. The evidence in the backyard backs him up, except for the part about who went first. Nothing to prove either version. Anyway, I parked Carney in a back room on the second floor and he hasn't moved." She looks up at me. "I really don't know what to make of Carney, but I'll tell you this. He's too goddamned calm for a man who just crippled a suspect."

◆

I come through the door, chest out, ready to confront, then stop dead. The walls are covered with white-supremacist symbols and posters. A holy shit moment for sure, but not so much a surprise as a disappointment. I'd been hoping the goon squad assembled by Colton Steele and Thrace Overby came together spontaneously. Now I understand that it's bigger than little Baxter. All the more reason to cleanse my city. On the other side of the room, a seated Carney raises a pamphlet.

"Good reading, captain. About the Rothschild family, how they knew the outcome of the Battle of Waterloo in advance and bet big on the British. Then they created the Federal Reserve and merged with George Soros in a war against Christianity. Right before their proxies took over the banks and they assassinated six presidents."

I step farther into the room, closing the door behind me. "Let's hear it."

"Not much to tell. Stepanik opened the door after Udell knocked. He seemed arrogant at first, but when Udell told him she had a warrant for his DNA, he jumped back and slammed the door. Evidence of a guilty mind, right?"

"Keep going."

"Udell ordered me to cover the back." He puts a little emphasis on the word *ordered,* just to make sure I get the point. "There's a shed in the back and I positioned myself behind it. A few minutes later, a woman carrying a child came through the back door and ran across the yard. A few minutes after that—it's hard to be exact about time when your adrenaline's up—Stepanik followed. He came through the door and stepped into the yard, carrying an AR-15 in his right hand with the barrel pointed at the ground.

I ordered him to put it down. He didn't, but he let me come to within a few yards. To where I couldn't miss."

I listen, thoroughly repulsed, as Carney recounts the conversation that followed. Any normal human being, listening to Debbie Cole's story, would react compassionately. Any normal human being would want to help her. Not men like Brim Houseman and Al Stepanik. They recognized opportunity when they saw it. And that one of them wears a Baxter Police Department uniform will stay with me for a long time. I'm buoyed only by the fact that Debbie Cole fought back in the end.

"What I think, captain, is that he wanted me to kill him. And I have to admit that I was tempted when he lifted that rifle. But I assumed you had questions for him, so . . ."

"So, you disabled him the way you disabled Brim Houseman."

"That's pretty much it." He waves his hand. "I've been right here, enjoying the ambience ever since."

"Great. Now tell me when you plan to quit."

Carney's laugh is spontaneous and genuine. The man's not handsome in a conventional sense. His nose is too wide, his jaw too strong, his eyes a little too narrow. But he projects a quiet confidence that I'm pretty sure women find attractive and men find intimidating. Seemingly affable, you sense that he can turn whenever he decides he's had enough.

"I signed up to work undercover and now my cover's broken. Leaked, captain. So, what next? Become another line detective? Maybe work the burglary desk? I can't see it."

"I need you to testify, Carney, and I think you know it."

"I do."

"Then you understand why I can't have you out there managing a casino in Boomtown. Being undercover provided you with cover. Working your way into the Baxter underworld was part of your job. That ceases to be true on the day you quit. At that point, you're just another criminal."

Carney lays the pamphlet on a table. That's another thing about the man. He's never spontaneous, always calculated. Maybe that's how he survived working undercover in Philadelphia.

"I see your point."

"Does that mean you plan to seek gainful employment when you quit the job?"

"I do, captain, but I haven't decided what."

"You need time, Carney, and I'm gonna to give it to you. First thing, you'll prepare a written statement about what happened here. Then you'll review every other report you've written, assuming as you do, that a defense lawyer will eventually have access to those reports. That done, you'll be given paid leave while you process the trauma. That will last two weeks, at least. So, reconsider your decision while you're enjoying your leisure. Reconsider carefully. Because if you fuck up my cases, I'll bury you." My turn to smile. "I can do malicious prosecution with the best of them."

◆

I spend the next hour firming up plans for late this afternoon, then join Zoe, Danny, and Gretchen for lunch at a newly opened Thai restaurant. I think I expected quaint, with round-bellied Buddhas and servers in shiny red dresses slit up the side. What I find is a sleek, ultramodern space with lacquered tables side by side along the center. An abstract mural covers the wall behind the bar, while a pair of enormous chandeliers, made from hundreds of gold leaves, cast a soft and flattering glow over the restaurant's patrons. Zoe looks especially good, a reminder of how badly I've neglected my home life.

Danny's super-excited about his coming time at Aspirants Baseball Camp. He's researched the camp online and decided their essential claim, that college and major league scouts attend, holds up. Last week I passed the open door to his room and glimpsed an image on his computer's monitor. Danny on a pitcher's mound wearing the uniform of the St. Louis Cardinals.

I didn't linger or ask any questions about how he did it, AI or Photoshop or whatever. Instead, I found myself struck by Danny's ability to dream. Most of the time, I consider my son grounded, maybe too grounded for a boy his age. Now I know he can revert to that eight-year-old with stars in his eyes. That he can—and probably does—imagine himself throwing the last pitch of some distant World Series.

Zoe's sitting next to me, smiling softly, and I take her hand for a moment as I imagine a future for myself outside the Baxter PD. Ex-detective Blanche Weber did it. As tough as they come, she quit the job to open a private security business. I visited her about a month ago. Pregnant, she was seated in an office that rendered mine unfit for human habitation. Blanche projected an enthusiasm for her job that I'm not close to matching, despite all the headaches. I think it has something to do with being the captain of your fate.

I lean back as our lunches are served, admitting to myself that I almost never think about the future. Instead, I wander through an eternal present, lurching from one nightmare to another, carrying light into a darkness people with any common sense instinctively shun.

"What are you thinking about?" Zoe asks. "You seem lost in space."

"What I've done, what I still have to do. It doesn't get any prettier."

Gretchen raises her chopsticks. She's handling them as if she was born with a pair of chopsticks in her hand. "But you're winning, right? You're getting rid of the Commandos."

"Is that what you call them?" I ask.

Danny answers. "Yeah, the Commandos. They're not allowed on the school grounds unless they're called by the administration. So, they hang out a couple of blocks away and hassle some of the kids?"

"Some?"

"Kids who look gay . . ."

"Or dye their hair pink or blue," Gretchen says. "Or have tattoos and piercings. They frisk them, search purses and backpacks. One girl said they need probable cause to search her purse and they slapped her face."

I lay my fork down (and that's right, no chopsticks) and lean toward Gretchen. "Why didn't you mention this before? I could have stopped it."

"But you are stopping it," Danny points out. "You told me you were after the ass . . . the jerks. They had to go and you would make it happen."

"When did I say that?"

"A couple of weeks ago."

Now it's Gretchen's turn. "I mean, that's your job, right? You're the good guys."

◆

We're once again gathered in the squad room. Myself, Patrick O'Malley, Sam Barret, Cade Barrow, and Laura Udell. Tom Carney's not with us, but the boss, Vern Taney, stands next to me at the front of the room. Stu Harrington's been added as well, along with Chuck Breyer, our one-and-only vice cop. We're going in force again, but not to the squad room this time. Just a few minutes ago, I received a call from Gianni Vetto, staked out with a view of a bar named Duke's.

It was Gianni who first called Duke's to my attention, describing it as the favored after-tour hangout for Baxter's rogue cops. According to Gianni, we can expect to find ten or twelve men inside right now, along with our target. That would be Louis Abott, who killed Ed Smith outside the Fulton Funeral Home. We're going to arrest him in front of his buddies, including some who were present when we arrested Guardino, Jackson, Buell, and Worth. What's more, our beloved commissioner will be present when the arrests are made. I tried to talk him out of going, but he insisted.

"I'm gambling," he admitted, "and hoping. Hoping that an all-in attack will drive these assholes out of town. I don't want to pick them off one by one, then let the results play out in courtrooms and disciplinary hearing rooms. We'd be looking at months, many months in some cases. Time for them to regroup, to develop strategies, to hire lawyers. No good, Delia. I know, and don't ask me how, that these assholes have support on the city council, support coming down through Bute Stafford. So, let's end it, if not tonight, within the next couple of days."

I don't pursue the issue. Captain Rawling and Lieutenant Steele have been neutralized. Both have been transferred to our traffic department and rumor has it that Rawling will turn in his papers within a few days. That leaves one more ranking officer still working, but Overby's days are surely numbered. Between the bribe Overby demanded of Tom Carney, and the bribe offered to Violet Grinnell at Baxter's licensing department, Overby can expect to spend at least a few years in prison.

◆

We pack into a traffic van, with Pat O'Malley driving, and head for Duke's at six thirty. The bar's located behind a line of stores on Baxter Boulevard, a hidden strip mall consisting of three attached businesses. A dog grooming operation lies to the north of the bar, an insurance brokerage to the south. Both are closed, as expected.

O'Malley circles an assortment of pickups and cars parked in front of the bar, pulling to a stop only a few feet from the door. We exit beneath gloomy skies that promise rain and head through a relatively narrow door that forces us to enter in single file. At his insistence, Vern leads the way, advancing far enough into the room to allow the rest of us to fan out behind him. I take a position to Vern's left, my head swiveling as I gauge the reaction of the bar's patrons.

Some appear stunned by this turn of events, but a few surrender to a rage they've probably been nurturing all their lives. We're well armed, while they're out of uniform, but some are likely carrying their weapons. We have no rule against off-duty cops bearing arms.

"What the fuck are you doing?" The challenge comes, not from one of the cops, but the bartender, a sixty-plus man with a soccer ball for a head and a basketball for a belly.

Vern speaks first and I'm not surprised by him knowing the bartender's name. "You need to keep your hands on the bar, Cheater. Your hands on the bar and your mouth shut."

Cheater's mouth works for a moment, but he doesn't speak. He doesn't take his hands off the bar, either. Still, his defiant question inspires others to make the same demand, and one, the cop nearest Vern, to stand. I don't know the man's name, but I recognize him. He's Vern's size and a decade younger. He's also drunk, obviously drunk, or maybe he would have looked in Vern's eyes and thought twice before issuing the ultimate demand.

"You need to leave, old man."

Back in the day, Vern was said to be the fastest man on the Goldman High football team. Faster than the quarterback and the running backs and the wide receivers. Or so he's told me on the few occasions when both of us were feeling no pain. Now he proves it by taking a quick step forward and slamming his fist into the man's face. Vern moves quickly, maybe too fast for a man his age, but there's no denying the result. The cop who challenged him manages to turn his head just far enough for Vern's knuckles to slam into his left ear. He goes down hard, eyes still open, tries to rise, falls back, tries and falls again, finally admits defeat, and drops his head to the floor.

Duke's patrons react with a collective gasp, then seem to freeze, as if their brains were spinning as fast as the brain of the cop on the floor. They come back to themselves one after another, eyes refocusing as they finally understand what's happening. We didn't come to Duke's for a debate.

"Delia," Vern says as he steps back.

◆

"Louis Abott, I'm arresting you for the murder of Ed Smith. Stand up and put your hands on your head."

Abott's easy to spot, what with the hawk nose and sharp cheekbones. I watch him literally quake. Last time I saw him, he seemed confused. Now the threat of spending many years in prison has sharpened his focus. He's seated at the end of the bar closest to us.

At my prearranged signal, Cade Barrow and Chuck Breyer move toward Abott. The man's wearing a leather jacket, but there's an obvious bulge on his right hip. Does he want to save Baxter the cost of a trial by reaching for that weapon? Personally, I don't care how it goes.

I'm expecting some resistance, but Abott doesn't move, maybe can't move. He doesn't resist when Cade bends him forward over the bar top, when Breyer disarms him, when Cade stands him up while Breyer frisks him, turns out his pockets, finally handcuffs him behind his back. Abott turns his head to look from one of his brothers to another, his eyes pleading, and I watch those brothers stir. The line between control and chaos is a thin one, but if it comes, it comes. I'm prepared, physically and emotionally. My hand drops to my weapon's grip as I watch Laura Udell lead Abott through the door and into the parking lot. I feel the room relax once the door closes and know the immediate crisis has passed. Vern glances at me and shakes his head, then opens his clenched fist to reveal a handful of FREE OUR POLICE cards, the ones with the blond cop holding a nightstick on a diagonal across his chest. I don't know where he got them, but now he tosses them high in the air. I watch them twist and dip as they drop to the tables.

"Your day is done," Vern says, his voice somehow calm and penetrating at the same time. "Four of your buddies have already been charged with police brutality. Two more have been arrested, one charged with murder, the other soon to be charged with the same crime. Saul Rawling and Colton Steele have been transferred and effectively demoted, so there's no protection for you at the top. What comes next?" Vern looks at me again. "Delia."

"We're going to review every tour you worked. We're going to examine dashcams and GPS data. We're going to interview whoever rode with you. We're going to let it be known that victims of police brutality can report incidents without fear of reprisal. We're going to brace the owners of every bar, casino, and brothel in Boomtown."

I take a step forward, leaving my threat to hang in the air for a moment. "If you're clean, you have nothing to worry about. If not, you need to protect yourselves. We'll be looking at active-duty personnel first. If you're no longer a member of the Baxter Police Department, we'll get to you when we get to you. If we get to you at all. Think it through, and think fast, because the dominoes are already falling. Guardino, Jackson, Buell, and Worth? Your pals? How long before one or another decides that cooperation is in his best interest? How about Abott or Stepanik, both facing murder raps? Think hard, think fast."

Vern takes the last shot. "You'll need to check in before you begin your next tour. We'll be shifting you around. Also, from here on, you'll be riding with reliable partners, veterans who actually care about their city, and you will never become sergeants or detectives, or posted to a special unit. Any hope you might have for advancement? Give it up and get the fuck out of my city."

CHAPTER FORTY-EIGHT

CARNEY

Back at the house, I'm parked behind a desk in the squad room and told not to leave. This from a detective named Sam Barret who assures me that he's just following orders. Orders from Delia Mariola herself. But if I want something to eat or drink, he'll send out to Lena's Luncheonette.

"The doughnuts," he tells me, "are the best in the city."

"Great, but can you tell me how long I'll be here?"

"That's up to the captain."

"And if I decide to stand up and walk the fuck out, like right now, you're prepared to stop me?"

Barret's young and good-looking, his chocolate-brown suit freshly pressed. He seems disappointed. He wasn't expecting me to challenge an order from the commander. But as I'm not under arrest, he's not prepared to stop me, either.

"I'll take the doughnuts," I finally tell him. "Cream-filled if they've got 'em. And coffee. Lots of coffee."

◆

The doughnuts prove delicious, as advertised. The coffee's decent, too, but I'm interrupted as I lift a second doughnut from a full box. The interruption arrives by way of a woman who introduces herself as Marcia Blackstone, Captain Mariola's personal assistant. She lays two files on the desk, both with my name on the outside cover. I don't have to ask what's inside. They contain the reports on my interactions with Violet at the licensing desk, and with Thrace Overby in my office at the casino. Again, I don't have to ask what I'm supposed to do with them. I'm to review them and make any corrections that need making. Meantime, I haven't started the paperwork on the Stepanik shooting.

"Also, this." Marcia hands me a thumb drive that surely contains the video and audio I recorded. Mariola wants to be sure that my written account and the recordings are free of conflict. Still, I can't resist busting Marcia's chops. I'm that bored.

"What am I supposed to do with these?"

A shrug, then, "I don't know."

"Don't you think you should find out?"

"I can't." She leans forward, her smile conspiratorial, and half whispers. "The captain's with the task force. They're gonna arrest Louis Abott."

The confidence demands a reward and I raise the box. "Have a doughnut."

"Thanks."

◆

I take the job seriously, running through my encounter with Violet first. My report is accurate enough. Overby directs me to Violet. I meet her at the city's licensing division. She hands me the license. Day, date, and time of day are all there. I add a handwritten description of Violet on the day we met. Maybe five five, a hundred and thirty pounds, thin nose, receding chin, hair dyed red, eyeglasses with neon-blue frames. Pretty much the same description I gave to Mariola, but now it's in writing.

I turn next to Overby, running the video and comparing it to my written statement. No discrepancies, not even an inch of daylight. The video and audio will do most of the work, but the data can't be put into evidence without my testimony. Guaranteed, Overby's defense counsel will try to portray me as bent, a crooked cop running an illegal casino. I'll have to weather the incoming negativity and hope a jury won't dismiss my testimony. But the data speaks for itself. I don't offer anything. Instead, Overby demands a bribe, and not just once.

From the material in hand, I begin an account of my confrontation with Stepanik. Two hours later, when Sam Barret shows up, I've completed the report, uploaded the data to the Stepanik crime file, and printed a version with only a small number of typos.

I stand up, ready to leave. "Everything's here and ready to go. Just like I'm ready to go."

"Not quite yet. We're gonna need you to stick around. Got an ADA wants a meetup."

"Who's 'we'? And I'm hoping it doesn't include you."

Barret only smiles. "Word out there? Tom Carney's an asshole. Thanks for proving it." Point made, he turns and walks back to his own desk.

◆

I don't like taking orders, even, or maybe especially, from my superiors. Barret's not a superior, but I know the order came from Mariola. I know, too, that she's right. Stepanik will have to be arraigned, likewise Overby when he's finally arrested. A grand jury will meet soon afterward and the district attorney needs to be fully prepared. Only an hour ago, I watched Bute Stafford defend Stepanik and Abott in the course of a KBAX interview. He called them heroes, not for the first time, and demanded that Commissioner Taney be fired for attacking the heart and soul of the Baxter PD.

So, yeah, ducks-in-order time. Fortunately, the wait is short and the ADA who shows up is affable. His name is David Weymouth, a short man in reasonably good shape, though almost completely bald on top. He's already familiar with Overby's file, but has only a basic outline of my encounter with Stepanik. He takes his time, first reading my written report, then questioning me closely. When I tell him that I'd never heard Stepanik's name before this morning, he seems pleased. No vendetta here, and no pesky witnesses to dispute my version.

My undercover work does trouble him, but I assure him that I kept my handlers fully informed. Weymouth isn't totally satisfied, but he doesn't probe for the fine details. If I lie under oath? That's on me, as long as I haven't told him in advance. On the other hand, if I do tell him and he still allows me to testify, he'll be suborning perjury and could be disbarred.

◆

It's closing in on seven thirty when David Weymouth decides to call it a night. There'll be another conference on the day before I testify, and I've given him my cell number. I think he knows that

I'm eager to cooperate, that I want to see scumbags like Stepanik and Overby in prison. Stepanik for life, Overby for as long as possible.

Mariola and her raiding party have returned and the squad room's become busy. Stu Harrington and Laura Udell are huddled around Harrington's desk, along with several detectives. They don't acknowledge me, but I don't care. My time here is short and I should already be on my way. Instead, I take a minute to call Vangi.

"Hey, baby," I say when I hear her voice, "I've been missing you."

"We can fix that in about thirty minutes."

"No good. You need to stay away from me. For the next few days, at least."

"That bad?"

"Lot of motivation out there. Lotta seriously pissed off men. Cops and robbers both. If I can sneak out, maybe I'll come to you. Assuming you're . . . receiving visitors."

"Okay, I understand. And by the way, Zack Butler really liked you. He says you remind him of him."

After I hang up, I call Zacariah at the Blue Skies. He answers on the second ring, his tone matter-of-fact. "Hey, boss, what's up."

"Crank around?" Crank Rivera's one of two people I hired to maintain security at the casino. Prison-seasoned, I know I can rely on him to stay cool. When Zacariah puts him on a moment later, I explain the situation and what I want him to do. He doesn't speak until I finish.

"Got it, boss. No fear."

◆

Good enough for me and I head for a back door that leads into the parking lot. As I come down the stairs, I see Mariola and our commissioner open the door and step onto the parking lot. They're talking, but I can't make out the words. Not about me, though. I'm not that important.

I'm thinking about the Blue Skies as I walk into a soft mist that clings to my face and hair. I don't plan on giving the casino up, the casino or the bar. Mariola's right, though. I have to remain out of sight. Can Zacariah be trusted to manage long-term? Do I need a working partner to handle day-to-day operations? Does the bar generate enough profit to justify a partnership?

Mariola and Taney are stopped alongside a Jeep Cherokee as I cross the lot. I'm hoping to escape unnoticed. No such luck. Taney spots me first, then Mariola. I smile, but keep moving until Mariola waves me over.

"Great day, captain." I don't know if I'm allowed to address the commissioner, so I simply nod.

Mariola ignores my comment. "Did you watch Bute Stafford this afternoon?"

"Yeah. In the squad room." Where I was stashed for many hours.

"The way he's calling it, the entire department is corrupt and the arrests we're making are part of a turf war. No good guys anywhere." She pauses, but I have nothing to say. "Stafford's lies? They're for right now and they're effective. The truth, though? The truth'll come in the form of evidence. It'll emerge in dribs and drabs over weeks."

Another pause. Same result. I'm going to be warned and I'm anxious to get it done. I haven't eaten anything since Barret brought me the doughnuts.

"I need you to do your Caesar's-wife bit. Beyond reproach."

I didn't know I had a Caesar's-wife bit, a point I don't bother to make. Back in Philly, I avoided bosses for reasons I've already mentioned. That doesn't mean I'm dumb enough to argue when a superior officer makes a demand.

"I hear ya, boss. Loud and clear."

◆

I believe Mariola was urging me to enjoy my time off. Especially because I was on paid leave. Stay home, cash your check at the end of the week, watch a little TV. But I've never been good at listening and as the mist builds into a light rain, I head for a barbecue joint, Killer BBQ. The killer in this case is named Sam. No last name, but Sam smokes his own meat in a wood-fired smoker, then cooks it in a back tent. It's eaten at long, communal tables in a tent that fronts Tenth Avenue, two blocks from my trailer.

I grab an open-faced brisket sandwich and potato salad, along with a soda, and carry it on a paper tray into the front tent. After the Stepanik shooting, Mariola kept me away from the reporters who surely covered the arrest. I'm grateful as I begin to cut the sandwich, smothered in onion gravy, with a plastic knife and fork. Two men seated to my left ignore me, as do a couple sitting across from me. I'm on my own. Time to think.

It's easy for Mariola to advise me to spend the next couple of weeks in front of my TV, maybe half-stoned on whatever substance I like to abuse. The problem is that Stepanik and Abott were no threat to me. Same for the four cops we arrested this morning. But Thrace Overby's still out there and he has good reason to wish me gone.

I'm not a passive type and I've already taken steps to ensure that my time on Earth continues. I've ordered Crank to sit on my trailer at Eighth Avenue. Scrunched down behind the steering wheel of his ancient Chrysler 300, he'll be virtually invisible, what with the rain. Even so, I don't intend to sleep in my own bed tonight, despite having no ready alternative. Vangi's place is off the table. I won't put her in the line of fire, not only because I care about the woman, but also because Overby may have connected us. He might be watching her place right now, hoping I'll show up.

I run through the list of my few acquaintances until I hit on Benny Kaplan. Benny's probably still pissed at my leaving abruptly, but his wife, Sarah, took my side. I don't have a direct line to Sarah, but if Benny turns me down, I might drive down to Kaplan Refrigeration and ask her directly. And there's another possibility I might try. Benny's always had a sharp eye for the bottom line. Put enough money in his hand, he'll let me sleep in his own bed. Though probably not with Sarah in it.

I take out my phone, ready to dial, when it begins to vibrate. Now I remember switching the ring setting from sound to vibrate when I set out for Stepanik's.

"Hey, Carney, where have you been? This is my third call tryin' to reach you."

It's Crank and he's pissed. Reasonably so. "My fault, Crank. So, what's up?"

"You called it right. Three guys—I'm not close enough to recognize anyone, what with the rain—are inside your trailer. I think they jimmied the door, but they could've had a key."

"Any spotters outside?"

"Think so. One man sitting in a Nissan. Been there for almost an hour."

"Can he be seen from the trailer?"

"Uh-uh. He's parked on Main Street and your trailer's halfway down Eighth Avenue."

The man in the Nissan's job is to spot me as I approach, then warn the men inside the trailer. A simple job that's about to become a lot more complicated.

"You wanna walk away, no hard feelings, Crank. What I need from you carries some risk. Not a lot, but some."

"I'm insulted you should say that, boss. Let's bury these assholes."

"Okay, so here's what I need you to do."

◆

The Nissan's parked on the east side of Main Street about twenty yards from the turn onto Eighth Avenue. Despite the weather, a dozen hookers parade up and down Main Street beneath umbrellas. Pink and red and every shade of blue from teal to cobalt. Perfect cover for Crank as he comes up the sidewalk. I'm walking on the other side of the road, shielded by cars and vans that occupy every foot of curb space. To my left, a chain-link fence topped with razor wire seals off the construction site. The evening shift is hard at work inside and one of the plant's enormous doors is open. Better still, some sort of hammer, out of sight, is smashing into a metal object, the result loud enough to be heard on Main Street.

There are no stores on this side of Main Street, no sidewalk either. I tiptoe along the curb, shielding myself alongside parked cars and pickups, until I can see the man in the Nissan. He's sitting behind the wheel, smoking a cigarette, eyes flicking from mirror to mirror. Relaxed, for sure, and probably bored. Stakeouts are incredible boring, especially if you're working solo.

Crank saunters forward until he's alongside the Nissan. Then he flashes a broad grin, steps toward the vehicle, and taps on the window. The man behind the wheel is startled and he immediately turns away from me. Bad move, really bad. I cross Main Street in a few strides and slam the muzzle of my Glock into the window. Tempered glass, it shatters, breaking into thousands of tiny shards.

The man inside freezes, as expected, and I don't give him a chance to recover. I grab him by the chin, yank his head through the window, and place the Glock's muzzle on his temple.

"Unlock the doors. Do it now."

"What the fuck? I'm a cop."

"Me, too." I slap my Glock into the top of his head. Hard enough to hurt, but not draw blood. "Unlock the door. And don't be stupid. If it comes down to me or you, it's gonna be you."

The locks release with an audible snap and Crank's right on it. He opens the front door on the passenger side and leans in. A few seconds later, he raises his right hand to reveal a small automatic with a stubby suppressor attached to the barrel.

I open the door and drag the man outside. On the sidewalk, the hookers have drawn together, a crowd of gawkers. That changes when I raise my badge. They don't know who I am, or who I'm holding at gunpoint, but they're familiar with Baxter cops, including the ones who'd beat the hell out of them for the fun of it. They glance from one to another, then disperse.

"Tell me your name and rank?" I tap him on the head again, just in case he didn't get it the first time.

"Kyle Barber."

"Your rank?"

"Patrolman."

"Okay, Patrolman Barber, what we're gonna do is get in the back seat and have a friendly conversation. I'm sayin' friendly because I'm an optimist by nature. But it doesn't have to work out that way."

◆

I'm in the back with the muzzle of Kyle Barber's silenced automatic pressed into his ribs. Crank's in front, keeping one eye on the street. No surprises, that's the idea. Barber's leaning forward. He has no choice since I've cuffed his hands behind his back.

"First thing, Kyle, I know there are three men in my trailer. I also know that you're acting as their spotter. I know something else, too. If I'd walked into my little home away from home, unsuspecting, I wouldn't walk out. So, we can skip the fishing expedition. First thing, I want to know who's in command of this operation."

"I don't know what you're talking about."

I'm not here for a debate. I jam the auto between his thighs, hard, and pull the hammer back. "You don't cooperate, I'm gonna put a round in your balls."

"All right, just don't . . ."

He doesn't tell me don't what, but I'm sure I have a grip on his ultimate aim. Eunuch, apparently, has no appeal.

"Who's in charge?"

"Sergeant Overby."

"Is he inside my trailer?"

"No."

"Where is he?"

"In a bar."

"C'mon, Kyle, we're almost there. What bar?"

◆

I don't have Mariola's number. I have to settle for Stu Harrington. He's home and not at all happy to hear from me. Tough shit. With three people waiting to kill me in my home, I can't worry about his dinner getting cold.

"Three men?" he asks. "Exactly three?"

"Exactly."

"And how do you know this?"

"A spotter parked on Main Street. Patrolman Kyle Barber. He was kind enough to warn me after a minimum of persuasion. He's a cop, by the way. The men in my home are cops, too."

Harrington sighs, a distinctly feminine sound I somehow find endearing. "Is he alive? Kyle Barber?"

"Last I spoke to him, he was fine. You'll find him in the trunk of a blood-red Nissan."

"Look, Carney, I'm ordering you to wait until I can send enough backup to resolve this without anyone getting shot. You understand? I'm ordering you to stick around."

"No can do, buddy. You'll have to deal with this on your own. I've got an errand to run." I give it a beat. "They meant to kill me, Stu. I have to take that seriously. This whole experience, it's a puzzle. But one you have to take apart instead of put together. I'm going after the last piece."

"By yourself?"

"Wouldn't have it any other way."

◆

I walk fast because of the rain, as if I can miraculously avoid being drenched, to Baxter Boulevard where it curls under the construction site. One block farther and I'm in front of Packers

Tavern where I often met George Pratt, now deceased. It's also where Thrace Overby has decided to hole up. An alibi's the whole point and he could have chosen any public space in the city. I suspect he chose Packers because it's so close to my trailer. Get there first, be sure the shooters are well away from the scene, control the investigation to the best of his ability.

All along, I've suspected that Mariola's been using me as bait. And here we are. Or, here I am. If I hadn't anticipated an attempt by Overby to remove me and my testimony from the penal equation, I'd already be dead and my killers vanished. This is a situation that might have easily been averted if Mariola had gone public with the audio and video I recorded in my office. There'd no longer be a reason for Overby to act. She didn't, though.

Nothing inside Packers has changed since I was last inside. The long bar, the scattered tables, the booths along the wall, the cattle drive mural behind the bar where a bartender mixes drinks. His name is Bear and his gaze jumps from my face to the badge I've pinned to my jacket.

Overby's sitting at the bar, staring at a Texas longhorn with murder in its eyes. He remains unaware of my presence until I'm right on top of him. Then, his brown eyes seeming without light, he turns slowly, his overall expression a valiant attempt at indifference. *What the fuck do you want?* But his already-thin lips form a dark, narrow line, like a scar, above his chin. Call it a tell. Or maybe an appropriate reaction to my being wet, my hair plastered to my skull, my jacket glued to the shirt beneath.

We stare at each other for long minute, until he finally asks, "What do you want?"

"It's on the record, Thrace. Every word, video and audio. I gave them Violet, too. You think she's standing tall for you?" I can't be certain, but I throw it in anyway. "Violet's already given a taped statement. You're done, so killing me never made a lot of sense. And by the way, Kyle Barber's in the trunk of the Nissan. And his buddies in my trailer? Let's just say their ambush has morphed into a trap. And me, I'm here to arrest you."

Overby takes his time as he considers his options. By now, Ally has sent one of his people to find out why he can't reach Mike and his buddy out in Coombs County. Does Overby know what they discovered? Does he now hate me enough to draw down, to hell with the consequences? I've come after him alone, which has to sting. I'm not only making his arrest personal, I'm showing contempt for all that macho he tries so hard to project.

"That bullshit you pulled off, it's entrapment," he finally says. "You lured me into accepting a bribe. And it's you who led the bitch to Violet. If the tapes are thrown out, then Violet goes, too." He folds his arms across his chest. He's going to surrender. "After it's all over, I'm gonna sue this city for everything it has."

I might point out that I never offered a bribe, that he twice demanded a payoff. I don't. Instead, I slap him in the face, hard enough to produce a loud crack that might be mistaken for a gunshot. Taken completely off guard, his legs wobble, only the bar holding him up.

Overby raises his hands to his cheek, now red and beginning to swell. Slowly, he replaces the shock with rage. He has to do something, but what? Throw a punch? Reach for his weapon? The answer never comes.

I'm surprised, myself, when an enormous hand grabs Overby by the collar and yanks him onto the bar top. A minute later, Overby's weapon, a Browning by the look of it, is sliding the length of the bar. Now, every eye in Packers Tavern is focused on Bear.

"This motherfucker's got his hand out every time he walks through the door." Bear's shouting. "Even tonight. Anyone think this asshole paid for his dinner or his drinks?" Then to me. "Take him, Carney. And keep me up to date. I wanna be there when he's sentenced."

◆

I walk Overby out the door, his hands now cuffed behind his back, and into the rain. He doesn't attempt to pull away, most likely because I've got the fingers of my left hand wrapped around his arm just above the elbow, a pain-compliance technique surely familiar to him.

"People like you just can't get it," he finally informs me. "You dream of a society held together by . . . by love, maybe, or duty, or cooperation. Yeah, cooperation. Like it's in everybody's interest to respect the rights of others, so I know all the good people will do the right thing. But the truth you don't want to face is that societies are held together by force and the threat of force. Here's the penal code. Obey it or else."

"And your threats are immediate? Obey or get the crap beaten out of you?"

"Respect, Carney. Order begins with respect. The policeman on the ground is the first line of defense."

I don't bother to respond with the obvious, that force pays well, too. The rain's steady now, and the flashing red-and-blue lights of several parked cruisers light up the raindrops as they fall. No sirens, but the trunk of the red Nissan has been raised. Presumably, Kyle Barber is in custody.

I discover more cruisers on Eighth Avenue in front of my trailer. The cruisers are empty, the cops still wrangling with three men in civilian dress who profess outraged innocence. They're claiming to be my friends, that I've asked them to wait for me, that it's a great big mistake.

Standing with her back to me, Mariola's slow to turn around. She's wearing a trench coat worthy of a 1940s gumshoe and a Stetson she must've borrowed from someone else. Mariola grins when she finally turns on her heel, then laughs out loud when she discovers Overby. I'm beginning to love the woman.

"You were ordered to stay at the scene," she notes for the record.

"Can't argue the point."

"Then you deliberately disobeyed a direct order." It's not a question, the way she puts it.

"Right, and that's not something you would ever do, right? It's not something you can condone. But I understand your position. Truly, I do. You're claiming that an order is an order, not a suggestion. And I have to admit, I'm not surprised by your stand, captain. After all, you're not the one they meant to kill. You're not the sacrificial lamb." I give Overby's arm a shake. "You could have arrested Overby days ago, but you left him on the street."

Mariola stares at me for a moment, then says, "It's over, Carney, and the good guys won. A chance for you to relax while you consider your options. But not right away. No, for the next couple of days you'll have to immerse yourself in the cleanup. It seems that the boys . . ." She flips her hand to indicate the three men now in custody. "It seems the boys did a job on your trailer. In fact, they've torn the interior to pieces. With a crowbar." Another smile. "Didn't spare the urine, either."

CHAPTER FORTY-NINE

DELIA

AUGUST 15, SIX WEEKS LATER

For the last hour, my little home has been ground zero for a morning thunderstorm. Unrelenting summer rain pounds on the roof, the raindrops so dense they reduce the house across the street to a shadow within a shadow. I'm not bothered by the rain. Thunderstorms in the Midwest are naturally ferocious. It's the thunder part that's got me hopping. Danny and Mike have been at baseball camp in California for two days and Danny's going to call for the first time. Gretchen's here, and Zoe, of course, and we don't want the face-to-face connection drowned by thunderclaps so furious I half expect the roof to collapse. They're coming one after another, bringing the lawn and the road outside into sharp relief. In the yard across the street, the branches of a dogwood tree shake wildly as if struck by multiple tasers.

"This is crazy," Gretchen observes. "I mean what are the odds we'll have a storm just when Danny's about to call."

I might remind her that the unrelenting heat and humidity, the conditions that gave rise to the storm, aren't overly concerned with a phone call from a seventeen-year-old boy. Even if he's fifteen hundred miles away from his family.

We're huddled around my kitchen table, staring at an open laptop as we sip from mugs of cinnamon-flavored coffee. Danny was terribly nervous when I drove him to the airport, fifty miles away. Pitching for his high school team was a given. Competing with players drawn from all over the country raises the stakes. And my reminding him of a letter from camp, one that advised him to think of the camp as a place to hone his skills, never made it past his smell test.

"So, how come they needed to send the letter?" He'd raised a finger. "The scouts? They can't recommend everyone, can they? So, you can talk about honing skills, but you really wanna look better than everyone else. You wanna be the can't-miss kid."

◆

The laptop's ready to receive Danny's call, but it's my own cell that lights up, with the storm at its height.

Tom Carney reporting, as demanded by yours truly. After Overby's arrest, Carney was placed on paid leave for one month. Afterward, he'd come back to work or turn in his papers. But as the days passed, and Carney announced that he'd never return to active duty, considerations of what he might do instead resulted in his leave being extended for another ninety days. But only as long as he stayed in touch with me, personally, and avoided contact with the police.

"Still breathing, Carney?"

"Sure am, lieutenant."

Not captain, not any more. Mayor Venn's hanging on by a thread, and while firing his commissioner would amount to conceding his failures, a sacrifice was certainly in order. I wasn't fired, but my position, chief of detectives, has been eliminated and my rank dropped, without loss of pay, to lieutenant. I am now heading our newly formed homicide division.

Personally, I'm thrilled. I wasn't meant to be a bureaucrat, and the past months have proved that. Ordered by Vern to personally take command of the many investigations spinning off the murder of Rowan Krauss, I relished every minute, especially the victory part. Returning to my old desk and hours upon hours of daily paperwork inspired something close to dread.

Abott and Stepanik have been charged with murder. They await trial in our county jail. Thus far, their efforts to secure a reasonably favorable plea bargain have failed. Thrace Overby, on the other hand, indicted on multiple counts of bribery and extortion, has implicated Colton Steele in exchange for a short sentence to be served in the Baxter jail instead of a state prison. Steele, in turn, pled not guilty to a multicount indictment and is out on bail. Perhaps, if he has a great lawyer, he'll be able to explain the twenty-two thousand dollars we found in his basement. Stuffed into a heating duct.

Perhaps most important, the bad apples are deserting the barrel. More than a dozen of our robocops have already resigned, their hope to avoid the fates of Buell, Guardino, Worth, and Jackson. Out of sight, out of mind? Not happening. If we can indict any one of them, he'll be arrested and brought back.

"So, what's new, Carney? What do I need to know?"

A thunderclap brings our conversation to a brief halt. "I've changed my place of residence," Carney finally announces.

"Does that mean you've moved?"

"Yeah, to Poplar Street in the Gardens."

"Seriously? The Gardens?"

"Don't knock it, lieutenant. I've got a whole house for half the rent on my trailer in Boomtown. And I don't know . . . I kind of like my neighbors. Lot of interesting folk peddling drugs. I'll keep you informed."

◆

"Delia." Gretchen's voice sounds from behind me. "Danny's calling."

That's it for Carney. I hang up and hustle back to the table. Gretchen's pulled up three chairs across from the open laptop, the center chair pushed back far enough to allow me, Zoe, and Gretchen to be seen at the same time. I find myself breathless for a moment until Danny's face appears on the monitor. His eyes are bright, though anxious, and he seems fully present and distracted at the same time. I'm sitting in the middle, slightly behind Gretchen and Zoe, and I join in the collective hello.

Only just seventeen, Danny's too young to face serious pressure, his boyhood still ongoing. But there he is, on display. I have to think he's feeling every ounce of the weight. No choice, though, not when he's competing in a sport where professionalism begins in high school. Not when elite players sign long-term, two-hundred-million-dollar contracts. Higher stakes inevitably lead to larger talent pools. Gold mountain again.

"So, tell us," Gretchen demands. "Are you a superstar yet?"

Danny's laugh is cut short by a thunderclap. He pauses for a moment, then goes on. "Not so you'd notice. I mean half the kids are only here because their families have the money to pay the fees. They're okay, but they'll never be good enough, not even for a college scholarship."

"But the other half?" I have to ask the question.

"They're really good, every one of them. I throw harder than most, but they've already got secondary pitches, sliders and curveballs." A smile now. "Of course, not everyone here is a pitcher, but it's the same for position players. And ya know the funny thing? Everybody understands the deal. Many are called, but few are chosen. We're not all gonna make it. I mean there's talent coming from all over the world. Japan and Korea, and every Spanish-speaking country in the Caribbean." Another laugh. "And then you have Max Kepler, from Germany. He's a ten-year outfielder with the Twins."

Zoe speaks, her tone soft. "What about in games? How are you doing?"

"That's just it. I'm not pitching in games. Everything's happening off the field. They've got me working on balance, release point, arm slot, improving my changeup, throwing sliders that finish in the left-hand batter's box. It's good, right? These are things I have to learn. Only the coaches are bossy as hell. With everyone, Mom. They teach, you learn." A sigh now, and a shake of his head. "Funny thing, though, with the other kids, the good ones. Everybody understands the competition, but we're close anyway. After dinner, the pitchers get together and talk about pitching, about grips, about release points, spin rate. It's like there's nothing else happening in the world."

Out of breath, Danny finally pauses, leaving Zoe to ask, "Are you going to play?"

"I'm playing already, only at shortstop." Now a true Danny laugh, wry and self-amused. "My arm's strong enough to handle the position, but I do have one little problem. I can't hit for . . . to save my life."

◆

Danny's okay. That's the collective judgment when we sit down to breakfast. Maybe not at the plate, though. Unlike college or the pros, high school pitchers have to hit in Baxter. Danny's always done fairly well, batting against Baxter high school pitching. Now he's up against other kids with serious talent and learning the true height of the ladder he has to climb, hitting and pitching.

Gretchen lifts a forkful of cheddar-jalapeño waffle to her mouth, then stops with her mouth open. "Danny's not gonna fall apart. He won't be discouraged, only more determined. So, it's good, really. That he got this lesson before his senior year. Gives him time to make good on his commitment."

"Great," I answer. "Only you need to make sure he keeps his grades up. Just in case."

Being Danny's mom, I'm allowed the last word and we eat in silence for a few minutes, until Zoe asks, "What's going on with Stepanik?"

Zoe's being specific because the numerous cases have become the property of defense lawyers and prosecutors. They're currently engaged in the plea-bargain tango. What do you have? What will you give for what I have? Good for you, bad for him. Either way, cops don't have a serious role in the proceedings, and won't until we testify at trial. Stepanik's the exception. We know Stepanik regularly transported Debbie Cole from Brim Houseman's house in the Gardens to a client somewhere in Baxter. I've wanted the name of that client since Brim named Stepanik as the man who picked Debbie up and brought her home. The sad part is that we've learned his name, but there's nothing we can do about it.

Denied bail and looking at life without parole, Stepanik proved to be anything but loyal. He began playing let's make a deal almost before the cell door clanged. Through his attorney, of course, a woman named Clarissa Leland. So, what did he have to offer? His statement came in the form of a proffer. He would give up the name of Cole's john in return for a reduced sentence with the chance of parole after fifteen years. Great, but not what the prosecutors wanted. They wanted the name of Stepanik's co-conspirators in the murder of Rowan Krauss, and Stepanik readily agreed. Then it all went south.

After weeks of negotiation, Stepanik named Thrace Overby as his one-and-only contact, but offered no proof. No written documents, no emails, no text messages, no recordings. No evidence and no arrest. Overby, of course, has problems of his own, but unless new facts emerge, he will never be charged with Debbie Cole's murder.

Nor will Debbie's client. I'd been hoping that Overby would name Bute Stafford. But, no, Bute's still out there, still on the attack. And the man identified by Stepanik, Ian Rodgers, one of the city's more active developers, won't even be questioned. Proffers are confidential, a communication between lawyers, and can't be introduced as evidence in court. No, to charge Ian Rodgers, prosecutors would have to accept a plea bargain. That's not going to happen because Stepanik has nothing to offer. His proffer has been rejected and he's headed for a trial he's almost sure to lose.

I've run through this with my family, including Gretchen, several times. Without actually naming Debbie Cole's client. I'm about to do it again when my phone rings. It's Patrick O'Malley. Pat's one of the detectives in a division that's too small to label a squad. There are four of us, me, Pat, Laura Udell, and Chuck Breyer, formerly the sole member of our vice unit. We're a good fit. Laura's a bulldog, tireless and unrelenting. Chuck's network of informants reaches past the city and into the surrounding counties. Pat's slower than he used to be and he wasn't all that fast to begin with. His value shows itself in the box. The man's able to create an instant rapport with the suspects he interrogates. He's everybody's daddy.

"Hey, Pat, what's up?"

"Got a body, Delia. In the Gardens."

A bolt of lightning, followed by a deafening crash, reminds me of how much I want to enjoy my day off. Duty calls, of course, but maybe not too loud. "We have a mystery on our hands?"

"Not so you'd notice. Tweakers in an abandoned house, adding booze and oxy to the mix. Up for several days by the look of it. There's a dispute over the remaining meth, as you'd expect, and Malcolm Dunn stabs a man yet to be identified, who bled out before the ambulance arrived."

"You have Dunn in custody?"

"Sure do. And he's showing remorse. Claims he only meant to scare the victim, but . . ."

"But you are not in need of my aid." I glance out the window at near-horizontal rain. The limbs of the dogwood across the street continue to wave wildly. Only this time I know what they're saying: *Yes, yes, yes.*

"Nope, just letting you know."

Behind me, I hear Gretchen half shout, "Last waffle comin' out. Anybody want it?"

"Not me," Zoe says. "I'm stuffed."

Gretchen does her part. "Me, neither. Enough for one morning."

And Delia Mariola? I'm thinking, if it gets any better, I'm gonna go out and buy a ten-dollar Powerball. Rain or no rain.

A. F. CARTER lives and works in New York City.

Other titles in A. F. Carter's Delia Mariola series are available now from The Mysterious Press

A twisted tale set in a tough town, *The Yards* is a multiple-voiced mystery with two unforgettable women at its core; its suspenseful, thrilling, and unpredictable plot will keep the reader guessing until the very last page.

"A breathless suspenser that's also a painfully acute evocation of the wrong side of the tracks."
—**KIRKUS**

Tough, thrilling, and filled with memorable characters, *The Hostage* is a gritty mystery set in the same hardscrabble town as 2021's *The Yards*, which *Kirkus* praised as "a breathless suspenser that's also a painfully acute evocation of the wrong side of the tracks."

"*The Hostage* will keep you absolutely nailed to your page or screen. Smart, urgent, and sneakily deep."
—**C.J. BOX**, #1 NYT Best-Selling author of *Shadows Reel*